Birth of the Legend:
Book Four of the Sophie Lee Saga

The Sophie Lee Saga, Volume 4

Stormi Lewis

Published by C.S. Press, 2023.

This is a work of fiction. Similarities to real people, places, or events are entirely coincidental. Other readers gave written consent to participate in this saga.

BIRTH OF THE LEGEND: BOOK FOUR OF THE SOPHIE LEE SAGA

First edition. May 5, 2023.
Second edition January 16, 2026

Copyright © 2023 Stormi Lewis.

Written by Stormi Lewis.

No part of this work may be used for AI training or reproduced in any manner whatsoever without written permission, except in the case of brief quotations embodied in critical reviews and articles.

For information, contact Stormi Lewis:
cspresspublishing@gmail.com

This work is 100% organic. No part of it was created by AI.

Discover us online:

https://linktr.ee/chasingstormi

STORMI LEWIS

To the OG Storm Chaser, who gave me my love of stories and books, always made sure that I knew she loved me, was always proud of me, and the spirit to all of my writing. I will see you in my dreams whenever you can take a break from chasing around Elvis and drinking coffee with your loved ones in Heaven.

To Shyera McCollugh Thomas, who convinced me to go back to my roots, and gave me the greatest gift I could ever ask for. Pure happiness, pandemic and all.

To booktok and authortok, who are forever teaching me new things and are helping me reach my author goals.

To Joshua, for starting something that made this book even more exciting to write and gave me my identity on booktok.

To the applicants willing to be a part of this story, and the supporters who let me add them to show my appreciation.

To the clue players that were willing to put up with my shenanigans and supporting me during the rough times of trying to finish this book through constant migraines and all.

To my beta readers, that gave me valuable feedback to make this book the best version of itself for you.

To all the booktokers who have bail money waiting...You know who you are. And always support me no matter what crazy I throw into the world. The ones I reach out to when I'm at my lowest, losing my mind, or just need a virtual hug. You will always have a special place in my heart. Period.

To my Instagram Support Team, who let me reach out for the good, the bad, and the breakdowns to help build me back up and get me back on track.

To the following Kickstarter supporters who helped make this book a reality: Kayla Cotrell, Sheyla Rochelle, Colleen Moore, Francesco Tehrani, Hana Correa, Kourtney Staton, Diane Gilbert, Rochelle Moore, Cassandra Peters, Marsha Renfro, Dani Breault, Bonnie Webber, Amanda Ross, Sherry Mock, Andy Bowen, Ali Kiki, Carrie Adkins, Nicole Lourenco da

BIRTH OF THE LEGEND

Silva, W.L. Brooks, and Caitlin Denman.

To my Patreon OGs: Monica Rollins, Marissa Atchison, Jenny Oliver, Amanda Shafer, Casandra Peters, Sharon Laundry and Ali Kiki for supporting everything I put out, helping me with ideas, and being a part of my author journey.

Lastly, to my Storm Chasers (aka: found family), who never stop conquering their personal storms while supporting my passions and personal growth. I would not be here without you.

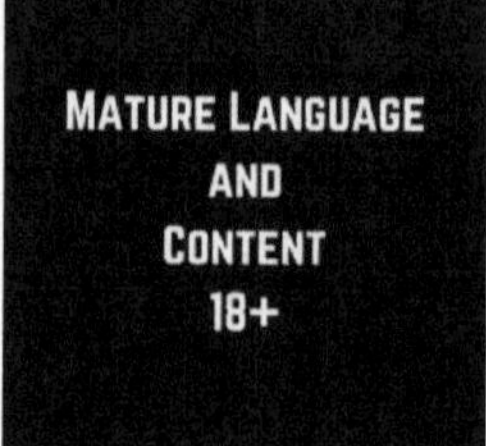

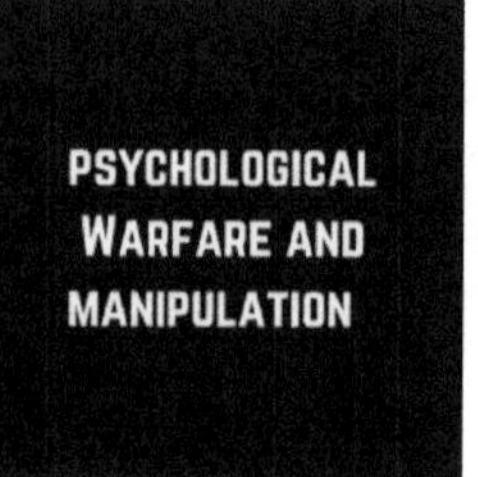

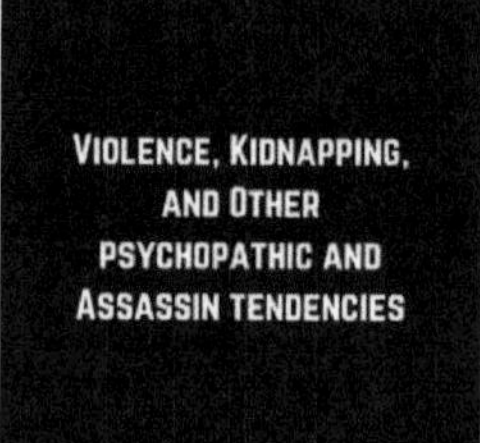

Full list of Trigger Warnings is listed at
https://linktr.ee/chasingstormi

BIRTH OF THE LEGEND

It's believed that stories are gifted to those with the courage to share them to paper. They are the stories of the realms and their existence. The people who read these stories give them the life force they need to thrive. Some have more power than others. A secret society, known only as the Guild, was created to keep the more powerful safe. They assign them watchers, and no one is the wiser of the power they hold. Including themselves. However, what happens when the Guild is corrupted, and their secrets are spilled?...

Will the raven awake in time? And will she save them or destroy them all?...

Let the legend begin....

<u>One</u>

There was nothing more they could do. The dream realm was locked, and Sophie was on her own. Jess clung to Jack with Corbin close by as they stared into the fire and intently watched the battle play out. Corbin absent-mindedly reached over to occasionally relieve Jack of the pain Jess caused him from crushing his thigh in her hands from the anticipation. Emotions were off the charts, but Corbin held on until Sophie finally reached James.

Everyone held their breath as Algos crushed Sophie's windpipe with his bare hands. Jess jumped up to interfere, but a skeletal hand pushed her back down before Corbin could get to her.

"I can't just sit here and do nothing!" demanded Jess.

"You can, and you will," John ordered. His hood wasn't on, and Jack nearly gasped. He had forgotten how much he looked like his father. John didn't take his eyes off the fire that grew high within the fireplace. He felt his granddaughter grow too weak for her own good.

"Not getting along with your new pet?" Clarice asked as she came into the room. Sophie looked in her direction and became madder by the second, but she had nothing left to give. She looked at James with tears of apology in her eyes.

The dead held their breath, forced to see how this was going to play out.

"You may have been right," Algos said. "She's more trouble than she's worth."

"Go." John whispered into Jess's ear so only she would hear. She closed her eyes and focused on the last image of her daughter she had seen.

Clarice threw her head back in a cackle. "That's a first," she said, coming to stand right next to him. She tilted her head at Sophie to study her. Only it wasn't Sophie who looked back at her. It was Jess. Clarice took in a sharp gasp at the sight, but remained by her father.

"Help me," she heard Jess whisper in her ear. Clearly a trick. Clearly, her sister did not know her as well as she had always claimed.

"So, what are you going to do with her?" Clarice asked casually as she turned her back dangerously to her father and took a few steps away from him.

"She's obviously been tainted," Algos said in great disappointment. "I will have to just destroy this one and start from scratch," he said with a shrug, as if Sophie were just a mere science project and not a human at all.

Clarice nodded her head and let out a heavy, thoughtful sigh. "Yeah," she murmured. "That's what I thought."

Algos didn't feel her take his trusty switchblade from his pocket. He didn't hear her open it while he spoke. He didn't hear her quickly spin behind him before jabbing it into the back of his neck and twisting it as hard as she could. All Algos felt was the numbness that quickly consumed his body, forcing him to let go of Sophie and fall to his knees before falling face first.

Algos couldn't talk. He couldn't move. She had taken him out just like he had taken his own father out. *Like some sort of hereditary, poetic justice*, he thought. Then he saw something walking towards him. A tiny, blurred figure. As it got closer, it bent down and got right in his face. A little boy in a red jacket, with ash brown hair and aero blue eyes, was staring back at him innocently. "Train goes fast," Peter hissed to him before his eyes turned red, and the most sinister grin crossed his face. He jammed his hand into Algos's chest and ripped out his heart. It was the last thing Algos saw, even though no one else did. But someone else did see. John knew exactly who took Algos, and it wasn't Peter.

Clarice had stepped back from the body and watched her own father's nasty poison take over his body and eat itself from the inside out. Sophie was busy gasping for air and getting to her feet to prepare to take Clarice on. Corbin and Jack looked at Jess, unsure of what her reaction would be.

"That's my girl," Jess whispered with pride as she opened her eyes.

"You're free," Clarice told Sophie flatly, not even looking her in the eye. "Go."

"I'm not done yet," Sophie warned.

"Sophie Lee," she heard her mother warn. "Please!"

"You killed Mario," Sophie said, ignoring her mother's warning.

"Yeah, and I can't bring him back, now, can I?" Clarice retorted as she bent down and grabbed the keys from her father's jacket and tossed them at Sophie. "Get out!" she barked and went to leave the room. Clarice paused only for a second. "You're not my concern," she added over her shoulder. "Tell your mother I kept my promise and to leave me alone." Then she walked out of the room, leaving Sophie feeling conflicted about letting the murderer of her godfather leave with no harm done to her, like she had promised.

"A little help here!" James called out to her. Sophie reluctantly took her eyes off of Clarice and rushed over to grab the only chair to stand on as she unlocked the locks and helped James get his feet back on the floor. He rubbed his wrists, trying to get the feeling back into them.

The fire died. There was no more to watch. Or so they thought. "Well, that was surprising," Jack offered.

"I told you to have more faith," Jess countered, and stood up. "Who's hungry?" she asked. Jack looked at Corbin, and Corbin looked at John, but John was already gone.

"I could use a bite," Corbin offered with a shrug.

"Good! I'm starving!" Jess announced with a smile as she swung her arms while she headed towards their new kitchen. She couldn't look at the old one, knowing Mario had given his life up for the cause in it. Things would never be the same without him. Jess paused briefly at the thought before opening up the refrigerator and pulling out supplies.

Jack observed his wife. *This will not end well,* he thought.

"Agreed," Corbin replied. Jess was too busy in the kitchen to notice either of them.

Corbin felt Clarice's jealousy, frustration, and emptiness all at once. It was like a gut punch he'd never experienced before, but he quickly replaced it with surprise, followed by happiness and determination. Something wasn't right. He just didn't know *what* exactly.

Mario felt the warmth and heat of the light, but couldn't open his eyes to save his life. Not that he was still living.

"That was dumb," a female voice offered flatly. Mario could not share any snappy comeback. His body had nothing left to give. He heard the heavy sigh and felt the woman's hand grab onto his arm gently. "You have a lot to learn, Newbie," she said before the light grew brighter. Mario felt her transfer her own energy into his lifeless body.

"I'd do it again," he finally countered, and she let go immediately.

"Yeah. I know," she eventually added. He heard the disappointment in her voice.

"She did it, didn't she?" he asked with hope.

"Clarice took the final blow, but yes. Sophie did what she needed to do," the woman replied heavily.

Mario finally found the energy to open his eyes. He found Air Force blue eyes full of conflict staring back at him, in a face he recognized from rare photos at once. "I'm sorry about your son,

Angie," Mario whispered, realizing that she had the greatest loss of them all. Losing a child.

"It had to be done," she finally replied, before holding out her hand to help him up. "Be more careful with her," Angie warned in her motherly tone. "I won't be around to always save you," she added with a stern look. He knew she meant it.

"I think I'm about nine lives short at this point," Mario chuckled to break the ice.

"Then I suggest you use this one more wisely," Angie said sulking before turning around to lead the way. The corners of her lips raised. The boy had a point. At least she only had to die once. Mario's blind love was going to get him killed for good if he didn't straighten up, but there's always a learning curve in the beginning. She had one herself. "We've got work to do," she said over her shoulder as they walked into the bright light and disappeared.

Dr. Liz Banks sat in a dungeon of a lab, secluded from the rest of the world, staring down at her latest test subject. A young college student with curly red hair, porcelain skin, and the slightest hints of freckles on her cheeks.

Algos chose her for several reasons. One being that she was a psychology student that studied serial killers. It was Liz's job to see if she could flip the switch from simply studying them to becoming one. Most people would say it was morally wrong, but Liz saw it for what it was. Science. *Who's to say that if she could flip the switch to being a serial killer, someone couldn't switch it back?* However, that wasn't her current project.

"Dr. Banks," boomed a loud male voice, forcing her to jump. Liz turned around to find an over-muscular tree in a suit too small for him and sunglass, despite being inside. Next to him stood a very miserable looking short man, whose suit was too big for his build. His eyes were sunken in, and he looked like he hadn't slept in days. He was opening his briefcase.

"Yes?" she replied skeptically.

A distinct voice responded. It was from the squeaky looking gentleman as he handed over an envelope to her. "I am to deliver this to you should anything happen to Mr. Hersteller."

"And what has happened to Mr. Hersteller?" Liz asked dryly. She didn't realize that she was in a completely unique area from the rest of the bunker. Or that Clarice had killed her own father to save the girl she had spent almost half her life hunting. She didn't know that Sophie had come and wiped out over one hundred soldiers single-handedly. In fact, Liz knew nothing outside of being assigned to this project, and that Algos would do whatever it took to make it succeed.

"Instructions are inside," was the only reply she got.

Liz opened the envelope with great irritation as she skimmed the words on the sheet of paper from inside. "Fine," she finally resigned. At least she could do her work without being constantly checked on by Algos.

"Duke will stay and make sure you carry things out as planned," the lawyer sighed as he turned to exit the lab.

"Duke can go take a flying leap wherever he would like, but he will *NOT* be babysitting me while I work!" she snapped.

The over-muscular giant sneered, but made no sound.

"You'll want to re-read that paper carefully, Dr. Banks. Have a nice day," the squeaky man stated before leaving her with one of Algos' goon enforcers. Liz glared at him with hatred. Duke was pretty sure if she could shoot daggers from her eyes, he'd be dead. Lucky for him, Liz had not been enhanced like some others.

"Stay out of my way," she barked at him.

Duke simply nodded and went to find a quiet corner to observe and do the job Algos over generously paid him to do. Liz looked down at her subject and took a deep breath in order to regain her focus. She brushed a loose red curl from the girl's face. "It's time to play," Liz whispered softly into her ear before getting back to work.

Clarice took her feet off the desk and pushed the intercom button. "Who is this, again?" she asked, softer than she had intended. *What the hell is wrong with me?*

"Mason, Ma'am," the male voice spoke back in hesitation.

"Well, Mason, how many are left at the moment?" Clarice asked a little sharper.

"Not many, Ma'am," Mason answered honestly.

Clarice paused for a second before responding. "Who's left from the lab?"

"Emma," Mason answered in reluctance.

"Who?" Clarice snapped.

"The redhead," Mason confirmed. Everyone knew how much Clarice despised Emma, minus Emma.

"Figures," Clarice mumbled. "Collect everyone left and tell her to find us a new home. Stat."

"New home?" Mason asked in confusion.

"Yes, Mason," Clarice said flatly. "We're not done, but this place is unstable. It's time to move."

"Yes, Ma'am," Mason responded with a hint of doubt in his voice before he got to work.

Clarice looked down at her father's desk. It was a complete mess. Most likely from Eddie looking for a way out. *Eddie...* Clarice shook her head. Now was not the time. She gathered the papers and threw them into a box when a picture escaped and fell to the floor. On it was a picture of a little girl, around the age of eleven, with long, light brown hair and petite elfish facial features. On the back of the picture had one word. *Karmen.*

"Well, who are you?" Clarice asked in curiosity as she held the picture closer to get a better look. "I guess we're going to find out," she added with a scowl as she stuck the picture inside her breast pocket and gathered what she could of potential clues her father had left behind for her to continue on with his legacy.

He chose her to do so. *Her. Just like she always wanted.* A ping of guilt tugged at her stomach for having just murdered him to save her sister's spawn, but it didn't last. It had to be done. Even Clarice knew that. Deep down. Now, to figure out what she was supposed to do next...

James held up Sophie as they walked to gather the backpack. Winter had been delayed this year, but the cold would not hold back anymore. James shivered as the cold cut through him. He was regretting not grabbing a coat before he took off. He heard Sophie giggle next to him and moved in closer as they walked through the forest. *God, he loved that sound.*

"I've got you covered," she said with a smile as she reached for the backpack and pulled out the heavy coat that was shoved inside.

"What about you?" he asked, his eyebrows drawing together.

"I'm warmer than you would think," she said with her typical grin as she held out the coat for him.

"Maybe you should share some of that warmth," he replied, flashing his boyish grin to match hers.

"Oh yeah?" she breathed with anticipation.

"Yeah," he whispered as he stepped closer to her and breathed warm air against her lips.

"I might be able to help you out," she whispered as her grin grew wider and their lips were just an inch apart.

James pulled her into his arms and crushed his mouth against hers. He felt her knees grow weak as she leaned into him and kissed him feverishly back. *It had been too long. Way too long.*

Sophie grew hotter by the second. She felt the energy he offered, and she took it greedily.

"STOP! You're killing him!" screamed a familiar voice in her ears. When she opened her eyes, red flames consumed her pupils. Sophie closed them immediately and pushed James back into a tree behind him. *Something was wrong. Very wrong.*

"Hey!" James gasped as he struggled to get air back into his lungs.

After a beat, Sophie giggled through her lie. "I needed to

breathe."

But James knew better. She was taking his life, and he was eager to give it. Like a fisherman drawn to a siren, he was answering her call. The fog of ecstasy quickly faded, and all he felt was her fear and guilt. "Hey," he whispered to her, still fighting to get some air into his lungs. He took a step towards her and nearly fell to the ground. Sophie caught him before his knees touched the ground. "We're okay," James whispered as his lips parted and he reached out to touch her cheek.

"I know," she whispered back with a wavering smile and a voice full of doubt to match.

"I'm okay," he said more sternly, his eye contact unwavering from Sophie's.

"Let's go," she said, changing the subject as she carried James the rest of the way to the nearest bus stop.

She struggled to open her eyes. She heard the beeping of medical machines and felt the iv in her arm. *Where the hell am I?* When her eyes finally focused under the florescent lighting, she saw an average, thin brunette buzzing around in a lab coat with a clipboard and fiddling with the medical equipment. Suddenly, she stopped and turned to look directly at her.

"Hello, Claudia," the woman said. "You and I are about to become great friends."

Normally Claudia would have panicked and tried to get away, but something in her brain released a huge amount of endorphins throughout her body. *Finally*, she thought...

<u>Two</u>

S hyera MacThom was a nobody working in the New York Public Library on Fifth Avenue in Manhattan. Or at least that's how she viewed herself, which made being a librarian a perfect fit. At first sight, people only saw a young thirty-one-year-old who stood at 5'7", with a short black afro, skin autumn brown and as smooth as a moonstone, and eyes that shone hazel in the sunlight. Her background was a mixture of African American and Seminole Indian, and her gold hoop earrings hung delicately from her ears. She was a queenly figure. Her luxurious curves made men go weak in the knees, which was a bonus for her husband. And the perfect resting spots for her adorable three children when they required snuggles.

She was helping little Jeremy Riker gather his millionth read from a top shelf. "This one, huh?" she asked, with the corner of her lips curling up as she looked down at him through her thick, black-rimmed glasses.

"Yes! I need it!" Jeremy danced around excitedly.

"Jeremy, you know you have a lifetime to enjoy the books from the library. You don't have to conquer them all in one day, right?" she teased as she went to hand him his book, but it fell from her hands and she closed her eyes as she stumbled onto the shelves. When she opened them, red flames consumed each iris. "The raven is awake, and she's missing her master," Shyera announced in a robotic voice. Jeremy stumbled back with fear.

Shyera closed her eyes and shook her head. "Jeremy, ask Miss Cassandra to check you out. I have something to take care of." The little boy crouched down and snatched the book into his trembling hands before taking off.

Shyera looked around with dilated eyes and called Cassandra over her shoulder as she headed for the door. "I'm taking that sabbatical," she announced, not slowing down to grab her things.

The redhead sitting behind the front desk jerked her head up immediately. "The one you might not come back from?" she asked nervously.

"Feed Annabelle for me, and watch my things," was Shyera's only reply. She opened the front door and vanished. It wasn't the busy streets of New York that greeted her. Instead, it was the black fog of the dream realm. She was granted access without question, just as planned...

John felt the shift before anyone else. Trouble was coming. Algos was the least of their worries. He only hoped it wasn't Sophie he was feeling.

"Where is Rebecca?" a council member screamed. "Why has she left?"

John had no answer to give, but he was nervous, too. He knew Rebecca's backstory. How powerful she truly was. He also knew Sophie was on a much higher level, with no idea of just how high.

"Corbin cannot defeat what is coming!" another shrieked. "He is so limited compared to her!"

"We all have our parts," John reminded them.

"Another has awakened!" one council member screeched. "His replacement is awake!"

"It is not our problem," John lied as he stared off into the fog. *Someone else was here. Someone who didn't belong.*

"What if they are worse?" another squealed. "What if they come for us again?"

John slammed his hand on the table before them, forcing the entire dream realm to shake. "You will address me with respect," he warned. "Or you can join the others."

The enormous hooded figure shrunk back into its chair. "Your priorities have shifted," the council member snapped.

"You know nothing of my priorities, or me," John warned. "My job is to keep this realm balanced and thriving, and at the moment, I sense an intruder."

The eleven other members gasped and shrieked as they began all shouting at once.

"They're here to destroy us!"

"They're here to control us!" they all yelled. "We're not safe!"

"SILENCE!" John screamed, taking their voices away. After a beat, he continued. "We will sort this out, and it will restore balance."

The council members looked at each other, providing an enormous amount of doubt to fill the air.

"Have I ever let you down?" John snarled in frustration.

"You left us to save her!" one shouted back.

"Exposing those that dared to betray us and keeping this realm safe. Did I not?" John snapped back.

Whispers broke out amongst the members.

"You don't have to know what I do or why. Just that I provide results. That is why I was chosen. That is why I remain so many years later," he added with emphasis. "If you have a problem, then you can join the others. My spot is promised. Yours is not," he reminded them.

Silence filled the air, and John took a breath. "We need to find who doesn't belong. Call for Corbin." They grumbled as they left John alone.

He would have to be careful. They could not know that his humanity had returned after the time spent with Sophie. John had memories again. He knew his family. He could no longer stay impartial. If they found out, balance would be lost. The dream realm would collapse. And his family would pay the biggest price of all.

James looked out the window of the bus as Sophie slept on his shoulder. He could feel her more than ever. Sophie's fear. Her guilt. She wanted to flee for their safety. He had to stop it before she could make it a reality.

"Corbin," James whispered, and closed his eyes. The usual wooden door greeted him. James quickly built an imaginary wall around his mind. They were so eager to feed off of his emotions, but he was here for answers. James pushed the door open without waiting for an invitation. Corbin Dallas was buried in books at his desk, with his blonde head down and none the wiser.

"So, is this going to be a thing? Where no one knocks anymore?" Corbin asked dryly and clearly distracted. He turned around to find a very concerned looking James. Only Corbin couldn't feel a thing. He tilted his head as he scrutinized the young man. "Interesting," he whispered to himself.

"I need help," James interjected, ignoring him.

"How did you do that?" Corbin asked, both curious and relieved to have a break from feeling everyone around him.

"I need help," James repeated more sternly, his eyebrows pulling together.

Corbin put the book in his hands down and gave James his full attention. "How may I assist?" he asked, still trying to figure out what James had done to block him from absorbing his emotions.

"Something happened," James started.

"What?" Corbin demanded as he stood up abruptly.

"Sophie. She..." James tried.

"What about Sophie?" Jack cut in, interrupting them both.

James looked nervously at Jack and Corbin. It was one thing to tell the dream doctor what happened when he kissed Sophie. It was another to tell her father. Even though Jack still didn't look any older than James, it was still a line he wasn't willing to cross.

"She just seems a little different," James tried again. "More aware," he offered.

"Aware how?" Corbin asked, crossing his arms and scowling. Jack or not, Corbin needed to know what he was dealing with.

James looked at Jack and decided that Sophie was still more important. Even if it costed him his life. "It's like she has a new electrical current of some sort. She absorbs energy. Energy from surrounding life."

Jack looked at Corbin with concern. "What does that mean?" Jack asked as his muscles tensed and his brows wrinkled.

"I'm not sure," Corbin replied honestly. "It may be an aftermath of whatever she did before she woke up," he added.

"Is it long term?" James asked.

Jack looked at James. He tried to sense how bad the problem was, but for the first time, he felt nothing coming from James. *Maybe it wasn't as bad as he was assuming.*

"It's hard to say," Corbin replied, disrupting Jack's thoughts. "Only Sophie knows what really happened, and we may still never truly know, even if she tells us."

"Not helpful, Doc," James countered sourly. "I'm not really worried, but she is, and you know Sophie..." he broke off.

Jack created a table and invited James to sit next to him at it. Corbin couldn't help with this, but Jack could. He produced two beers, just like Mario used to, and pushed one over to James.

James hesitated, but knew the gesture meant more than a typical invitation. This was the reminiscence of his friendship with Mario, and he was offering it to James. With limitations, of course. He was engaged to his daughter, and some lines just didn't get crossed in

James's mind. He took a seat and a swig of beer as he waited to hear what fatherly advice Jack offered.

"Son, the Harris women are a different breed, in more ways than one," Jack snickered as he took a swig of his own beer. "The universe needs balance," he continued. "There are people that are created to fight for that balance, and those chosen to be by their side to keep *them* in balance while they fight."

"I'm sorry, what?" James asked, trying to follow.

"Sophie's mom kept the world in balance, despite having Algos as a father," Jack clarified. "I was chosen to keep her balanced. Sometimes good has to be evil in order to fight evil, and it's not always easy for them to come back from that by themselves. They need someone like us to help them get back to being balanced. Sophie carries this trait. You were chosen to give her the balance she needs to get the job done."

"And how exactly do I do that?" James asked, pushing his beer to the side and leaning forward onto his elbows. His eyes focused on Jack's face intently.

"That, I'm afraid, I can't answer," Jack said. "Sophie is like her mother, but also not her mother. It's your job to figure out what provides *Sophie* balance. What works for my wife won't work for my daughter. Though equally stubborn, they are unique and require different needs."

James hesitated before asking, "And what if I can't do it?"

"Then you're not the chosen one," Jack offered, shrugging and taking another sip.

Corbin looked at Jack in shock, but Jack just shook his head ever so slightly to deter him.

"Do you want to be the one?" Jack asked after a pause.

"You know I do," James said, baring his teeth.

"Then trial and error, my boy," Jack uttered with a weary smile. "Don't think I could balance Jess overnight," he laughed as he played some memories through his head that James couldn't see.

"And what if she doesn't *want* balance?" James inquired, interrupting Jack's trip down memory lane.

"They won't always want it," Jack said with a knowing smile. "But they need it, and we need to give it to them. That's why we're chosen," he emphasized.

"So, I didn't meet Sophie by accident?" James asked in shock.

"It doesn't matter the answer," Jack replied, putting his hand on James's shoulder. "Trust me. I spent several years trying to figure it out myself. You won't get the answer. And frankly, it means nothing if it wasn't by accident. Does it change the love you have for her?"

"No," James answered truthfully. "But it might change hers for me," he said flatly as he stared at his hands.

"Only if you let it," Jack replied, squeezing his shoulder and sitting back for another sip of beer.

"Have you met your daughter?" James asked sarcastically.

Jack spit out the beer in his mouth. "Her mother was no walk in the park, so I can imagine," he laughed with his own grin. He sensed Jess in the background and waved his hand behind his back to stop her.

"What if she leaves again?" James asked, shoving a hand through his hair, not looking Jack in the eye.

"Go find her," Jack advised. "Listen, they take a while to accept who they are and what they are capable of. Let alone why they need us," he concluded. "It's not an easy road, but it's a road worth traveling. If you want to be Sophie's balance, then you need to do that. No matter the cost. Do you understand?" Jack questioned, his jaw setting and giving James a warning gaze.

James looked up, giving Jack a curt nod. "Yes, sir," he countered.

"She'll fight you like hell on wheels until she realizes that it's what's best for you both, so you have to be patient and persistent," Jack warned.

"I understand," James said, thrusting his chest out, suddenly calm and focused. "Thanks for the beer," he said, holding out his hand to Jack and giving it a squeeze before he stood up to go back through the door.

"But she's okay, right?" Jack asked, growing still as his forehead wrinkled.

"She's adjusting, but she's good. I'll keep her safe," James answered back. "And balanced," he added with his boyish grin before he turned and went through the door.

"He's not the one, is he?" Jess asked, wrapping her arms around herself.

"I don't think you give him enough credit," Jack replied, still staring at the door James had left through. "You Harris girls don't exactly accept us with open arms," he reminded her. He felt the pang of guilt come from his wife, but it was the truth, and she needed to remember that part.

"I said I was sorry," she finally whispered.

"We're just lucky I'm here to tell the tale," Jack laughed as he stood up and took his wife into his arms to kiss her passionately.

"Is she okay?" Jess breathed out once they parted.

"I didn't feel alarm with him, so I think it's just more of the adjustment phase," Jack answered with a shrug and kissed his wife again. Corbin left the room feeling less sure.

"Benjamin Miller, if you don't put on your doctor hat right now, so help me, you will *not* see this child born!" shouted Tina from down the hall.

"Going well, I see," Daryl said with a grimace. Although he looked like the typical biker bouncer, Daryl was the biggest teddy bear when needed. And now he was concerned for Ben's safety in Tina's pregnant hands.

Sally and Donna sat calmly, sipping their hot tea at the table, and exchanging knowing looks. "Roger, Dear," Sally called over her shoulder. "I think Ben needs some help calming down."

"Coming, Dear," Roger called out in amusement as he headed down the hall.

"I thought women didn't get this violent until labor?" Daryl pouted. Both women giggled at him. "Oh, goodie," he grumbled as he walked away.

"Do you think they're okay?" Donna asked Sally.

"You'll have to be more specific," Sally giggled.

"Sophie and James," Donna clarified.

"My son is more savvy than most realize," Sally offered. "I'm sure they're fine," she lied.

"How can you be so sure?" Donna asked.

"Because someone has to be," Sally replied, and took another sip of her tea. She hadn't known Sophie for long, but Sally knew the intensity of their love. They're either both alive or both dead. Sally refused to accept the latter and put her energy into the chaos that currently surrounded her instead. A new mom with an overprotective new dad that was driving each other and everyone else crazy. This she could control, so this is what she focused on.

Just then, something metal came soaring out of the open door. Everyone cringed at the sound. "Should we...?" Donna started to ask.

"They have to learn," Sally giggled, shaking her head 'no'. "So, what should we do for dinner?" she asked, changing the subject.

Three

"We're here," James whispered into Sophie's ear as he nudged her with his shoulder.

"Already?" she asked, confused, as she tried to get her foggy brain to focus.

"Well, we're halfway," he clarified. "I need food and an actual bed."

"We need to get you checked out," Sophie said firmly as she sat up suddenly and brushed her hand down his cheek. He felt her concern and guilt swallowing them both up. *When did he become so in tune with her?*

"I'm okay. Honest," James assured as he took her hand and kissed it. "But I need food, and so do you. Let's go, Princess," he added for good measure.

Sophie narrowed her eyes as her eyebrows came together, because he was using Mario's trick to let her know she was being unreasonable and needed to follow suit for both their sakes. "Fine," she mumbled as she grabbed the bag and led the way off the bus. She could feel his boyish grin a mile wide, shining from behind her. Sophie couldn't help but smile herself. "What are you in the mood for, nerd boy?" she giggled as she led the way away from the bus.

"You," James growled, pulling her unexpectedly into a passionate kiss before she could protest. Sophie tried to push him away for fear of hurting him, but quickly lost the ability as need and desire took over. When James felt the heat brew within her, he pulled back. "Italian," he said, rubbing his nose softly against hers. *Balance*, he thought to himself proudly.

A mixture of relief and frustration pushed from Sophie's body and James laughed as he took it in. "You're mean," she pouted and spun to smack him in the face with her ponytail. Sophie left him to freeze alone as she led the way to find them food. James just whistled and kicked the rocks as he walked behind her, secretly plotting his next move.

Ben came sulking out of the room and joined the women at the table.

"Tea?" Donna offered.

"I think I need something stronger," Ben mumbled as he slumped into one of the chairs. Like magic, Daryl placed an open beer before him. "You get it," he winced as he nodded at Daryl. Daryl put a sympathetic hand on his back before pulling out a chair and sitting down to join them. Cecil set a fresh plate of nachos in front of everyone and took a seat himself.

"I don't understand the fuss," Ben started, but Sally held her hand up to stop him.

"Ben, have you ever known Tina not to handle herself?" she asked in her motherly voice.

"No, but..." Ben started. Daryl kicked him under the table. "Hey!"

"Have you ever known her to break at a single touch?" Donna asked.

"No," Ben answered, confused.

"Son, you've got your 'freaking out dad hat' on as she keeps putting it, and we need you to put on your 'doctor hat' for a second," Cecil said bluntly, using air quotes. "Is a woman's body able to handle pregnancy and still manage everyday tasks and then some?"

"Of course," Ben replied as his eyebrows drew together.

"Is Tina different from any other woman?" Cecil continued.

"Well," Ben started, but Daryl kicked him under the table again. "Cut it out!" he finally snapped. Daryl shrugged in innocence.

"From a doctor's point of view, is Tina able to carry this child?" Cecil tried again.

"Oh, of course. She's as healthy as a horse," Ben replied, lifting his chin and leaning back in his chair.

"Then knock it off with the over protective routine. You're driving her and all of us nuts!" Cecil ended with a raised voice.

Ben's eyebrows came to a perfect "w" almost before he let

them relax. "I'm just a little nervous, I guess. We're not in normal circumstances," he finally admitted to himself and everyone else.

"You know how they always say it takes a village to raise a child?" Donna asked softly before showing off all the people in the room and then some with her best Vanna White impression. "You have a village. Relax a little," she replied flatly.

"You're staying?" Ben asked as his eyes widened and his mouth dropped open a little. He assumed everyone would just be on their way once Sophie took out Algos. If Sophie took out Algos.

"You're stuck with us, Kid," Daryl laughed as he slapped Ben on the back, causing him to almost knock over his beer.

"No matter the outcome, this is our home. You are a part of that home, and can stay as long as you want," Donna explained. "But you are required to come back often. Especially after the baby comes," she demanded.

Ben knew it to be true. Donna was as sweet as Sally. However, also like Sally, she was not to be crossed. Her added enthusiasm for guns and knives helped him not crossing her, too. "Deal," he finally said with a smile as he relaxed in his chair and took another sip of his beer, suddenly at ease.

"Now, go apologize to your wife, kiss her, and tell her it's going to be okay," Sally ordered. "This will be a phrase used often in the next nine months. Start practicing now," she added firmly.

"Yes, ma'am," Ben said with a smile and rushed down the hall to do just that.

"Are we going to talk about..." Cecil started.

"Nope," both women said in unison as they sipped their tea. The men drank their beer in silence.

Clarice packed up what she considered useful. She ordered Mason to oversee the move to their new temporary location as she went off to find a cheap hotel in Provolone to get some sleep and plan her next move. She was sure that James and Sophie were long gone, getting back to their family. *Family.* Something Clarice was completely out of now, minus the niece, she finally stopped hunting.

She waited to feel sick to her stomach over killing her own father. The one person who she had spent a lifetime trying to gain approval of, but nothing came. No guilt. No remorse. *But he had left what was the last of his legacy to her? Why did murdering him not phase her?*

She absent-mindedly rubbed the new gold necklace around her neck as she walked down the streets of sleepy Provolone. She flipped their family symbol between her fingers as she walked.

It was dinnertime. The college kids were out lighting up the town and blowing off steam. Clarice stopped to look up at the building off the beaten path that clearly no one willingly stayed on. It reeked of sweat, filth, and cheap thrills. Even holy cities had spots of glorified sinning. Whether or not they admitted to it. The corner of her lips curled up at the irony of the situation as she got a room.

The man working the front desk had looked so shocked that she was there at all, let alone checking in as one. He sat in a chair that looked like it came out of the dumpster, and wore a wife beater stained with god knows what, with hair poking out of every opening. He reminded her of Danny DeVito, if he never made it as an actor and sold his soul to the devil in order to reign over this hellhole of a motel. Clarice had assured him she would put the room to good use, but tonight she needed sleep.

"Whatever," he snarled in his food. The wife beater was two sizes too small as he tossed the key to her.

He was generous enough to give her a king-sized bed, anyway. Holding down the vomit that threatened to escape her lips as she flirted with him hadn't hurt. He tried to act like he didn't care, but she knew men as well as she knew how to take a life in mere seconds without leaving a mark. It had been worth the upgrade. Something told her this was his best room, despite the horrific view from within. Jess would have pitched a fit, no doubt. *Jess.*

Clarice threw her bag into the sorry excuse of a chair in the corner. The chair protested loudly as it moved closer to the wall from her anger, and she fell onto the bed as she let out a frustrated scream.

"Knock it off!" a male husky voice answered back on the other side of the paper-thin wall.

Note to self, sound proof walls in the new place. She glared at the faded horrible seventy's flowered paper that stared back at her before she kicked off her shoes and laid back to get some shut-eye. Good thing she was used to sleeping on a terrible excuse for a bed. This was just like home. *Home.* Clarice gave out a frustrated sigh and closed her eyes.

When she opened them, she found the wooden door before her.

"No!" Clarice screamed out into the nothingness.

"Open it," her sister demanded loudly in her head.

"Screw you!" Clarice yelled back as she tried to force herself awake. She wasn't ready to face her sister. Not right now.

"Open it, or I will open it for you," Jess warned.

Clarice crossed her arms in front of her chest. "You'd put me in the hospital after all I have done for you?" Clarice snapped back.

"Please open it," Corbin pleaded in her head. She drew in a sharp breath. *That wasn't fair. That wasn't fair at all.*

"Why should I?" she asked, trying to collect herself.

"Although your stubbornness is cute, you need to put it aside and talk to your sister," he added softly.

Cute? Did he really just say that? She hated he knew he affected her at all. Clarice took a step back as adrenaline shot through her body unexpectedly. *How much did he know?*

"Please," Corbin begged in her head one more time.

Clarice gave a heavy sigh before reaching out and opening the door. Jess was waiting impatiently on the other side with her own arms crossed in front of her chest.

"So, you came to see me after all," Jess started.

"Don't start with me," Clarice snapped. "You weren't going to let me not come in here."

Jess dropped her arms to her side as obvious hurt crossed her face. "I just wanted to make sure you were okay," she said as if she were a child that was sad she had disappointed a parent.

"I'm fine," Clarice said, a little softer than intended. "You didn't have to use Wonder Boy, though."

"Wonder Boy?" Jess asked, confused.

"Hey, Sis," Jack said, interrupting them both.

Clarice glared at Jack. "You don't call me that," she snarled.

"Well, we didn't exactly spend a lot of time together before I had to leave," Jack interjected quickly. "At least I don't call you Clare

Bear," he offered with a smile. Jess glared at him, but Clarice's frown turned into a sneer for just a split second before it went back to deadpan. A habit she had picked up the day Algos murdered her mother in front of her. Jess missed it. Jack didn't.

Corbin debated if he should stay hidden or join them. *Would it be too obvious?* He talked to Clarice without Jess knowing, but he wasn't sure how long he could keep it up. *Maybe he should just wait.*

"What do you want?" Clarice asked, annoyed, interrupting his thoughts.

"I just wanted to make sure you were okay," Jess replied softly. "I know that was...difficult."

"Not as much as you'd think," Clarice said with a shrug as she turned back to the door.

"Clarice," Jess said with pleading concern oozing in her voice.

Clarice's shoulders fell forward, and she turned around slowly to face her sister. "Listen," she started. "You forced my hand. I had to make a choice. You didn't have to try your ghost trickery, by the way," she added with obvious irritation. "I was going to do it anyway," Clarice added, glaring at her sister. "And the deal was you left me alone. I'm not after your stupid spawn of a child, so you're supposed to leave me alone. Remember?" she ended with emphasis.

"Clarice," Jess said wide-eyed as she took a step towards her sister.

Corbin couldn't breathe. So much hurt was coursing through both of them, it was literally crushing his lungs.

Clarice threw her hands up. "I did what you asked. Why can't you do what I ask?" she yelled, unable to even look at her.

Tears filled Jess's eyes. "Because you're my sister. And it

couldn't have been easy to do, no matter how horrible of a person he was," Jess started.

"Don't!" Clarice cut her off, throwing her hand up to stop her from continuing. "You know nothing about him."

"I know everything about him!" Jess shouted back as her eyes glowed red. "Don't make it like I didn't," she hissed.

"Ladies," Jack tried to interject, placing himself between the women.

Corbin appeared without warning, gently wrapping his arm around Clarice's waist and pulling her back towards him. "Calm down," he warned Jess, but her eyes just grew brighter.

Clarice's eyes may not physically change, but she was seeing red herself. "You're just pissed because he chose me!" she shouted at Jess. Clarice attempted to wiggle out of Corbin's grip to take a step in her direction, but Corbin just tightened his grip, making her red waver from anger to desire for a split second.

"What are you talking..." was all Jess got out before she saw the necklace around Clarice's neck. "What is that?" she snapped, nodding towards the necklace.

Corbin looked down to see the symbol they knew all too well. "Oh Clarice," he whispered in her ear.

Tears stained Clarice's cheeks as she thrashed in Corbin's grip. "He chose ME!" she screamed at them all as saliva flew from her mouth like a rabid dog. "Me! NOT YOU! ME!"

Jess's eyes extinguished as they filled with tears and concern. "Is that what you really believe?" she choked out.

"YES!" Clarice demanded. "He left a note! Me! Not you! Me!" she repeated.

Jess wasn't sure who she was trying to convince more. "Clare Bear," Jess whispered softly, but that just made Clarice thrash harder and scream louder. It was obvious that Algos still had plans. Plans that involved destroying her sister beyond recognition, but now was not the time for Clarice to see that. "Let her go," Jess said through her grief.

Corbin reluctantly let go and Clarice fell back a few steps, trying to catch her footing.

"Guess you weren't the favorite after all!" Clarice snarled back. "Now, leave me alone!" she demanded one last time as she faced the door, yanked it open and let it slam behind her, shaking the dream realm in her wake.

"She doesn't mean it," Jack whispered as he put a reassuring hand on Jess's shoulder.

"I'm not so sure about that," Jess replied, defeated, and walked out of the room.

Corbin was still staring at the door, willing Clarice to come back.

"You okay?" Jack asked him, interrupting his thoughts.

"It just really hurts," Corbin whispered, still staring at the door.

"I see that," Jack replied, but when Corbin turned to look him in the eyes and see what he knew, Jack was already gone.

So much for not being obvious.

Four

Clarice sat up immediately, angrier than she had ever been in her life. *He chose me! Not her. ME!* Tears ran uncontrollably down her cheeks as she gasped for air to get back into her lungs. Their father finally chose her. The note had said "C" not "J". He chose her. *Hadn't he?* Doubt seeped in, and she devoured it as aggressively as she swallowed the surrounding air. Once she could breathe again, she wiped away unending tears. "She's just jealous," Clarice sobbed out loud.

"Shhh," she heard Corbin whisper in her ear. She felt an imaginary hand brush across her forehead, forcing immediate calm to consume her body. Clarice fell backwards with her head hitting the pillows behind her. This was not the first time she had felt him force her to sleep. It was the first time that she had felt as if she was being cradled in his arms. As if he were actually there to physically hold her.

"I've got you," were the last words she heard whispered in her ear before she drifted into a deep, drama free sleep.

Stacey Bowen's sky blue eyes squinted at the computer screen before her, with the tip of her nose wrinkled up. She chewed vigorously on the gummy bear in her mouth. God, did she miss Tina. She was much better than Stacey, with solving puzzles. Stacey shoved back her chair in irritation and stood to take a break. Her exquisite curves were hidden under her lab coat, and she was fine with that. Those curves were for her husband, and devour them, he did.

She used a pencil to scratch her scalp, hiding under a messy bun made up of Stacey's shoulder length black hair. Her blonde highlights shimmered in the florescent lighting. Although her temporary supervisor at the FBI gave regular lectures on how to "dress for the part you wanted", Tina had always let Stacey be herself. God, she missed Tina. As if on cue, the burner phone vibrated in her pocket. Stacey grabbed it, eager to hear her friend's voice.

"Hello," she said cautiously, despite knowing who would be on the other side.

"Hey lackey," Tina giggled.

Stacey snorted in response before casually asking, "How's it going?"

"Ben's driving us crazy, but otherwise, okay," Tina replied. "Still no word," she said with a mixture of frustration and sadness in her voice. "How are you doing?" she asked, quickly changing the subject.

"I used to love puzzles, but this one..." Stacey dropped off.

"Yeah, I know. Just keep working," Tina assured.

"But if no one made it back, is it even worth it?" Stacey asked in a hushed voice. She was by herself, but you never knew. Even in the FBI.

"Just keep working," Tina emphasized. "And Stacey," she added.

"Yeah?"

"Please stay safe," Tina said in a motherly tone.

"Always," Stacey replied with a before hanging up. Now, to get back to work.

Sophie entered the hotel room nervously. She loved James, and she wanted him. Badly. But something was wrong. Something was causing her to drain the life out of him. Literally. And that was just a kiss! *I can't avoid him forever.*

James felt her nervousness. He felt her energy like never before. *Balance.* He had to prove to her he was her balance. But his lust for her was taking over like he'd never felt before. He dropped his bag and helped take Sophie's from her back.

"We should get something to eat," she offered as she crossed her arms in front of her to protect them both.

"Oh, I plan on it," he said in a deep tone that oozed with desire.

Sophie spun around to see an unfamiliar creature standing

behind her. James's eyes were dark, and his breathing picked up speed. Something was definitely wrong. "James," Sophie said cautiously, taking a few steps back.

Her reaction stopped him dead in his tracks. He closed his eyes and slowed down his breathing. *What's wrong with me?* "I'm sorry," he said without opening his eyes. "I need some food," he added quickly. He grabbed her by the hand before she could protest and dragged her down the stairs and back out into the streets.

Sophie watched him cautiously. *Had she done this to him?* "Are you okay?" she asked as her eyes filled with tears.

He paused and took her face in his hands as he pulled her into a gentle kiss. James felt her protest, but only for a second, before she leaned into the kiss and searched his mouth feverishly with her tongue. He reached around and cupped her butt in his hands as he pulled her closer to him. James felt her grow dangerously hot again, and he stepped back, making sure not to let go of her. *Balance.* "I think I just have missed you a little too much," he said, giving her his boyish grin that made her knees go weak.

"I missed you, too," she breathed as she struggled to get air back in her lungs.

The cold air whipped around them, nearly cutting them in two. "Let's get inside," he said, grabbing her hand and pulling her into the restaurant.

They avoided talking about the future. They avoided talking about Clarice and everything that had just happened. James listened, but his mind remained elsewhere. *Balance.* She was more powerful, and he seemed to feel everything she had become and what she was becoming. *How the hell do you balance that?* He had about an hour to figure it out, or they were both doomed. He kept her distracted as he contemplated his options. There weren't many.

Claudia sat up to take the doctor lady in. "Who are you supposed to be?" she asked sarcastically.

"My name is Dr. Liz Banks, but my friends call me Lizzy," the woman replied as she continued to check Claudia's vitals.

"Are we friends?" Claudia asked, watching her closely.

Liz stopped for a second. "I hope we will be," she finally replied before going back to work.

"Where am I?" Claudia questioned, taking in her surroundings.

"My employer's lab," Liz replied casually.

"And I'm the lab rat?" Claudia asked with a scowl.

"You're so much more than that," Liz answered, giving her a genuine smile.

Claudia began pulling the cords and iv off her.

"Please don't," Liz said as she rushed to replace them. "I really need your baseline vitals. It'll just be a few more minutes."

"Baseline for what?" Claudia demanded in a raised voice. Her lips pursed together tightly as her muscles tensed and her left eyebrow raised.

"To finding out how amazing you truly are," Liz replied in pride.

"What the hell did you do to me?" Claudia hissed as her eyes narrowed, and her tone sent a shiver down Liz's spine.

"I set you free," Liz said, sticking her chin up in the air.

Claudia closed her eyes to take in what was just told to her. Free was definitely a word that fit how she was feeling at the moment, but she would not give this woman the satisfaction of knowing she agreed. Not until she knew exactly what was going on. "Free, how?" she whispered, not opening her eyes.

Liz paused for a second before responding. "My employer saw people were their best when inhibitions were taken away and they answered their true calling," Liz stated matter-of-factly. "He hired me to help flip that switch for you. It's up to you to see what you can accomplish with your new freedom," she replied flatly.

Claudia opened her eyes. "Who's your employer? Where are they?" she asked, strangely calm.

"Dead," Liz replied bluntly.

Claudia gave out a sarcastic laugh. "Well, isn't that perfect!" she exclaimed.

"Actually, it is," Liz said with a sheepish smile. "He wouldn't let you truly be yourself without his own agenda. Now, you can be."

"And you're going to let me?" Claudia asked, raising her left eyebrow at her again.

"Of course!" Liz responded with enthusiasm. "How else will I know if I achieved success or not?"

"Spoken like a true scientist," Claudia replied dryly.

"I know, right?" laughed Liz.

Claudia tilted her head and took in the doctor. "Then why do I feel the need to murder someone?" she asked, sitting up straighter.

"Maybe that's what your calling is," Liz responded honestly.

"Then what makes you safe?" she asked, staring at the doctor like she was her next meal.

"You will never hurt me, Claudia," Liz answered with confidence. "It's not in you to kill the person who gave you your true freedom."

"What's that supposed to mean?" she asked with annoyance.

"It means I'm going to be by your side as we figure out what you're truly capable of. If that's being a psychopathic serial killer, then I will be the one helping you hide bodies and figuring out your signature. If it's to save the world, I will be by your side figuring that out, too. Either way, I'm your new best friend," Liz said bluntly.

"Why do I feel you made option one more doable?" Claudia asked her warily.

"I just flipped the switch," Liz lied calmly. "But if that's what you want to start with, I'm fine with it. Ready to see what you can do?"

Claudia's lips pulled into a sneer. *You have no idea...*

Jack found Corbin sitting at his desk, buried in books. "Hey, buddy. We need to talk," he stated as he slapped his friend on the back. He felt every muscle in Corbin's body tighten, but he pretended to keep reading the book in front of him.

"Oh?" Corbin asked casually. "What about?"

Jack smiled his familiar grin. *Game on, my friend.* "You know, the usual," Jack said softly, pulling up a chair next to his friend. "Let's just start with Clarice."

Corbin tried to act indifferent. He knew Jack was looking for a response, and he needed to make sure he didn't give it to him. "Is something wrong?" Corbin asked, as nonchalant as possible.

"She's fine," Jack assured. He noticed Corbin slump a little, and exhale a breath he probably didn't even realize that he was holding. "I don't think I ever told you about the first time I met Clarice," Jack continued.

Corbin let out a laugh. "How is this important to anything going on?" he asked, waving his hands around the empty space.

"Oh, it matters," Jack laughed. "We were all in high school," he started. "Clarice, a couple of years ahead of us."

"Any embarrassing stories to share?" Corbin asked, placing his chin in his hand, and looking at Jack with great interest.

Jack rolled his eyes and shook his head. "Not today, my friend," he sighed. "The girls always had boys chasing after them," Jack started. Corbin frowned and went to turn back to his book, but Jack gently pulled the book away and closed it in his lap. "I don't think they ever realized that he had made them that way," Jack continued, and Corbin jerked up his head to stare at Jack in shock. Jack just gave him a knowing nod. "Yeah, I know, trust me," Jack continued, shaking his head in disbelief. "I never figured out why he had altered them. I assumed it was to make them more potent at helping him lure in his prey," he added with anger radiating from his voice.

"She doesn't know?" Corbin asked angrily.

"Neither of them know," Jack confirmed with a shake of his head. "My daughter has no clue it was passed onto her, either," he added, to let him know just how far it went. "So, it's easy to get caught up in them. Wanting to protect them. Save them."

"So, you think James isn't meant for Sophie?" Corbin asked, trying to change the subject and still get his answers.

"I didn't say that," Jack replied honestly. "You see," he

continued, "everyone's naturally attracted to them, but they determine who stands by them in the end," Jack said, leaning in and focusing so hard on Corbin, forcing him to shift uncomfortably under his stare. "And when they have chosen you, the universe graces you with whatever abilities are necessary to help them accomplish what they are destined to do," Jack said, drawing out his point.

Corbin looked confused. "What does that mean?"

Jack tilted his head from side to side in contemplation. "It's in the beholder's need from what I have found," he finally replied honestly. "I had to inform James that what they gave me to keep Jess balanced will not be the same for Sophie."

"Which means, in theory, would also not be the same for Clarice," Corbin stated as he stared off into space and nodded as he took in the information.

"Correct," replied Jack, watching his friend.

Corbin grew still, minus the pen he kept spinning in his hand. "So, how did you know you were supposed to be with Jess, if everyone felt the way you did?" he asked, looking inquisitively at Jack. "For scientific purposes," he added quickly.

Jack stared at Corbin. Searching him, but he got nothing in return. Corbin knew Jack could sense other's emotions. That's what helped him keep Jess balanced. Of course, Corbin would keep himself safe. So, instead, Jack just smiled. "When lust no longer existed, and I knew that even if she didn't choose me, I would always want nothing but happiness for her. Whatever that looked like," Jack said with a shrug. "When I knew if giving my last breath would mean she could keep going, and there was no hesitation to do just that," he sighed. "For scientific purposes," he said as he nodded at Corbin, fighting to keep the grin off his face.

That's what Jack wanted him to know. Corbin nodded slowly, knowing he had already reached that point, which is probably why Jack was here in the first place. "And how did you survive patiently waiting for her to choose you?" he asked Jack, not daring to look him in the eye and give his hand away.

Jack remained quiet, forcing his friend to look at him. When Corbin finally looked at him, Jack smiled. "Who said I waited?"

The men chuckled and nodded in silent agreement. Then Corbin turned to face Jack fully. "Jess is going to kill me," he whispered softly, betrayed by the fear in his voice.

Jack reached out and put his hand on Corbin's shoulder. "Why do you think I'm here?" Jack laughed lightly. "You're putting me to work, again," he said in an assured voice. "Clarice has waited a long time for you."

"Too bad I'm dead," Corbin mumbled. He felt Jack squeeze his shoulder, forcing him to look him in the eyes again.

"That's the thing that I love most about them," Jack said firmly. "When they choose you, the universe has one hell of a way of rewarding you for sticking around to do your part. Even in death," he said, winking at his friend before dropping his hand and standing.

"Does that mean..." Corbin started.

Jack threw his hands up in surrender. "Each situation is different," Jack replied honestly. "I didn't realize that we would be here in all honesty," he said, dropping his eyes with a hint of sorrow. "But I know there's a price to be paid to retain balance. As long as you're willing to pay the prices for the gifts you gain along the way, and you're willing to do your part, the possibilities are shockingly endless,"

Jack finished with a shrug.

Corbin looked down at the desk next to him, and when he started to ask Jack another question, he was alone in his office. A single paper floated down in front of him, and Corbin instinctively grabbed it. He read the words scribbled in Jack's unmistakable handwriting and watched the paper turn into ice blue flames the second the last period was digested. Jack's warning ringing in Corbin's ears.

The price would be hefty for crossing over and dealing with the living. Even Corbin knew that. The question was if he was willing to pay it, and without hesitation, the answer would always be yes. Corbin closed his eyes and let the secret words Jack sent him sink into his mind. He had work to do. Work to get the woman he loved with all his heart to love him back.

Five

James kept his arm around Sophie's shoulder as they walked back to the hotel. She had relaxed over dinner as they made mindless small talk and just enjoyed having a normal "date" for a change. No Algos. No Clarice. No ghosts. Just the two of them. Pretending to be normal.

However, Sophie was far from normal. No one was more aware of that than James as they walked down the sidewalk back to the hotel. Never mind that she had a psychopathic serial killer for a grandfather who had murdered her own parents to have her for himself. And that same asshole had genetically altered his own daughter to be the perfect assassin that got passed down to Sophie. This. This was different, though. It was almost like a beast had awakened between them. One that fed off carnal lust and life itself. One that would destroy them both if he couldn't tame it.

Ugh! He hated that word. People always assumed that they needed to break an animal's spirit. Make it compliant to their own desires instead of letting the animal be what it was designed to be. And they wondered why the animal fell back to its natural instincts and became a "things gone wrong" kind of news story. *That's it!*

Sophie felt his walking speed increase. She wasn't sure if it was from the cold that seemed to have pushed out fall and taken over, or if it was something else. They'd had such a nice evening. She wanted to keep it that way. She didn't want to think about reality. Sophie wanted to stay in this bubble of normalcy for as long as possible.

"What's the rush?" she giggled as she picked up her own speed to keep up with him.

"It's been a long day, Babe," he said with a fake yawn. "I'm ready for some pjs, tv, and snuggles. You?" He felt her tense up under his arm. James instinctively massaged her shoulder as they walked.

"Sleep, huh?" she asked, trying to gauge him out of the corner of her eye as she kept looking ahead at the couple holding hands ahead of them.

Balance. "Let's go find a nice Romcom to watch. What do you say?" he asked as he watched the same couple ahead of them. James felt her shoulders slump forward under his touch as she relaxed at the thought of a snuggle session instead. Maybe she realized she was more tempted to lose control when she was lost in the moment, too. Either way, he just wanted her to relax again.

"Sounds great," Sophie finally replied, looking into his eyes and giving him her grin in response. They walked in silence while they pretended to be a normal couple, like the people who surrounded them.

Clarice woke up feeling refreshed. A flash of her sister floated in front of her eyes that just made her blood boil. She felt an imaginary hand brush down her cheek, and Corbin quickly replaced the image.

"Nice try," Clarice barked as she gathered her things and headed out the door.

"Let her be," Jack warned his wife.

"I don't know what you're talking about," Jess replied innocently as she pretended to clean up the kitchen that didn't need cleaning.

"Uh huh," Jack replied, flicking the paper and continued to pretend to read it at the table.

Jess sighed heavily before she turned around to lean against the counter like her friend did so many times throughout their life together. *Mario.*

"She needs to know I still love her," Jess said as her body became rigid and she shook her head to shake her grief away.

"She's no different than you. The more you push, the more she'll hate you in the end," Jack said point blank as he stared at the paper in front of him. This was not the time for kitten gloves. He felt the glare of his wife's eyes, but he felt her emotionally agree with him despite his blunt delivery.

"Then I need a distraction," she said moping.

"I might have one for you," John interrupted as he entered their staged getaway.

Jack jumped up and Jess froze by the counter. Despite now knowing he was Jack's dad, the council never came to anyone. Ever. It was against the rules.

"Relax," John said with furrowed eyebrows. "This is business that I can't trust my council with."

Jess and Jack looked nervously at each other.

John pushed his hand out in front of himself. "You're still under my protection, and always will be. No one can change that," he replied sternly. Jack sat back down at the table and pulled out the chair for his father, but he didn't take it.

"There's an intruder in the realm," John continued, glowering at Jack.

"An intruder?" Jess asked. She pushed off the counter and crossed her arms protectively in front of her stomach.

"Yes," John answered with unmistakable tension in his voice. He pulled his hand through his grey hair, pulling the hood off his head. "I don't know why they are here, or what trouble this will cause," he said, displeased. He was bothered. They both knew it.

"We will look into it," Jack assured.

"Why can't you trust your council?" Jess asked as she stared at the face she hadn't seen since she was in high school. It was obvious he wasn't telling them everything.

John jerked his head in her direction and she immediately stared at the ground. "You know why," he hissed.

Jack got up immediately and placed himself between his father and Jess. "We will look into it," Jack said sharply, warning him to back down.

"See that you do," John snapped back, and then he disappeared into a black fog.

They both hesitated a moment before Jess replied, "Sorry. It just came out."

"I know," he said, turning to her and taking her chin in his hand before giving her a gentle kiss on the lips. "Just be more specific when asking for a distraction. This wasn't what I had in mind," he said grinning, taking her hand and helping her out of the chair.

"You're telling me!" exclaimed Jess as they held hands and went for a stroll to see who had invaded the dream realm, and why.

Shyera knew she had to tread lightly. She also knew the head of the council would feel her long before he could find her. She still had to work quickly. Shyera needed to find the raven. She saw a timid young girl with platinum blonde hair pulled back into a ponytail. The girl took Shyera in before heading in her direction. "Excuse me, do you know where I am at?" Shyera lied.

"Are you new?" the girl asked softly.

"I think so," Shyera answered shyly.

"Oh! My name is Giselle. Some people call this the dream realm. It's kind of an in between," the girl replied.

"In between for what?" Shyera asked curiously.

Giselle thought for a second before answering. "Well, I'm not sure. Some are chosen to be here. Some chose to be here. I guess it depends on what unfinished business you have left to do," she said with a shrug. "Or what we're chosen to do," Giselle added as an afterthought.

"Interesting," Shyera replied, deep in thought.

"I'm sorry, I didn't get your name?" Giselle asked, interrupting her thoughts.

"Shyera," she replied with a sweet smile.

"So nice to meet you," Giselle giggled softly as she offered her hand to Shyera.

She looked hesitantly at Giselle's offered hand. "This is really overwhelming," Shyera said, still looking at Giselle's hand. "Can you show me around?"

Giselle dropped her hand, thought for a second, and suddenly pulled Shyera into her arms. "I know it's overwhelming, but you're in a good place," she whispered softly into her ear. She pulled Shyera away from her suddenly to take her in. "Let's get you that tour!" Giselle said excitedly as she took Shyera's hand and dragged her away.

No one can know she's here. Not yet.

James held the hotel door open for Sophie like the true gentleman he was. Her giggle lit the fire within him so strongly, he had to fight to keep it under control. God, he loved that sound. Sophie grabbed her bag and raced for the bathroom, and locking the door behind her, laughing as she went. *Balance.*

James laughed in amusement and shook his head as he shut the door and locked it. He quickly stripped and put on his pajamas and jumped under the covers. When the bathroom door finally opened and Sophie came out with just James's boxers and t-shirt she had gained on her first night at his parent's house, his heart stopped beating. *Damn!*

After a longer pause than he had intended, he held open the covers as she ran and jumped in next to him. She nestled down against him and put her head on his chest. She listened to his heart race just being so close to her, and he felt her smile of approval against his chest. "You're in a good mood," he chuckled as he handed her the remote.

"Smart, but I'm going to let you choose," Sophie said smugly.

"Very well. Challenge accepted," James answered with determination. He saw *Cutting Edge* and clicked the accept button.

"What is this?" Sophie asked with curiosity.

"Oh, you'll love this. It's a movie about a stuck up ice skater who was denied an Olympic gold medal after she fell. She becomes too difficult to work with," he said, tickling her side. Sophie giggled and wiggled in response. "So they bring in a former Olympic hockey player who doesn't put up with her crap, and they build chemistry on the rink and outside of it," he finished proudly.

"Do you think you're the hockey player?" Sophie snickered.

"Obviously!" James retorted.

"Why can't I be the hockey player?" Sophie asked, suddenly sitting up and pretending to be annoyed.

James brushed the hair away from her face. "You're way too pretty," he added slyly.

She glared at him, which was chased by a snort. "Nice save," she said as she settled back in against his side.

"Watch the movie, nerd girl," James countered as he pulled her in as close as possible.

"Again!" Angie demanded impatiently.

"I'm trying!" snapped Corbin, but Angie crossed her arms, looking terribly unimpressed.

"Are you?" she mocked.

With irritation from the sarcastic tone she gave him, ice blue flames shot out of his palm and danced in a circle before him. A portal. He had finally done it!

"Don't get too excited until you verify it's the one you intended," she replied flatly.

He used his second hand, placing next to the first, and widened the portal to see where it had gained him access to. Only the sight of Clarice, sleeping in a nighty, tangled in sheets, had him embarrassed, and losing the connection immediately.

Angie watched with interest, leaning into one of her hips. "Well," she said, intrigued. "When I told you to let your heart decide, I wasn't expecting that. I was thinking like Costa Rica or something," she stated as the corner of her lip twitched in amusement.

"Don't," he snarled as icy blue flames darted uncontrollably across his eyes.

"Oh, put your kitten paws away," Angie snickered, waving her hand and diffusing his flames immediately.

What the hell? "Why are you even helping me?" Corbin asked in annoyance as he walked over to the table and grabbed the beer bottle to take an angry swig.

Angie took a little pity on him. "Because Rebecca is missing, and you're the next line of defense," she said, still staring at where the portal had been, realizing something much more important was going to come from this. "You can't save people if you don't know how to use what you've got, and you came to me because there is no one else," Angie said, still seeing Clarice's image burned in a vision before her.

Sensing her distraction, Corbin spun around. "What?" he exasperated.

"You didn't tell me," she said, turning her head to take him in.

"Tell you what?" Corbin asked, trying to play innocent.

"You know what," Angie said as her eyes narrowed like a teacher who just caught a student cheating on a test.

"There's nothing to tell," Corbin said, dropping his eyes from her heated gaze. "I'm just preparing," he mumbled.

"Oh, you're preparing alright, but for a different war entirely," she giggled.

"Do you know anything about her?" Corbin asked, realizing that he wasn't aware of how much access Angie was granted to her own granddaughter. "I know we have more free rein here," Corbin added softly.

"That you do," she said, looking back at where her granddaughter had laid, sleeping. Her voice cracking, as water filled her eyes, but she quickly blinked it away.

"I'm sorry," Corbin whispered. He wasn't sure what to say.

"Don't be," Angie said, waving her hand around the empty space before her. "We all make choices we believe to be the right ones at the time."

Corbin knew Angie took her own life. He knew she had a vision of Peter asking her to join him before Algos made it impossible to do so, and that Angie had been taken to a realm that didn't allow the same access to the living as the dream realm did. Cutting her off from all the family outside of Peter. Corbin also knew that Angie was currently trying to convince herself that it had been the right choice. Why he could feel her, he wasn't sure, but it definitely made her less annoying suddenly.

"Well," Corbin offered cautiously. "She's as stubborn and mouthy as you are," he offered with a shrug. Angie let out a hearty laugh and covered her mouth immediately. "I know she has good in her, despite Algos trying to steal it from her," Corbin continued confidently. "I know I love her, and I need her like the air I breathe, which says a lot since I'm already dead," he chuckled. Angie let another hearty laugh escape through her hand, and she threw her other one over it as her eyes grew wide with surprise. "I know that because of your love and patience," he emphasized, looking intensely at her, "you will teach me what I need to know in order to keep her safe until my existence is no longer needed."

Angie looked over at him, dropping her hands and smiling at him wearily. Tears of thankfulness streaking her cheek before she brushed them away quickly. "Do you know what your greatest gift is in here?" she asked him.

His eyebrows furrowed. "No," he replied.

"You're an oneironaut, my dear boy," Angie said, showing a wicked smile. "You know this world better than anyone, which means you can manipulate it to do your bidding. That is your greatest gift. You showed it respect in life, so now it returns the favor. Not even John can do it to the full extent you can," Angie declared, wiggling her eyebrows. Corbin swallowed a laugh, thrown off by her sudden playfulness. "So, are you ready to play on a Doctor Strange level?" she asked, full of hope and excitement.

"Oh, hell yeah!" Corbin replied, and with that tiny nugget of knowledge, the surrounding realm began to do his bidding eagerly. A different energy began to spread through it, as if showing approval of him finally answering his calling. John felt the shift and smiled sheepishly.

"That's my boy," he whispered to no one.

<u>Six</u>

James felt his t-shirt get wet with Sophie's tears as she watched the skaters epic fight scene towards the end of the movie. He knew she was enjoying it, because James felt everything she felt while Sophie watched it. He wasn't sure why he could suddenly feel everything she was, but he wasn't complaining. James knew Sophie kept a lot of things to herself. Mostly out of habit, but also because she didn't always understand or know what to do with what she had at hand. Sophie became overwhelmed often and felt she had to figure things out by herself first in order to have a better understanding of what was going on. James was guessing it came from her upbringing and running from a psychopath. He hoped that one day he could prove to Sophie that she could come to him. James hated lying to her, but this was something he knew he had to keep to himself. At least for now. He couldn't afford her shutting down and locking him out again.

When the room got dark with the rolling credits, Sophie pulled up and put her lips feverishly on James's to claim his mouth for herself. James tensed up with surprise before eagerly accepting. She kept her hands on his chest, knotting his shirt within her fist. He felt her need. Her need to be loved by him. For him to know how much she loved him back.

James ran his hands eagerly up and down her back, sliding them under her t-shirt. Her back was bare, with no sports bra to fight with. Without taking her mouth off of his, she got up and straddled him excitedly. They both moaned as she rubbed her sex against him, making him harden even more. James tossed his head back with his eyes closed, trying to slow down his racing heart before he had a heart attack, but Sophie took his face in her hands and crushed her mouth against his once more as they moaned together from their contact.

"Oh, Sophie," James moaned against her mouth.

"I can't stop," she whined back.

"Then don't," he grunted as he flipped her onto her back and pinned her hands beside her head. When he looked down, he saw the flames ignite in her eyes. "No, you don't," he snarled as he quickly straddled her and pushed himself against her. She needed to feel what she did to him. How she changed him. How much he needed her to stay with him. She tossed her head back and arched her back welcomingly. He heard her moan in acceptance, and it just made him want her more.

He moved slowly against her, matching her rhythm, and he felt her madness grow. James grabbed at the bottom of her shirt and yanked it off before she could even think to react. She frantically grabbed at his shirt to do the same. Sophie sat up and placed her hands on his chest and they saw the flames ignite at her touch on his skin. It burned, but James didn't care. He grabbed her hands and forced them down, along with her back to the bed as he took her mouth with his. He leaned down and growled with dominance in her ear, "You're mine. I need you to be mine."

"I am," she moaned in response. She kept her eyes closed, trying to control herself, but she needed this. They needed this.

"Then stay with me," he begged.

Sophie opened her eyes to find icy blue flames staring back at her. "Always," she eagerly submitted. *Did he not understand how much she loved him?*

James switched gears and worked his way down her naked chest. Taunting and teasing her nipples as he sucked on her breasts, making her nearly explode on the spot. "James!" she cried out.

"You're mine," he declared as he kissed against her left breast. "That means I can do whatever I want," he said triumphantly.

Her body grew hot as it seemed to combust into actual flames, but for every flame that ignited, James kissed and nibbled it away until she turned ice blue to match his eyes.

"How?" Sophie gasped before tossing her head back and losing her mind.

"Balance," James mouthed against her belly button. She took in a sharp breath as he did. *Oh, this was going to be fun...*

He continued to work his way down both her inner thighs slowly, as he held her firmly in place despite all of her attempts to wiggle free. *How was he stronger than her?* He had her shorts and panties off and held her back down before she could stop him.

"James, please!" she whimpered.

"Don't worry, Babe. I've got you," James said as he rubbed his nose against her sweet spot. God, she smelled good. He heard her gasp as he tasted her sweetness. Sophie grabbed for the pillow to put over her mouth in habit, but it burst to flames by her touch. She breathed out heavily as she grabbed the sheets beneath her, trying to focus enough not to set the damn bed on fire underneath them.

"James," she whimpered again, just before he felt her quiver under his touch.

"Come for me, Baby," he pleaded. She couldn't help but fulfill his command. She let go of the bed and the room lit up in a blinding crystal blue light as she screamed out his name. Within seconds, she felt him slide into her while she continued to vibrate in his arms.

She was warm and ready, and so was he. He thrust into her gently and slowly as they quickly built up a rhythm together. They were always in sync. "James," she whimpered again as a second wave made its way slowly through her.

"Stay with me," he begged again. Sophie opened her eyes to find not only ice blue flames greeting her, but the man she loved begging her to stay with him. Forever.

Sophie wrapped her hands around his neck and pulled him close. "I'm forever yours. There's nowhere else I will ever go," she assured.

It was the words he needed to hear. Permission to be hers in return. He willingly gave himself to her as she accepted him readily. They both screamed out each other's names as they rode together in ecstasy. The room exploded in an icy blue light as they became one.

___

James fell onto her naked chest in exhaustion, trying to catch his breath. Sophie giggled and ran her fingers through his hair as she gathered her own breath. Soon after, he pushed off her and pulled her up against his own sweaty and bare body, and they fell into a deep sleep of a future including them both holding hands and rocking in rocking chairs on a deck of their log cabin in the mountains. No serial killers. No ghosts. Just them.

Clarice needed to blow off some steam. She needed to release the aching for something she would never be able to have. *Or someone.* Clarice tightened her leather jacket around her as the frosty night air cut through her. Even the sinning side of town was near closing. She needed a drink. And she wasn't in the mood to put up with any more goodie two shoes. So, Clarice headed down the alley further into the stench of filth, sweat, desire, and alcohol into a hole in the wall bar.

It was small, but still fairly packed with people. She felt multiple suspects check out her curves being on display in tight black jeans, a shiny silk top, black high heel boots, and a leather jacket. Her hair was naturally curled to perfection and her eyes begged for someone to dare to take it all off of her. She sauntered over to the bar and ordered a whiskey neat. Clarice even noticed the bartender's eagerness from his pants as he leaned on the bar to give her the drink.

"Haven't seen you around here," he said in a husky voice. His greasy chin length hair hung over his green eyes full of desire. His lips curled up on the ends as he flexed his muscles in the black t-shirt that was too small for his frame while he leaned as close as he could to her.

Clarice smiled and chugged the whiskey down before slamming the glass back on the bar. She leaned over towards him and slid the glass back to him. She whispered sweetly into his ear, "That's because it's my first time." Clarice lingered a second more before pulling back with a wicked smile on her face. She watched him uncontrollably shudder in response.

"How long are you here for?" he stammered.

"I have a better question," Clarice said in a husky voice, pushing her breasts in his direction. "When does this place close?"

She heard him gasp. Clarice waited patiently for him to recover. He cleared his throat before asking, "Looking to leave already?"

"Just starving," Clarice said, looking down at the glass and casually running her finger around the rim and sticking it in her mouth to slowly suck on it when pulling it out.

The man swallowed hard. "I can have them fix you up something if it's not too complicated," he offered.

Clarice laughed out loud before leaning on the bar, pushing her breasts together. She wrinkled up her nose and breathed, "I'm not hungry for food."

She watched him swallow hard again. "Yeah?" he asked for clarification.

"Oh yeah," she said, as her wicked smile grew wider.

The man took the towel around his belt off and tossed it to the woman tending bar with him. "Mickey, you're closing," he yelled as he jumped the bar and held out his arm. Clarice took it, and they walked back to her place.

The door flung open and Clarice and the bartender entered, kissing, biting, and pawing each other like wild animals. He fumbled with her clothing, and she sighed with frustration, waiting for him to get his act together. After a few minutes of waiting, Clarice gave up and shoved him up against the wall to help her in undressing them both. She rubbed her nose against his neck before kissing him passionately. She heard him moan in agreement.

"Oh, Clarice," he muttered.

Clarice's eyes opened immediately. She never told him her name. Still kissing down his body, she reached over to the nightstand and quickly grabbed the knife from underneath it and held the knife at his throat with just enough force that, with the slightest twist, his life would be gone.

"Who are you?" she hissed.

"Easy slick," the man gasped. "You'll kill us both."

Clarice narrowed her eyes and searched the man before her. He still looked like the bartender, but he talked like Corbin. She saw red immediately, as she added more pressure to his neck and barked, "What do you want?"

"I'm sorry," the man said with sorrow in his eyes. "I just needed to check on you."

"Like this?" Clarice shouted in fury. Her eyes looked like a wild animal more than a human.

"You're right. I don't know what came over me," Corbin confessed, staring at the floor. He couldn't look at her, but he heard her breathing slow down. "Don't kill him because of me." When his eyes met hers again, Corbin was gone, and it was the bartender, terrified and confused, looking back at her.

"Get out," snapped Clarice as she let go of his neck. The bartender scurried to collect the clothing that had been tossed and left the door open as he ran out of it. Clarice watched him leave. After a second, she went and slammed the door close. "And you," she shouted to no one. "You don't have the same effect looking like that, just so you know." She threw the knife and it stuck in the front door as she screamed out her frustration, turned off the light, and crawled warily into bed.

"Noted," she heard the smile of Corbin's voice in her ear.

"Shut up!" she warned as she flopped onto her side and pulled the covers over her head. She still felt his finger brush against her forehead, forcing her into a relaxing sleep before she had a chance to protest.

James opened his eyes to a wooden door. "Really?" he exasperated.

"Please," he heard Corbin plead.

James envisioned a brick wall to protect his brain, reached out, and opened the door. He saw Corbin sulking at his desk with his head in his hands, clearly distraught. "What's going on, Doc?" he asked slowly, as he watched the distraught doctor.

Corbin held his face in his own hands. "How do you do it?" he asked James.

"Um, you're going to have to be more specific," James replied in confusion.

"How do you come in here and get to keep your feelings and emotions to yourself?" Corbin asked, dropping his hands and looking at James in desperation.

"What's going on, Corbin?" James asked more firmly.

Corbin slumped at his desk, staring at nothing in particular. "I understand I volunteered to come here. To help save Sophie. But even a man deserves some privacy from time to time."

"I'm sorry, Doc. I'm not following," James replied softly, trying to figure out what the heck Corbin was talking about.

"The gift of the dream realm is that you gain powers specific to you. To help you provide balance while you're here. It seems great, and easy to understand that it comes with responsibility," Corbin said, staring down at his own empty hands.

James studied the doctor, who was clearly suffering from that responsibility. The responsibility Corbin took on to help blindly protect the woman James loved. He needed a friend. Someone impartial to talk with that wouldn't make him feel bad about whatever he was facing. James looked around and pulled up an empty chair next to him, and sat down to be the sounding board Corbin needed.

Corbin gave him a weary smile. "They don't tell you it comes with a price," he said, more frustrated than anything.

"What's the price you have to pay?" James asked with a raised eyebrow.

Corbin sighed, and his shoulders slumped over even more. "I feel everything in here. Most of us do. We feed off of the energy of each other in order to help provide balance. When one is weak, another can provide power to keep the system going."

"Like electricity?" James asked, intrigued.

"Basically, yes," Corbin replied. "But power here is based on emotions and thoughts. None I get to keep to myself," he said with a hint of bitterness.

"What do you need to keep from everyone?" James asked, confused. "Does it put Sophie in danger?" he demanded.

Corbin shook his head immediately. "I committed my death to Sophie. Do you think I would do anything to put that child in harm's way?" he asked as he sat up straight and looked wide eyed at James.

"Good point," James said. Guilt seeped in and broke through the brick wall he had held strong around his mind.

Corbin looked at him with interest. "She's really a weak spot for you, isn't she?"

"Isn't every woman you love with all your heart?" chuckled James.

"Love," Corbin whispered to himself.

James started to see more of the picture. "You're right," James offered with sympathy. "A man needs some things to keep to himself." *Poor guy.* James leaned forward with a raised eyebrow. "Anyone I know?" he asked with a growing smile. Corbin pulled at the collar of his shirt and squirmed in his chair a bit. *That's a yes.* "Are they worthy of your love?" James pressed on blindly.

"Everyone's worthy of love, aren't they?" Corbin whispered. "If that's what it is," he added.

"Oh, Doc," James said in amusement and put a hand on his shoulder. "Whether you admit it to me, yourself, or anyone else, it's getting there if it's not already."

"How do you know?" Corbin asked, jerking his head up.

James laughed. "Your heart will tell you, regardless. We don't really get to choose those things. Even if they aren't the right ones. But when they are, you will know above all else," he offered with a smile. Then he had a disturbing thought. "It's not Sophie, is it?" he asked concerned.

"No offense, but definitely not!" Corbin said. "Sophie's like the niece I never had," he added with a look of disgust and shaking his head at the thought.

James laughed out loud. "As long as we're on the same page for that one," he grinned. "Regardless of who it is, I can see that being an issue in here. You're both dead. Live it up! But can the dead love like...normal people?"

Corbin stayed quiet.

"Are they dead?" James asked after a second or two of uncomfortable silence.

"I don't know if we can," Corbin offered with a change of subject. "Either way, I can't exactly keep it to myself while I figure things out."

"Can't you?" James offered. Corbin looked at him with curiosity. James let out a deep and dramatic sigh. "Listen," he started. "I know the need to keep some things to yourself. I also know you can read me when I'm in here," he scolded. Corbin, consumed with guilt, looked back at his messy desk. "So," James continued, "I make a conscious effort to protect my brain once I get here."

"That's it?" Corbin asked in surprise, staring at the boy before him.

"Your protection might take a lot more effort considering the circumstances, but I don't see why it wouldn't work the same for you,"

James shrugged. "They say emotions come from the heart, but you and I both know it's the brain that does most of the magic," he winked.

"That is true," Corbin said with a smile. James felt his spirit raise, which made him think about getting some answers for himself.

"So, feeling everything between people is really a thing in here?" he asked curiously.

"You have no idea," Corbin replied in exasperation.

"Is it something that can happen on the other side?" James asked with hesitation.

"I wouldn't think to the same degree," Corbin answered bluntly. Then the importance of the question sunk in. "Is it?" he asked James with a frown.

"Would coming in here increase that probability?" James suggested.

"I don't see how," Corbin replied, sitting back in his chair and rubbing his finger across his chin. "It's simply permission between the living and the dead to connect. Nothing more." The thought of feeling Clarice more clearly came to mind. "Are your friends experiencing the same thing?" he asked with a hint of worry.

"We haven't talked to anyone yet," James answered honestly. "We're still in Utah. She needed the rest."

"Is she okay?" Corbin asked in a sharper tone.

James made sure his wall was strong again before he answered. Sophie consumed with red flames and everything else that had transpired in less than twenty-four hours flashed before his eyes. "She's still adjusting to waking up," he answered honestly.

"Meaning?" Corbin pressed.

"You said people have powers unique to them in here, right?"

James asked, looking at the desk as he thought.

"Yes," Corbin replied impatiently.

"But only in here?" James asked slowly, waving his hand around the empty space before him.

"James," Corbin cut in. "What's going on with Sophie?"

"You've seen her eyes, right?" James asked, finally looking back at Corbin.

"The red and blue?" Corbin asked, thrown off guard. "You see them?"

"Only when she gets really emotional," James offered.

"But out there?" Corbin asked for clarification.

"She was fighting Algos," James half lied.

"But not after?" Corbin asked firmly.

"No," James lied, already having his answer. James knew powers and things of that nature were just fictional tales in real life. But that was before he met his future ghost in-laws, was dragged into the dream realm repeatedly, and met a girl that was enhanced more than anything he had seen in the movies. Even Dr. Corbin Dallas knew Sophie shouldn't be able to do the things she could do in the dream realm amongst the living, but the rules never quite applied to Sophie to begin with. James would protect her at all costs. Even if it cost him his own life.

"So, is that all?" Corbin asked, interrupting James's thoughts.

"It was just new is all," James replied honestly.

"She was pretty exhausted by the time she got to him," Corbin offered, deep in thought. "She may have needed to tap into the power just to keep her going. To stop Algos and save you. I hear love is a very powerful thing," he replied, more to himself than to James.

"That it is," James answered honestly. "Feeling better?" he asked, to change the subject.

"I don't know about better, but thanks for listening," Corbin replied sincerely. "It was definitely needed."

"Any time, Doc," James said, giving him a light pat on the back. "Can I get back to my girl now?" he asked with his boyish grin.

"My apologies," Corbin chuckled. "Please do."

James eagerly stood up and opened the door. He woke up to Sophie breathing restfully in his arms. He pulled her closer, kissed her on her head, and whispered, "I love you." She moaned blissfully and wiggled closer to him in response.

Seven

Corbin sat in his office, thinking long and hard about all the information and advice James had provided. First, he needed to figure out if dragging the living into the dream realm increased their connection to them. That would help him determine what he was feeling exactly for those he was crossing. *Clarice.* Corbin shook his head in an attempt to ignore the obvious.

Second, no matter the answer to the first question, Corbin needed to work on keeping at least a small portion of his feelings and thoughts to himself. For his own sanity. It wasn't maintaining balance for everyone to know his business while he was figuring things out. Especially Jack and Jess. That much he knew.

Third, James had alluded that Sophie was showing signs of

having powers where she shouldn't be. Amongst the living. It was true, Sophie was stronger than anything he had come across. Even Rebecca. But the universe wouldn't tolerate such imbalance, and it could cost Sophie her life. He had dedicated his life to keeping her safe, and he took pride in always keeping his promises. The one person who might help him get those answers was Rebecca, but he would have to find out what happened to her first. She wasn't gone. Well, technically, she didn't appear to be in the dream realm, but she wasn't gone for good. He wouldn't be able to feel the energy she left behind if that was the case. It would have faded, and yet, he was the only one that seemed to still feel her energy at all. He needed to know why.

Corbin didn't dare write down his list of things to do like he normally did. This needed to be kept to himself. He quickly pushed number two to number one on his list of things to do and began looking into how he could protect his feelings and thoughts in a world that made it impossible to do so.

There were certain things John knew. First, Rebecca was missing and needed to be found. ASAP. Second, someone had invaded the dream realm with no consequences and John didn't know which side they were on. Third, another raven had awakened. Now Sophie was powerful. More powerful than Rebecca. However, that did not guarantee that she was the chosen one. And last, someone had already replaced Algos. John didn't know who, but he could assume that they came with alterations, whether given by the universe or Algos himself. Either way, his realm was going to be in danger, and he needed to be prepared for anything.

But there was a problem. John should have lost his memories of his family once he took back his spot as head council and he didn't. He remembered his son as clearly as the day he was born, and that meant he couldn't stay impartial. The realm was designed with checks and balances, allowing certain members to feel everything around them and maintain control when members got off course. Corbin was on his predetermined path, but this was going to put John in danger and put his family in danger as a result.

Without Rebecca, he had no one to trust. Not even his own son. His feelings would give him away in a heartbeat if he knew the truth. Sophie was changing. John had seen it for himself. He wasn't even sure if she could be the one to save him either, to be honest. He needed to find Rebecca. And he needed to discover the identity of the intruder before his council did. Luckily, he knew Jess would come through for him. If he could just keep her focused enough. Which meant keeping Corbin hidden until he did what needed to be done on his end. Even if he didn't know what that was just yet. He let out a heavy sigh.

Sophie opened her eyes immediately and closed them again to appear before him. No door was needed.

"Are you okay?" she asked eagerly.

John spun around in shock and nearly fell over. Her hair was shorter, but she still looked like herself. Only with her newly gained one red flaming eye and one blue.

"Are you okay?" she asked, more as a command than a question.

"Sophie?" he asked, trying to catch his bearings.

"John," she stated sternly. "What's wrong?"

Fear consumed him for a split second before he regained his composure. "Nothing, sweet child. What are you doing in my realm, uninvited?" he asked curiously.

"Don't lie to me," she warned. "You called me," Sophie added with frustration.

"I did?" he inquired. John grew still and stared off into the distance, blinking slowly.

"John!" Sophie snapped as her eyes glowed red with frustration. "Tell me what's wrong."

"Do not throw around your powers in here at me, young lady," John cautioned in such a tone that had the fire within her blow out instantly.

"I'm sorry," Sophie replied, adverting her gaze. "I'm a little off today. I can just feel how distressed you are, and you're not exactly the best at communication," she said as her eyebrows drew together. Sophie studied her grandfather.

"You can feel me?" John asked. He chewed on the inside of his cheek as he thought. "Out there?" he clarified, although speaking more to himself than to Sophie.

She nodded slowly. "I think it's the bloodline," she smiled with her usual grin. He couldn't help but return a grin of his own.

"Listen, little one," John started, "Being in charge of a realm comes with some complicated issues from time to time. Nothing I can't handle. However, I can't have you coming in here unannounced every time you feel me trying to sort things out. It makes me look bad, and my council will get the wrong idea. Do you understand?" he stated in a much softer tone.

After some thought, Sophie finally nodded. "But will you let me know if you're actually in trouble? I really can't afford to lose anyone else," she choked out.

He gave a quick look around before pulling her into his arms and whispering, "I give you my word." John kissed her on the top of the head and pushed her back before his own tears gave him away. "Now, get out of here. I'm sure you have better things to do," and with the flip of his wrist, he kicked her out before she could protest.

John made sure Sophie remained asleep in James's arms, but it was unexpected pieces he would add to his puzzle. *Puzzles.* It might be time to go visit Miss Miller...

Tina was resting comfortably next to Ben. It was still a little too early to determine the sex of the baby, but Little Bear, the name everyone insisted on calling it in the meantime, was holding up strong. Motion sickness was easing up, and everyone insisted she was glowing. Tina was just excited to not be hurling her guts and sweating all the dang time. When she opened her eyes, she saw the most beautiful pearl door.

"Well, this is different," Tina muttered in hesitation as she put a protective hand over her stomach.

"Relax, Tina Miller," she heard a male voice say. "I'm a friend of Sophie's, and we need your help. Please open the door."

"Yeah, I've heard that before. I'm gonna need more than that," Tina called out, putting her free hand on her hip and taking her usual stubborn stance.

There was a brief pause before the voice continued, "You

tricked Ben into going on a date with you by pretending to be violently ill with food poisoning, and had him take you to the hospital and..."

"Okay! Opening the door!" Tina screamed out. "Jesus! Did Sophie tell the world?" she muttered to herself. She slowly opened her eyes and gave them the opportunity to adjust to the brightness that was the dream realm.

"In her defense," the voice continued softly, "Sophie didn't tell me. It was a memory. I just read it in a book and found it to be quite amusing. Sounds like something my wife did to me."

Tina looked up to find a thin figure that looked similar to Jack, had he aged any older, standing before her in a white suit. She gasped at the sight.

"I hear the family resemblance is dead on," he said, smiling at his own joke.

Tina stood in shock.

"My name is John," the man said, extending his hand to her. "And I hear you like puzzles."

"I used to," Tina said with a weary smile.

"I understand completely," John replied. "But my family once again needs you to solve another one. Maybe Stacey can help you with this one, too?"

Tina froze, and her eyes narrowed. "Stacey, who?" she replied coldly.

John put his hands up and took a couple of steps back, like he had seen Ben and all of them do so many times as a sign of retreat and truce. "I will be honest with you if you will let me trust you with what I'm about to tell you," he stated sincerely. "I don't have anyone else to tell."

Tina cocked her head to the side as she studied him. Her senses were on overload since she was carrying another human being, and even the baby was telling her to listen because he was telling the truth. "Go on," she drawled.

John sighed heavily before he continued. "I was chosen to be head of the council of death for whatever reason. I didn't get a say, and the price was to not remember anything in order to remain impartial and always maintain order. However, since being pulled in by Sophie to help save her from herself, I should have gone back to forgetting everything once I returned, and I did not."

Tina's eyes widened. Even she could quickly calculate the danger this could create.

"As you are calculating, in a realm where feelings are community property, it won't be long before it is found out that I didn't become a blank slate, and I am no longer impartial. Which will put Jack and Jess in danger."

"What do I need to do?" Tina asked, fully engaged.

"Well, there' are a couple of things going on," John confessed. "We will need Ben's help, too."

Tina gave John the side eye, and he put his hands up to prove he would not put him in harm's way. "Sophie can feel me. Out there," he added, jabbing his chin towards the pearl door.

"So, they're okay?" Tina cut off with relief.

"You haven't heard from them yet?" John asked as his eyebrows drew together.

"James said everything was fine, but they were delayed getting back. I can tell something is wrong. I just don't know what. What do you mean, she can feel you?" The question was finally registering in

Tina's mind, and might be the reason they were staying away.

"No one should have powers out there that have powers in here," John clarified. "Period."

"Have you seen her eyes?" Tina asked a bit sarcastically.

"You see them out there, too?" John asked in a hushed tone as he shook his head softly. A heaviness that he couldn't avoid quickly consumed his whole body.

Tina's eyes widened as she realized what John was telling her. She put a hand over her stomach and began walking around aimlessly. John quickly produced a chair for her to sit on. Tina took it anxiously and put her head between her knees.

"Are you okay?" John asked her.

"It's just the baby," Tina replied, still keeping her head down.

"It's not the baby," John answered in a low whisper. He was right beside her.

When she sat up, her eyes were closed. She opened them slowly. "What's wrong with her?" Tina asked as a sob escaped her.

"I'm not sure. This has never happened before," John answered her truthfully. "And with Rebecca gone, we need to see if Ben can come up with a way to shut her down. Just in case," he added grimly.

"*SHUT HER DOWN*?" Tina sobbed in half anger and half terror.

John crouched down to her level and stroked her back. "Listen to me," he whispered, but with a strong hint of warning. "She is my flesh and blood, and I *will* do anything and everything to save her. But if I can't...You and your baby must live. It's already been decided."

"*What*..." Tina went to scream, but this time John put his hand over her mouth and looked around anxiously. When he looked back at her, she gave him a confirmed nod and he removed it. "What the hell does that mean?" she hissed back as tears ran down her cheeks.

"Child, Algos isn't the only psychopath on the planet. He was not the first, and he will not be the last. As much as Sophie has been designed to stop what's coming today, someone has to be prepared to stop what's coming tomorrow. You were chosen for a reason, just like I was. It's not fair. Sometimes, it down right sucks. But we all have a purpose. To save as many lives as possible when no one else can. I'm asking you to save some right now. Will you help me?" John asked, leaning forward and holding her eyes in an intense gaze.

Tina looked down at her stomach and back at John. She let out a heavy sigh before answering him. "We will solve your puzzle and shut her down."

John nodded in confirmation and stood up. Tina followed in suit.

"But I will also find a way to save her. Save all of us," she announced, sticking her chin into the air and giving a quick nod at him.

John smiled at her. "Why do you think I came to you?" he said with a wink and brushed her head with his finger, putting her into the deepest sleep. She would need it to hit the ground running tomorrow.

There were two reasons Clarice couldn't leave Utah yet. One was a med student, Ashley Jacobs. She watched the thirty-seven-year-old leave the gym and get in her car before the sun was even up. *Dedication. A good sign.* Average height, and her mid-length blonde hair pulled back into a sweaty bun, she brushed the sweat from her forehead before driving away. Clarice kept a safe distance and followed her back to the school campus, where Ashley showered and put on her white lab coat before following the herd of students into the lab. Clarice leaned against the wall and waited patiently.

She had looked long and hard the last several days for the perfect person to head her pet project. No one fit better than Ashley Jacobs. Known for always putting others before herself, her lovely athletic curves and sassy mouth were not to be messed with.

Clarice listened to the instructor, who clearly hated his life, teach about the effects of certain chemicals on the human body. "Miss Jacobs!" he snapped unexpectedly. Clarice's ears perked up.

"Yep," she heard Ashley reply just as dryly, with a hint of sarcasm.

"Would you like to join the rest of the class in learning today?" he challenged her.

"Naw, I'm good," Ashley sassed back. A ripple of stifled giggles went through the room.

"*QUIET!*" the instructor shouted. "And why is that, Miss Jacobs?"

"Oh, because you're absolutely wrong, and I prefer to learn the correct information, so I'll just go to the library," Ashley retorted with a shrug.

The corner of Clarice's lips curled up as she turned to peek through the window of the classroom. Ashley hadn't looked up from her textbook, but all eyes were on her, and the instructor was furious and about to seriously strike the girl. Clarice was seconds from kicking down the door when she heard Ashley speak again.

"It's bad enough that you're teaching us the wrong information, but do you really want to add physical abuse and an arrest to your record? Because as I see it," Ashley said, looking the instructor in the eyes, "I have thirty-four eye-witnesses that can vouch for me since I'm about to get you fired. For three weeks you have given us seventeen different wrong answers that would have us killing patients instead of saving them, which will be followed by lawsuits, and this college being forced to shut down. Who do you think is going to survive this?" she asked, unwavering eye contact.

The instructor's face was blood red, and spit flew from his mouth as he shouted, "*GET OUT!*"

"Gladly," Ashley replied dryly, as she gathered her things and went out the door. Clarice was waiting for her on the other side, applauding as she exited.

"Nicely done," Clarice said, showing no emotion.

Ashley paid her no attention and headed straight for the office. Clarice kept up and walked next to her. "What do you want?" Ashely finally asked.

"For you to come save some lives," Clarice said with a shrug.

"And you are?" Ashley asked dryly, keeping her eyes forward.

"Clarice."

"Clarice, who?" Ashley sighed.

"Just Clarice."

"What? Like Madonna or Cher?" Ashley laughed.

Clarice's lips curled up again. "Something like that."

"I'm not a doctor," Ashley stated flatly.

"Not yet," Clarice noted. "But isn't it more fun to practice and get it right until you are?"

Ashley paused. "I thought you wanted me to save people?" she asked with a raised eyebrow.

"Oh, I do," Clarice replied with a nod.

"I don't know what I'm doing," Ashley said, with the corner of her mouth curving down.

Clarice looked back at the classroom before she looked back at Ashley. Her lips were pursed together, and she cocked her head while raising an eyebrow. "I doubt that."

"Why me?" Ashley finally asked, pulling her head back and eyeing Clarice.

"You're smart, and I like you," Clarice shrugged. "I *really* don't like people, but I have a very important project that needs to be worked on. I'm pretty sure that you're the only one I can trust to do it and do it right. So, do you wanna do it or not?"

"I can see why you have a lot of friends," Ashley replied sarcastically.

Clarice glared. "Who says I don't?"

Ashley studied Clarice long and hard and looked back at the classroom. "I still want to get my piece of paper," she said, staring at the door. "Stupid places require it."

"I agree," Clarice said with a smile, knowing she had Ashley in her pocket.

"Please tell me we're getting out of this hellhole," Ashley said, looking back at her new friend.

"Relax. I know you only stay for your family, and I will compensate them while you work for me, but yes. I hope you like to travel. We tend to do that a lot," Clarice said as she wrapped her arm around a now confused and scared Ashley. "I do my homework, too," she whispered in Ashley's ear as she guided her out the door.

Eight

Tina woke up refreshed, but with a heavy heart. "What's wrong?" she heard Ben almost demand more than ask as he grabbed her hand and took it in his own.

She sighed heavily. "We have a new project."

Ben didn't get angry often, but Tina watched his face change instantly. "Tell the ghosts they're on their own! You can't be taking chances like that, now," he ended in a snarl.

Tina squeezed his hand and tried not to giggle. "First of all, even the doctor in you knows that's a ridiculous request. And second of all, this is another puzzle that actually is for you more than me."

His eyebrows raised as he almost dropped her hand completely. "Me?" Ben asked, pulling his head back with wide eyes.

"Sophie's not quite herself," Tina began slowly. "Apparently, the council," she said, putting much angered emphasis on the last word, "would like to have a backup plan in case Sophie gets out of control and can't be stopped."

"Like a kill switch?" Ben asked in horror.

"Exactly like a kill switch," Tina grimaced.

"I will do no such thing!" he shouted in horror as he stepped back and crossed his arms in front of him.

"Benjamin Miller, look at me," Tina commanded.

He did, but with narrowed eyes full of frustration and anger.

"Have you ever known me not to have a Plan B to their ridiculousness?" Tina asked with a cheeky smile.

Ben didn't move, but replied, "I'm listening," with a raised eyebrow.

"They are right," Tina replied before quickly putting up her finger to silence him and force him to listen to her. "Should something go wrong, she might need to be, let's say, slowed down a bit. Like maybe put to sleep for a bit, but much more safely than when she does it herself," she added, freezing her husband with the intensity of her stare. "Can you at least work on that part in case my puzzle piece doesn't work?" Tina added with a plea.

Ben thought for a moment before finally nodding in agreement. "Wait! What are you doing?" he asked with concern.

Tina crawled out of bed and kissed him gently on the cheek. "Only using my brain to cause mischief. I promise," she whispered with a reassuring smile. "Now, please come take advantage of me before my belly grows too much to let it be as much fun," she added, throwing him a devilish look.

"Yes, ma'am," Ben said, giving her a smile back before picking her up and carrying her back to bed.

𝄾

Sophie rolled over to an empty bed. She heard James in the bathroom and she took a second to relish in the glow of their lovemaking. *How could a single person make her feel so happy and loved?* But as she rolled over and ran her hands over the sheet where he should lay, her hand touched something else that had her sitting up in alarm.

James felt the shift in her without even seeing her and he rushed out of the bathroom to find her pushed up against the wall, holding clumps of torched hair. Her burnt hair in her hands and tears running down her cheeks, unable to speak.

Fear hit his gut like a wrecking ball had punched him. "Hey Babe," he whispered softly, as if coming up to a terrified child or wounded animal.

Sophie shook her head wildly, signaling him not to come closer. She looked down at the torched hair in her hand that she could still smell. The stench of scorched hair permeated the room and burned her nostrils. She looked up and found James just inches in front of her. *How was he so close without her hearing or knowing?* "No, James," Sophie stammered.

"Babe, you won't hurt me," he whispered, feeling the fear from her and knowing what she feared most. She looked at him with wild eyes. They dilated wide, and he felt her body begin to heat up. "I'm not okay," she shrieked in hysteria.

Without hesitation, he pulled her into his arms and pushed his love onto her, forcing the lava red to turn icy blue immediately. He rubbed his hand down the back of her head as she sobbed wildly in his arms. "That's it. Let it out," James cooed at her. Sophie was a fighter, but she couldn't fight until she came to terms with the fear of the unknown. James didn't care how long it took for her to release all the stress and everything else she had been holding in. He would hold on to her for as long as she needed, because that was what he was meant to do. Be there for her. To balance her out when she felt like she couldn't do it herself.

Sophie was so tired she couldn't stand it, so she let James hold on to her. Let him sway with her like her father used to. Hum to her. Calm her. While she bawled until there wasn't a tear left to cry out. Eventually, she turned her cheek and rested on his shoulder as they swayed in the middle of the hotel room in silence.

"Well, I hope you prefer my shorter hair," Sophie sniffled in an attempt to lighten the mood. She felt him smile against her head as they continued to dance in silence.

"Still plenty to tug on," James teased in a low voice as he tugged gently at the back of her hair. A motion that ignited warmth for them both below the belt.

Sophie tried to muffle her giggle against his shoulder, but it didn't work.

"Better?" he asked her.

"I'm always better with you," Sophie said, smiling against his shoulder. She still couldn't make herself look at him. Not just yet.

"Back at ya, Babe," he whispered in a voice so low that heat ignited from between her legs.

Sophie forced herself to push away from him. "You can't keep doing that," she said with a frown, trying not to giggle and stay focused.

"Do what?" James asked with a shrug of innocence.

Sophie took several steps back, trying to put some distance between them, and she watched his own eyes dilate like an animal stalking a prey at night. "Stop it!" she warned, but the giggling made it a lot less convincing.

James's boyish grin stretched across his face as he watched her every move, but he remained silent.

"You cannot distract me with sex every time I burst into a ball of fire!" Sophie yelled out. She was being honest, but he was forcing out her customary grin, making her fail miserably.

"Says who?" James asked with his grin growing wider, as he shifted his weight between his feet, ready to attack.

She watched his body tense like a cheetah just before it pounces, and she held her hands in front of her, trying not to giggle with the anticipation of his touch. "Because we can't be having sex in the middle of public, for starters!" Sophie half giggled and whined.

James tilted his head, not taking his eyes off her. "True," he said casually. "But we're not in public now," he said with so much lust and desire that Sophie almost burst into flames right then and there. He came at her faster than he's ever moved, and he gently tossed her on the bed to devour her and take her as his own.

She may be different, but he was too, and she needed to find out why. To save him from himself. But she was already losing her mind and herself to his heat and need for her. Hopefully, she would remember when she woke up again.

"What would you like to try first?" Liz asked Claudia.

Claudia's eyebrows furrowed as she thought, but she honestly didn't know, and thinking this hard was giving her a headache. Liz could tell.

"How are you at shooting guns?" Liz offered with a shrug.

Claudia put a finger to her chin as a memory flashed before her eyes. Her eyes quickly dilated before going back to normal. She was a young girl on a farm with a younger blonde boy. They were laughing in a field and chasing the goats around when a tall elderly man in overalls came up to them. He asked the boy if he wanted to go shooting with him. The boy would only go if Claudia went too, and it had turned out that Claudia was actually the better shot. Although it was just a flash of a memory, it was very vivid, and seemed to wake up a part of her brain that had been sleeping all these years. "I think I can," Claudia half lied.

She still didn't understand why she had such a thirst to kill, and yet Liz was not an option. It was confusing and provided her with no trust for the woman what so ever. Claudia would keep her cards close to her chest until she could find out more of what was going on, and exactly what she was capable of before she decided if the doctor needed to be cut loose.

"Long range or short?" Liz asked with more excitement than Claudia was expecting.

"Long..." Claudia replied slowly, biting on her cheek and giving a quick nod. She had to admit, it was nice to have someone as excited about her new thirst as Claudia was. Liz was definitely along for the ride. But that wasn't a free pass to freedom, either.

"Long it is!" Liz announced as she grabbed Claudia's hand and yanked her down the hallway. Liz grabbed some sniper rifles out of a cage before she hauled Claudia out of the lab to take her out for a test run.

Erica Jackson was your typical twenty-eight-year-old that was of average height, slender build, with somewhat wavy, shoulder-length, dark brown hair, and green eyes with a touch of hazel in them. She was fine minding her own business, usually wearing a hoodie and leggings or sweats, and blaring music in her Skull Candy headphones. She kept to herself messing around on Pinterest, writing stories, and watching gameplay videos on YouTube and playing Otome games.

So, when she opened her eyes and found herself in a glass coffin with a pounding headache, it took her a second to recall how she had gotten there. The last thing Erica remembered was walking to the library and then waking up here. But something had her attention immediately. Actually, several things.

Roaches. Roaches were now crawling all over her body. Erica closed her eyes tightly and tried to tell herself she was having a nightmare. However, the roaches and her panic remained. She let out a scream and began banging on the surrounding glass while swatting at the ones that attempted to crawl into her mouth and nose. Erica didn't know there were cameras surrounding her, and a psychopath sitting behind the wall watching her be eating alive just on the other side. A killer she knew from booktok.

❧

Clarice had Ashley packing up her things, and Mason coordinating with her to get her to the new lab. Now, for the second thing, she needed in order to get the hell out of this small town USA. The only lead she could find to the little girl in the photo on her father's desk. *Karmen.* The wind picked up and chilled her to her bones. She zipped up her jacket and began heading back to the hotel.

❧

Lauren Dempster sat eagerly waiting at a small coffee shop with a hot coffee in one hand and a book in another. Her Scottish accent, French violet hair, and right pure blue eye and left cinnamon brown eye made her stick out like a sore thumb in this small town that wasn't exactly known for their diversity. Luckily for Lauren, it was just a pit stop on their travels across the USA.

She had talked her BFF, Kayleigh King, into coming in from Wales, UK, to travel with her and see some of their favorite bookstores and authors. Both being thirty-five and the exact same height of 5'5", they often joke they're sisters from different mothers. Kayleigh's somewhat matching brown hair with aqua blue and indigo highlights flowing just past her shoulders. Although Kayleigh doesn't pay as much attention to her surroundings, Lauren loves listening to her rock out to her 80s/90s/00s music. However, Lauren was eager to get out of the cold and move on to their next destination.

"Sorry, I'm late," Kayleigh huffed, as her warm breath clouded the air between them as she set a bag on the table.

"If you keep buying books along the way, you're going to need to have an affair with a billionaire just to get them shipped back to you," Lauren teased.

"I don't know what you're talking about," Kayleigh replied in fake innocence as she eagerly took the other hot coffee sitting on the table in her hands. "And why are we sitting out here purposely freezing to death?"

Lauren smiled wickedly, trying to not let her teeth chatter and ruin the effect. She nodded behind Kayleigh. "The bus will be here in less than five minutes and we're getting our butts on it and getting out of here."

"Oh, thank God!" Kayleigh sighed, warming up her hands with the coffee. She laughed a little, seeing their luggage at the side of the table. When Lauren was done, she was done. And Lauren was done with Utah. Kayleigh blew some of the steam off the top of her cup and took a sip.

Clarice walked back, noticing two colorful ladies sitting outside having a cup of coffee. Clearly not the brightest of the bunch to be drinking in such cold weather outside, but she couldn't say much. She was walking a few blocks in it herself, because old habits die hard and she never parked near where she slept.

She heard the whistle of the bullet before she saw it whiz by her eyeball into the back of the first lady's head. Only it wasn't a normal bullet. It should have gone straight through and taken them both out simultaneously. Instead, there was a pause. A minor ticking. And then an explosion.

The second woman, still with her cup of coffee close to her lips and clearly in partial shock, hyperventilated and made a horrible sound as if trying to scream but wasn't able to. She finally sobbed hysterically. Her friend's brain matter and blood covered her face and clothes. And Clarice. She felt the warmth of it all on her face and in her hair.

She heard a second whistle and turned to see which direction it was coming from. Clarice squinted at the split second reflection of light on the roof of a building across the street. A female figure dressed in all black stood up. She had studied Sophie from the day she was born and knew it wasn't her, although she had plenty of reason to shoot at Clarice.

She felt her back drenched in what she assumed to be the second woman's body fluids. The figure wiggled her fingers at her in a wave as a single strand of red curly hair escaped her hood when she took off running. Clarice heard people scrambling and hiding behind her, and she couldn't afford to stick out right now. "Damn it!" she muttered before pretending to take cover.

Clarice was completely drenched in blood and guts, and would surely be held forever in questioning. She heard the sirens just down the street. Clarice really needed Eddie to get her out of here. *Eddie....*

"Enough!" she yelled at herself. She crawled past the table to give the bodies a quick scan before leaving the scene. As suspected, the second lady took a bullet to the head as well. Same fashion, with no bullet fragments left behind to study. "Well, that's convenient," she muttered to herself. Clarice took advantage of the chaos and crawled on her hands and knees around the corner and out of sight.

She looked down at her favorite leather jacket. "Okay, now, I'm just pissed," she declared to no one. She stripped down to her black t-shirt because it was the only thing that didn't show blood on it and wiped her face the best she could before throwing her clothing into the dumpster and setting it on fire with the lighter in her pocket. She walked away as she rubbed her arms and tried not to freeze to death before she got back to the motel.

Clarice suddenly felt warmth from another pair of hands rubbing her arms.

"So help me, Doc," she growled through chattering teeth.

"You can't get revenge if you get hyperthermia," he reminded her, and she kept quiet until she reached the front door. She raced up the stairs as quickly as she could and jumped into the shower.

"Damn it!" Clarice hissed again, as she wiped the steam from the mirror. She felt her eyes grow heavy and her knees grow weak. "NO!" she ordered.

"Are you okay?" she heard him ask her. His voice was full of concern.

It made her stomach flip a bit. She let out a sigh before she replied softly, "I'm okay."

"Can we talk?" he asked.

He's asking? Well, that's an improvement. "Are you going to let me put clothes on first?" she asked dryly.

"Oh, geez," he replied. She thought she heard actual embarrassment in his voice. "I'm sorry."

She let out a laugh. She couldn't help it. "Now, go away. Please.

I don't need you watching me get dressed."

"I never do! I swear!" she heard him contest.

"I know. Go." She waited a good thirty minutes. Just in case....

Claudia sat and stared at herself in the mirror. She studied herself, concentrating and trying to remember the person she was...before. She remembered being a straight-A student. Studying psychology and biology and trying to make the world a little better before she left by saving lives. Now she was taking them. Oddly, this felt more like who she was destined to be. For a brief second, she hoped her mother would understand. *Her mother....*

Her mother had married her father right out of high school. A bet that had gone drastically wrong. She was a cheerleader, and he was the bad boy from the wrong side of the tracks. But it was love at first date, and the rest was history. Her father worked odd jobs trying to provide for his family. Her mother took care of her and her brother. *Reece.*

The little brother who followed her around, and continued to have separation issues after their mother passed back when she was in high school. Claudia could get him to do pretty much anything, but with Reece, she always manipulated him with good intentions. Now look at her. Claudia's eyebrows came together as she scowled at the reflection that looked back at her. She had somehow become the complete opposite of her former self. *What had they done to her? And why her?*

Claudia tried really hard to think back. She remembered

cramming relentlessly in the library for finals. She had even made some sort of discovery that had escaped her brain, but was going to be her thesis for her senior year. Claudia had walked out of the library and said goodbye to her friends. She had seen him before she heard him coughing. He had asked her for a cough drop. She tried to find one for him, but he had taken her by surprise. And the look in his eyes as he watched her slip into the blackness.

Claudia had never seen him before. Not once. She had an impeccable memory for faces, and Claudia had never seen him. She would have never forgotten his face, half burnt and scarred. *Had she been a random target?* No. Liz had said she had been chosen. *But how?* As a scientist, it would have been more thrilling to grab a specimen that you could alter to a complete 180, but something told her there was something else. She would need to figure it out before she could let her plans play out completely. It was time to spend some quality time with Liz and find out how she became the chosen one....

Nine

Tina was glad that Ben had a project to obsess about other than her. She loved he was as excited and eager to be a new parent as she was, as unexpected as it was, but he was driving them all crazy, not just her. They didn't tell the others of their latest request from the dream realm. No one needed the added stress.

Despite James suddenly calling in daily to check in with everyone back at the hotel, even he couldn't charm away from them the unanswered question of when he and Sophie would return home where everyone awaited for them anxiously. He kept things simple and stated that Algos was gone, and he wanted to spend some time with his fiancé. Give her the break she had more than earned. Though everyone had agreed, they were smart enough to know there was more to the story.

He had a long conversation with Cecil, stating that Sophie was safe and doing okay, and if he was lying, he gave Cecil permission to murder him on the spot once they returned. That was good enough for Cecil, although Donna was a different story. Sophie refused to talk to anyone, because she wasn't sure she could keep from giving herself away, so they only heard from James with Sophie occasionally laughing in the background. It was always genuine, so everyone let it go. For now.

Tina snuck away and made a phone call to the only person who could help her with her own puzzle.

"What's up, Buttercup?" Stacey greeted her on the other end.

Tina giggled. She missed Stacey. "How's the progress?" she asked. She could almost see Stacey grimacing through the phone. "Yeah, that's what I thought. This might help some. This is all I could find on Rebecca. It's not much, but it should be a start. Good luck, my friend," she whispered before hanging up the burner phone.

"What are you up to?"

Tina nearly jumped at the sound of Donna's voice behind her. She turned around and saw Donna leaning against the door frame and with her arms crossed behind her. "Nothing," Tina shrugged with her best poker face.

"Your lying sucks since you got pregnant," Donna replied, deadpan faced.

"Seriously?" Tina asked in frustration. "Ben hasn't said anything."

"I love the boy, but he sees what he wants," Donna answered, with the corners of her mouth curling up. "What are you up to?" she repeated more sternly.

Tina sighed and rolled her eyes. "Okay, so like this prego thing has my senses on overload," she confessed.

Donna tried not to laugh, but nodded instead. "Go on."

Tina looked around before stepping closer to Donna. "I just have a bad feeling that makes me believe that we're not quite done," she finally confessed.

"Done with what?" Donna pressed, not moving a muscle. She wasn't pregnant, but she'd had the same feeling.

"Algos was a complete asshole," Tina said, rolling her eyes. "Who always had tricks up his sleeves. I think one of those tricks is waiting for Sophie. We just don't know it yet," she confessed, giving out a heavy sigh.

"I know I joined late to your side of the game, but I couldn't agree more," Donna said in confirmation. "I've been trying to figure out what he might have left behind to destroy her with," she said with her eyebrows coming together as she straightened up and stepped closer.

"Yeah, well," Tina continued. "It's nearly impossible to figure it out without being a psychopath yourself. So, I started looking around the family tree. Or what I could find of it. Try to track his moves from the start of the chess game to the end to see any patterns," Tina finished chewing on the inside of her cheek.

"And?" Donna prompted, leaning forward and raising her eyebrows.

Tina sulked. "I mean, he killed everyone, yes," she started, "but there should still be some sort of paper trail. Some sort of history of the original players."

"Let me guess," Donna interrupted, putting her hands on her

hips. "Not finding much?"

"No!" Tina was exasperated. "It's like someone purposely went through and destroyed records. Signs of any life or existence."

"So, you're using your connections still at the FBI?" Donna asked, concluding Tina's confession for her.

"Yeah, but don't tell Ben," Tina added urgently.

Donna smiled a sweet smile and held out her hand. Tina looked at it in confusion. "There's more than one way to get information," she said slyly. "Especially when it comes to people like that."

"I can't ask you to help," Tina said, shaking her head. "I don't know where this rabbit hole will go."

"You didn't ask. I'm telling you, we're doing this," Donna said more firmly, shoving her hand further out to Tina. "You're going to need me to keep the men out of this and stay safe." Tina looked from Donna's hand to her face before finally accepting it. A bit of relief rushed over her, knowing she wouldn't be alone in the darkness of getting lost in the history of the madman that still haunted them beyond death.

"Get dressed," James said as he tossed clothes at Sophie, who was sleeping blissfully naked under the sheets.

"What?" she asked, sitting up, trying to rub the confusion and sleep out of her eyes.

"Get dressed," James said again as he packed the backpack for the day.

"Where are we going?" Sophie asked, still trying to get her

bearings.

"Wherever you want," he said over his shoulder.

She was awake then. "I don't think I should be around people," she protested.

"So, we're going to live in this hotel room for the rest of our lives?" he asked her staring into her soul. "Not that I would complain to that," he added with a smile.

"I could hurt someone," Sophie replied with a mope.

"So, let's go figure out how to be around people and not hurt them," James offered with a shrug.

"Are you mad?!" Sophie shouted, jolting out of bed fully naked and mad as hell.

James stood up slowly, turned to face her, and crossed his arms in front of him to control himself from taking her right then and there.

"Listen," he started softly. "You made a good point last night. I can't just attack you and make mad passionate love to you in the middle of public. I don't think that's the kind of news my parents were looking for me to make," he said with a grimace. "So, we have to figure out how else to calm you when you heat up," James continued with a shrug and turned back around to return to packing. "And if we can't figure it out in time, I'll drag you into the alley, and *then* make passionate love to you until you calm down," he added with a smile. He felt her t-shirt hit him in the back of the head.

"Not funny," Sophie growled, but the corner of her lips were curling up and giving her away when he turned back around.

He grabbed and tossed the shirt back at her. "Get dressed, Babe," he said, winking at her. "Just because there are no psychopaths doesn't make it any less of an adventure."

_____

Sophie groaned and rolled her eyes before she stomped into the bathroom, but he could feel her energy coming to ease at the thought of figuring this out. The giggle that came from behind the closed door was just an added bonus.

Clarice never paid attention if what she had on when she fell asleep was what she got to wear in the realm or not, but she wasn't taking any chances. She put on her fighting gear just in case. When she was finished, she laid down, crossed her arms over her chest, and closed her eyes.

"Okay, Doc," she whispered and waited. It wasn't long before she felt the need for sleep consume her. And when she opened her eyes, it wasn't the normal house wooden door that greeted her. It was a door that looked like it should be on the front of a bar.

"Doc?" Clarice called out.

"Yep, come on in," she heard him call out. Clarice looked around cautiously before opening the door.

She was not expecting what greeted her on the other side. An actual bar. But not the raunchy bars she would visit when she had an itch that needed to be scratched. It was more like a classy jazz bar. With round booths covered in maroon velvet and an actual bar to sit and be served drinks. The bar stools had maroon leather coverings and shiny brass highlighted the place nicely. Soft jazz music played in the background. Corbin leaned behind the bar, fixing himself a drink. He looked up at her and scowled.

She automatically scowled back. "What?"

"You don't always have to dress to pick a fight, you know," he replied in a sulk.

"I'm sorry," Clarice replied as her eyebrows drew together and she stared at the floor. She felt judged and exposed at the exact same time. She didn't like it one bit.

"What do you want to drink?" Corbin interrupted, pretending to check his inventory.

She looked around. *What the heck is going on?* "Beer is fine," Clarice answered.

"Oh, okay," Corbin said, a little defeated.

Clearly, he had gone through a lot of effort for whatever this was supposed to be. "You know what, after today, I think I could use something harder. You look like you know what you're doing. Surprise me," she offered, a little nicer.

"Really?" he asked, jerking his head up and raising his eyebrows at her. Before giving her a chance to change her mind, he replied quickly with an, "Um, okay." He went to work as a smile threatened to creep across his lips. "So, tell me honestly, are you okay?" he asked, not looking at her.

"Something tells me you would know if I wasn't. Am I right?" Clarice asked, studying him. It was something that she wasn't sure she wanted the answer to, but she wasn't sure she didn't want the answer at the same time.

He thought for a second before he went back to working on his experiment. "It appears that is correct."

"I thought so," Clarice said, more to herself.

"Listen," Corbin began, as he poured contents into the shaker and shook it. "I had no right to do what I did the other night. My curiosity got the best of me, and...I'm sorry," he finally confessed, still unable to look her in the eye.

She felt his overwhelming guilt. It bothered her to know that he was so distraught over what had happened. Even though he was clearly in the wrong, it still didn't sit well with her. "Well, I would assume even being freshly dead has a learning curve," Clarice offered, but the words just made her feel worse. "Don't do it again," she added sharply and walked over to a booth to gain some space and try to force some oxygen back into her lungs. "So, what is this place?" she asked, quickly changing the subject.

"This," he said as he topped off her drink with a garnish and eagerly brought it to her, "is a safe place," Corbin said with a grin. He looked like a little boy that had made the greatest discovery known to humanity.

"Oh, is it now?" Clarice asked, taking the drink he offered and trying to control her sneer.

"You like bars, and I like jazz. Seemed like a suitable compromise," Corbin added with a shrug. "The dream realm is blocked, and we can talk about anything we need to in here," he finished as he took a nervous sip of his drink.

She was taking a drink and froze. He felt her breath quicken, and her heart threatened to beat out of her chest.

"Like who might be trying to kill you, for starters," he tossed out quickly. Corbin felt her catch her breath and relax. If he was going to figure out Clarice, he was going to have to tread lightly. Go at her pace. Follow her cues. This wasn't about him. It never was. It's always been about her. "I see we have a new player," he added sharply, failing miserably to control his anger.

"So, I noticed," Clarice replied, matching his anger as she went back to sipping on her drink. "This isn't bad," she added with some shock. "What's in it?"

"If I told you, you'd have to join me permanently, and I don't think you're ready for that yet," he said sheepishly as he continued to drink his own drink.

"Ha ha," she said, rolling her eyes and taking another sip. But the idea didn't sound terrible. He tried not to smile and give himself away. "Well, despite my niece having plenty of reasons to off me, it's not her," Clarice stated.

*So, Sophie's her niece...*Corbin nodded in agreement.

"But she's yet another annoying red head," Clarice replied, rolling her eyes. Jess flashed before her eyes, and Corbin rushed to her side. Clarice's heart rate raised again and her eyes filled with angry tears.

"Not in here," he whispered. Corbin took her hand in his and squeezed it, forcing Jess to disappear. "Keep going," he encouraged softly.

Clarice caught her breath and focused on the task at hand. "The bullets were handmade. Tiny bombs to drill into the skull at a certain point. A timer starts, and it goes off, leaving no evidence behind. That should be easy to track down," she said, looking at Corbin and getting lost in his sapphire blue eyes. Then he watched her eyebrows drop and her mouth curve into an instant grimace. "I need a new leather jacket," she pouted.

He tried not to laugh at her childlike response, but damn, was she cute. "We'll get you taken care of," he said, brushing a loose piece of hair from her face.

A realization finally sunk in and she pushed herself back from his trance. "Did you put something in my drink?" she asked, staring at the empty glass. She felt his hurt in response to her question.

"Only alcohol," he muttered as he took her empty glass and walked back to the bar, giving her the space she thought she needed.

"I'm sorry," she finally whispered, staring at the floor. For the first time, he felt guilt from her. Even if she didn't know what she was actually feeling.

"It's okay," he said as he washed the dishes. When he finished, it surprised him to find her sitting in front of him at the bar. He didn't hear her move across the floor. She was watching him intently.

"I'm...I'm not good...with people," she finally declared. Corbin hadn't given her anything that hard, but she had really let her walls down for some reason. At least more than normal. Maybe it was from the events of the day. Either way, he would take what he could get.

"Well, lucky for you, I'm not people," he said, drying his hands on the towel. He leaned over on the bar and got dangerously close to her face. "I'm a ghost," he added with a wink and a smile.

She giggled like a school girl and fell off the stool. Something wasn't right.

"Clarice, Honey," he said to her as he rushed to pick her up off the floor. "You said the bullets were handmade like a bomb, but do you think there was something else in them?"

"God, you're hot," Clarice said as she traced her finger around his face.

"You're not okay," Corbin said firmly as he picked her up and carried her swiftly to one booth. He held out his hand and his doctor's bag came flying out of nowhere into it. "Clarice, listen to me," Corbin ordered her.

"I think I might be falling in love with you," Clarice declared, making his heart stop beating.

He closed his eyes to focus and took a deep breath. When he opened them, his eyes were consumed by crystal ice blue flames. "You were covered in blood when they were shot, weren't you?" he asked her.

Clarice's head bobbed to the twist and turns of the flames in his eyes like a snake in a trance. "Yes," she replied. "It was all over my face. I tried to wipe it clean."

"Damn it!" Corbin hissed. "That's how you got infected."

"Don't you need a sample to study?" Clarice asked, as her head danced in response to the fire in his eyes.

"Do I have time to take one?" Corbin asked her.

"Probably not," she sighed.

"Then no," he said and went to put his glowing ice blue hand on her.

Clarice grabbed his hand, still in the trance. "We have to save Sophie," she sang.

"I'm saving you first," Corbin declared, and before she could say or do anything else, Corbin crushed his mouth on hers and took it as his own. He wrapped his glowing ice blue hands around her and feverishly ran them around her body, exploring every inch he could with her clothes still on.

Clarice threw her head back and gave him access to her neck as she climbed into his lap, straddling him, and found him eagerly waiting for her. She ran her fingers through his long blonde surfer hair and pulled his head back to claim his mouth in return. He was pulling the poison from her body and having one hell of a time doing so.

Clarice forced him on his back and began finding a rhythm as heat and desire consumed her. She needed him. Like never before. He tasted like nothing she had ever tasted in her life. Corbin gently flipped her onto her back and forced himself to pull away from her as he brushed the hair from her face and used the last of his energy to send her into a deep drama and poisoned free sleep. When she had safely disappeared from beneath him, he allowed his icy blue flame to die out, along with his own vitals and consciousness.

Ten

Shyera tried to keep up with Giselle, but the dream realm was much larger than even she had expected. "Hey," she called out, nodding her head over Giselle's left shoulder. "What's that bright blue door?"

Giselle turned to look. "What bright blue door?"

Crap. "I knew you were wearing me out. I didn't realize it was to the point of seeing things," Shyera giggled.

"Sorry," Giselle said, flashing a sheepish smile. "We don't get a lot of new people in...."

Man, did the girl get easily distracted? "What now?" Shyera asked with a hint of irritation.

"That's odd," Giselle said, more to herself.

Shyera waited, but the only response she got was a confused Giselle people watching around them. She watched two colorful ladies walk around aimlessly. One with French violet hair, and the other with brown hair and aqua blue and indigo highlights. Both were extremely confused and terrified. "What's wrong?" Shyera asked more sternly.

"We don't get a lot of new people in here," Giselle answered, still looking around.

Shyera knew that wasn't the end of the sentence. "But?" she prompted.

"Those two seem to be very new," Giselle replied, nodding her head in the ladies' direction

"So, maybe you should help welcome them. Like you did me," Shyera offered.

"You're probably right," Giselle said as she continued to watch the ladies looking just as confused as she was.

"I need a second to catch my breath," Shyera lied. "I'll meet up with you later," she said, offering a smile. Giselle nodded without making eye contact and headed over to introduce herself.

Shyera shuffled her feet around and waited for what felt like a good ten minutes before heading for the bright blue door that was glowing so brightly it lit up the entire realm. Only she was the only one that could apparently see it. *Interesting.*

She reached out her hand and turned the knob, and was surprised that the door willingly opened for her since she was unsure who exactly had made it. Shyera slid in quickly and closed the door behind her. Jazz music played softly in the background of what appeared to be a fabricated relic jazz bar. "Nice touch," she said as she ran her fingers across the bar's outlining brass.

When she turned around to take the room in, she saw a tall, muscular, blonde, laying on the floor completely unconscious. "And who are you?" she whispered to herself. She closed her eyes and stretched out her own energy to feel a pulse, but there wasn't much of one. "Well, that's not good for you," Shyera said as she opened her eyes and tilted her head to study the man lying on the floor.

A light blue flame flickered desperately for life through his veins. His breathing was shallow, and it was clear as day...He was dying.

"I don't have time for you," she whispered, not sure who she was trying to convince more. "I'm not here for you," Shyera said defiantly as she turned her back to him, placing her hands on the bar, and putting her head down.

Just then, a black raven flew in and landed by her right hand. Shyera turned to glare at it. "Don't start with me," she warned.

The bird tilted its head back and forth and blinked its eyes at her, but never made a sound.

"We don't have time. You've seen this place!" she hissed back over her shoulder as sadness quickly filled her eyes. This time, the raven squawked back.

Shyera put her head down and let out a deep sigh. "Yeah, and when the world ends, I'm blaming *you* for this," she returned. The bird simply stepped back and took off, disappearing into the darkness.

She turned around and stared at the man passed out across the room. "The gods have spoken, Stranger, and today's your lucky day," she said with a weary smile. "Just don't take me out, too, with whatever stunt you did to put yourself in this position or we'll all be in trouble," she warned as she strode across the room with determination. As she did, her eyes lit up with red fire, and her hair turned into red flames. She held out her hands, and a red light shot out from her palms, jolting fire into Corbin's body and forcing it to jerk into the air like a rag doll.

Shyera chanted under her breath as she swallowed the toxins Corbin had taken from Clarice, taking a small piece of each of them into her. The price she paid for every life she messed with. When Corbin's body recharged on its own and icy blue flames quickly raced through his veins, Shyera lowered him down onto a velvet round bench, closed her hands into fists, and closed the circuit of power. The blackness swallowed the flames that had previously consumed her pupils.

"Stop messing with what you clearly can't handle," she warned before she slid out the door and was gone before he ever fully woke up and knew she was there. But her words would continue to haunt him until he figured out how to handle the gifts he was given....

"Peter!" Angie called once Mario and Angie returned to their usual bright, all white, meeting room. It wasn't as cozy as the cabin set up Mario was used to in the dream realm, but it still had its perks. Comfy white couches that never seemed to get dirty, tables and chairs. Lots of white. Lots and lots of white. But it was peaceful, and he didn't have a choice either way.

A very tall, very muscular man entered the room. With eyes that were as blue and sparkly as diamonds that even Mario got lost in them. "You rang," he said with a wide, perfect grin, as he strolled in and kissed Angie on the cheek. *Good grief! Could he be any more perfect?*

Angie smiled with genuine happiness, and Mario guessed any woman would. He looked down at himself in comparison. Although he had upgraded from his shabby black combat attire that Clarice had murdered him in, to a cleaner lighter grey, his body still wasn't in its twenty something shape by far.

Sensing Mario's distress, Angie added, "It's always good to see you, Son." Mario's head jerked up. He hadn't been here long. He was still learning a lot. Mario had heard the stories, but he didn't know this Peter was *the Peter* that was Algos's first human sacrifice. Things were making a lot more sense. "I need you to go with Mario, here, and find Rebecca," Angie ordered.

"She's missing?" Peter asked in alarm. Angie's look of warning had him silenced immediately. Mario knew the dream realm was ridiculous about their "need to know" policy, but here was a whole different level of absurdity. He wasn't sure why he was here, or how long he would last, honestly. This wasn't exactly his cup of tea. Never had been.

"Together, you should be able to locate her and bring her back," Angie continued, breaking Mario's thoughts. "And keep your thoughts to yourself," she whispered to Peter. He gave a nod of acknowledgement and eyed Mario with suspicion. "Is he even ready?"

Angie looked at him with a similar doubt. "We're about to find out."

"I'm right here, ya know," Mario grumbled in annoyance.

Angie ignored him and turned to Peter. "You know what will happen if you fail," she reminded him wearily.

"I am well aware," Peter nodded with determination.

"If someone would like to tell me, that would be helpful," Mario said, standing up in irritation, and was quickly knocked back down onto the couch by an invisible hand. He glared at the sky but said nothing. *You brought me here.* He scowled and crossed his arms.

Angie took her son's face in her hands and kissed him on the cheek. "Safe travels," she whispered as she blinked away the tears that threatened to fall. He placed his hands over hers and squeezed tightly before stepping back.

"Come on, Newbie," he said cheerfully. "We have a damsel to go save!"

"No," Mario said stubbornly. "And I have a name," he scoffed. But he was shoved off the couch and out the door before he could protest anymore.

❧

Karmen Beaufort was not your typical eleven-year-old. Though she had difficulty expressing the information that zoomed through her incredibly intelligent brain on an ongoing basis to others, her test scores were off the charts. They would find out that she had a unique balance of autism and genius.

Karmen kept to herself, usually with her nose in a book, drawing or painting, or helping her foster dad piece together cars. She had already helped to rewire the entire house to be more efficient, and that's only what people already knew she was capable of. It was enough to make them terrified of her, which is why her foster parents didn't share any of the rest.

They hadn't had Karmen long, but it had been long enough to

know that in the wrong hands, she would be dangerous. Daniel and Denise Lackey fought hard to get her out of the system. They agreed to keep her in the house and have teachers come to her. They had already gained her late one night when her parents were found brutally murdered.

The police found Karmen, the sole survivor, sitting in their blood, holding their hands in hers, rocking and humming as tears streamed down her bloodied cheeks. It took Daniel and Denise less than forty-eight hours to realize why Karmen had been left to survive, and they couldn't, with clear conscious, let anything happen to her. That had been two years ago.

The nightmares of the man with the cane had faded as Karmen continued to draw and paint pictures of a red-headed girl in black with one red eye and one blue eye traveling between wooden doors. She painted a blonde man that looked more like a surfer than anything else, and some other ghostly like figures. She often drew a short, curvy woman with gorgeous curly short hair that was as dark as her skin, always surrounded by fog. The Lackeys assumed it was just a creative outlet for Karmen.

However, the thing Karmen drew and painted the most was the man with the cane's daughter, who was looking for Karmen at that very moment. The only problem was that Karmen and Clarice weren't the only people who knew it. And Karmen only knew how to talk through her pictures....

Clarice finally stirred from her drunken deep sleep. "What the hell?" she asked, placing her hand to her forehead to steady the room that was spinning around her. Flashes of Corbin's body on hers. The taste of his lips against hers. The feel of his body, hard and wanting, pressed against hers. But it had just been a dream. *Hadn't it?*

Clarice remembered the assassination after meeting with Ashley clear as day. The mysterious redhead on the roof who had taken the shots close enough to easily take her out, but hadn't. Stripping her close off in the alley and coming to the room to quickly shower and lie down. As for the rest, it was a hazy blur that refused to surface. *Was it because nothing happened? Or was it because something had and Corbin was blocking it?*

"Corbin," Clarice hissed in a mixture of apprehension and annoyance, but there was no answer. She couldn't even feel him like she did before. *Was something wrong? Was he in trouble?* The feeling didn't set well with her for some reason, and the only person she knew she could ask, she couldn't ask at all. *Jess.*

Sophie wasn't a safe option either, but there might be another. Clarice laid back down, and hoped secretly that the system worked the same for Jack as it seemed to for Corbin. She closed her eyes and let out a nervous breath. "Hey brother, I need your help," she whispered and waited as patiently as she had ever waited in her life for a response.

Jack heard her call for him and stopped dead in his tracks. Jess turned to look at him. "What is it?" she asked with a frown.

Knowing better than to tell the truth without knowing what the truth truly entailed, Jack simply replied, "Corbin needs some help with something. He needs your nerdy scientist to help him run some numbers," he said, flashing her a smile and kissing her on the cheek.

"Be careful," he warned her. Then he disappeared before Jess could say anything else.

Clarice opened her eyes to the wooden door and eagerly opened it to find Jack looking at her curiously, standing with his hands on his hips. "You must be desperate to be coming to me," he said, watching her carefully as he took a seat at the kitchen table that appeared out of nowhere. Clarice glared at him.

"Yeah, well, still not in the mood to deal with your wife at the moment," she snapped. "And something tells me that your buddy, Corbin, might be in some trouble," she finished, crossing her arms in front of her chest as she took a seat across from him. Jack sat up straighter.

"I'm listening," was all he dared to say.

"There's a new player," Clarice started. "Nothing I can't handle," she added quickly, glaring at Jack. He had opened his mouth, but then shut it and remained quiet. "She took out two innocents when I passed," she finished in a flat tone.

"Innocents..," Jack repeated, watching her. He'd never heard Clarice use that word. Ever.

Clarice rolled her eyes. "She was clearly out to get my attention, and she got it," Clarice muttered through her anger. "Anyway," she pushed through, "Corbin wanted to talk about it afterwards, but I think something went wrong."

Jack leaned in closer. "You don't remember what happened?" he asked softly.

Clarice stood up and paced the room. "Something definitely doesn't feel right, and I didn't wake up like I usually do. So, I'm telling you," she said, looking at Jack with more plead in her eyes than she intended. "I think he's in trouble, and I know how close you two are," she replied, and headed for the door.

Interesting, Jack thought. "Am I the only one?" he asked.

Clarice froze.

Didn't think so. "That you've told," Jack added, to switch the subject.

Clarice let her shoulders sag a bit. "Yeah. I didn't know who else to tell," she said, looking down at the black invisible floor beneath her.

She heard Jack stand up from behind her and walk over to her. He placed a hand on her shoulder. "I'll find him," he whispered. Clarice could only nod before jerking the door open and stepping out, leaving Jack to his thoughts.

He couldn't feel Corbin at all, which wasn't a good sign. He had sensed long ago that Corbin was starting to feel for Clarice. The problem in here was that you could get drunk on your "power", and Corbin had more than most.

When Algos pulled Clarice in against her will, it formed a unique connection between the two. At least, it was Jack's hypothesis. Clarice gave Jack the confirmation he needed. Only Jack never equated that their connection would change Clarice like it appeared to be doing. However, hypothesis needed to be tested, even he knew that, and those were tests Jess wouldn't stand for. There were no guarantees that these changes were permanent either.

Regardless, Corbin seemed to be in trouble, and that needed to be Jack's priority. *But how was he supposed to find someone who appeared to already have no energy trail left in him?* That usually meant only one thing. Jack was already too late.

However, before Jack had an opportunity to go look for his friend, he was shocked by a surge of energy that tossed him across the room and into the wall behind him. His body slid down the wall as it fell to the ground. Thankfully, he felt Corbin's life force return.

"Well, hello intruder," Jack muttered as he got to his feet. "Thank you for saving my friend," he talked to no one with honest appreciation. "But I'm a little more interested in knowing which side you reside on."

Shyera's eyes narrowed at the sound of Jack's voice ringing in her ears, but knew there was no way he could find her. Not yet, at least. Time was running out. Shyera had to move fast. She spotted Giselle talking to the new ladies of the realm and beelined it to the opposite side of them. Shyera didn't respond, because she wasn't exactly sure what the answer was herself....

"Well?" Liz asked, watching Claudia.

"Meh," she responded without hesitation. "Not much fun being so far away," she answered honestly.

"So you prefer to be closer? To watch the torture first-hand?" Liz asked, more to herself than to Claudia as she paced around the lab deep in thought. "Well, that's a start," she said with a decisive nod. "What would you like to try next?"

"Why do you care so much about what I like or don't like?" Claudia asked with a hint of irritation mixed with curiosity. She couldn't help but wonder what the good doctor got out of all of this.

Liz turned around and looked her dead in the eyes. "I don't

know what your full past was before we met, but for me, I was already being compared to a goddess long before I was even old enough to go to school," she started looking over her shoulder as if staring at a ghost. "My mother," Liz added to answer Claudia's curious stare. "It was predetermined long ago that I would automatically follow my mother's footsteps, which was fine because I love the work. But sometimes just because you're expected to follow in someone else's footsteps, doesn't mean you don't want to have a piece that is your own, ya know?" Liz asked with a shrug, now looking at the floor. "I may look like her, but I'm still not her. I can never be her. And maybe, just maybe, if I did something that really mattered, then I would matter outside of her shadow."

"Like making a psychopath?" Claudia asked, trying to hide her smirk.

Liz snorted. "Yeah. Like making a psychopath," she said, looking back at Claudia.

Claudia knew how Liz felt. Her past had a similar storyline to it. It made her understand the doctor a little more, and almost trust her a little more, too. For what petty emotions she could muster as an ultimate psychopath. It didn't take away her desire not to fully trust Dr. Liz Banks, but it took the edge off to allow her to hang around a little longer.

"I don't enjoy being so far away," Claudia confirmed for the doctor. "The bullets were cool, but I think I'd like to try a more hands on approach, maybe?"

The corner of Liz's lips curled up into a smile. "Okay. Let me see what we can do."

Clarice tried to push Corbin out of her mind during the day. She had Ashley on her way to her new lab safely and saw no signs of the new redheaded player that seemed desperate to get Clarice's attention. *What for?* Clarice wasn't sure, but she was pretty sure she didn't want to be involved. She had her own plans.

She watched a bouncy brunette exit the coffee shop after grabbing her morning latte and head over to her full-time job as a nanny for the Lackeys. The foster parents that held the girl who her father kept a picture of in his office. *Karmen.* Funny how she had been so close to them, and Clarice still knew nothing of what her father wanted from the girl.

Based on the information Clarice was able to find on such short notice, Karmen Beaufort was the only survivor of a mass murder in her own home. Handy work that had her father's signature all over it. *But why let the child live?* There was always a reason for everything he did. It was just a matter of untwisting the twisted to see what that reasoning was.

Karmen didn't go to school. She never left the house. The records on her were sealed heavily, and no one knew more than the basics. She was eleven-years-old, and teachers came to her. The Lackeys were a white, middle-aged, middle-class couple who both worked. Vanessa Jones was the twenty-something nanny that stayed with her while they worked. When the Lackey's came home, they gave their undivided attention to her until she fell asleep. If Karmen went outside, it was in the high fenced backyard where no one would know she was back there.

Clarice wasn't sure if this was because of her father's visit, or if there was more to the story. Either way, her only way to get to Karmen would be through Miss Vanessa. So, Clarice waited casually in her rental car for Vanessa to be done with her shift and go about her evening.

<u>Eleven</u>

James and Sophie had spent the day out in public without a hitch. It was quite refreshing. It almost had Sophie believing they could return home, and she could enjoy watching Tina's belly grow larger. Maybe she could even feel the baby eventually start to kick. They could finally be...normal. The sun was going down, and they were both getting hungry.

"What do you feel like doing?" James asked her, squeezing her hand as they walked down the filling sidewalk. It was interesting to watch how much life this smaller town had to provide once the sun hid behind the mountains.

Sophie's eyes lit up at a sign that promised live music, beer, and great food. "This!" she exclaimed, dragging him behind her. He laughed at her enthusiasm as he jogged to stay in step with her. It was nice to see her back to her old self.

They sat in the corner booth and ordered some appetizers as a live band set up to play for the evening. However, a figure sitting at the bar caught James's eye that made him lose his appetite immediately....

Clarice leaned against the bar, eying the crowd carefully. She saw a happy Sophie and James enter, but they were too distracted to notice her. *Seriously? Why have they not left yet? Ugh!* She turned her back to them and ordered a whiskey straight from the bartender. She didn't have to see Vanessa to know she had entered. It was her usual Friday night with her girlfriends, and they had started the party early, apparently. The corner of Clarice's lips curled up before she took a sip of her drink.

"Nice necklace," cooed a female voice to her left. Clarice didn't answer and continued to sip her drink. She saw the red curly hair out of the corner of her eye and knew exactly who it was. The new player. "Man, it gets crowded quick in here," she commented. Clarice remained quiet. "Not much for words, huh?" the woman snickered.

"Not when it's not worth my time," Clarice sneered back. She saw the woman's lips twitch out of the corner of her eye.

"Bartender! A refill for my sister, and a jack neat for myself, please," she called out, smiling sweetly, pressing her breasts together as she leaned over to hand him cash. The young man nodded eagerly, unable to lift his eyes to meet her gaze before he raced off to get their drinks.

"Sisters, huh?" Clarice laughed. "I've already got one of those, and we don't exactly get along."

"Well, that's because she doesn't understand you like I do," said the woman, not making eye contact still as the boy came running over with their drinks, nearly spilling them. "Thank you," the woman said sweetly to him, winking and pursing her lips at him. "Don't let these get empty," she added, circling her finger around the rim of the glass. He nodded and went off to help some other customers.

Clarice sighed dramatically before turning around to face the woman, already causing her too much grief. "And what is it you think you know, *sister*?" she asked, adding an emphasis to the last word with great distaste.

"Well, for starters," the redhead said with a smirk, "you think that necklace is yours, and it's not."

Anger flashed across Clarice's eyes, but she remained as cool as a cucumber. "Do tell," she stated with a deadpan face.

"Your father always had more than one plan. We both know that," the woman continued, batting her lashes as she sipped her drink. "But he never respected you for your true worth and potential."

"Oh, let me guess, but you can?" Clarice answered, batting her eyes and matching the woman's innocence.

"But of course," the woman replied with a shrug. "Think of all the fun we can have!"

"And if I refuse?" Clarice asked dryly.

"Well, eventually, you will have to be dealt with like all the others," the woman added with a shrug and chugged the rest of her drink before setting it on the bar.

The woman had already been following Clarice. *Who else was she after that Clarice knew?* "What a tempting offer. Do I have time to think about it?" Clarice asked over enthusiastically as she also chugged the rest of her drink.

The woman narrowed her eyes, as if seeing right through Clarice's lie before Clarice realized she was even giving it. "Not long," the woman finally offered.

The bar was quickly filling up as the band was starting their show.

"Why are you here?" asked an exasperated James, grabbing Clarice's arm and pulling her attention away from the woman to her left. However, when she spun back around, the woman was already long gone.

"Well, why make friends when you have plenty of enemies?" Clarice snarled as she turned around to face James. "Why are you?" she asked, glaring back at him.

"If she sees you, she'll lose it, and..." he started, looking back to make sure that Sophie didn't see who he was talking to.

There was something much more concerning to him than her anger at seeing Clarice. Even Clarice could hear it in his voice. "James, what's going on?" she asked sternly.

He looked her dead in the eyes. "Just go. Before it's too late."

"Too late?" Clarice snickered, but his look of warning had her quiet in seconds. "What's wrong with Sophie?" she demanded.

"It's not your concern. Just go," James commanded before working his way through the crowd back to Sophie.

Just then, a girl screamed and everyone turned to look and see where the call of distress had come from. A male about 5'9", in his late twenties, with a stout figure, emerald green eyes and a buzz cut, held a knife to some poor girl's neck. Everyone looked at the girl except James, who locked his eyes on Sophie's slow burning red irises.

"Sophie," he gasped, and Clarice followed his stare.

"That's still going on?" she asked, studying her niece. James's silence was more concerning than Clarice cared for.

"Please get out of here," he hissed as he pushed his way through the crowd trying to get to Sophie. People were panicking and looking for the nearest exit.

Clarice turned to see where the nanny was, but she only saw the back of her going out the side door.

"Sophie!" she heard James call out in a panic. Clarice tore her eyes away to see the back of Sophie race out the door and out of James's reach.

Clarice looked back at the side door, and then at the front door. "Damn it," she muttered to herself before she took off, running out the side door and back around towards the front.

The man was dragging the girl as a shield in front of him as he nervously backed away from Sophie. Clarice would have too at the site of her. Sophie's hair whipped wildly around her despite there being no wind to cause the reaction, and her eyes glowed a dangerous fiery red as she stalked him like prey.

"She said you were crazy, but..." was all he said, but it was enough to catch Clarice's ear and had her pretty sure who had sent him to poke at her niece.

"We really have got to stop meeting like this," Clarice called out. James finally had caught up to them and went to take a step forward, but Clarice stuck her hand out, stopping him. Something told her that Sophie may not exactly be in total control, but she knew all too well what it would do to her if she hurt the man she loved. Clarice shook her head, and James froze.

Sophie's lips curled up into a sinister grin. "You can wait your turn," she called over her shoulder.

"Oh, I'm sure," Clarice said flatly, "but is this really how you want to honor Eddie's memory?" she tossed out for good measure.

Sophie froze, and her fingers twitched at the name. "You don't get to say his name," she hissed angrily over her shoulder.

"Why?" Clarice taunted. "Cause the truth sucks, and is a lot less fun than taking this sucker's life?" She let go of James, but held up a finger, warning him to stay put as she strode dangerously up behind Sophie and passed her and the guy that nervously looked between them both while still holding the knife to the crying girl's throat. "Trust me, niece," Clarice warned as she wandered off to the side, but still within plenty of striking distance to the man holding the girl, who had all but crumpled under his arm. She didn't look at Sophie, but crossed her arms and continued to stare at the strangers before her.

"There's a difference between killing because you have to and killing because you want to, and once you cross that line...once you let that feeling ever so slightly justify your actions, you can't go back. You lose everything," she said, tossing a nod towards James. "And you can't go back. Trust me."

Sophie's eyes were consumed with blackness minus the red flames that burned in the center. Her veins glowed like lava, and she looked more like a fictional demon than an actual person, but even Clarice saw her hesitation as she took in the words Clarice had said.

Sophie tilted her head to study the woman that had taken her godfather from her. The woman she had sworn to take a life for a life and had yet to do so. Even in this state of desire and need to take this man's life for putting an innocent in danger, the obvious anguish in Clarice's voice from her ongoing life decisions couldn't be missed. Sophie wanted so badly to take his life and right the wrong. She wanted it more than she wanted James. *Why?*

"What did she want from you?" Clarice asked the man holding the knife, breaking Sophie's train of thought.

"To get you both outside," the young man said shamefully over his shoulder. Clarice remained off to the side, but between the three of them.

"And the price?" she asked with a scowl.

The young man sighed. "Something I couldn't pay unless I did."

Clarice nodded, as if knowing what exactly that was. "So, what's it gonna be?" Clarice called out, turning to finally face Sophie and keeping her arms crossed.

Sophie fisted her hands, closed her eyes, and took a deep breath. *Could she live with herself if she chose this instead of James and everyone else?* Balance. She heard his words echo in her head. When she opened her eyes, she stared at the knife still in his hand and when she turned her head; it went flying in the direction of her glance. The girl elbowed him hard in the gut and took off running to James, who just caught her and spun her to the next person behind him as he ran towards Sophie.

Clarice nodded with a smile of pride sneaking across her lips, before she reached down into her pocket, grabbed the switchblade, and spun and jabbed it into the back of the stranger's neck.

The man fell to his knees before he fell forward and landed face first in the street in the middle of the surrounding crowd. Sophie and

James stared at her in shock.

"What?" Clarice asked with a shrug. "I said *you* shouldn't kill him. Not that he shouldn't die." Then she spun around on her heels and walked away. She might have felt guilty had she known the mystery woman wasn't in the crowd hiding and watching. Or that she had already planned on killing the poor man, anyway. Something told her the redhead would have been much more torturous since she was proving to want to outdo her father more than Clarice ever desired to.

Sophie watched Clarice walk away for the second time, hating her aunt a little less.

"You okay?" James asked her as he looked deep into her now electric blue eyes.

Her eyebrows creased, and she scowled. "Yes. I think." Despite having James gazing at her, she couldn't take her eyes off of Clarice as she disappeared into the night.

"That's almost convincing," James countered with his own frown.

Sophie turned to look at him and gave a giggle. "I'm sorry. Yes, I'm okay."

"I'm sorry. I didn't know she was still here," he said, looking down at the ground.

"Why *is* she still here? I'm pretty sure the bunker isn't foundationally safe," Sophie stated as she looked around him back towards where Clarice had disappeared to.

Her tone seemed more curious than angry. James wasn't sure if he should be concerned or not. "She didn't say when I went to get our drinks from the bar. She was sitting there talking to some redhead, and she didn't seem too happy about it," he ended with a shrug.

Sophie looked at him like Tina did when she was trying to solve a puzzle. "What do you think she's up to?"

However, before he could even answer, she had grabbed his hand and was dragging him behind her as she chased after her aunt.

"Well, isn't that interesting," Claudia said, studying Sophie as she stalked Robert Wheeler. *Who knew some unsuspecting poor sap would come in so handy?* Although Sophie was on her list, she had more important things to take care of first.

It surprised her to see Clarice, of all people, come to Sophie's rescue. However, it wouldn't take much salt to pour on Sophie's wounds to make her not allow Clarice to walk away ever again, and that would be useful. But for now, Clarice could live. It was much more fun to play with her, anyway.

Claudia briefly wondered if this fell in the same category as playing with her food. Then she giggled. Boy, did her mother like to lecture her on that one. However, her father had always stepped in and reminded her mother that Claudia needed to still be a kid every once in a while.

For a moment, Claudia missed her father. However, it was gone almost as fast as it appeared. She wondered briefly if that was going to be a good thing or a bad thing, but quickly went back to taking mental notes of her subjects in the test she had set up for them.

It had taken forever to shake Liz. Claudia needed to see for herself what she was actually up against. The old man had left a letter for her, too. Telling her what he wanted from her. She had her own ideas, though. Better ones.

He was dead. *Why should she be left to clean up his messes and carry on his legacy, because he made his children hate him in the end? Hell, Clarice killed him, for crying out loud!* But that was neither here nor there for Claudia. She had her own plans, and she wasn't ready to share them with Liz until she knew if she really needed her or not.

So, instead, she just watched. Impressed with both prey. They would be trouble if they got together, but it would be entirely too easy to make sure that never happened. Claudia wasn't worried. She smirked as she watched Clarice kill Robert without hesitation. If she wasn't such a damn wildcard, Claudia could find use for her.

However, she was in no mood to deal with someone who clearly swayed so easily when it came to family. *Family.* She wondered what hers would think of what had become of her, but within seconds the brainwaves shifted, making her not care either way. Or at least that's what everyone thought.

"Well, great," Clarice muttered as she slammed the door behind her. She had lost Vanessa in the chaos, and Sophie's "show" in front of the bar didn't leave room to hangout anymore in town. *What's wrong with her?*

Clarice wasn't blind when Sophie fought them in the bunker. She had noticed the one blue glowing eye and the one red, but there was no blue to be seen tonight. She had seen her sister turn red and Corbin blue. Since Jess had the blood of a psychopath in her, Clarice guessed red wasn't the best color to be glowing. However, all of that glowing had taken place in the dream realm. Not here in her world. *Corbin.*

Just when she got ready to call his name, the hair on the back of her neck prickled up and she sensed she was about to have company. She shut off the lights and hid behind the door.

When it creaked open, Clarice grabbed the hand still on the handle and swung the body onto the bed. She felt male arms wrap around her immediately, as James grunted against her struggling, "It's just us."

Clarice sighed heavily, and her shoulders slumped forward. "Let go of me," she hissed, and James obliged. When Clarice flipped on the lights, Sophie was lying on the bed, making the place her home with her standard grin shining back at Clarice.

"What's up, Auntie?" she asked sweetly.

"Oh my God, never call me that!" Clarice groaned as she walked over and grabbed a glass before pouring herself a long whiskey neat and sitting down at the sad excuse of a table in the corner.

"It's not polite to not share," Sophie pretended to pout.

"Are you even old enough?" Clarice sneered as she took a drink, knowing very well Sophie was. Barely. "What do you want?"

"Why are you still here?" Sophie asked matter-of-factly.

"Why are *you*?" Clarice countered. "My guess is it's all your moodiness," she added, waving her hand around in the air.

Sophie grimaced, but the guilt in her eyes answered the question for Clarice.

"How long?" Clarice asked her.

"What?" Sophie questioned.

"How long?" Clarice repeated more firmly before taking a

drink.

"Since I woke up," Sophie confided.

"Are we sure?..." James started.

"I can't help you," Clarice cut in. "I honestly don't know what all he did." There was no point beating around the bush. "But you shouldn't stay. That show of yours is going to have you on everybody's radar. We're both already on one, and until I figure out who and why, it isn't safe."

"What?" James asked.

Clarice took another drink. "Until you get yourself under control, you need to hide," was all she said, but it was how she said it.

James and Sophie looked at each other. Since when did Clarice care what happened to them?

"No one remembers tonight," Sophie assured. "What are you going to do?" she asked Clarice.

"I'm going to find out what's going on and take care of it," Clarice added with a shrug and downed the last of her drink. "Now, if you'll kindly leave, I need some sleep." She wasn't ignoring Sophie's comment. Clarice was just too exhausted to deal with it right now.

"Is that the only reason you're still here?" Sophie asked, not sure what kind of answer she was looking for.

"Listen, Kid," Clarice started, but when she saw Sophie tense up, she realized her mistake. "I'm sorry," she whispered in honest sincerity. She stood up and walked towards the door. "I gave your mother my word that you would remain safe. It appears someone wants to make me work to keep that promise, so until I resolve it, I will have to remain. Now," Clarice said, yanking the door open. "I need sleep," she stated flatly, keeping her eyes out towards the dark hall scanning it before Sophie got off the bed reluctantly.

James took her hand and led her out of the room. "Keep your head down," Clarice warned, still looking down the hall. "I'll let you know when it's clear." She shut the door in Sophie's face before she could respond.

James observed her. "Come on," he said, gently tugging on her hand. "Did you expect much else?" he added in a soft whisper.

"I don't know what I expected," Sophie murmured back, as she squeezed his hand and followed him down the dark hallway.

Clarice leaned her head against the door behind her. Sophie was hurting, and it was Clarice who had taken her last lifeline to family away. At least she still had James, and Clarice had great faith that Tina and Ben would be on top of it. *Unless they didn't know. Was that why they weren't leaving?*

Clarice shook her head to clear it as she walked over and dramatically fell onto her crappy bed, face first. She didn't bother to change her clothes. She simply grabbed the pillow and shoved her face into it, hoping to smother the uncomfortable feelings that stirred from within. Sleep. She just needed sleep....

Twelve

When Corbin finally came to, he sat up immediately. *Clarice.* After closing his eyes, he searched for her. Corbin found her struggling to find sleep in her hotel room. He breathed a sigh of relief. *She's safe.* Corbin reached out and brushed the wet hair away from her forehead, and she sat up immediately.

"Who's there?" she demanded.

"Easy, Slick," she heard Corbin whisper in her ear. "It's just me. I needed to make sure you were okay."

"Yeah, well, I'm not," she mumbled, burying her face into the pillow.

"Wanna come have a drink?" he asked hopefully. She froze. "Or just talk," Corbin corrected, realizing their last drink didn't exactly end so well.

Clarice wanted to talk, but her body told her she needed to sleep more. He felt her exhaustion and decided to try something different.

"Here," she heard him whisper in her ear. It felt like Corbin had curled up behind her and taken her into his arms. *How was this possible?* She felt the sweaty hair that was stuck around her face be pulled away as her temperature dropped, making her more comfortable. "Tell me about it," Corbin whispered in her ear.

Clarice felt silly talking to herself, but she told him about what happened at the bar. About the mysterious redhead, and about Sophie. How she didn't seem to be herself anymore, and how Sophie was scared of herself. Corbin listened as he fought to keep her cool. It was clear she was struggling between trying to help Sophie and leaving her be. He didn't interject. Just simply held her and listened.

"I can't help her," Clarice finally whispered before drifting to sleep.

"Sleep," Corbin said softly, and so she did. A deep sleep. As she dreamt of a life with a man who was already dead.

Mario reluctantly followed Peter through different realms, trying not to be alarmed by how many truly existed. Yet, there was no energy trace of Rebecca that Peter could pick up.

"What's on your mind?" Peter asked, cutting into Mario's thoughts.

"Who says I have anything on my mind?" Mario asked, crossing his arms in front of his chest and taking a step back from Peter. He wasn't good with people he didn't know, and Mario had lost everyone he loved in order to buy them more time. He just didn't realize it would end him up here.

The corner of Peter's lips curved into a grin. "Nothing at all," he said with a shrug. "But I can't imagine what it was like to leave everyone you loved to be stuck with me," he added.

Was he in my head? "Listen, it's nothing personal," Mario said in a low whisper. This realm was very dark, with shadows lurking and watching them with red glowing eyes from every angle as they walked along the abandoned road before them with no end in sight.

"If it makes you feel any better, I didn't exactly signup for the job either," Peter chuckled.

Mario kept his eyes on the surrounding shadows, but he never heard the full story of Peter or what had happened. Only that he was another unwilling victim of Algos, who happened to also be family. *A brother, maybe?*

As if reading Mario, yet again, Peter replied, "I was Algos's little brother. I happened to really enjoy trains. Algos thought I would enjoy seeing them up close and in person. We just didn't agree on how close I needed to see them as they sped down the track," Peter said, with a hint of irritation in his voice.

Mario stopped and looked at Peter. "Damn."

Peter slowed down his pace to allow Mario to shake off the shock and join him again. Once he did, Peter continued. "I was too little to see it coming," he added, as if to console Mario.

"Aren't you a little mad that you weren't the one to take him out in return?" Mario asked in curiosity. He would have been.

"It's not my path," Peter replied, but the hint of irritation told Mario otherwise.

"So, what is your path?" Mario inquired, as he raised an eyebrow and edged closer to Peter.

"To help you find yours," Peter replied simply with a shrug.

Mario stopped and crossed his arms while narrowed his eyes. "And if I don't want to go down any more paths?" he asked curtly.

Peter laughed in delight. "You already have," he said with a smile, and continued to walk down the road before them.

Mario glared at the man that seemed to stroll through this realm without a care. Hell, he had already died. TWICE! *What more did he have to offer at this point?* He looked at the sky. "You're going to kill me off again, aren't you?" he mumbled. Mario felt a small kick in the butt that pushed him forward. Apparently the Powers That Be had control in all realms. He glared up at the sky before giving out a heavy sigh and jogging to catch back up to Peter.

John walked the realm quietly in disguise. There was no need to upset his people any more than Algos already had, but there was an intruder among them. He needed to find out if they were here to do harm or not. John also needed to find Rebecca. He knew that Corbin, whether he was aware or not, was doing what he was meant to do. Help Clarice find her way.

Algos may have loved chess, but this game was turning into something completely different. With new players still in hiding, everyone was in danger, including his family. Remembering who they were wasn't helping him to keep them safe, either. John was curious why the gods had allowed him to keep his memories this time, or if that was another consequence of being near Sophie. *Sophie.*

Had their interaction changed each other? Had he set these changes in motion? Or were they always meant to cross paths? They used to give him a hint to the endgame, but it was radio silent, and he was a player like anyone else. That fact alone scared the hell out of him.

His council could never find out. They would rebel and he would lose his control. That would have consequences he couldn't afford to pay. No one could. *But would the gods allow it to get that far? Had they not chosen him, and forced him to be stuck here for so long, if not to carry this out to the end?* That was what John had always believed. Had he just been another pawn in a very sick psychological warfare game?

It was best to have faith than to believe you were a pawn of nothingness, and that was what John did. Which meant he had to have faith he could keep his people safe, family included. And he had to have faith that Clarice and the others would step up and help get Sophie under control before too much damage was caused that couldn't be reversed.

There was also a raven to be reckoned with. Rebecca had only been half-raven, and it had been enough of a nightmare for John. Whoever woke up was a hundred percent, and more dangerous than anything he had ever come across. They had to figure out who it was, and fast. Without the right people to guide them, all the worlds would be destroyed. And if it was Sophie that would have to face them, well...they needed to get Sophie under control as well.

John closed his eyes to clear his mind and concentrate, but there was no energy trace to track. Whoever was here was being smart enough not to use their gifts to help them be found. "Damn it," he mumbled.

Just then, he heard a faint but familiar voice call to him. "John...help me," it begged in his ears.

"Rebecca!" he yelled back. There was no answer.

Liz continued to document her findings in her encrypted journal. Claudia was doing well. She definitely had the thirst of a psychopathic serial killer. Although they hadn't found her specific signature yet, she definitely preferred being up close and personal. Claudia's planning was always dead on, and very creative. No one ever sees her coming. Yet, there would always be a fault to this experiment. Liz had made herself safe by messing with Claudia's nerves to recognize Liz's scent, the sound of her voice, and her touch. She had creatively programmed Claudia to never physically desire to kill her.

As evil as Liz worked to make her, there would always be uncontrolled variables. Humanity's need for freewill. Basically, deadening and destroying her frontal lobe allowed Claudia to lack a conscious since her emotional responses were blunted. Nothing would trigger her to think her behavior was not appropriate, or cause her to avoid the decision to take a life. Or at least that was the desired outcome of the experiment.

Yet, there was no actual proof Claudia wasn't having flashbacks to her old life. Not that she was confessing anything to her own doctor.

Liz did her best to kill the frontal lobe in order to bring out Claudia's aggression without making her completely brain dead. And several studies stated that such an injury led to a majority of the serial killers and psychopaths that had roamed the earth. Yet, her mother had once confirmed Algos had no damage. He just simply had a black, soulless heart. *The heart.*

An organ often contributed to helping people fall in love and making decisions their brains couldn't agree with. Of course, when it came to science, that was just rubbish. Then again, the dream realm didn't exactly fit into the scientific world, either, but had proven to exist all the same.

Liz had to question that even destroying the frontal lobe may not destroy a woman's need to have a choice, or any human, for that fact. The brain was the most unknown organ in the body. No one truly knew everything it could do, despite all the studying they had done on it. It could very well be a human's need to have a choice over their fate that would make this experiment never truly successful. To know that for certain, she would have to get Claudia to confide in her. For science.

Liz tapped a pencil against her mouth, deep in thought as the computer quickly encrypted the notes she had just left. She may not be able to completely make a psychopathic serial killer, but she would get Claudia pretty damn close. When the computer chimed, insuring her notes were secure, her lips curled up into a smile as she closed the laptop.

"See, Mother," she announced to no one. "I will do the one thing you never could." Someone else would have to worry about switching Claudia back, if it was even medically possible. But for now, she had a psychopath to nurture to maturity. And Liz was going to do the best possible job of achieving just that. For science.

Ashley got settled in her new digs. They were a definite upgrade from what she had left behind, and it was right next to her supposed lab. Mason knocked on her door lightly before coming into full sight of her already opened door.

"Hey, whatever your name is," Ashley said with irritation.

"Mason," he offered with a frown.

"She said I get to work in a lab. Why can't I see it?" Ashley demanded, with her hands on her hips.

"First," Mason acknowledged, crossing his arms, trying to show authority over Ashley. It just made her laugh. *Great. She thinks she's above me.* "Clarice was very specific that you get settled first."

"Yeah, well, considered me settled. I want to see my lab," Ashley said, squinting her eyes and staring Mason down, proving dominance. There was no way this twerp was going to run over her in her own area of expertise.

"Listen," Mason started, holding up his hand to ward off any attacks. Or so he thought.

"You listen," Ashley interrupted. "I'm easy to get along with, but you're not my boss. Let's be *VERY* clear about that."

Mason glared at her, but eventually just gave up. He would let Clarice deal with her when she arrived. "Fine," he retorted. "Second, this project is very important to Clarice, so it would be in your best interest to treat both her and them with respect."

Ashley nodded in agreement. Mason looked a little taken aback at her willingness to agree over anything with him, but he took the win, turned on his heels, and led the way. When they entered the lab, it had been divided it into several sections. The smell of sterilization was overwhelming, but Ashley didn't mind. It meant Clarice was as serious about Ashley's work as she was. It was also filled with every piece of equipment imaginable, and then some.

Mason stopped before the last door. "Please keep your voice down when you speak to them." Ashley nodded, trying to reign in her excitement.

She watched Mason punch in a code, and the automatic door opened. The temperature was much cooler, and the medical machines were buzzing like crazy as they worked hard to preserve whatever was wrapped in dressings. Ashley swallowed hard. She had never worked on a live person before.

"And what is it I'm supposed to do, exactly?" Ashley asked in a whisper, realizing that Clarice never really told her.

"Save them," Mason shrugged without looking at her.

"What happened to them?" Ashley asked, with her morbid curiosity coming to life.

"They were experimenting, and something went...wrong," Mason offered carefully. "Clarice still needs their services, so it's your job to save them and bring them back to life."

"I'm sorry, what?" Ashley asked, turning to stare at Mason. "Are they dead?"

Mason smirked, knowing he had an upper hand on her. He leaned in so that their noses were barely an inch apart. "Not yet," he whispered. "But I wouldn't be the one to kill them if I were you," he warned wickedly before he headed for the door. "You're the only one to be in this room at all times outside myself and Clarice. Enjoy." With that, Mason was gone, and Ashley was left with the mysterious creature lying in the hospital bed.

"Well, um, hi," Ashley whispered. "My name is Ashley, and it looks like we're about to become friends," she said with a nervous laugh. No response. "Okay, well, if we're going to be friends, you're going to have to get better at laughing at my jokes," she said with a grimace. "Guess we should try to figure out how to make sure you can do that first, because that's definitely a priority." She pushed up her sleeves and got to work.

"So?" Liz asked. "What do you want to try next?"

Claudia put a finger to her chin as she paced the room to think for a bit. After a few minutes she finally offered, "What if we take in some of the scenery?" she suggested with a shrug.

"Okay...." Liz said, not sure where this was headed.

"Let's stop by the hardware store on the way. Might need some supplies," Claudia offered with a smirk.

"That's my girl," Liz said with an approving smile as she grabbed the keys to her car and held the door open for Claudia to lead the way.

Nikki Johnson had her arms wrapped tightly around her

husband's waist as they rode his motorcycle down a secluded back road. Although winter had arrived, Mother Nature had surprised everyone with a warmer than normal day, inspiring an impromptu ride. She was thirty-seven, 5'2" and a mom to five. Her hazel eyes hid behind her sunglasses as her dark brown hair, just past her shoulders, was tied up into a messy bun so she could enjoy the warm sun and wind on her face.

With an autoimmune disorder, Nikki took what moments she could get to enjoy to the fullest. She loved volleyball, softball, sunflowers, the beach, cruises, and stitching. She wasn't about to let any short straws stop her from living life to the fullest. Or at least as full as she could.

"Wanna go faster?" her husband yelled over the roar of the wind.

"Hell yeah!" she shouted back.

He leaned forward in order to help the bike gain more momentum, and Nikki held her chin up to welcome the sun. There was a snapping sound that was ever so quick and clean. But it wouldn't be until her husband felt the back of his neck, his shirt, and his cheeks feel warm and wet with liquid that would force him to slow the bike down and spin it to a halt.

In the process, his wife's headless body fell off the side of the bike, and he stared at it in horror. After what seemed like an eternity, he forced himself to look in the direction from which they had come, to see his wife's head, with her eyes closed and a smile on her face, laying in the middle of the road.

Someone had tied piano wire to the speed limit sign on one side of the road and pulled it straight across the trees tightly to catch them as they drove by. The only reason he survived was because he had leaned forward to make them go faster. To make her happy. *Oh God.* He scrambled off the bike and threw up until his guts had nothing left to offer. Then he fell to his knees and bawled. *Who was supposed to die? And why?*

Suddenly, he spun around frantically. The piano wire had been lying next to his wife's head the whole time. *Did they rig it to take them out and run? Or did they pull it to watch them die in person and were still there watching?*

<u>Thirteen</u>

Vanessa had Karmen in the backyard. She had been so agitated lately. She was coloring pictures like a mad person, but always with the same characters. The Lackeys claimed it was just a creative outlet for Karmen, but sometimes Vanessa wondered if there was more to the story.

It was hard enough to get Karmen to engage when she was stressed out like this, but today seemed extra difficult. Karmen refused to go anywhere without a pad and pencils, and screeched in a high pitch holler and rocked back and forth until they were placed safely in her hands. Vanessa had baited Karmen outside with her favorite snack, but Karmen only got as far as the table before sitting down to color another picture.

Vanessa let out a heavy sigh and looked to the sky, secretly wishing for extra patience and help. Normally, Karmen was the sweetest kid on the planet, but right now, no one could reach her. Vanessa's phone buzzed in her hand letting her know someone was ringing the doorbell. She went over to the table and got down on Karmen's eye level.

"Hey, Sweetie," Vanessa whispered. "Someone's at the door, and I need to see what they..." Vanessa couldn't finish her sentence. She was staring at Karmen's picture. It was of Vanessa opening the door to the figure Karmen had been drawing for weeks. Karmen beat her palm aggressively against the face of the woman she had just drawn and began rocking back and forth. Vanessa's stomach dropped. She didn't know what to do.

At the sound of Karmen shrieking, Clarice kicked open the door instead of knocking as she had originally intended, and raced into the house, pulling the 9mm out of the back holster hidden under her new jacket. She searched the living room quietly and quickly as she made her way towards the sound in the back of the house. Vanessa threw herself in front of the child and shielded her the best she could.

When she saw Vanessa and Karmen alone, she did something she's never done before. Clarice immediately spun her gun up along with her hands, showing she meant them no harm, and quickly put it away.

"Sorry about the door," Clarice added roughly. "I heard the yelling, and I was just making sure that you were..." but the drawing on the table caught her eye. The girl had drawn her to perfection without ever having laid eyes on her, and suddenly it was very clear why her father had made her an orphan once he had located her.

Clarice forced herself to swallow. Her throat was suddenly parched. "Hey, nice drawing."

Karmen poked her head around Vanessa's body to peer at Clarice through her very long lashes. Her rocking had come to a halt.

Vanessa puffed out her chest defiantly, knowing she had no weapons at all to protect the child. "What do you want?" she demanded.

Clarice didn't take her eyes off the child. For some reason, she couldn't. With her very distinct elfish features, the child reminded Clarice of Kira on *The Dark Crystal* movie. It was the one thing that she remembered doing with her mother. So she forced herself to look back at the drawings instead.

"Relax," Clarice offered Vanessa dryly. "I'm not the one you need to worry about." She reached for the tablet slowly. "Do you mind if I look at the rest?" she asked, not daring to look at Karmen any more than she had to.

Karmen pushed the tablet towards her. Clarice picked it up and began flipping through it. "Karmen never leaves the house, right?" she confirmed with Vanessa. The woman crossed her arms and glared at Clarice defiantly.

"So, that's a yes," Clarice sneered. "Well, here's the problem," Clarice said, putting the tablet back down on the table to show them both. "These are very accurate and beautifully drawn, but Karmen has never met them," Clarice started. "However, this is my niece, Sophie," she said, identifying the redhead with one blue eye and one red eye. "This is Wonder Boy, Corbin. He's...well, he's kind of a pain in the ass in honesty, but he's cute, and also very dead."

Vanessa's eyes got wide at the last word.

"I don't know this person. She looks like a new player I haven't met yet, but what she's drawing is known as the dream realm. It's like the in between, where the living and the dead can sort of mingle," Clarice said, flinching, knowing just how crazy she sounded, but Vanessa had to understand why Karmen wasn't safe anymore.

"And I know how crazy this all sounds, but Karmen, here, is drawing a war that's been going on for a while, and unfortunately it is why she's with the Lackey's now," Clarice finished with a rush.

Vanessa grew pale and stared at Karmen, who only continued to study Clarice without looking directly at her. She seemed more fascinated that her drawing had come to life than what it all actually meant. *Did she understand what she was capable of? Or was she just an innocent bystander? What kind of god would give her this kind of gift in a package that made her a clueless target?* Vanessa turned to look at Clarice. "So, what side are you on?" she asked in a panic.

"What?" Clarice asked, lost in the picture of Corbin and the stranger that seemed to have been standing over him, consuming his power and enjoying it.

"What side are you on?" Vanessa demanded.

"I don't do sides," Clarice stated dryly, still studying the picture. *What the hell was she doing to him? Was it sexual? Did he like it?* It wasn't like she could be with him, anyway....

"Bullshit." Vanessa's words cut through Clarice's thoughts and she turned to take in the very irritated nanny that was suddenly in her face now without her realizing it. "Which side are you on?"

"I don't do sides," Clarice said more firmly. "I don't have to fight this battle. I only have to keep my niece safe out of obligation," Clarice said with a hint of irritation. *Why won't people just leave me alone?!*

"Wow," Vanessa said, putting her hands on her hips. "How many times do you still tell yourself that?"

"Excuse me?" Clarice asked, getting very irritated.

"I only asked because clearly even you don't believe your own lies," Vanessa laughed and shrugged. She turned to look at Karmen and looked back at Clarice. "Listen," she said more softly. "You came here for a reason, whether or not you want to admit it to yourself, and I think that reason was to save her," she stated firmly, jerking her head in Karmen's direction.

This time they both looked at Karmen, and Clarice finally caught on to where Vanessa was going with all of this. She walked back with her hands up. "No," Clarice stated firmly. "Listen, you just need to tell the Lackeys to get her out of here. There's someone in the area and I will take care of her. Just give me a couple of weeks."

"And then what?" Vanessa asked, snapping her head back to glare back at Clarice. "If you figured it out, then so will others. There will *always* be someone else. We don't have your skill set. And I know for a *FACT* we can't deal with the dead!" Vanessa exclaimed.

They were too busy arguing to notice Karmen had come out from behind Vanessa. It wasn't until Clarice felt a tiny hand slide into hers that she jerked her head down to see what was happening. It was Karmen, looking up at her, blinking her big innocent cornflower blue eyes up at her.

"No," Clarice said decisively as she tried to pull her hand away, but the girl had a death grip like Clarice had never felt before. So Clarice turned to Vanessa. "I can't track a psychopath with a child. You know that, right?" she asked in desperation.

Vanessa just grinned and shrugged. "Yeah," she said, wrinkling her nose. "She's autistic, and once her mind is made up, you have a better chance of redesigning the White House in six hours," Vanessa giggled.

Clarice glared back at her and then looked back down at Karmen. She sighed heavily and rolled her eyes while slumping her shoulders. "Go pack your things," she said with a grudge. "But you'll have to stay with some friends while I take care of some business, so don't think I'm going to be with you 24/7," Clarice replied steadfastly. Karmen squeezed her hand and nearly broke it into tiny pieces before humming and heading to her room to pack.

"You're doing the right thing," Vanessa said, patting Clarice on the back as she walked past her to help Karmen pack.

Clarice already regretted the additional responsibility, but the child would definitely come in handy. If nothing else, she could finally have tabs on Corbin. Not that it was a primary goal of hers. But definitely a bonus....

Donna knew Cecil wouldn't like her reaching out to some of her contacts, especially about what she was asking for. So, she just would not tell him. They all knew she wore the pants in the relationship, anyway. There was a reason she ran the operation side of things. She was good at getting answers. She had her ways, and everyone left it at that.

Over the years, some had lived to tell the tale, while others not so much. However, no one would ever know what would happen, because Donna was entirely too smart for her own good. She had taken in Mario when he was a scrappy teenager and taught him to do the same.

He only hadn't made it because he gave his life, not once, but twice, for the daughter he helped to raise. Now it was her turn to return the favor. No matter how old she got, some informants could still be played like a fiddle, and Mike was one of those informants. When she was done with him, he would join the rest, but for now, she still had some use for him.

The hotel was so easy to sneak out of with no one noticing, especially at night. Donna made her way to their usual spot and strolled in five minutes late, unsurprisingly.

"You're late!" the muscular man, with a brown crew cut and walnut eyes, barked. He was dressed in all black biker gear, leaning up against a counter of an abandoned building. He stood around 5'7", and looked too preppy and pretty to be doing the outfit he wore justice. Even if his body filled every inch nicely.

Donna didn't skip a beat, as she ran her finger up the man's bicep casually and leaned in to whisper in his ear. "I always make it worth your while, don't I?" she asked innocently.

She did nothing with the man. She never cheated on Cecil and had no intention of starting now. But Mike was that kind of man that you could easily keep toying into believing that if he did you one more favor, he would get some. And the day he refused was the day he met his maker. Apparently, he wasn't ready for the game to quit just yet, and that worked out for Donna.

"Who are we killing today?" he leered.

Donna laughed. "Just some intel. However, some say it doesn't exist. I thought you could prove them wrong," she said sheepishly, holding out a piece of paper.

Mike's eyes glittered at the prospect of being her favorite. "They really can't find anything?" he asked eagerly.

"Not a single bread crumb. Can you believe it?" she asked in pretend bafflement.

"Are you just teasing me?" he asked, suddenly suspicious.

"Like I don't have better things to do," she said with a warning.

He eyed her with some hesitation, then snatched the paper out of her hand. "How long do I have?"

"The sooner the better," she said honestly. "It's the largest missing piece to my current puzzle, so I need it pretty badly," she added in a husky voice. Donna watched the hair on his neck stand at attention and the shiver that went through his body. He also couldn't hide the bulge that suddenly grew in his pants, although he crossed his legs in an attempt to do so.

"Let me see what I can do," Mike said in his best version of a flat voice as he rolled his eyes.

Donna's lips curled into a smile. "Thanks, Mikey," she said, and kissed him on the cheek before walking away.

"That's it?!" he yelled after her.

Donna kept her back to him, stuck her hand in the air, and wiggled her fingers in a wave as she exited and headed back to the hotel to shower the scum off and go make love to the man she actually loved with her whole heart and soul.

Sophie had been silent and in a funk since seeing Clarice. She didn't trust herself and nothing James tried seemed to bring her out of it. He held her and listened to her breathe unevenly, knowing she was having a hard time sleeping. He was about to call Corbin for help when he finally heard her settle on her own. Or so he thought.

Sophie opened her eyes to a wooden door and opened it eagerly. She was expecting to find her parents on the other side, but found Ben slumped over some desk with his head in his hands and clearly in distress. "Ben? What's wrong?" she asked eagerly. He jerked his head up in response and looked at her in confusion.

"Sophie?"

"Last time I checked," she said with a frown. "Is Tina okay?"

"Why haven't you come back?" Ben countered.

"I'm...not well," she finally confessed.

"What's wrong?" he demanded as he got up and stalked over towards her.

Sophie threw up her hands immediately and yelled, "Stop!"

He froze. She watched his eyebrows draw down in determination as he took another step.

"Ben, please," she begged as tears streaked her cheeks.

Water filled his own eyes in response. "That bad?" he asked.

"Worse," she choked.

There was a deafening pause.

"They've asked me to figure out how to shut you down," Ben finally confessed.

She didn't look shocked when she tore her eyes from the invisible floor they stood on. "You should," she said steadily, as she stared him down.

"I won't do it at the price of your life," he said with his voice cracking.

"You do whatever it takes to keep your child safe," she hissed, though the tears running down her cheeks said otherwise.

"Sophie," he whispered.

"Benjamin," she growled, "I can't control whatever is going on, and if it doesn't kill me, hurting any of you will. So, please, for me, if it comes between saving me or saving our family, I *NEED* you to make the choice that you know I would make if I could."

The coldness in her voice sent a chill that cut Ben to his bone, but he knew exactly what she was asking of him.

"Benjamin!" Sophie demanded.

"I promise!" he snapped back.

"Don't call for me again," she warned. "It's not safe."

"I did...." But Sophie was gone before Ben could finish his sentence. He woke up next to Tina snoring softly beside him. "I didn't," he whispered to himself. *Or did he?....*

A knock on the door stirred them both awake, and James whispered into Sophie's ear, "Be still. I'll see who it is."

"Nice try," Sophie snorted.

Yet, somehow, they both got to the door at the exact same time. *How had he gotten so fast?* Sophie hid behind the door as James opened it as far as the chain would allow, surprised to see what was waiting on the other side.

"Open the door," Sophie heard Clarice's voice snap on the other side. *What the hell?*

James closed it, only to open it again and have it nearly shoved into his face. Luckily, Sophie moved out of the way in time. Clarice shoved a little girl a head of her in before looking up and down the hallway and closing the door quickly behind her.

Sophie and James looked in shock at the little girl with elfish features who was humming and taking the room in. She was bending to look at everything from all angles and rubbed her index finger over it repeatedly before moving onto the next object that seemed to catch her eye.

"I thought I told you to leave," Clarice said in irritation.

Neither of them answered. They were still staring at the girl who was roaming around, touching everything with great curiosity and rocking slightly.

"Hey!" Clarice said, snapping her fingers at them both.

James and Sophie turned their heads back to stare at her.

"I told you to leave," Clarice repeated in annoyance.

"You have a child with you?" Sophie almost laughed out.

"We are still working on things," James answered Clarice's question, but turned back to watch the child in fascination.

"Well, since you didn't the first time, you have to keep her with you," Clarice said, nodding in Karmen's direction.

James snapped his head back to stare at Clarice.

"I'm sorry, what?" Sophie asked, suddenly very focused.

"Keep *her* with *you*," Clarice articulated, as she pulled her shoulders back. "I can't fix *your* situation and keep you both safe," she said, looking between Sophie and Karmen. "So, you all need to let me do what I need to do," she said, crossing her arms and staring down her niece.

"Did you forget that I have issues of my own?" Sophie asked, wiggling her fingers in exasperation at her aunt.

"So, look at that ridiculous face and you'll be fine," Clarice said, only briefly glancing at Karmen before looking back at her niece.

"Um," James cut in. "Is there something we should know about her?"

"Like what?" Clarice asked defensively, not sure how much she should share.

"Oh, I don't know," James said sarcastically. "Like how she's unique, and if she needs any help or anything," he added, looking at Clarice with annoyance.

"Or why you have her at all?" Sophie asked, crossing her own arms and mimicking her aunt's glare.

"Don't do that," Clarice hissed. "You look like your mother."

Sophie snorted.

Clarice squinted her eyes harder, but Sophie didn't back down. *God, she's just like Jess.* "Fine," Clarice finally conceded and rolled her eyes. "Karmen, Sophie wants to see the drawing you drew of her," she said, softer than either Sophie or James had ever heard her speak.

Karmen's humming grew louder, and after a few minutes of spinning in the middle of the floor, she made her way to the bed and opened up her backpack and pulled out her drawing tablet. Sophie and James slowly walked over to the bed and sat down. Karmen opened the tablet to a specific page and pushed it in Sophie's direction. She patted the page enthusiastically on the face of the drawing, grunting, and then withdrew to go stand next to Clarice and rock and hum and a quieter volume.

Sophie's eyes widen and her mouth dropped open as she took the tablet into her hands. Her heart raced as her mouth went dry. The accuracy, down to the one red eye and one blue eye. Sophie swallowed desperately to get her mouth wet enough to talk again. "She saw me at the bar?" she whispered.

"Nope," Clarice answered. "Karmen, here, has never left her foster parent's house until this afternoon when she was forced into my hands. Keep flipping the pages," she said, almost with a hint of pride.

Sophie turned the tablet so James could see, too, as she flipped through the pages. Algos, Clarice, Sophie, Corbin, Jess, Jack, and someone none of them had seen before. At least not yet.

"She draws the dream realm, too?" Sophie finally breathed out.

"So, you see why she needs to be with someone to keep her safe," Clarice replied, placing her hands on her hips, as her jaw line hardened.

"But I'm not that person right now," Sophie said in alarm, staring at Clarice.

"You're more adept than me," Clarice said in a softer tone than she had intended.

They all looked at Karmen, who just looked up at Clarice, but Clarice broke her stare and turned to Sophie. "Someone is still trying to get our attention, and not for the right reasons. I need to find out why and put a stop to it. Do you really want me doing that with a child?" she asked in a more chilled tone. Sophie frowned.

"If you would just let us help," James started.

"I am," Clarice snapped, turning her heat in his direction. "I'm asking you to take this," she said, jerking her head in Karmen's direction, "and do what you do best, while I do what I do best. I don't know what she wants, or why. All I know is she plays as nice as Algos, and you're not up for the game right now," Clarice added, looking back down at Sophie.

She hated that Clarice was right, but she was. "Fine," Sophie agreed reluctantly.

Clarice got down on Karmen's level, like she had watched Vanessa and the Lackeys do so many times. "You're going to stay with Sophie and James while I take care of some business," she said in a much softer tone. Karmen rolled her head around, hummed loudly and rocked back and forth aggressively.

"Yeah, I know," Clarice said with a sneer. "But they grow on you," she laughed. Karmen got a little quieter at the notion. "I need you to keep drawing those gorgeous pictures for me though, okay? Because Sophie's going to call and tell me all about how amazing they are, so I don't miss a thing. Deal?" Clarice held out her hand in a high-five position.

Karmen rolled her head around and squealed in what seemed like excitement before slapping Clarice's hand in an enthusiastic gesture.

"That's my girl," Clarice said with a smile as she stood up and faced Sophie and James, who stared at her in shock. Clarice glared in response. "What?" she snapped. They both just shook their heads. She stalked over to James and shoved a piece of paper into his hands. "I mean it. You'd better call me. Every picture. Dream realm or not. I need to know every single picture. She'll rat you out if you don't," Clarice said with warning.

"I don't doubt that," James said, trying to stifle his laughter as he went to take the paper from her.

______

Clarice pulled the paper to her chest and whispered. "Every picture. Corbin and all."

James's brain flickered to life, but he simply took the piece of paper and nodded confirmation. So, this was what had Corbin all twisted up inside. Had him wanting to cover his tracks in a realm that read his every thought and feeling. He was in love with Clarice, and apparently Clarice was finding herself starting to feel the same way. There was hope for lost souls after all...He didn't have to look to know it was a way to contact her while she was hunting whoever was hunting them.

"Keep her safe," Clarice warned as she walked to the door. She opened it and looked both ways, but before she left, she added, "That includes you, too." The door was closed before anyone could respond.

Sophie turned to make a comment, but James just held up his hand. "Oh, you know she wasn't talking about me," he laughed out loud.

Sophie scowled but ended up laughing herself. "That was a weird request about the pictures, wasn't it?"

"Not really," James shrugged as he added the number to his phone and handed the paper over to Sophie to do the same.

Sophie dramatically gasped. "OMG! What do you know?" she demanded, tackling him on the bed and pinning him down.

He laughed at her response. "I love your enthusiasm, but we have tiny eyes, remember?" he reminded her lovingly and looking in Karmen's direction, who had taken to sitting at the table and began pulling out a piece of paper with some writing on it.

"I don't know how to take care of children, let alone one with special needs," Sophie whispered as she climbed off James.

He took her hand and led her towards the table where Karmen sat waiting for them patiently. They looked down at the paper she had pulled out. James couldn't help but laugh.

"That's okay," he chuckled, getting on Karmen's level as he had seen Clarice do. "Thank you Karmen."

Karmen didn't look him in the eyes but nodded repeatedly and got out another book and began flipping through it. The piece of paper was Karmen's regular schedule and the other instructions that Vanessa had written out. The booklet was of things Karmen loved, like the cars she worked on with Mr. Lackey, the Lackeys themselves, and her favorite desserts, etc.

"This one comes with instructions," James said with his grin, as he stood up to show Sophie the list.

Sophie got down to see Karmen's book of favorite things. "Oooo, desserts are my favorite, too. Did you know chocolate saves lives?" she giggled.

Karmen's lips curled up into a sheepish smile.

Fourteen

Amanda Harris was forty-one and the fun size of 5'2". Her hazel eyes were glazed over as she listened to another rude ass customer. *God, she needed another job.* She smiled her fake "customer service" smile and nodded while she half listened to the woman in front of her explain why Amanda was so incompetent as an employee and a person in general, patiently waiting for the window that always eventually came.

Amanda took a breath and ran her hand through her shoulder length dark brown hair that was now sticking to her back, signaling the end of her shift. "Now, Miss Peterson," Amanda said sweetly once the woman was finished. "You and I both know that you are not only a month out of the return policy, but a year and a half. If you really had a problem with the product, we both know you would have been back way before today. You are welcome to cry a river to my manager, but in the end, she will tell you the exact same thing as I am. You used it until you couldn't any more. You thought we'd be dumb enough to just take you at your word and give you your money back. But you see, Miss Peterson, this is a business. Not a charity. No business is going to buy your story, so either buy a new product or become a better con artist."

"Well, I have never!" gasped the woman.

"Be sure to take the survey at the end of your receipt," Amanda said sarcastically as she waved and rushed to the time clock.

"Taco Tuesday?" asked her friend Lauren.

"Are you seriously asking me that question?" Amanda countered.

"Yeah, I don't know what came over me," Lauren laughed.

The girls headed out for tacos, margaritas, and laughs. Then Amanda headed home to do her usual winding down routine. Remove the makeup, get into comfy pjs, smoke her trusty weed, and read her current book that allowed her gutter mind to roam freely without ridicule. Once snuggled in bed, she pulled the covers up high and opened to the last page she was on. She eagerly took a puff to help her wash away every person who felt righteous enough to tell her she was worthless and call her every name in the book just because she worked in customer service. But something wasn't right. It didn't taste right. It didn't feel right either.

Instead of feeling her usual instant calm, she started to feel panic. Like her lungs were literally catching on fire and burning faster with each breath she took. Blood filled her eyes, taking away her sight instantly. She felt it spill out of her eyes and run out of her nose as she tasted it on her lips. *What the hell was happening?!*

She desperately tried not to gasp for air since it made her lungs burn that much worse as she desperately reached for the phone next to her bed. A phone that was no longer there. Nothing was there. Amanda flailed around, searching, and found nothing but a clean, sleek surface. *Wasn't stuff there just a second ago?....*

Panic took over, and that was the end. The doctors would find no lungs, because there would be none left. Liz and Claudia came in from around the corner.

"What about this one?" Liz asked her.

Claudia studied the body for a long time. "Closer," was her only response.

Peter stretched out his arm as Mario tossed him a long, broken off tree branch just in time to spear a two headed lion through both its heads before he got swallowed up. Mario slid down the tree trunk, completely drained. Peter dragged his own spent body over to join him as they watched the world around them crumble. Only an occasional burst of fire that lit up the black sky like the fourth of July showed any sign of existing life left outside of the two of them.

"How do we even know she's still alive?" Mario asked wearily. "And if you say we don't, you can just kill me right now," he added sourly.

"Relax, my friend," Peter gave an exhausted laugh. "I still feel her. It's not much, but it's enough."

Mario was too tired to do anything but roll his head against the tree and glare at the prodigal child next to him. "I'm sorry, but if you can 'feel her' then why do we have to roam all over the place looking for her, again?" he asked as anger boiled in his blood.

Peter rolled his head against the tree trunk to look at Mario. "It's not as exact as a GPS," Peter said with a scowl. "And it's too faint to get a solid read to begin with," he added with his own irritation.

"How do you feel her in the first place?" Mario asked, suddenly curious. *Maybe it would be a good way to keep tabs on Sophie, no matter where he was.*

"Not everyone has the same abilities," Peter quickly replied.

"Is yours mind reading?" Mario mumbled.

"Not exactly," Peter said with a grin.

"Great," Mario snarled.

"Easy, tiger," Peter said, holding his hands up. "I really am on your side. No matter what you believe." The look on Mario's face let Peter know he wouldn't be gaining his trust any time soon, so he pressed on. "Some people who can heal others also have a price to pay. In order to maintain balance," he clarified. "There's always a check and balance to the system to make sure no one part can overpower the other. So if you heal, you also are forced to take a piece of that person with you. You're connected for life."

"So, you saved Rebecca?" Mario asked, studying Peter.

"Other way around," Peter said, staring off into the distance as if reliving the moment all over again, but the story seemed to stop there.

"But you feel her?" Mario questioned, a little irritated that show and tell seemed to come with limitations just like everything else.

"It's a two-way street," Peter said, looking back at Mario with a weary smile.

"So, am I a healer?" Mario asked cautiously.

"I don't know," Peter answered honestly.

"How do we find out?" Mario asked with a scowl.

"Unfortunately, not until the time demands it," Peter said, wrinkling his nose and shrugging his shoulder.

Mario's face went deadpan. "You're completely useless, you know that?"

"So, you keep telling me," Peter laughed back. "But we can't stay here."

"What if I don't want to keep looking for Rebecca?" Mario asked, crossing his arms in front of his chest and staring Peter down.

Peter's grin seemed to widen even more as he jumped up with renewed energy, and he held out his hand to help Mario up. "Because quitting now means quitting on Sophie, and if we don't find Rebecca soon, we can't save either of them."

Mario's eyes widened at his goddaughter's name before a flame burst within them. It was the first time Peter had seen a flicker of Mario's power, and Mario still didn't know he had any. "What do you know?" Mario barked. He caught a flash of blue sparkle in Peter's eyes before it quickly disappeared.

"Something called a raven is awake," Peter said calmly. "Rebecca knows more than any of us, which is why we need to find her, like yesterday."

"What the hell is a raven?" Mario demanded.

"I don't know," Peter lied. "Without finding more, Sophie and everyone, us included, are in danger. Someone has replaced Algos, and they may be the raven. If that's the case, then the dream realm is in danger and so are we," he finished.

Peter hated lying, but half-truths were permitted if it provided the end goals, and the end goals were always to save humanity and all the realms that existed around them. Peter needed Mario to fight. Mario would only fight for one person. Sophie.

If Sophie drifted to the dark side before the end of the war was finished, Peter knew his assignment. This was why he had been sacrificed all those years ago. He had been prepped his whole life to take out his great niece, should it come to that. However, Rebecca was the answer to preventing it. So, they needed to find Rebecca. Now....

Ashley buzzed around the room, checking vitals. The skin graphs were holding up nicely, and her other tests were showing positive signs. It was hard to tell how much brain damage there was while the patient remained asleep, but it would be entirely too painful to be awake right now while their body healed from the majority of their injuries. So, to keep them both entertained, Ashley played music, read spicy and true crime books, and told them about her sessions at the built in gym and how she kept smoking out Mason, which was always a personal triumph.

Every time she was about to ease up on Mason, he made some snide remark that changed Ashley's mind. So, he really just did it to himself, she told her coma patient, who she was fondly calling, Zack. She didn't know his original name. No one seemed to know, or was willing to tell her for fear of losing their own life.

Today, she was feeling Ruelle, and they were listening to *The World We Made* when she noticed his brain waves spike. "Like this one, huh?" Ashley asked with interest. "Yeah, it's one of my go-to's, too," she said with a devilish grin. "I listen to it when I'm working out or need some motivation."

Zack's eyes fluttered wildly underneath the bandages.

"Hey," Ashley whispered softly, placing her hand gently over his wrapped hand. "I don't know what you think is trapped inside, but there's nothing wrong with you. And this world may be fucked up, but it was fucked up long before you ever entered it. So, if you're upset because you're taking the lyrics to heart, knock it off right now," she demanded. "Don't think I can't kick your ass just cause you're wrapped up and helplessly in my care at the moment," she huffed, putting her hands on her hips.

His bandages stilled, and she thought she almost saw a smile underneath as well, but it was gone as quickly as it had appeared, so she turned her back on him and went back to business. She didn't notice him barely raise his head to sneak a peek through the slit of the bandages at the blonde that wasn't paying attention to him when she should have been. Or feel his sudden desire to slit her throat and find the girl that had put him here, and gleefully watch as he squeezed the life from her body.

Sarah O'Donnell was a loving thirty-seven-year-old free spirit with no filter, and the best ride or die friend a person could ask for.

Her turquoise blue eyes usually sparkled with mischief, and her long pastel pink hair matched her pistol of an attitude. She pushed her glasses back into place before she headed on another peaceful journey through her trusty woods.

This was an activity Sarah did often. She needed to clear her head and recharge from the negativity that the world was becoming. The solitude of the woods helped ground her again to fight whatever was thrown at her, and it was her favorite past time outside of reading. She just didn't realize that today would be her last one.

The twig snapped beneath her, and she fell into a pit fall trap deep into the woods. It would be eight days before the dogs would find her. Only pieces of her Phoenix tattoo that used to be across her back and what would finally be determined to be the words "Live Free Love Completely" that had been tattooed on her right foot would be what helped her family identify her body at the morgue.

Karmen woke in the middle of the night covered in sweat. She rolled over and saw James holding Sophie in his arms in the bed next to hers. They had upgraded to a double bedroom so Karmen could have her own bed. She wiped the hair that was stuck to her face away and slid out of the sheets down to the floor where her backpack laid safely.

As quietly as possible, she pulled out her tablet and pencils. Karmen's eyes glazed over, and she rocked in a rhythmic motion while she drew like a madman. She colored a picture of a tall, muscular blonde man spearing a two headed lion, and another blonde woman in a lab coat working on a person in a hospital bed wrapped up like a mummy.

Sophie sat up when she heard Karmen's feet touch the ground, waking James up with her movement. They both quietly walked towards where Karmen was sitting. When Sophie went to speak to her, James grabbed her softly by her wrist and pulled her back into his arms. "Ssshhh," he whispered in her ear, stopping her.

Karmen frantically drew Sarah O'Donnell laying at the bottom of a deadfall trap, and began hyperventilating as she drew a short, curvy woman sitting on a porch, sipping what looked like hot chocolate. Sophie pushed away from James and fell to the floor in front of Karmen's eyesight. She looked at James when she noticed Karmen's eyes were not her usual light blue color.

"Karmen," she whispered, looking back at Karmen. "Honey, what's wrong?" She was careful not to touch her.

Karmen was gasping for air, and her moaning was getting louder.

James joined Sophie. "Karmen," he said a little more forcefully. "Where is she?" he tried.

Karmen's face was turning a purplish blue. Sophie reached for her.

"I don't think we're supposed to..." James started.

"I'm not going to watch her die," Sophie hissed back. She carefully ran her fingertip down Karmen's arm. Karmen's head snap to stare at the crystal blue spark that seemed to glow from Sophie's finger and Karmen's breathing slowed at the distraction. She dropped her pencil to touch Sophie's finger as her rocking came to a halt.

"Karmen," Sophie said softly as she brought her finger to the last picture that Karmen drew. "Do you know where this is?" she asked in a whisper, looking directly into Karmen's blinking cornflower blue eyes.

Karmen looked down at the picture Sophie was pointing at, almost surprised that it was there at all. Her eyebrows furrowed as she concentrated.

"I don't think it's a conscious thing," James whispered with interest.

"God, Tina would love you," Sophie said smiling, thinking of her friend. Karmen looked at her with a frustrated scowl. She looked back at the picture and picked up the pencil with determination and rocked ever so slightly. She pushed Sophie's hand away and pushed Sophie away all together.

James reached down and pulled Sophie back by her shoulders. "I think she wants some privacy," he said, trying not to laugh.

"Apparently," Sophie said, annoyed as she got up and walked to the other side of the room to give Karmen some space.

"Don't take it personal," James said with his boyish grin and kissing her on the cheek, but Sophie still scowled.

"I'm not," she muttered.

"Yeah, I can tell," he laughed. "Nice way to get her calmed down. How did you do it?"

The question got her to stop glaring at him. "I don't know," Sophie answered honestly, looking at the girl still glaring at the paper. "I know this sounds crazy, but it's like I heard her tell me," she said in a whisper.

James turned to look at the little girl. At this point, crazy didn't mean what it used to since he had met Sophie, so nothing really surprised him anymore. Hell, he was shooting crystal blue flames these days, along with suddenly being able to keep up with her when needed.

In fact, it seemed he could do a lot of things when she needed balance. He was told by Jack not to think about it too much, and he was trying not to. Just to focus on what it meant to keep Sophie balanced. But even he couldn't ignore the fact that she shouldn't be able to do half the things she could now.

So, was he always supposed to meet Sophie? Or was he given these gifts to help keep her balanced because she chose him to begin with? Did Jack tell him not to think about it because it would make him lose his mind and not be able to do what needed to be done? Or because the truth would destroy him in the end? AND this is why Jack said not to think about it...It was way too easy to get lost in the madness when there was plenty of madness already in play. *However, could he really live with himself if he didn't know the truth?*

He felt a tiny hand inside his own and he looked down. Karmen was holding up the picture with an added symbol of Kentucky in the corner. The look of triumph was quite obvious on the little girl's face. "Kentucky it is," James said with a wide grin, taking the picture from Karmen. "Thank you," he added with a nod of appreciation. Karmen didn't look him in the eye, but nodded back to him before crawling back into bed. She was passed out within seconds.

Sophie grabbed the picture from him as James went to get his phone. "Well, clearly *you're* the favorite," she said, unable to disguise her hurt.

"Don't be so sure," he offered sternly as he took the picture back and snapped a picture, along with the others.

Sophie crossed her arms and sat on their bed, watching the little girl sleep.

You need someone in Kentucky for this one. She's still warm. -J

"Clarice?" Sophie whispered, when James climbed into bed next to her.

"Yep," he replied. He pulled the reluctant Sophie into his arms. "So, what are we going to do tomorrow?" he whispered in her ear.

"Well, we can't take her out, and we can't keep her locked up in here all day, every day," Sophie frowned, still staring at Karmen.

"Road trip?" James offered softly as he swayed back and forth gently with her.

"Where?" she laughed. "There's someone apparently taking people out," Sophie said still frowning, and watching Karmen like a hawk.

"Who's currently on their way to Kentucky if Karmen's as accurate as Clarice believes," James offered with a little hope in his voice. "So, maybe some fresh air and a little rock climbing would do everyone some good while there's some space to be had."

Sophie finally took her eyes off of Karmen to look at James over her shoulder, who had clearly lost his mind. James just sighed and rolled his eyes. It may be 2 a.m. and dark, but she could still see the white of his eyes all the same.

"We wouldn't be out in the open, and my money's on us keeping her safe," he said, nodding his chin in Karmen's direction.

"I'm not exactly on my A game," Sophie hissed at him with a glare.

"You haven't sparked once since she's been here," he hissed back and stuck his tongue out for good measure. She copied the gesture and sighed in resignation.

"Fine," Sophie mumbled. "But not all day," she added more sternly.

"Yes, Mom," he added with a squeeze. "Now, let's get some sleep. We'll need it for tomorrow." He slid his hand over her mouth, knowing she would giggle as he pulled her down onto the bed with him. They both froze and stared over at Karmen. She was snoring heavily, as if an earthquake couldn't wake her.

"That must really wear her out," Sophie whispered with concern.

"Yeah," James agreed. "We'll have to take extra care of her."

"Yeah," Sophie said with a frown as she turned her back to Karmen and laid her cheek on James's chest. He could feel her uneasiness, but it smoothed as she listened to the steady beating of his heart. She was asleep in no time. James, however, had work to do. He closed his eyes and reached out to the person he knew he needed the most. *Corbin.*

Fifteen

Clarice looked at the text message James sent and studied the pictures closely. She didn't recognize any of the people. Although the blonde with the lion looked a little too much like Algos for her own liking, but that was a matter to deal with at a later time. James thought the girl on the porch was "still warm" and in Kentucky, and Clarice was too far away to be comfortable letting the girl possibly die in her absence. She needed to call Mason and send him on a job.

Amanda Ryan West was forty-one, fun-size five feet, and had

curves that drove the men around her crazy. Her family fondly called her Peaches, and she was currently the caregiver to her great uncle and his wife, who were in their mid-nineties when she wasn't caring for everyone else. Despite being allergic to almost everything outside, including the sun itself, she loved living in the quietness of eastern KY at the top of the Appalachian Mountains.

She was allergic to her five rescue kitties, but Amanda didn't care about that either. Life was meant to be lived. Not locked up in the dungeon just because you drew the short genetic straw. *So what if she couldn't be in direct sunlight for more than three minutes, and lived lathered up in sunscreen and wearing flopping hats?* As long as the allergens and sun were low enough, you would still find her sitting on her porch enjoying her books and the birds in her spare time.

It was still nice enough to sit outside before winter would drive everyone in for good, and Amanda would not miss any of her chances of sitting outside. She grabbed her current read and favorite throw in one hand, and a nice cup of hot chocolate in the other, and headed for the porch before the sun would rise too high, forcing her to leave for the day.

As she read and sipped on the hot chocolate, Amanda became extremely drowsy. So drowsy that she eventually fell over, spilling what was left of her hot chocolate across the porch and falling out of the chair she was sitting in. She was passed out cold.

When Amanda tried to open her eyes, it was pitch black. Whatever she was currently laying on was extremely hard. She tried to move, but she was wedged in tight. She felt her hot breath bounce right back in her face. *Surely not....*

Amanda felt around and was greeted by the ringing of hard

plastic underneath her. Panic quickly set in, because she knew exactly where she was. She tried to push the lid open, but it was locked closed. Her breathing grew rapid as tears ran down her cheeks. *Who the hell would lock her in a tanning bed? Was this some sort of joke?*

"Hello?" she called out. No response. She banged her hands harder against the plastic beneath her and scream louder. Still no response. *Breathe. It's not on.*

She heard a door open above her, and footsteps coming down some very loud creaking stairs. "Hello?" Amanda called out desperately. "I need help," she said in a shaky voice.

The only response that greeted her was the turning of the dial and the awaking of the surrounding bulbs. "NO!" Amanda screamed out. "You don't understand!" she pleaded.

It wasn't long before she was screaming in agony and bawling as she quickly realized whoever was there wasn't there to help her, but to watch her suffer. Her body instantly broke out into blisters and hives as she franticly wiggled to get free somehow. She didn't hear the footsteps retreat up towards the door, or the fact that it didn't close. Amanda was too busy bawling and screaming in agony until her body couldn't take anymore.

"Well?" Liz finally asked once the girl grew quiet.

Claudia stared at the closed tanning bed. The corners of her lips curled up into a smile. "Getting warmer," she smirked before she walked past Liz and left Amanda's body to rot without a care in the world.

Mason was able to track down Amanda West, but only after she had clearly been taken. He dreaded dialing Clarice. He knew she wouldn't be happy.

"Let me guess," he heard her frustration on the other side.

"She's already gone," Mason responded as equally frustrated. "Looks like they poisoned her and dragged her somewhere just an hour or so ago, so she should be close. I'll keep looking."

"Looks like she already got another girl here. Pit fall trap," Clarice grumbled. Mason was surprised she wasn't barking at him like she used to when her father was still around.

"They must have a plane," he added.

"You think there's more than one?" Clarice asked with interest.

"There has to be," Mason said cautiously. "There's no way they can kill this quickly and this spread out. Right?"

What the hell was going on? "Has what's her name found any connection yet?" Clarice snapped.

Mason smirked. "Not yet," he replied, knowing she was talking about Emma. He didn't know what Emma had done other than exist, but Emma still got the old Clarice when everyone else seemed to get an updated version.

"What's taking her so damn long?" Clarice growled with growing irritation.

"There's no connection," Mason quickly added to calm her down. "Literally none. And I'm not just saying that. The only thing that seemed to tie any of these people together is that they were part of some booktok community on the TikTok app, but half of them didn't even really know the other. There is absolutely no tie to you, Sophie, or anyone else in your family. None."

"Then why?" Clarice laughed. "There's no guarantee that you would catch our attention?"

"Do you think they know they have it yet?" he asked. "We might still have the upper hand."

"Let's pretend we do until we know otherwise," Clarice said in resignation. "And keep digging," she added as an afterthought.

"Of course," Mason replied.

"Oh, and Mason," Clarice said.

"Already in the car and tracking them," he reported.

"Try to find this one before it's too late," Clarice said softly.

"Doing my best, Ma'am," Mason whispered back.

However, Mason wasn't able to keep his promise. By his calculations, he was about thirty minutes too slow. Amanda was already burnt to a crisp. He said a silent prayer and disposed of the body properly so it wouldn't be told in the news like the last one.

There were no clues to where they were going next, or why Amanda was chosen. Mason was also losing his patience with these new players. He cleaned up the scene and wiped down his own traces before he left while Amanda roamed the dream realm, aimlessly trying to figure out where she was and why.

James eagerly opened the wooden door in front of him, only to find Jack instead of Corbin.

"James!" Jack said, a bit alarmed. "Is everything alright?"

Thrown off by not seeing Corbin, James stepped back a couple of steps. "No," he replied quickly. "I was just looking for Corbin."

"Oh," Jack said looking at the floor. "I'm afraid he's not available at the moment. Is there something I can help you with?"

"Probably not," James said with a bit of disappointment as he turned to grab for the door handle.

"Apparently the realm disagrees, because it gave you me instead, so why don't you be honest with me, and let's talk about what you want to actually discuss," Jack said waving his hand to supply some nice plush chairs, a table, and a couple of beers.

"Is that how it works?" James asked, turning around and not letting his guard down.

"Is how what works?" Jack asked, puzzled as he took a seat and cracked open a beer.

"You told us to call you when we needed you, but it's really the realm that decides?" James asked as he followed Jack's lead and took a seat.

Jack shrugged. "Depends on the true intent, I guess."

"How can you stand it in here?" James asked, shaking his head as he cracked opened his own beer and took a swig.

Jack threw him a grin that matched Sophie's and simply said, "Sophie."

James smile wide and laughed. "Enough said."

"So, why do you need Corbin?"

James shifted in his seat.

"Ah, Clarice," Jack chuckled.

"He told you?" James asked in shock.

Jack leaned forward, placing his elbows on his knees and wrinkling his nose up. "Not exactly," Jack confessed.

"Poor guy," James whispered.

"To his defense, he did a pretty good job until recently," Jack snickered. "What's going on?" he asked again.

"I don't think I should," James started. "Jess and all."

Jack nodded in understanding and leaned back in his chair, and took a sip of his beer. He thought long and hard. "There's more though, that you wanted to talk about," Jack declared, already knowing the answer even though James had him blocked. A father always knows.

James's eyes flickered in fear, but he just sipped his beer. Jack knew he would have to gain the first to get to the second. He still had to earn James's trust, and that was hard to do, considering the circumstances. Jack would have to confess his own sins, because he was pretty sure he knew why James was here. It was what Jack had to come to terms with in order to be with Jess. Jack leaned forward again.

"Believe it or not," he whispered, "when it comes to Clarice, I'm much more clearheaded than my wife and can keep secrets when needed," Jack added with a wink. "So, tell me what you think I need to know, and I will answer your questions that will help you on why balance is so important with Sophie and yourself and why you're the one to accomplish that."

James narrowed his eyes as ice blue flames lit his pupils. Jack was taken aback by the response, because he had never seen a living being have that power, even in the dream realm. "Get out of my head," James warned.

"I'm not in your head," Jack replied sternly. "I'm simply guessing, because I've been where you are, and it's a logical assumption. I'm a scientist by nature. Now, please calm yourself before I have to calm you," he warned.

The flames disbursed, and James took a deep breath before

telling Jack about Karmen, what she had been drawing, that it was Clarice that had dropped her off to them, and how adamant Clarice was about wanting to know if Karmen drew Corbin. There was a new player on their side randomly killing people, and Clarice was trying to track them down so Sophie could be safe.

James showed Jack the pictures from his phone of some of the new players that seemed to be in his own realm. Jack soaked it all in and took mental notes. He had no idea how the blonde spearing the two headed lion came into play. Nothing like that was here in this realm, but he was guessing the 5'7", woman with autumn brown skin and as smooth as a moonstone, who had short black afro hair and hazel eyes was the intruder that his father had sensed enter the realm. She looked like a queen of some sort.

"Minus these two, I believe these are on your playing field," Jack pointed out. "I don't think this one is on ours, but John sensed this one enter, and thanks to you, we now know who we're looking for. Thank you for that," Jack replied with a reassuring smile. "You say this girl, Karmen, right? She's just now seeing the actions of the new player killing, but not the player themself?" he asked, intrigued.

"It doesn't appear so," James offered with a grimace. "She goes into quite a trance to get the information. It takes a lot out of her. I've never seen anything like it before. It's pretty obvious Algos found out about her. Killed her parents to get to her. Left her as the only survivor. Just hadn't taken her for himself yet."

"You don't say?" Jack asked, creasing his eyebrows. *That didn't sound like Algos at all.* "I don't think this new player is a fluke," he said as he jumped out of his chair and paced.

"You don't think..." James couldn't finish the sentence.

Jack stopped and stared right at James. "The game's not done."

Ben was sitting at his desk with his head in his hands when Roger walked in. Neither one of them wanted this assignment, but if worse came to worst and Sophie couldn't stay focused, they needed to shut her down. At least as safely as possible. It was going to cost him his child, and Ben his best friend, which is why Roger had every intention of taking the brunt of the end results, no matter how disastrous they ended up being.

"How goes it?" Roger asked quietly.

"Peachy," Ben replied sarcastically.

Roger sighed and pulled up a chair to sit next to him. "What do you have so far?"

"Well, for starters," Ben said with a grimace, "Sophie was impossible to catch even before she started malfunctioning, and she's not even here to test because she's thankfully trying to keep my baby safe. Which I appreciate," he threw in as an after-thought. "However, it's not exactly helping me come up with a way to safely put her to sleep if she can't do it herself."

"Put her to sleep..." Roger said in half a trance.

"Well, she was putting herself to sleep when she was overloaded," Ben reminded Roger. "That seems like the safest way to keep her alive and still have her safe from herself and others, right?"

Roger smiled the widest grin Ben had seen since he played with James as a kid. "Ben," he said, slapping Ben on the back. "That is the best idea you could have come up with!"

"Yeah, but if no one can catch her," Ben protested. "Cheetah speed, remember?"

"You let me worry about that. Just get to working on a formula. Get with that Travis fella that Dr. Elaine sent to us. He'll be an excellent asset in this project, and with Algos gone, his safety won't be an issue." Roger pushed back the chair and raced out of the room before Ben could get another word in.

❧

Donna kissed Cecil on the cheek and headed for the door.

"Um, where do you think you're going?" he asked with his eyebrows furrowed and a frown.

When she spun around, her long grey braid flung over her shoulder and she placed her hands on her hips. "I'm sorry. Did you want to save Sophie or not?" she asked with a glare as she tilted her head and stared down at her husband. He knew better than to ask any more questions.

"Do you need backup?" he asked her as he swallowed the lump in his throat.

"Do I ever?" she replied with a devilish grin.

"No, but sometimes I like to pretend you do," he said in a pout.

Donna sauntered over to him like a tiger walking the land she owned. She gave him a long, passionate kiss. "And when I do, you're the first person I call. You know that," she breathed against his lips.

His knees nearly buckled, sending him straight to the floor. "Yes, Ma'am," he gasped.

She leaned in against his ear and whispered, "I'll be back soon.

Don't worry," and kissed him on the cheek once more before leaving him quivering and eager for her return so he could show her just how much he loved her.

<u>Sixteen</u>

Mike was pacing the empty warehouse when Donna arrived. "You're late!" he barked.

"And I can leave right now if you don't adjust your attitude," she warned, glaring him down as she challenged him from the door frame, not fully in or out.

"Get in already!" he pleaded as he rushed towards her and handed her a very thin vanilla envelope.

She glared at the contents. "What's this?" she asked in annoyance.

"Everything there is. Your friend wasn't kidding," Mike said, looking around. "But don't ask me for anything else. This cost me big."

He was truly scared. Donna had never seen him so scared.

What the heck was in this thing? Was it even safe to take back to Tina?

"What's the summary?" Donna demanded. It was better to know what she was carrying before she took it back.

"No!" Mike replied. "I'm dead already, and so are you if you open that. There's a reason there's not much. He was really fucked up, and no one lived. Stop looking. Everyone who does dies. Please Donna," he said, grabbing her by the arms and shaking her. "Don't! I have to get out of here." And with that, he raced through the door and was gone.

Donna looked instinctively around, but she saw and heard no one. Then she looked at the thin 8x11 yellow envelope in her hand. Tina wouldn't stop digging. She was worse than Donna herself. Especially when it came to Sophie.

However, Donna needed to open this and see what was in it before she took it back to where her family was. There was only one place to do that, and it wasn't walking distance. She sighed and rolled her eyes, knowing Cecil would throw a fit. Donna put the envelope in her purse and pulled out the burner phone.

Taking longer than expected. Be back as soon as possible. I love you. -D

At least with their usual safety protocols in place, he wouldn't respond. Therefore, she wouldn't get an earful until she made it back to the hotel. Now, to go to the one place no one would ever expect her to go. Home....

❦

"Clarice," she heard Corbin call her name in her head.

"Go away," she snapped. "I'm busy." She was walking the scene of where Sarah O'Donnell had fallen in the deadfall trap.

"It's okay, I'll wait," she heard him taunt her.

"Just because you're dead doesn't mean I can't kill you again," she hissed as she tried to focus on the scene before her. She heard him chuckle, but remain silent afterwards.

After about five minutes, she sighed dramatically to the heavens and yelled out to no one, "What?"

"I just wanted to make sure you were okay," he said. She could hear his stupid grin through his voice.

"Are you kidding me right now?" she asked, exasperated.

"Nope," he laughed. "But also that I think I found something out about your redhead."

She stopped and screamed out at the top of her lungs. After taking a second to compose herself, she calmly stated, "Next time, maybe just start with that."

Nothing.

"Are you going to tell me, Wonder Boy?" she asked through gritted teeth.

"Why do you call me that?" she heard him ask in curiosity.

She grabbed the bridge of her nose to calm the wild range of emotions suddenly coursing through her. "So help me," she breathed out. He apparently decided to give her a pass.

"Come join me," he offered more softly. "I promise to behave."

Clarice wasn't so sure she wanted him to, and she wasn't sure how she felt about that either. "I'm trying to track a killer at the moment," she said in hesitation.

"I know," he said. "I'm trying to help."

She looked at the scene once more. There wasn't anything else she could get from it, anyway. Might as well see what Corbin had to offer. She took a deep breath and looked around. "Give me a couple of minutes to get back to the hotel," she murmured.

"Oh! I learned a new trick!" Corbin said in excitement.

Clarice squinted at the tree before her, unsure of what she was seeing. It looked out of focus compared to the surrounding ones. Clarice rubbed her eyes.

"No! It's me!" she heard him exclaim eagerly, like an excited child.

"Nice?" she offered, more as a question than a statement, not really sure what he was expecting from her.

"Walk through it," she heard him encourage her.

Oh, hell no. "Maybe after you've had more practice?" she proposed as nicely as she could.

"I can do this," he snapped.

"I'm not sure I can," she snapped back.

"Have a little faith," he replied, but she could hear the mixture of hurt and frustration in his voice and it unwantedly tugged at her heart.

"That's not fair and you know it," she muttered.

No response.

"How do I know I'll be in one piece when I get to the other side?" she asked no one.

"You think I wouldn't test it before trying it with you?" he asked. She could almost feel the heartbreak from within her own chest. Giving him what he wanted had to be better than feeling whatever this kind of hell that she was feeling inside.

Without asking anymore questions, she took in a deep breath, ran towards the tree and was caught in large, warm, muscular arms that were oddly familiar. "You didn't have to give it a running go," he laughed lightly into her hair, but he also didn't let her go.

She pushed away a little flustered and brushed off absolutely nothing off her clothes just to keep her hands from reaching out and ripping off his own clothing. "Yeah, well. You didn't exactly give me instructions," she said with a mild scowl and not daring to look him in the eyes. *Why does he have any kind of effect on me?*

"Right, well," Corbin said, cutting into her thoughts. "I found out some information about your mystery redhead," he said, turning around and walking behind the bar to fix them some drinks.

Clarice looked up. It was their place. The place he made for them. She eyed him suspiciously. "I don't recall that ending up too well last time," she said, watching him make the blue drink she loved so much.

Corbin looked up and faked hurt before smiling his stupid grin. "That was the poisoned blood. Not my mixology, but nice try," he said, sliding her drink down to her.

She caught it and stared at it. It almost sparkled in her hand.

"And I'm surprised you remember anything with as drunk as you were," he laughed, trying to lighten the mood, but her cheeks were getting as hot as fire and they both felt the warmth of that moment as if it were happening all over again. So, to help her out, Corbin walked to the farthest part of the room and sat in a booth. Giving her the option of joining him or not. She chose not. For now.

"And?" she prompted.

"Her name is Claudia Hayes. She's actually a missing grad student. Her friends said she insisted on walking back to the dorm after they were studying in the library for finals, but she never made it back," he said as he took a sip. Clarice took a sip as well. "Two guesses who took her, and the first one doesn't count," he added with a frown.

"Yeah, I was guessing," she muttered. "So, what makes her so fucking special?" she asked bitterly.

"Oh, absolutely nothing," he assured. "Nothing you couldn't handle, of course," he added with a grin before casually sipping his drink.

She looked at him in shock and quickly took a sip. "Nice try, but Daddy Dearest always has an alternative motive. So, seriously. What's her talent? Stop ass kissing. It gets you nowhere," she added with a smirk.

Corbin tilted his head. "I take offense. I have gotten nowhere near your ass."

Clarice nearly spit out the sip of delicious blue liquid she had in her mouth, but was able to choke it down instead. Not nearly as gracefully as she had hoped, though.

He smiled, considering that a point, in whatever game this was they were playing.

"She was a straight-A student and studying psychology and biology. She wanted to help understand what made a person a psychopath, and how to prevent it. One took her mother unexpectedly. Her father and brother still live in a small town in Wisconsin called Two Rivers."

"When did she go missing?" Clarice asked, picking up her drink and pacing the floor between them.

"It was right before winter break," Corbin said, taking a sip and trying not to draw attention to the fact that she was making her way closer to him.

"He knew," she whispered.

Corbin put his drink down. "Knew what?"

"He knew he couldn't flip Sophie, so he had to come up with a backup plan," Clarice said with a hint of anger. She put the empty glass down on the booth's table and stood across from Corbin.

"Well, he had to assume it might be a possibility," Corbin countered.

"No," Clarice said firmly, daring to look straight into Corbin's eyes as she placed her hands on the table and leaned in towards him. She was furious, and she didn't have to have the flames for him to see that. "He *KNEW*," she emphasized.

"How would he know for sure?" Corbin asked, confused.

"Because he had already discovered Karmen, and she showed him," Clarice hissed, angry spit flying from her mouth.

Corbin was alarmed by the new player's name, and how upset Clarice was becoming. "Who's Karmen?" he asked her softly, reaching out to place his hand over hers. She looked down at it, hesitated, and pulled it away, suddenly unsure of how many people who should know about Karmen and her "gifts".

"Thank you for the information," Clarice said, quickly changing the subject. "I need to get back and check on Sophie." She raced for the door.

"I only want to help you, Clarice," Corbin said eagerly, getting up and chasing after her.

Clarice froze. "I know. I appreciate it," she breathed over her shoulder. "But you're here, and I'm..." she couldn't finish the sentence. She didn't like the feelings that were stirring inside of her. "I need to go."

"Clarice!" he called out, but she yanked open the door and stumbled back out into the woods, nearly falling right in the deadfall trap. His hand clung to hers still within the doorframe, and she gasped at the sight before her. He yanked her back towards him and wrapped her in his arms immediately, holding her tightly as they both breathed heavily. "Don't. Do. That. Again. Please." he begged.

She couldn't even respond.

Jack turned to rush off, but James grabbed him by the arm. "I need to know," he said in a plea. "You promised."

Jack closed his eyes and took a deep breath before he sat back down. "As a scientist, it's hard to give much stock to things like 'love at first sight' and things of that nature, but that's exactly what it was. Now, I could give you the scientific mumbo jumbo of why our bodies react to the female species, but there is definitely something unique about the Harris women," Jack began. He picked up his beer and took a sip, making a face. It was warm and gross.

"I was a hopeless romantic by nature," Jack continued with a smile on his face, "so I was willing to wave it away a little more than I should have, probably. I knew Algos messed with the girls psychologically, but it wasn't until I started working for him that I found the hidden file about what had happened to Jess while we were dating. I watched her like a hawk for months that turned into years, but even I couldn't deny the fact that whatever he did either didn't work or was lying dormant." He paused with a scowl.

"They say never fall in love with your subject, but I was already in love before I started," Jack smiled, looking off into space. "I wondered if it was one of the things that Algos had done to her. If he had *made* her that way to make her more potent, ya know?" he said, taking a second to look at James to make sure he understood where he was coming from.

James nodded, so Jack resumed staring off into space as he went down memory lane. "I ran so many tests that she doesn't even know about, so I only tell you this so that you understand what our role is," Jack warned, looking back at James. James nodded again to confirm he understood, but didn't dare interrupt.

"But at some point, I realized that no test was going to talk me out of loving her," Jack chuckled. "None. It wasn't my choice, regardless. A partnership takes two people. She had to want it as bad as I did, but it wasn't something that could be forced upon her, either. Once she made her choice, I had one to make myself. Take on a family of psychopaths to be with the woman that I literally couldn't breathe and my heart would stop beating if I ever had to go without, or I walked away before we both kept getting hurt further." Jack paused. "So, we can clearly see how that turned out," he replied in amusement, looking at James, "but the Harris girls come with a package deal attached to them. You see," Jack continued, "they're incredibly strong, stubborn, and feel everything to their core. And that was even before they were enhanced," he let out a laugh. "So, they require a special someone to provide the balance they need to anchor them, and allow them to do all the things destiny requires them to do."

"How do you keep Jess balanced?" James asked.

"Depends on the day and the mood, my boy," Jack smiled. "My wife was emotionally damaged and destroyed by someone who thought it was okay because it was fun for them. So, they have a hard time trusting people like us that come along, only wanting what's best for them, and helping them succeed."

"That's why she runs," James whispered.

"That's our fault," Jack moped. "We taught her she always had to. We weren't sure you were going to come along, or who you were going to be. They have to choose us."

"Choose us?" James asked.

"Yes," Jack answered. "Plenty of men have loved them throughout their lives."

Eddie.

"But they have to choose their own protector. The one who will keep them balanced when their emotions take over and they lose sight of who they truly are," Jack continued on, ignoring James's realization. "However, once we are chosen, the universe steps in to give us a little help, and gives us gifts so we can help maintain their balance."

"What do you mean?" James asked, confused.

"Out there, once she chose me, I could keep her calm with my words and touch. Keep her grounded," Jack offered. "In here, we're assigned certain gifts. Sometimes it's something we're good at, something we love, but we're usually assigned a single gift."

"So, what's yours?" James asked with a mischievous smile.

"Nice try," Jack laughed. "But I can tell you this," he said, leaning in closer to James, causing him to do the same. "I've never had just one, and they change based on her needs for that moment," he whispered with a wink before he sat back. "So, she's clearly chosen you. The only question is, are you up for the task?"

James gave his boyish grin. "Yes, Sir," he confirmed happily. *That's what was going on. He was changing, because she was changing. Not to go against her, but to help her.*

"Is everything okay?" Jack asked with a hint of concern.

"She's good," James confirmed. "She's just adjusting, but I've got her," he affirmed as he got up and reached for the door.

"You would tell us if there was something wrong, right?" Jack called after him.

James turned around. "This is a Sophie battle, Jack. And based on what you just told me, fate is stepping in and I'm the only one to help her through it. I would move heaven and earth for your daughter, because I love her more than the air I breathe. This time, you're going to have to have faith in me," he said right before he turned around and opened the door. Sophie was still sleeping soundly next to him, and Karmen was passed out in the bed next to them.

They would need supplies for their hike. James would sneak out and get some before the girls woke up. It was going to be a great day.

Seventeen

ophie found herself surrounded by blackness and staring at Rein.

"Don't look so disappointed," Rein sneered.

"What do you want?" Sophie demanded.

Rein laughed a deep throat cackle. "You called me," she replied, shaking her head.

"I don't need you right now," Sophie hissed at her.

"Your conscious says otherwise," Rein responded flatly with a shrug.

"Karmen," Sophie whispered in panic as she looked all around her.

Rein rolled her eyes. "The twerp is fine," she offered in

annoyance.

Sophie let out a breath, and noticed Rein watching her far too closely. "Losing control, already?" she asked Sophie with great interest. Sophie turned her back to Rein and tried to gather herself. *Was she trapped again?*

"Oh my God," Rein cackled like a hyena. "You are a hot mess! Maybe you should let me have a go. Clearly, you can't handle it."

Sophie's eyes lit up with fire as she spun around to face Rein. "Watch yourself," she hissed at her.

"Or what?" Rein taunted.

Sophie's entire body lit up into red flames as she lifted a few feet above Rein. "You really want to find out?" Sophie dared back. Then she felt a tiny hand inside hers and when she woke up, she was staring into Karmen's large cornflower blue eyes.

"Karmen, No!" Sophie shouted.

Karmen grunted loudly and tried to wiggle desperately out of Sophie's grasp, but she held on tightly while she inspected Karmen carefully. She expected to find burn marks, but found nothing. Once Sophie was satisfied, she released Karmen, who rushed over to the corner of the room screaming loudly. As she did, James came through the door with his arms full of bags. He dropped them immediately at the sight of Karmen running for safety, and Sophie's tear-stained cheeks.

She narrowed her eyes at him before hissing, "Don't leave me alone with her again. It's not safe." Then she turned around and stalked to the bathroom and slammed the door shut.

James fought the need to follow Sophie to make her hurt less, and turned his attention to Karmen, who was so overwhelmed with emotion, Sophie's emotions, that she was banging her head on the wall with no other way to express what was happening. James ran to her and slid his hand between Karmen's head and the wall and felt the bones crack at her force.

"Karmen," he whispered calmly, but her screams drowned him out. Sophie would not be able to help them, but maybe he could try. James was Sophie's balance, so maybe...He closed his eyes and tried to imagine his other hand lighting up ever so gently to distract her into calmness. It shocked James when he opened his eyes to find it actually worked. Karmen was cradling her fingertip to the palm of his hand that was radiating the softest of a blue light. "What happened?" he asked in a whisper, not sure she could give him any kind of answer.

However, when Karmen sat back on her heels, she was in a trance and ready to help. She got up and went to where her tablet and pencils were waiting for her. James hung back and gave Karmen space as she feverishly drew a picture for him. When she was done, Karmen blinked back to the present and got out of the chair to hand the picture to James.

There was an older version of Sophie on what would have been the ground, with her original black bob and a red suit, looking much like she had when they first met. The sneer on her face reminded him more of Algos than of the Sophie he knew and loved. Their Sophie was above her, engulfed in red flames, holding onto Karmen's hand, but he recognized the anger within her eyes. Two Sophies, with Karmen in harm's way. Karmen sat on the bed, rocking and humming herself to peace.

"She thought she hurt you," James breathed out as he looked at Karmen. She didn't look him in the eye, but held up her arms so he could see she wasn't harmed as she continued to rock back and forth and stare at the closed bathroom door. James swallowed as he looked back at the picture.

Was this why she was glitching? She was battling with herself? She had been in a coma for longer than any of them desired, especially him. Sophie never told him what happened while she was asleep, just that she was stuck.

James stared at the other Sophie, pretty sure of what she was supposed to represent. All the things Sophie would have become if Algos had gotten her instead of Jess and Jack having their backup plan to hide her until Mario could rescue her to keep her safe.

Only this wasn't about the choices that could have been made if things had played out differently. If Karmen could see her, then she was as real as they were, and that was the scary part. Sophie wouldn't tell him, because she would insist on dealing with this by herself like she was used to doing. However, she wasn't alone any more, and James would spend the rest of his life proving that to her if he needed to.

James folded up the piece of paper and put it in his bag for safekeeping. He balled his previously broken hand into a fist, noticing he was healing even faster than Sophie could. This was something he was going to have to pay attention to, but for now, there were other things to take care of first.

"We're going on a trip today," he announced to Karmen. "Can you get ready to play outside while I go check on Sophie?" he asked her. She gave a solid grunt and an almost nod between the rocking as she got off the bed and got ready.

Karmen wouldn't make eye contact with James, but she continued to stare at the bathroom door. James got down on Karmen's level and forced her to look at him. "She'll be okay," he assured her without touching her. "She doesn't enjoy hurting people, especially those she cares about, and it was just a bit much for her."

Karmen looked past him to stare back at the closed bathroom door. James smiled and got up to coax Sophie out of the bathroom. He knocked gently with his knuckles. "Hey, Babe," he said, leaning his head against the door. "Can I come in?"

"Just take her and go," Sophie said as her voice cracked.

"Yeah, no," James said as he jiggled the handle just hard enough to shake the lock free, and he slid in, closing the door behind him. He turned around to find Sophie slumped on the floor with her head laying on her knees.

"Destroying property will not make me go with you," she said in a mumble.

"Oh, I know," he said with his boyish grin as he picked her up by the shoulders and threw her over his shoulder.

"What are you doing?" she yelled in shock and half giggling.

"You're coming one way or another," James said defiantly, giving her butt a smack. She squealed and tried to wiggle out of his hands with no success.

"Put me down!" she warned, but her bark was much worse than her actual bite. They both knew it when it came to him.

"Hey, if you're going to act like a toddler, then I'm going to treat you like a toddler," James said, smiling, enjoying that he was finally having the upper hand with the woman he loved.

"So help me..." Sophie yelled. Then she finally stilled. "It's not safe," she whispered in defeat.

James slid her down the front of his chest to sit her on the bathroom counter and put his arms up against the mirror to keep her trapped. "Look at me," he ordered her.

Her eyebrows came together as she stuck out her bottom lip. "No," she said stubbornly.

"Okay, then," he said, acting like he was going to throw her over his shoulder again. She glared at him, but there wasn't any hatred behind it. She was scared.

"You didn't leave a single mark," he said, staring deep into her eyes.

Sophie blinked. She knew she hadn't seen anything, but how were her flames not harmful to James and Karmen? As if reading her mind, James responded, "I don't think you can hurt those you care about."

"One, get out of my head," she warned, and he saw she meant it. "Two, how can that be?"

"Let's go out to the mountains where no one is to find out," he said with his boyish grin that she couldn't resist. "Come on. You know you're curious," he taunted. "We'll take turns making sure Karmen's safe, but I think it's time to see what we both can actually do, don't you? We can't stay away from the fam forever. Tina will come hunt us down sooner than later. I promise you," he chuckled as he leaned his head against her forehead.

"She will, won't she?" Sophie giggled.

"I didn't want to mess with her before she was a mama bear," James admitted.

"Okay," Sophie giggled, leaning back and pushing him away. "You're right. She scares me, too."

James stepped back and held out his hand to help her down.

She took it readily and hopped down.

"Oh," James said before opening the door. "Karmen hasn't stopped staring at the door since you went behind it, so don't tell me you're not a favorite," he informed her before he stepped out. "Ready?" he asked Karmen. Sophie was still standing in the bathroom with her mouth hanging open.

Donna stepped into a small house that from the outside looked like no one had lived there in years, and was greeted by a shotgun barrel pointed at her head with the hammer cocked. "Hey, Mama," Donna said with a deep sigh. "Long time no see."

"What the hell are you doing here?" hissed an elderly woman, still hiding in the shadows.

"Just thought I'd check in on you," Donna said, faking a small smile.

"Horse shit," snapped the old woman.

"I just need an hour or two," Donna confessed. There was a long pause before she heard the safety put back on the shotgun. She watched her mom lay it down in the corner behind the door.

"Come on then," resigned the elder lady, who was a carbon copy of Donna, with a few extra years on her. She stopped asking her daughter questions around the time she ran away to elope with Cecil. Though the woman never would understand their love for each other, she had come to terms not to mess with it anymore.

"So, how are things?" Donna asked as her mom turned on lights, bringing her childhood to light around her.

"Like you care," the old woman muttered, but they both knew she did. Donna sent her money regularly, made sure she had everything she ever needed, including the bodyguard that was always smart enough to stay out of sight unless truly needed. He kept tabs and reported back to Donna regularly. It was just safer this way.

Donna ignored the comment and took a seat at the kitchen table. Her dad had passed years ago, and her mother kept to herself minus a few close friends. Like mother, like daughter. She opened up the file and began looking through it when a cold glass of tea was sat on the table next to her.

"Do I even want to know?" her mother asked, with a subtle hint of worry.

"Nope," Donna said, reaching for the tea. "But it's not about me, it's about Sophie."

Her mother nodded and opened the fridge to make them some sandwiches. Donna had brought Mario to meet her mother a few times, mostly to prove he never had it as bad as he thought. She gave a much different level of "tough love" than Donna did, and it usually only took a visit or two during his rebellious years to straighten him out. Hell, who was she kidding? Mario was rebellious until the day he died. Donna grinned at the thought of her old friend.

When Mario acquired Sophie, this was one of his first stops. Mostly because no one would ever guess it. They never knew Donna and Cecil had raised Mario. They made sure of that. So, her mother knew better than to dig deeper. Sophie and Mario were off limits as topic of discussions, but even her mother would fight to protect them if it came down to it.

A plate clattered on the table with a ham sandwich on it. "I'm going to watch tv," her mother muttered, as she headed for the living room. She listened to old episodes of *Murder She Wrote* play in the background. Donna smiled broadly as fond childhood memories floated in front of her eyes. Then she shook her head and looked down at the folder before her.

She looked at the family tree that represented Algos's side of the family. No history of evil psychopathic tendencies until he was born. No head injury or any brain damage. Satan just having a go at living top side. She reviewed his psych records from the asylum, and didn't find much more than what she already knew.

Rebecca's side included mostly blank spaces. A great grandmother, Maxine, and a grandmother, Ruby. No mentions of husbands, although someone had to of hooked up for the line to continue. Rebecca's mother died in childbirth, and they marked her father as *unknown.* Ruby took Rebecca after her daughter died and raised Rebecca as her own.

Apparently, Ruby wouldn't approve of Algos, and it would cost the old woman her life in the end. The witness to their courthouse marriage would be one of the college schmucks from campus shortly after they graduated, on Rebecca's terms.

There was some speculation of witchcraft amongst the women of Rebecca's side of the family, but nothing would save them from dying "mysterious deaths", aka Algos got his way. There wasn't anything in the file itself that should have scared Mike as badly as it did. *So, what's NOT here that scared him to his core?....*

Suddenly, a fierce tapping at the window had Donna jumping out of her skin. A raven sat on the windowsill, tilting its head from side to side and almost staring Donna down in a challenge.

"What in the world?" she heard her mother say as she got up from her recliner.

Donna stepped closer to get a better look at the raven when its eyes burst into flames before her. It began tapping its beak repeatedly against the window. Donna backed away slowly. "Mom, bring me your gun," she said with a hint of urgency.

"Are you trying to burn my freaking house down?" her mother shouted at her.

"What?" Donna asked in confusion, turning to face her mother. The file that was on the table was now in flames, and they both raced to the sink. Donna grabbed a towel while her mother quickly filled a glass with water and threw it at the table.

When the fire was out, the papers were just ashes, and Donna turned to the window. The raven was gone. "I'm sorry, mom, I think I need to go," she said, quickly kissing her mother on the cheek, grabbing her jacket, and racing out the door.

"Love you, too," her mother muttered after her.

Donna raced into the night, but found only blackness. The raven was long gone, and Donna had chills down to her bones. It wasn't Algos that scared Mike. It was the secret Rebecca was carrying, even in death.

Donna threw on her jacket and wondered if going back was putting everyone in danger, or if this was just a warning to Donna. She couldn't go back until she knew it was safe, and the kind of help she needed was going to be of the afterlife kind. Donna closed her eyes and whispered for Corbin, but when she opened them, there wasn't a wooden door that greeted her. It was two elderly women, with short white hair, black robes, and dilated eyes.

"Welcome, my child," they cooed in unison. "We have you to replace our child." Lightning struck all around Donna. When the light show faded, the only thing that remained was the scorched ground where she had been standing.

Eighteen

A woman with long, hazelnut curly hair with white streaks stumbled out of the woods and fell to her knees. Her frame was small, and her bright pure blue eyes illuminated in the moonlight. A red flame glowed in each pupil with fear, for she didn't know who or where she was....

John felt the immediate shift. Something was wrong. Terribly wrong. He closed his eyes and summoned Angie.

She appeared in the darkness, her light nearly blinding him. "You know this isn't how it works," she said in dismay.

"Do you feel that?" he asked, cutting her off.

Angie paused to see if she could sense what had John so terrified. "I don't feel anything," she said slowly.

"Well, I do," John said as his eyes lit up in icy blue fire. "She's gone."

"Gone? What do you mean, gone?" Angie asked in sudden alarm.

"I heard her cry out not that long ago, but now she's gone," John said, looking at Angie as his body lit up, matching his eyes.

"Calm down before you destroy us both," Angie warned, taking a few steps back. John quickly closed his eyes and waited a beat before opening them again.

"Call them back," he ordered. "She's not in any realm."

"Then where is she?" Angie asked in frustration.

"Only Sophie and Clarice can find her," he replied dryly.

"No!" Angie gasped, covering her mouth with a shaking hand.

"We're too late," John said, looking down at the nothingness underneath him. "Prepare them. We don't know where she's been, or what state she's in," he said, unable to look at her. Angie nodded and turned to walk away.

"And the girl?" she asked over her shoulder.

"They're the least of our concerns," John breathed out before the black mist consumed him and left Angie alone.

She fell to her knees and tried to catch her breath. "I'm so sorry," she whispered in a shaky voice. A single tear escaped and ran down her cheek before she bowed her head and was gone.

Cindy Kukas loved to live life to the fullest, and today was no different. She strutted her heavenly curved 5'7" frame down to the tattoo parlor to celebrate her 60th birthday with a new tattoo of the green ribbon that represents bipolar awareness with the bipolar symbol on one end, and the suicide semicolon on the other. She was bipolar, herself, and proudly represented for those still too scared or unable to speak up just yet. With her ocean blue and Bob Seger t-shirt on, she went in to see her pal Braydon. His pierced face lit up immediately.

"Hey mama hen! How goes it?" he asked her.

"Oh, you know. The usual. Had to get Maxwell out of the house for a bit so he'd stop being so naughty," she said, looking down at the Yorkie that gave no shame in return. He knew he was mama's favorite.

"Maxwell," Braydon laughed, knowing it would do no good. Maxwell just gave him a bark in response.

"So, are you ready for me today?" Cindy asked him.

"Ready for the birthday queen? Am I ever!" Braydon exclaimed, as he fluffed out a glittering blue cape and clipped it around her. He placed a beautiful crystal crown on her head before letting her sit down. She giggled like a schoolgirl, and it pleased Braydon he could give her such joy. She deserved nothing but the best.

"You'd better not screw it up!" Cindy lectured, wagging her finger and trying to sound as fierce as possible. Or I will tell your mama on you!"

Braydon smiled from ear to ear. "Yes, your majesty," he said, giving her a bow. He cleaned off her arm, pulled up his stool, gave her headphones blaring some Bob Seger, shook out his arms, and got to work.

Cindy laid back, closed her eyes, and twitched her right foot in tune to the music to keep herself distracted while Braydon worked on her. He had already done other tattoos for her, and had done them well, including the names of her grandchildren. She knew she was in excellent hands.

Cindy didn't hear Braydon get up and leave. She didn't notice a woman come in and pick up a different barred needle that drew a smiley face and the words "I'll See You Soon" on her arm. Cindy did, however, notice when she started to feel ill, and there was no one working on her arm.

She opened her eyes and looked around. Braydon was nowhere to be found. She looked down at her arm and saw the smiley face. "Now, what the hell?" Cindy called out. "Braydon! Get in here!" But Braydon would never come. His lifeless body would remain just outside the doorway out in the hall.

Cindy became dizzy and nauseous. She felt weak suddenly, and it was nearly impossible to breathe. "Maxwell!" she called out, suddenly realizing that she never heard her trusty companion. Maxwell was dead on the other side of the room.

Cindy was consumed with shock and confusion as both her pulse and breathing increased. "Help!" she screamed as she tried to get out of the chair, but immediately fell to the floor. Her shiny birthday crown slid across the room to Maxwell's lifeless body, and tears ran down her cheeks just before her body began convulsing. In less than a couple of minutes, Cindy was gone. Never to make it to sixty-one.

"Well?" Liz asked eagerly.

Claudia studied the frail, quickly cooling body before her. "Meh," she replied with a shrug before turning on her heels and walking away. Liz quickly followed.

The coroner would determine that someone had laced the ink with a blood thinner that had seeped into poor Cindy's veins, causing the hemorrhaging. However, with no other cases of its kind in the area, and no solid leads, the case went cold, and Cindy joined everyone else in the dream realm without knowing why.

"So, what happens now?" demanded Mario.

"Nothing," Angie stated flatly. "We're too late. We just have to wait and see."

"I'm sorry, what?" asked Mario, as his eyes lit up on fire. Angie knew he had no idea of his power yet, but she always needed him to stay in control.

"Calm down," she ordered him. Peter put a hand on his shoulder, but he just shrugged it off.

"My goddaughter is in danger, and we're just going to sit here and do nothing?" he hissed through gritted teeth.

Peter placed himself in front of his mother instinctively. "Hey, calm down. We're not letting anything happen to her," he lied. "We just have limited access at the moment." He watched Mario carefully, ready to engage if needed.

"What the hell does that mean?" Mario asked, raising his voice. They felt the heat of his power rise around them both.

Angie stepped around Peter, and when he went to fight her in protest, she flicked her wrist, freezing him against his will.

"Mario," she said calmly. "This realm doesn't work the same as your last one. We don't get to interact with the living as much as we would like," she began to explain in a motherly tone. "Sophie isn't in danger. She will be our savior. But she will need your help to succeed, so I'm going to need you to calm down in order to figure out how to best help her with our limitations. Can you do that?" Angie asked him softly.

Mario wasn't happy, but he was contemplating her words and the temperature dropped around them. He closed his eyes and took a deep breath in and out before responding, "How do we help?"

Peter let out the breath he was holding. Mario's love for Sophie might give him more power than even Peter was capable of handling. He was pretty sure that even *they* were highly underestimating how far Mario would go to keep Sophie safe. This would have to be discussed with his mother later, but for now, they needed a plan. One that Mario would accept and still get the job done.

"I thought you'd never ask," Angie said slyly.

She had been playing this game long enough to know how to push the needed sides into doing her bidding, but Peter had been playing since he was a toddler. Waiting for his calling to come in order to stop his brother from all the harm he had caused. He never would have guessed it would have included helping Mario find his way, or destroying his great niece he never got to meet if she lost her way.

However, even his own mother didn't know all the details, and that was how it was to remain. It didn't mean he wouldn't do what he could to save as many as possible, but his brother would be stopped. One way or another.

🔥

Even Shyera couldn't ignore the increase of body count within the dream realm. It was multiplying quickly, and she was no closer to finding the raven. If she didn't find her fast, there wouldn't be any realms left in the wake.

"Getting a little crowded in here," Jack said as he approached her from behind. Shyera didn't move. She just kept watching the new arrivals wonder around lost and confused.

"I wouldn't know," she said. "I just got here myself," she added, trying to sound as confused as possible.

"Well, we both know that's not true," he said with a grin as he walked around to face her.

Shyera didn't look him in the eye. She knew better. "It feels like I just got here," she said, still examining the ghostly images around her.

"Why are you here?" Jack asked more harshly. "Because we did not invite you like the rest," he added, to prove she couldn't fool him.

"I'm not here for you," she said, still not looking at him.

"So, who are you here for?" he asked cautiously.

"Someone who doesn't belong," she replied dryly.

"You're the only one that doesn't belong here," Jack said, gathering his energy just in case.

"There's no need for that," Shyera said as she finally looked him in the eye. "You wouldn't win anyway," she said with a wicked grin, and flicking her wrist to show a small ball of flame dancing on her palm. "Now, put yours away, and I'll put mine away," she warned.

Jack raised his hands in retreat, but kept his energy close. She smiled, but kept her flame dancing on her palm. Jack chuckled and let the power around him go. Shyera closed her fist, and the flame went out.

"How did you get in?" he asked curiously.

"I had permission," she said as she went back to scanning the surrounding ghosts.

Jack waited for more explanation, but got none. "Well, maybe if you tell me who you're looking for, I can help?" he offered. He took a step back when she tossed her head back and laughed.

"You don't have the power to help me look," she finally offered. "But thanks," she added more softly. "I really mean no harm."

"Well, you could have just asked us," he stated simply as he watched her scan the surrounding people.

"Looks like you have your own problems to be focusing on," Shyera replied, nodding her chin at the increase of guests around them.

Jack frowned as he looked around. "So, it seems," he mumbled. "You wouldn't know anything about this, would you?"

"This has nothing to do with me or my raven," she stated, although she wasn't entirely sure. She hoped she was right. It was easier for her to be good than not.

"Raven? What's a raven?" Jack asked curiously. He had heard the term, but couldn't get an exact answer from anyone when he asked.

Shyera studied him. "It's not your concern," she finally offered.

Jack studied her in return before stating, "Oh, I think we both know that's not true."

Shyera looked around, but saw no sign of decision making to push her either way. So she closed her eyes and let out a breath.

"A raven is someone with the ability to cross between the living and the dead, with unimaginable power to either save or destroy both," she said with a scowl. "This one has no master at the moment, and so I must locate them in order to make sure everything survives."

The alarm on Jack's face told her he knew more than he had offered, and the corner of her lips curled up into a wicked smile. *Sophie.* She read in his mind. He swallowed, trying to keep his cool.

"Who's Sophie?" she asked, intrigued.

"Not your concern," Jack said as the flames ignited in his eyes.

"It does if she's my missing raven," Shyera said with red flames matching Jack's blue.

Jess came running to his side. "Jack!" she said as her veins ignited red.

Shyera stared at Jess and laughed. This one was more powerful, but she couldn't back down. Not now.

Jack stuck his hand in front of her to stop her. To protect her. "We're fine," he said, still staring at Shyera. "She doesn't mean us harm," he reminded them all. Jack and Jess continued to stare at Shyera as she stood her ground. "She already saved Corbin," he added. Jess looked at him in shock. After a minute, blue chased the red from her veins, but uncertainty kept her lit like a glow stick.

Shyera tilted her head as she watched the change take place. *Well, that's interesting....*

"I don't mean harm," she confirmed. "I'm simply trying to find my raven before it's too late."

"Raven?" Jess asked, confused.

They didn't know the danger that awaited them. Shyera felt a little guilty, but knew the rules and the price of interfering. Her own family was at risk.

"Someone who can cross between the living and the dead with

some killer powers," Shyera offered.

Sophie! she heard again inside her head. Red chased through Jess's veins again, but Shyera held up her hands indicating she meant no harm. It helps no one to start a war when it wasn't needed. Jack watched her, but still held Jess back.

"You're her balance," Shyera whispered, fascinated. "Her protector," she added in a softer tone. "You're lucky," Shyera offered to Jess, throwing her off and turning her power down to a dim glow.

"I think it might help everyone if we had a conversation, so we can help you do what you need to do," Jack offered honestly. Even Shyera felt the truth behind his words.

Shyera looked between the two of them. "I can't help you," she said in resignation. "My own family is in danger until she's located." She felt the tug at both their hearts.

"How many?" Jess asked. Shyera looked at her, confused. "Children," Jess clarified.

Shyera shifted the weight between her feet. "Three," she finally offered.

"We have one," Jess said in a softer tone. "Sophie."

Realization reached Shyera's eyes. "I'm not here to harm the raven," Shyera confirmed for them. "Without a master, they need to find their way. Tame their power. Save everyone. If your Sophie is the raven, then she's more of a gift than you could ever imagine," she offered with a smile.

"What happens if she's not?" Jack asked cautiously.

"If I don't find the raven in time?" Shyera asked, confirming their concerns. "Then one was designed to stop her."

Jess's knees went weak, and Jack caught her before she hit the ground. When they looked up, Shyera was gone. They couldn't feel her to find her without her power on.

"Jack," Jess said, looking desperately at her husband.

"We'll get to the bottom of it," he assured her, but he wasn't sure how well he could keep his promise.

Corbin pushed a drink towards Clarice. She let him hold her until the shaking slowed, but now she was sitting in a booth, trying to process all that was happening. "Drink this. It will help," he offered. She looked at the drink, but made no reach for it. "Are you sure you're okay?" he finally asked her. He could feel she wasn't, but she didn't need to know that.

Clarice swallowed. "I'm fine," she mumbled. "I need to get back. How can I go and not die?"

"I'm sorry," he apologized again. "The realm shifts. It's not exact science." She felt his guilt and knew just how bad he felt about her almost falling to her death.

"Just help me leave," Clarice said more softly. "Please."

He didn't want her to go, but she needed space. He knew that. "Come on," Corbin said with a nod towards the door. He reached out and opened the door to check it first. She was behind him, and eager to get out. "You're good," he said, looking at her with uncertainty.

"Thanks," she replied quickly, without looking at him. She went to rush past him, but stepped back to kiss him quickly on the cheek before disappearing out of sight.

His eyes widened, and he froze at her reaction. Corbin didn't know what had possessed her to do it, but he wasn't complaining. The door was still open, and he watched her until she got in the rental and drove away.

Corbin knew the rules. He knew it would cost him. But he always wondered how much was actually true. He slowly reached his fingers ever so slightly into the sunlight left behind her. He felt the warmth on the tip of his fingers just before the door slammed shut, blocking him from following her. *Maybe it was possible? But first, he would have to pay....*

Nineteen

Karmen sat in front with James, as Sophie looked out the window from the backseat. They had rented a Jeep for their excursion. Sophie was too preoccupied with her own thoughts to notice Karmen wasn't looking out the window. She was watching Sophie from the side mirror.

"So," James said, breaking the silence as they rode as far away from the city as possible. "What are we testing first?" He watched Sophie grin from the rearview mirror.

"We can't go crazy. We're not alone," she reminded him, not taking her eyes off the view as she quickly calculated what their options were.

"Karmen, what do you think we should try?" he asked his

copilot. He heard her giggle amongst her steady humming. He was pretty sure she was as excited as they were.

"Here," he heard Sophie request from the backseat, so he slowed the car down and pulled over. They were in the mountains, and able to test, causing no harm. Or so they hoped. Everyone got out of the Jeep with an extra buzz of excitement.

"Speed?" James asked Sophie.

"You will find that's only useful in spurts, not for long-term," Sophie said, with the corner of her lips curled up. "If you're going to stop me from getting out of control, we need to think more outside the box," she replied.

"Scared I'll beat you?" he asked with his boyish grin.

Sophie laughed in a mocking tone. "Doubtful," she retorted. "But it uses up your energy quickly and we shouldn't be here when it gets dark. It will be too cold for Karmen," she reminded him.

James looked at Karmen, who looked a little annoyed that she was the deciding factor in anything, before she went to go play with some rocks off to the side. "I don't think she likes we use her as an excuse," James chuckled in a low tone.

"Well, she can get over it," Sophie said, putting her hands on her hips and standing firm.

"Hey, I'm not arguing, Boss," James laughed as he held up his hands cautiously.

"Focus," Sophie said, giving him her mom's look and shaking her head at him, but her smile betrayed her attempt at being serious. "What's the farthest thing you can see?" she asked.

His brows furrowed at her. "What?"

"What's the farthest thing you can see?" she repeated.

James looked around him and noted a chipmunk several miles away. "There," he pointed. "But what does that have to do with anything?" he asked in confusion.

"Do you know how far away that is from here?" she asked him.

James's eyes widened with realization. "You want to see if I just have your similar gifts, or different ones," he said, intrigued. He had never considered what the options might be. *Did he just match her, or did he have anything to surpass her?* "But mine show up when yours does, it seems," he pointed out to her. "I changed when you did," James reminded her. "Your dad made it sound like that will be a regular thing."

Sophie froze. "I'm sorry, what?" she asked, letting her hands slide down from her hips as her eyes grew wide.

Shit. "He doesn't know anything," James started quickly, but the look on Sophie's face told him it was too late.

"You've been talking to my father? When?" she demanded. He saw the red flames light up in her pupils.

James threw his hands up again. "Easy, Tiger," he pleaded. "They don't know about us," he added more firmly. "But I had to know for myself if I was changing to help you or hurt you," James added honestly.

Sophie shook her head and stepped back, as if unable to accept the words he was saying.

"I know you think you are going to hurt me, and that terrifies you," James pressed on. "But you never stopped to think that I had the same fears," he said, as tears filled his eyes. "I knew I was changing, and I would die before hurting you."

Sophie looked at him. She felt his panic. His frustration. His fear of losing her. The red flames simmered as tears filled her own eyes. "Why do you think I'm so scared?" she gulped. "I can't lose myself and have it cost me you," she said as her voice cracked and her bottom lip quivered.

"But that's the thing," he said, rushing to her and taking her in his arms. "Do you want to know why I know that will never happen?" James whispered into her hair.

"Why?" she asked, swallowing the lump stuck in her throat.

"Because fate didn't throw us together," he lied. "You chose me. I get to change to help you be balanced, because *YOU* chose *ME*."

Sophie pulled away from him. "I don't understand," she said, shaking her head.

"Did you ever see your mom ever hurt your father?" James asked her.

Sophie thought long and hard before replying, "Not that I can remember."

"Even in death, they are stronger than ever, right?" he asked her.

Sophie giggled. "That they are," she confirmed.

"Your mother chose your dad, so fate helped him change to keep her balanced," James said with a shrug, as if it was no big deal.

Balance. Her mother had asked if James gave her balance. Her parents talked of it often. That her emotions couldn't get the best of her. Mario lectured her on it even after death. John also harped on her when she was stuck within herself. It all came down to that single word. *Balance.*

"So, he thinks everything is happening to provide balance?" she asked him.

———

"Even in death, he said he continues to change in order to provide balance," James assured her.

"So, I'm not glitching?" she asked him with sudden hope spreading from her core.

James gave her his boyish grin that always made her knees go weak. "No," he confirmed. "I don't think you're glitching. I think you're changing to stop something that requires you to have powers here and there," he said, confessing his theory. "And I think I'm getting to change to not only help keep you balance, but to help you when the time comes."

Sophie let out a sigh of relief, and James welcomed it as he pulled her closer. However, it was short-lived. Realization set in, and Sophie pushed away again. "What do you think is coming?" she asked nervously.

His face fell a little. "I honestly don't know, but something tells me it will not be good," he confessed. "With all the new players in Karmen's pictures so far, something tells me that the war isn't over, and it may cross both worlds, if not more."

Sophie looked in Karmen's direction. The little girl was very content drawing pictures in the dirt and playing with the surrounding rocks.

"Don't you think we should find out what we can do so far? To keep her and everyone safe?" James whispered to her. "Tina's baby needs to stay safe, too," he reminded her.

Sophie looked back at James with crystal blue flames lighting up her irises and determination etched on her face. "Let's see what you've got," she said, showing off her grin.

Stefanie Wheeler pulled up to the vacant house eagerly. God, she really needed this sale for her friend. How she got roped into covering her friend's real estate appointment was just something she stopped asking herself a long time ago.

Her friends knew they could call her at any time when in a pinch, because Stefanie would do anything to help a friend or family member out. Stefanie was average height, forty-two, with a full figure that made her husband grovel to please her, dark blue eyes and dark blonde curly hair that stopped around her shoulders. Today, she was dressed to the nines and ready to wow this client into buying this house.

Stefanie enjoyed painting furniture, swimming, and books. Today, she was saving her friend Kim, who was tending to her sick child at home. Most loved her for her sweetness, witty comebacks, and heart that always seemed way too big for such a hard knock town.

She straightened up her jacket as she walked up to the front door and extended her hand to a gorgeous redhead. "Hello! I'm Stefanie," she said with a smile.

"Claudia," the woman offered with a smile and nod as she stepped back to allow Stefanie to unlock the door and let them in.

Claudia trailed behind Stefanie as she explained all the benefits of the property with great confidence. Based on Stefanie's read, the woman was quiet but seemed interested. However, when Stefanie turned around to ask Claudia if she had questions, she felt a horrible stab in her stomach. She placed a hand over where it hurt and felt warm liquid fill her palm. Stefanie looked down to find dark red blood oozing out of her.

With a look of shock and confusion across her face, Stefanie looked up and asked, "Why?"

Claudia sighed in noninterest as she reached over to clean the knife off with Stefanie's jacket. With a shrug, she offered, "I'm bored." She tilted her head and watched with curiosity as Stefanie stumbled back and fell to her knees, and collapsed against the bed behind her. "Does it hurt?" Claudia asked her.

Stefanie didn't respond.

"I hear a gut wound is the worst way to go next to being eaten alive," Claudia announced, studying her carefully. "Mostly because there's nothing anyone can do," she continued.

Stefanie finally turned her head to stare at her in bewilderment, but she already couldn't speak. The blood was filling in cavities, making it impossible to do so.

"You will just simply bleed out. Here. All alone. It will be slow. Painful, but quite fascinating to watch if I had the time," Claudia said, looking at Stefanie as if she was a new creature man had yet to discover. She sighed heavily. "But unfortunately, I do not," Claudia announced before turning on her heels and leaving Stefanie to bleed out in the master bedroom of the empty house.

Claudia locked everything up before she left and headed to her next target. Stefanie tried to find her phone, only to realize that Claudia had taken it from her without her even realizing it. So, she sat and waited as she slowly bled out. And after her final breath, she found herself surrounded by fog, as ghostly figures roamed around her.

"Welcome to the dream realm," a blonde headed woman with emerald green eyes offered with a smile.

&

"What is it?" Tina asked Ben. She had been watching him work endlessly, night after night on some sort of serum to put Sophie to sleep, should it come to that.

Ben stepped back in shock.

"Ben!" Tina shouted at him. Her hormones were cutting into her patience.

"I think that will work," he whispered.

"You have it?" she asked eagerly, rushing to his side.

"I mean, it's pure guess not knowing what's going on with her now, but yeah," he half laughed from exhaustion.

"And it won't harm her?" Tina demanded.

"No," Ben confirmed shaking his head.

"What about the serum that Roger gave her to change her chemical makeup so she can never be cloned?" Tina asked him, trying not to sound too doubtful.

Ben looked at her with narrowed eyes. "Why do you think it took so damn long?" he asked her, irritated.

Tina smiled widely as she ran and jumped into her husband's arms. He swung her around a bit before setting her down carefully.

"Finally!" she exclaimed. "Now, let's go get them back!"

"Whoa! You're not going anywhere," Ben said, glaring at his wife.

"To hell I am!" she said, putting her hands on her hips and staring him down.

"Nice try, but I will not risk you and our baby," Ben challenged as he crossed his arms in front of his chest and widened his stance.

Tina glared at him before busting out laughing. "You're so cute when you think you're going to get your way," she said, waving her hand at him and walking out of the room.

"Hey!" Ben shouted before chasing after her.

They both ran into Cecil when they came around the corner. "Have you seen Donna?" he asked urgently.

"No, why?" Ben asked, but the look of distress gave them both the answer.

Cecil just looked around and paced wildly.

Tina's stomach dropped. Donna had told her to stay put. That she was going to get some information from a friend, but that was hours ago. Color drained from her face.

"Are you okay?" Ben asked her as he began dragging her to a chair.

"What do you know, Princess?" Cecil barked immediately.

Tina was having trouble swallowing.

"Easy, Cowboy," Ben warned him as he grabbed the blood pressure cuff and began examining his wife.

"Ben, stop," she whispered. "I'm fine."

"Where's my wife?" Cecil demanded in a snarl.

Daryl, Roger, and Sally appeared immediately at the commotion and placed themselves between Cecil and Tina.

"Easy, big guy," Daryl warned Cecil.

"Where's my wife?" Cecil shouted at Tina.

"I honestly don't know," Tina confessed. "She said she was getting some information from a friend about Sophie and her family. She didn't tell me more than that, but that was hours ago."

Daryl observed Cecil carefully. Cecil moped as his face grew more red. "God damn it!" he yelled.

"What's up, Boss?" Daryl asked him, ready to stop him from spiraling out of control if it came to that.

Cecil looked at Daryl like a rabid animal. "Her last text was that it was taking longer than expected, and she would reach out soon, but soon has long gone," he hissed.

"I'm sure she's fine," Daryl tried to assure him. "She's the only woman I *DON'T* worry about around here," he added, trying to calm his friend.

"She broke protocol!" Cecil snapped, glaring at Daryl with dilated eyes.

Daryl's stomach dropped. Donna wouldn't do that unless she was in trouble.

"What's going on?" Sally demanded, watching all parties carefully.

"Someone's taken Donna," Daryl whispered.

"Who would take her?" Roger asked urgently.

"Ask mama bear over there," Cecil shouted in Tina's direction.

"Knock it off!" Daryl warned him.

"It's true," Tina sobbed and covered her face with her hands.

Ben tried to grab her hands, but Tina just yanked them away and cried harder. Sally bent down and began rubbing her back gently. "What was she trying to find out, Love?" Sally asked her softly. Cecil went to cut in, but Sally held up her hand and gave him a look that made him retreat, slightly.

"We were trying to get the family background to help the boys out with a solution," Tina wailed. Her hormones made her even more ridiculously emotional. "But I couldn't find anything on Rebecca's side, so Donna offered to help me collect information," she sobbed.

"Rebecca?" Sally asked thoughtfully.

Tina sniffed and wiped her nose with her sleeve. "Sophie's alterations stem from her mother, but there was also a rumor that Rebecca had her own alterations. So, I tried to get more information, but there was nothing. Almost like Rebecca didn't even exist! And when Donna found out, she insisted that she could help," Tina informed them as tears stained her cheeks. Ben reached out and rubbed her leg gently.

"And now she's been taken!" Cecil shouted at her.

"Stop it right now!" Sally shouted back as she stood up and placed herself right in front of Tina.

"It was for Sophie," Daryl whispered softly to him.

"I don't care!" Cecil shouted back. "Donna's missing!" And with that, he stormed off downstairs.

"Let him cool off," Daryl warned before following his friend.

"What about Rebecca would have put Donna in danger?" Roger asked himself out loud.

"I don't know, but I think it's time to ask our ghostly friends," Sally said defiantly.

"I'll go," Ben offered, but Sally put a hand on his shoulder and shook her head.

"No, I will go," she said heatedly.

"Not without me!" Roger demanded.

"You just want to take another nap," Sally said, rolling her eyes, but her husband just scowled at her. "Fine. It's time to talk to James's future in-laws," she said as she grabbed her husband's hand and dragged him to their bedroom with Ben and Tina on their heels.

Twenty

Sally and Roger opened their eyes to a wooden door before them. "Ready?" Roger asked his wife as he took her hand in his. He did not know what was on the other side, but they couldn't keep sitting on the sidelines.

"Let's do this," she nodded in determination as she reached out and opened the door. Bright light flooded them instantly, making them blind. They both threw up their free hand to block their eyes as they waited for them to adjust. Once the light dimmed, Sally and Roger looked up to see Jess and Jack standing in front of them with concern etched on their faces.

"Is everyone okay?" Jess demanded, more than asked.

"No," Roger answered. "Donna's been taken, and we need your

help."

"Donna?" Jack asked alarmed.

"Yes," Sally said, irritated.

"We need to talk," Roger said to Jack in his doctor tone.

Sophie. "Alright," Jack replied slowly.

"If you have something to tell my husband, you can say it to my face," Jess snapped in irritation. Jack reached out and grabbed her arm immediately to calm her.

"Easy," he warned her.

"Your lack of honesty with us is why Donna is missing and our children are in danger," Sally cut in with her mama bear instincts igniting.

Jack threw up his hands in surrender and stood between the women. "Okay," he said with a weary smile. "First, we all need to calm down," he said, looking between Sally and Jess. "In here, our emotions are heightened and not always in the best way. There's no need to start something that will have to be finished. Our children don't deserve that."

Jack gave Jess a warning look over his shoulder. She glared at him, but he felt her lower her guard behind him. He smiled and winked his approval, and she stuck her tongue out at him, making him laugh.

Roger squeezed his wife's hand, and she also took in a deep breath to calm herself. Wherever this place was, it made her feel over protective and strange. "I'm sorry, Love," she said hesitantly.

"It's understandable," Jess replied wearily. The realm had shifted its energy since the intruder had entered, and everything and everyone was on edge. It was exhausting, but no one seemed to know how to fix it.

"Please," Jack cut in. "Start from the beginning," he said with an encouraging nod.

Roger and Sally took turns filling in the Harris couple, who resembled their own children. Roger explained they hadn't seen the children since they had left, but there was concern that something had happened that was preventing them from returning. They confessed Sophie's changes before she had gone to face Algos, but Roger would tell only Jack about the serum waiting to force his daughter to sleep should it come to that. He would understand as a father and a scientist. At least, that's what Roger hoped.

"You saw flames in her eyes?" Jess repeated in confusion.

"Yes," Sally was saying.

"That's not possible," Jess whispered to herself.

"I promise you, as a mother, it is," Sally insisted.

"What my wife means to say is no human should have powers like that," Jack clarified. "Powers are only assigned after a person is...well, after a person leaves," he concluded.

"Dead," Jess said, glaring at her husband with a hint of irritation. "I thought she was only ever in a coma?" she asked, jerking her head towards Roger.

"She was," Roger replied. "Ben and I monitored her the entire time. Not once was she ever completely gone. Not vitals wise, that is," he said with a grimace.

"You didn't give her anything, did you?" Jack asked, thinking about when he saw his daughter with his own eyes. He remembered the red flame and the blue. Something had awakened within her, and he still hadn't found the identity or reason of it.

"Only the serum that Elaine had designed to mask her DNA and never be identified," Roger replied.

"You what?!" Jess shouted as she stepped back in shock.

Jack grabbed her arm and pushed his calm through her. "It was just to keep her safe," Jack confessed. "I worked with her on it myself before we left. There wasn't anything that would have caused this," he assured her.

"You knew?" Jess gasped as tears quickly filled her eyes.

Jack gave his wife a stern stare. "You told me to do everything I could to keep her safe, and I did," he warned before turning back to Roger. "Are her eyes the only thing you've witnessed?"

"It's the only physical identifier I could see before she left," Roger confirmed. Jack gave him a nod.

"She had more power," Jess offered, staring into space as she remembered watching her daughter fight at the bunker. "Jack," she gasped as she snapped her head in his direction.

"What?" Sally asked in a shaky, raised voice.

Neither spoke.

"WHAT?!" Sally screamed out as she stomped forward in their direction.

"Someone has entered here that doesn't belong," Jack said slowly, still staring at his wife. "She's looking for someone who is something called a raven."

"What the hell is a raven?" Sally asked as her irritation grew.

Just then, Giselle stumbled into their space. "Oh, sorry!" she said, surprised. "Are these new guests, too?" she asked with a weary smile. The dream realm was growing, and not for the right reasons.

Sally was losing her patience with the cloak and dagger routine, and turned to the innocent girl who was taking her in. "What is a freaking raven?" she asked exasperated.

"A black bird that lives in the Northern Hemisphere," Giselle answered in confusion.

Sally turned to Roger. "I hate this place," she whispered. Roger and Jack tried not to chuckle.

Feeling like she hadn't given a satisfactory answer, Giselle continued. "They're typically confused with the crow, but ravens are much larger with a wider wingspan," she rattled on. Giselle was always known for her random facts, but she rarely got to showcase them here.

Jess smiled at her wearily before replying, "Thank you, Giselle."

However, Giselle was in her nerd mode and happily continued. "Their symbolism takes on various meanings in different cultures, but they typically symbolize the sun. I think it comes from their shiny coats and believing to have the ability to survive the sun," Giselle said with a shrug. "But they're very well-known surrounding death and eternal peace. Some people say if they eat the food you give them after a person passes, it shows they're safe and happy in the afterlife."

Jess went to interrupt Giselle, but Jack squeezed her arm and shook his head. He wanted to see where this was going.

Giselle's eyes grew bigger with excitement. "They're actually super smart and can do shape-shifting. People say they're spell-casters, but they carry great wisdom, affection, healing powers, fertility, longevity, and of course, death. It's granted the greatest of power and is a symbol of mystery, memory, and thought," she added with a triumphant nod. "Ooo, Native Americans believe they transport the energy of a message to its destiny, and they can even heal from a distance. Seems pretty fitting in here," Giselle giggled to herself.

Jess looked at Jack in alarm, but he shook his head at her, not taking his eyes off of Giselle.

"The Celtics believe that the Goddesses of war could change themselves into Ravens," Giselle continued as she went to what appeared to now be a kitchen and grabbed herself a drink from the fridge. Sally's jaw dropped, and Roger's eyes sparkled in fascination.

"Ravens really get a bad rap, ya know," she said with a mope before taking a sip. "People always say that if you see a raven in a dream, it promises death, but that's just not true in all cases," she said, pointing her can of pop at them. "It actually signifies attaining sovereignty of one who's worthy, and utterings of truth that others find unacceptable. You know," she said, taking another sip. "Even though they often eat the dead out of survival, they are a sign of transformation, which I find to be truly beautiful," she finished with a smile. "Although they're quite the tricksters, and not one to piss off because they are quite the fighters and protectors for fighting in what they believe in," she added with a warning.

"Fascinating," Roger whispered, trying to take in the fact that she appeared to be drinking a soda as a ghost.

"Giselle, Dear," Jack began. He paused to craft his question to get the best answer. "Why do you think someone would be in here looking for a raven?"

Giselle burrowed her brows in thought. "Maybe there's war coming, and the raven is the goddess to win it for everyone?" she offered slowly. "Only you would have to catch her early to make sure she was good and not evil," she added.

"You're sure it's a she?" Jess asked for clarification.

"Oh, yes," Giselle nodded. "It's always a female. Typically, the gifts are passed on to the next chosen child, but it can skip a generation," she shrugged.

Roger, Sally, Jack, and Jess looked at each other in a bit of alarm.

"You need to find Sophie," Jess begged Sally.

"Is your mother a raven?" Sally asked, putting the pieces together. "What has she done to Donna?"

"My mother?" Jess asked, confused.

Roger gave Jack a nod. "Was Donna looking into Rebecca?" Jack asked slowly.

"She was," Roger confirmed wearily.

"What about my mother?" Jess asked, taking a step back as her body grew rigid.

"Jess," Jack warned.

"No, I have a right to know!" Jess hissed back.

"We're just trying to keep the children safe," Roger started.

"Why do you need to know about my mother?" Jess asked, on the verge of hysteria.

"Have you lost your mind?" Sally interjected.

Jack pulled Jess close to him. "We know nothing about Rebecca. She was taken from Jess when she was too little to really remember, thanks to Algos," Jack offered with a glare. "She showed up here to block him from coming in here to torment Sophie and the rest of us, and the only thing we know was she was going to collect Sophie from wherever she was while she was in a coma. We haven't been able to locate her since," he said in a low, sadden tone.

A wave a guilt slapped Sally almost literally in her face. "Love, I'm so sorry," she breathed as she ripped Jess from Jack's arms and took her into her own. The men watched in astonishment that they could interact in such a way, but Jess soaked up Sally's warmth as tears stained her cheeks. "How awful to find her and lose her again!" she said, combing Jess's hair.

It was difficult to remember that they were around the same age, when Jess looked no different from Sophie or Tina. Sally wrapped as much love around Jess as she could, allowing Jess to quietly sob on her shoulder.

"I still don't understand how Donna went missing," Jack said as he felt the relief pounding off his wife.

"She said she was meeting someone that had some information on Rebecca," Roger offered in a low whisper. "Then she said it was taking longer than expected. That was the last communication that was ever given," he added in frustration. "You don't think she found out Rebecca was the raven and was taken, do you?" he asked softly.

"You know, that makes sense now," Giselle said as she took the last sip of her soda and tossed it in a trashcan.

"What makes sense?" Jack asked her.

"Ravens can cross easily between the living and the dead," Giselle added, as if that answered everything.

Jess raised her head. "What do you mean?" she asked.

"Rebecca was using hosts to help Sophie and her friends," Giselle replied matter-of-factly.

Jess's eyes ignited red. "You knew my mother was in here?" she sobbed as anger filled her core.

Giselle threw up her hands immediately and backed away. Sally held onto Jess as tightly as she could, but the heat coming off her was too much to bear.

"I only knew her as Rebecca," Giselle confessed quickly. "She found me when Sophie went missing. I didn't know!" she exclaimed. "She made me swear not to tell anyone," she pleaded. "I did it for Sophie!"

"Jess," Jack warned. "You're baking Sally, Dear," he reminded her.

Jess looked at the woman that had been holding her and saw the pain etched on her face. "I'm so sorry!" she gasped, stepping back. "Corbin!" she yelled, but he never came.

"I'm fine," Sally lied as she inspected her now burnt flesh.

"John!" Jess cried.

"Jess!" Jack ordered her.

"I can't fix her!" Jess snapped back.

John walked in with his hood down and fury on his face. "I am not here for you to..." but he froze at the sight of Sally and her burnt flesh. "Jessica," he scolded as he rushed to heal Sally.

Roger went to race to his wife, but the look on Jack's face kept him silent and frozen.

"How's that?" John asked as the blue flames floated over Sally's arms.

"Much better, thank you," Sally said in relief.

"You shouldn't be here, and need to leave," John replied quickly, opening the door behind them to encourage them to go.

"Our friend is missing, and we need your help," Sally said, standing her ground.

John shot a glare at Jack and Jess. "That is not our concern, I'm afraid," he said softly to ease the pain.

"It is when one of your own took her," Sally said firmly, placing her hands on her hips.

"Ma'am, none of my..." John started.

"She was investigating Rebecca and is gone," Sally cut him off, glaring into his soul. She may not be able to set people on fire in here, but that didn't mean they wouldn't get her wrath.

"Rebeca?" he asked, confused.

"They think Rebecca is the raven," Jess almost hissed. John would know more about her mother than anyone being the head of the council of death, and Jess was about to pin him to the wall if it meant getting the answers she needed, but his hesitation gave him away.

"She's part raven. There hasn't been a full raven in decades," John said in a hushed whisper. "And this is a conversation not to be had in here, right now," he warned. The ground beneath them shook and everyone grew quiet except Sally.

"We're not leaving without our friend," she ordered.

John glared at the woman who dared to defy him. "Your friend isn't here," he said firmly. "And I don't know where either of them are," he added to keep her from talking anymore. "We've been looking for Rebecca since she left, and now she is untraceable. Your concerns are not of mine, and you will leave my realm, or I will force you out," he finished with a warning.

"We will see what we can do," Jack interjected quickly, "but understand there are rules and we must obey them," he added with warning.

"They might just be holding someone's place," Giselle said as an after-thought before turning to walk away.

"What did you say, Child?" John asked, willing her to turn back around to them.

Giselle's eyes widen and she froze in fear.

"Giselle," Jack said gently as he stepped around his father and went to the girl. "What do you mean, 'holding someone's place'?" He sent her an encouraging nod and gave her a warm smile.

"When I found Corbin, after Rebecca disappeared," she started slowly. "One of the cloaked figures told me not to bother. He was holding someone's place. He was here, but he wasn't *REALLY* here," she gulped.

Jack looked at John. "Bill came and took Corbin's place, allowing him to come back. I had forgotten," he said, deep in thought.

"What the hell does that mean? Holding a place?" Sally snapped.

John turned to Sally with regret. They weren't supposed to know. This would cost him. "In some realms, one can't leave without being replaced by another." He threw up his hand and Sally found herself unable to speak anymore. "Depending on who came across who, Donna might be holding the place of someone who was allowed to escape," he continued. "There must always be balance, and right now I need you to find my granddaughter and keep her safe," he added.

Granddaughter? Sally and Roger's eyes widened with realization. All of Sophie's family lived in this strange world.

"John," Jack warned.

"I will pay the price," John hissed over his shoulder. "Please," he continued, looking into Sally's eyes. "We will do what we can to save your friend, but it won't matter if you don't find Sophie and Rebecca."

"Rebecca?" Jess asked, confused.

"We can't feel her because she's been transformed again like a phoenix," John clarified. "My guess is she's searching for Sophie, because even as a half raven, in the wrong hands, they are both in danger."

"Is she?" Jess whispered.

"We don't know if Sophie's the raven," John answered her question. "It's too soon to tell, but better to be on the safe side."

The ground rumbled beneath them, almost forcing them to fall over. John hung his head low. "You need to leave," he said regrettably. "I have to go pay for my confession," he said before turning into a black mist and disappearing at once.

"John!" Jack called out in concern, but there was nothing any of them could do.

"Please go," Jess pleaded. "I give you my word. We will find her. For the children," she added.

Sally gave Jess a quick hug and grabbed her husband's arm. "We need to go," she commanded.

"Jack," Roger said softly, putting his hand on his shoulder.

Jack looked at Roger. "You have my permission," he said with a weary smile and nod. "Keep them safe," he added before lightly touching each of their foreheads and sending them back through the door.

Both of them woke up in a gasp.

"Just breathe," Tina coached them.

"Ugh!" Sally groaned.

"Yeah," Ben said, annoyed as he continued to monitor their vitals, "not a fun ride."

Tina scowled at her husband. "Do they know where she is?" she asked Sally as guilt consumed her stomach.

"No, but they're going to look," Sally confirmed as she gathered her senses back. "We need to find Sophie and Rebeca."

"Rebecca?" Tina gasped. "How are we supposed to do that when she's not?.."

"Apparently she is now, and we need to find her before someone else who shouldn't does," Roger said, trying to get off the bed, but Ben pushed him down.

"Easy," Ben ordered. "It takes a few minutes to function again."

Tina grabbed her phone and called the only person she could think of.

"What's up, Buttercup?" Stacey asked on the other end.

"I need help to find Rebecca," Tina replied.

"She's not buried anywhere that I could find," Stacey whined. "I've looked everywhere!"

"She's not buried and we need to find her," Tina cut in.

"I'm sorry, what?" Stacey asked, clearly dropping whatever she had been holding in her other hand.

"Treat it like any other missing person," Tina replied as she walked out of the room. "And Stacey, watch your back," she added with serious concern. Tina heard her gulp on the other end.

"Sure, I mean I'm only looking for a zombie," Stacey tried not to giggle.

"She probably will look like a normal person," Tina giggled before hanging up the phone.

"Sure," Stacey tried to convince herself. "I need to ask for a raise," she mumbled as she slipped the burner phone back into her lab coat pocket, rolled up her sleeves, and got to work.

Twenty-One

Joshua Del Toro had just finished his last massage client, and he was looking forward to getting caught up on reading *The Calculating Stars* by Mary Robinette Kowal. It was his favorite book, and he was rereading it for the fourth time already. His brown eyes eagerly picked his favorite bench in the park, and he settled himself down onto it with excitement.

Winter would come soon, so he wanted to soak up the last of the sun he could get. Joshua knew the Mexican in him would eagerly accept the sun, making him a little darker even this late in the season. At twenty-four, he was living the life he always wanted, and now it was time to spoil himself for all the hard work he had done earlier today. Joshua took a deep breath and opened his book, ready to get lost in its story.

He wouldn't notice the redhead who casually passed behind him and stuck him in the neck with a syringe, sending a mauve liquid directly into his vein. The only thing he would feel was a small prick. As if a bee had stung him.

Joshua pulled his brows together as he raised his hand to rub the irritation away from his neck. However, by the time he would lower his hand to his lap, his eyes would be filled with a strange, warm liquid. When he looked down at his beloved book, spots of blood had rained on the pages.

"What the heck?" he said in confusion. He raised his hand to wipe what he thought to be the start of a bloody nose, but the drops would quickly become puddles as the words got lost in the blood pouring from his nose and eyes.

Joshua gagged as it ran down his throat, and he tried to cry out for help, but his mouth filled too quickly before any words could escape. His body convulsed violently as he slid to the ground. A woman screamed in terror at the sight of his flesh melting away.

Liz watched from the opposite bench with a scowl. "Hmmm," she said. "Might be a bit much."

"Ya think?" Claudia asked sarcastically as she sat down to watch the show. "We only need to put her to sleep. Not to take her out completely," she said in frustration.

"I am well aware of what you require," Liz snapped, not taking her eyes off of Joshua.

Both women sat with their arms crossed, and glared at Joshua as he made a final gurgling sound before his body gave up completely. Parts of his skin and muscle had burnt away, only leaving exposed bone behind.

"Very disappointing," Liz said once he was gone. Then both women got up in silence and went back to the lab to refine their serum.

Clarice stared at herself in the mirror. Her eyes were sunken in more than usual, and the black circles under her eyes were definitely growing darker. *What was wrong with her? She can't feel like she does for someone who's not even alive....*

The cell phone rang, forcing her to jump. "Damn it!" she mumbled and glared at the phone. *It could be about Karmen.* Clarice blew out a deep sigh and stuck out her tongue to the reflection that stared back at her before dragging herself to go answer. "What?" she snapped into the phone.

"There's been two more," she heard Mason announce in frustration.

"What the hell?!" Clarice yelled at the ceiling before rubbing a hand up and down her face. "Who?" she finally demanded.

"A realtor and a massage therapist who use booktok," he announced.

"There has to be another connection besides being a nerd on the internet," Clarice growled.

"Actually, no," Mason confirmed. "Never met in person, either," he added before she asked.

"There has to be a reason!" she exasperated.

"Booktok is much wider and influential than most realize," Mason said with an obvious scowl on the other end. "She wants someone to notice. It's just a matter of figuring out who exactly," he added.

Clarice's memories of Sophie always with her nose in a book flooded to the front of her mind. "Does Sophie use that stupid app?" she asked with a hint of curiosity.

"Even if she didn't, she would hear eventually. There's too many going not to make a connection," Mason replied. "Do you think she's trying to draw out Sophie?"

Clarice's eyebrows furrowed. "I think she wants her busy while she does whatever her actual plan is," she answered. "Keep tracking, but I'm guessing this is all a distraction. That's what I would do," Clarice said, thinking out loud.

"Yes, Ma'am," Mason replied with determination.

"Mason," Clarice said as an afterthought. "How is he?"

"Ashley's making substantial progress from what I can tell. He will be mobile sooner than expected," Mason reported.

Clarice's stomach dropped a bit. *What the hell was wrong with her?!* She cleared her throat to push the lump stuck in it. "Keep me posted," she said before hanging up. She knew he would without her asking, which is why she liked him. Emma, she desired much less. She was no Eddie at finding anyone. *Eddie.*

She felt wetness on her cheek and quickly wiped it away with her sleeve. *What the hell? Did she actually miss the troll?* "Get a grip," she muttered to herself. Clarice couldn't grow soft for anyone. Not now. Not ever. Her father was counting on her to take over. He had left her the necklace and note telling her such. *Or did he?....*

"Shut up," she snapped at no one.

Mario burst through the door, finding Angie sitting on the couch patiently waiting. "Tell me everything, *NOW*!" he demanded.

Angie watched the flames ignite in his eyes, but was aware he was clueless about what he was capable of. "Sit," she breathed as she patted the seat cushion next to her.

"Tell me!" he barked in warning. Angie simply nodded.

"Rebecca is a gifted soul, because they genetically passed her down the gift of being a raven. Well, a half raven," Angie started slowly. She would only give the illusion that he was getting a complete story. It was a story he wasn't prepared to hear. Not yet. "This allows her to have some powers that crossover between the living and the dead." Angie paused and watched Mario impatiently cross his arms in front of him. He wasn't exactly the storytelling type, clearly.

"However, it also means she can be caught between realms, which apparently happened," she said with a frown. "The problem is, if she loses too much power, her body will rebirth itself like a phoenix. I doubt she is even aware that this is the price." Angie stared at the floor in frustration.

"What's this got to do with Sophie?" Mario demanded. Angie lifted her eyes to meet his.

"Because the gift of the raven can be passed down to the next generation, or skip to the one following," Angie continued steadily, but choosing her words carefully. "And without a master to help guide the next raven into understanding their own powers, the raven can choose to give into the power and end up on the wrong side of it." Angie's face remained steady, despite the interrogation it was receiving from

Mario's razored glare.

"Sophie's showing signs of having powers she shouldn't have in her own world," Peter cut in as he entered the room to save his mother.

Mario looked over his shoulder, giving Angie a break from his heated stare, but didn't engage with a response. "So, why can't someone else help Sophie find her way?" he asked, putting his eyes back on Angie.

"If it were that easy, you wouldn't have been traipsing across realms looking for Rebecca," Angie retorted. She was losing her patience. This was a dangerous conversation to be having. It could cost them all everything, and Mario hadn't been here long enough to know or care about that fact.

"So, we lost Rebecca, and she has...been reborn, for a lack of better words," he concluded with a frown.

"She's most likely wondering around with no clue who or what she is, starting from scratch," Peter offered as he walked around Mario to put himself protectively in front of his mother.

Mario took notice of the gesture, but was too preoccupied to analyze it. He also noticed Angie's slight shake of the head, warning Peter not to be so obvious. Something had changed. They were scared. He would have to get his answers some other way. "Why can't we find her, now?" he resided in asking Peter.

"Because the realm connection is broken and lost," Peter offered. "She's just another random human in the pool of 7,937,081,566. Not knowing who or where she is right now is the worst needle in a haystack game to play," he said as his brows furrowed. Mario felt his frustration.

"Will she not look for Sophie?" Mario asked, remembering an earlier conversation he had heard.

"Eventually, she will be pulled towards Sophie, in need to connect with the next raven and pass on whatever gifts she has gained, before she passes on completely."

Jess. Mario's heart broke a little for the woman who always had a special place in his heart. She would lose her mother all over again. "So, what now?" Mario mumbled as feelings he hadn't felt in years began to oddly resurface.

"We wait," Angie said sternly. Mario's head shot up as he glared at her. Angie raised her hand to stop his protest before he could even speak it. "I know it's not your strong suit, but we don't have a choice," she said, closing her eyes to avoid his heated glare. "There are stronger rules with greater consequences here, and you must obey them if you want to remain in Sophie's life," Angie said as she opened her eyes to glare right back at him. She watched the shock and horror flash across his face.

"We'll be watching Sophie, waiting for Rebecca to find her," Peter assured him.

"And what happens if someone finds Rebecca first?" Mario snapped. He watched them both flinch. They knew that was a possibility. One they oddly were willing to accept.

"Sophie will remain safe," Peter assured. "I give my word."

"You're a psychopath's brother who didn't make it past your toddler years!" Mario exclaimed. "Are you kidding me?"

It was Angie's turn to put Mario in his place. Her body lit up in a blinding light, as she warned him, "Watch your tongue. You are in our house now, and you will not disrespect my son." Peter reached for his mother's hand, but she yanked it out of his reach.

Mario didn't flinch. They didn't scare him, but the energy that coursed through his veins at that very moment did. He felt a force turn him around and force him out of the room. At least in the dream realm, he wasn't a literal puppet to be moved around against his will. "Let go of me!" he snapped to no one. He felt the pressure release him, and he stalked away to calm down and come up with a plan to save his goddaughter.

Rebecca had been reborn, making her human again, and impossible to trace. John paced wearily in his own personal hiding place within the realm. A raven flew in out of nowhere and squawked at him. John simply held up his hand.

"Yes, I am aware," John sighed in exhaustion. The raven transformed into a figure he hadn't seen in decades. "Hello, Melanie," he whispered softly.

"John," the woman replied. She was only slightly shorter than John, and black curls cascaded past her shoulders. Her baby blue eyes sparkled with dark humor as her pale skin lit up the room. She was as beautiful as the day they had met. "You don't look well," she scolded.

John chuckled. "Nagging in death, I see," but the look he gave back was of heat and passion.

"Old habits die hard," the woman shrugged. The black gown that covered her flowed easily around her as she came closer. She gently placed her hand on his cheek and watched as they turned rose pink instantly. "What webs we have woven," she sighed.

John gently placed his hand over hers, paused, and then removed it. Melanie sighed, but nodded in agreement, before crossing past him to put some space between them. "What's the next step?" he asked her.

She hesitated. "How is he?" she asked, trying not to choke on the words.

John's heart broke a little. "You've seen him," he replied softly. "Strong. Stubborn. Everything he was as a child."

"Taking after you, clearly," Melanie replied in a playful voice.

John let out a hearty laugh. "Oh, there's both of us in there. Believe me." Melanie spun around at his words.

"So," she spoke slowly. "You remember." Her eyes searched his wildly.

John just blinked. It wasn't safe to say them out loud. Not here.

"But," she said in a rush, coming towards him, but he held up his hand to stop her.

"I met her," he quipped.

"You did?" she gasped. "What's she like?"

"A combination of both," he smiled wearily at her. "I think she's the reason for some of the chaos," he added, observing her.

"We still haven't located the raven, if that's what you're searching for," Melanie replied with a frown.

"So, not Jess?" he confirmed.

He saw her cheeks turn a rose color, showing her irritation in not being able to answer him, but it fleeted as quickly as it came. She simply shook her head and replied, "She hasn't chosen."

"So, you can't find the raven until they choose a side?" John asked eagerly.

Melanie switched back to her nonchalant persona. "It does make it easier. These being extenuating circumstances." She gave a shrug, but the anger in her baby blue eyes made them turn grey. Even John knew that was a sign of danger, as he took a few steps back.

Algos wasn't supposed to kill Rebecca before she knew she was half raven. Corbin wasn't supposed to volunteer to enter the dream realm. Rebecca wasn't supposed to interfere and save Corbin once he arrived. Jessica wasn't supposed to be enhanced, and Sophie was never supposed to gain powers. Especially powers she still kept in the regular world. As if reading his mind, Melanie flipped her grey eyes angrily onto John.

"What?" she hissed.

John immediately threw up his hands in retreat. "I just found out myself," John confessed eagerly.

"Do you know what this means?" she gasped, taking a few steps back.

"That she's the raven?" John guessed.

"No," Melanie gasped. "It's much worse!"

"Worse, how?" John demanded, rushing towards Melanie, but before he could grab her and stop her, Melanie transformed back into her raven form and took off, staying just outside of John's reach. He screamed out, "No!" as he tried to grab her and she disappeared into the blackness.

John fell to his knees and held onto the nothing with all his might as his emotions spiraled out of control. John only knew what Melanie chose to share with him before she passed from cancer. She had a sense about Jess and had made John promise that if Jess chose their son, he was to keep them safe at all costs.

But Algos stepped in and took him away before their relationship had barely begun. John was somehow selected to rule this realm at the cost of losing his memories. It had only been his encounter with saving Sophie from herself that had brought them all back. He should have lost them again once he returned, but he didn't. That put his family in more danger, should the powers above decide he couldn't maintain balance in this delicate world.

Yet, something was wrong. Something was very wrong. He had sensed it when Rebecca came to get them out of Sophie's artificial prison. Now Rebecca was human. Nothing was where it was supposed to be, and Sophie was at the root of it. Melanie had all but confirmed that.

By her reaction, it wasn't good. They had already lost Mario, and Corbin's path had changed to serve Clarice. A new psychopath was running around, going against her own destined path, and there was an intruder in his realm. An intruder he *had* to track down if he was going to get any answers.

He rarely prayed, knowing that it did no good in the end. The powers would take who they needed for their wars in the end, and the rest just had to try to survive in their absence.

John ducked his head down and pleaded with everything that was left in him. "Please, don't let me lose them again. Don't make me destroy the only reason for life that I have been given," he nearly sobbed his request. "And if you could send me the intruder, that'd be a nice bone to throw," he laughed hysterically.

He didn't expect an answer. He simply got to his feet, brushed down his robe, and turned around to find a young African American and Seminole Indian woman standing before him.

"You rang?" Shyera replied cautiously, as she tilted her head to study the man. Her power coursed through her, ready for a fight should it come to that.

John stood gaping at her, unable to believe they had given her so easily to him. Something was wrong. Something was very wrong indeed.

Twenty-two

Clarice splashed some cool water on her face, then looked at herself in the mirror. In the absence of her father, she was finally getting some meat on her bones. She no longer looked like a walking corpse. Her ash brown hair was getting quite long and hung past her shoulders, but it was stringy and needed to be cut. It hadn't been that long since she took her own father's life, and yet she was changing drastically by the minute.

Clarice saw the dark circles that remained under her eyes. Proof that she was getting little sleep. Not because of the guilt she should be feeling at this point, but rather over the consciousness that continued to grow inside her heart. She saw Jess's reflection behind her. "Go away," she growled at the ghost.

"I will not," Jess countered, crossing her arms.

"Fine," Clarice hissed, and turned on her heels to leave the bathroom, only to find Jess actually standing in front of her, smirking. Clarice copied her smirk and attempted to walk through her to make a point, but found she was as solid as the living. "What the hell?" she shouted in irritation.

"They sent me to talk to you. By any means necessary," Jess shrugged casually.

"By who?" Clarice demanded, crossing her arms in front of her chest and glaring down at the 20 something version of her dead little sister.

"The who isn't of importance. It's the why," Jess sighed wearily.

"I don't care what your problems are. Fix them yourself!" Clarice snapped as she pushed past Jess.

"They're not our problems. They're yours," Jess warned, putting her hands on her hips.

"My only problem is *you*!" Clarice exasperated as she slumped onto the bed.

"I'm not your enemy," Jess said with a hint of sorrow. Clarice ignored her. "Fine," she pushed on. "It seems like Algos left you a parting gift," she said, eyeing the necklace just briefly, and raising her eyes to meet Clarice's. "We don't know who it is. Only that they are killing the innocent far too rapidly to get your attention."

"Yeah, I noticed," Clarice mumbled.

Jess tilted her head to the left to eye her sister before continuing. "We're not sure what the reason is, but the dream realm is filling at an alarming rate," she pushed on, trying to sound as objective as possible.

"And you want me to do what?" Clarice sighed, glaring at her sister.

Jess hesitated, making Clarice cackle out loud.

"You want me to eliminate your problem," she said in a sarcastic laugh.

Jess closed her eyes and sighed.

"I thought killing was 'wrong'," Clarice snorted with air quotes and rolled her eyes.

"It is when it's unnecessary," Jess snapped back.

"But this is necessary," Clarice said, leaning forward and putting her elbows on her knees. "To keep your precious dream realm not too crowded?" she laughed sarcastically.

"They're killing the innocent," Jess protested. "They want to do God knows what to you and Sophie."

"Don't act like you care what happens to me," Clarice hissed as she sat up straight.

Jess's eyes watered, but she blinked the tears back. "I have *always* cared what happened to you, and you know it!" she retorted.

Clarice knew she was right, but she was still too stubborn and pissed to admit it. "And if I don't?" she came back.

"The council believes all the realms will fall if we don't stop this plan before it fully plays out," Jess said, staring at her sister. "Not *just* the *dream realm*," she emphasized. Clarice remained quiet. Thinking. "Everyone you know and love will be wiped out," Jess continued. "Everyone," she repeated.

"I love how you think I love anyone these days," Clarice replied, rolling her eyes.

Knowing that naming off the people she knew for a fact that

Clarice loved would only push her to do the contrary, she went in the opposite direction.

"Fine," Jess said casually, with a shrug. "What about the people that love you, regardless? Jack, Sophie, myself, mom, Corbin," she said, ticking each name off with a finger, knowing the last two would get her the most.

"Stop it," Clarice warned, and Jess fought not to smile. Clarice thought of Karmen, Corbin, her mother who she watched die in front of her, their brother, Eddie, and all the others that had cared for her no matter how mean and nasty she was to them and to herself.

"No one will survive this," Jess added sternly.

"Then *you* go deal with it!" Clarice snapped.

"We have another matter to address," Jess said grimly.

"And what matter is that?" Clarice commanded more than asked.

"I'm not entirely sure," Jess answered honestly. "Only that it holds just as much importance, so we really need your help right now." She looked pleadingly at her sister.

"Don't do that," Clarice sighed, waving her hand at her sister's face.

"Do what?" Jess asked, taken aback.

"Those stupid puppy dog eyes," Clarice growled. "It may work on Jack, but it doesn't work on me. Never has."

Jess bit her bottom lip to stop her from laughing at her sister. "I didn't know I had a puppy dog look," she finally admitted.

"Whatever!" Clarice exclaimed as she stood back up. "You used it on me and mom all the time, only I don't buy it," she sighed, but the corner of her lip curled up.

"I see," Jess said slowly. The two stared at each other without saying a word.

"It's really that bad, huh?" Clarice found herself asking to break the silence.

"Yes," Jess said, suddenly staring at the floor. "I think it's going to get a lot worse before it gets better," she sighed heavily.

Clarice watched her sister. There wasn't a lot she had witnessed Jess being bothered about outside of the assignments Algos sent them on. It had been years since she had witnessed so much distress on her sister's face.

"And if I agree," Clarice said in a tone so low, she barely heard herself speak.

Jess looked up. "I expect you to be the one still standing on the other side," said Jess, sticking up her chin in defiance. "And I might actually leave you alone," she added, knowing it was the thing Clarice had begged for the most in the recent time of coming together again.

Clarice started looking at the horrible seventies pattern on the bedroom floor. "You wouldn't have to leave me alone," she said, acting as if she was put out in doing so. "Just stop giving me a damn chore list every time you do," she replied dramatically and dared to look back up at Jess.

Jess bit the inside of her cheek to force her smile from emerging. "I'll work on it," she said with a solid nod. "But you really need to get some sleep. You look terrible," Jess added, waving a hand in front of Clarice's face to stop herself from crying.

"At least I'm alive," Clarice threw back and stuck out her tongue.

"Barely," Jess countered. "But I am sorry that I'm asking you to take a life," she added uncomfortably.

"It's what I do best," Clarice said with a shrug.

"No, it's not!" Jess snapped back.

"Oooo, and I was almost starting to like you," Clarice said as she flopped backwards on the bed.

"You love me," Jess protested as she followed.

"You're blood," Clarice laughed. "Nothing more," she lied miserably.

"Oh, okay," Jess replied, rolling her eyes. Clarice felt the bed dip as Jess laid next to her, just like she used to when they were kids.

"Is this weird?" Clarice asked, waving a hand at her.

"Lying next to you? Naw," Jess said. "I learned to block out your stench years ago," she laughed.

"Honey, being dead doesn't make you smell like roses," Clarice countered. She had missed their sisterly banter without realizing it, and blinked back the tears.

"You need to sleep," Jess demanded.

"You're not the boss of me!" Clarice protested, but felt Jess's finger swipe across her forehead before she could stop her. "Stay," Clarice begged as she drifted off into a deep sleep.

"Always," Jess whispered in her ear, and she felt Jess lay her head on her shoulder. Just like they used to when hiding from their psychopathic father.

The day in the mountains had been more of a bust than James and Sophie had hoped. As much as James tried to poke at Sophie to ignite any new enhancements she may have gained, Sophie knew he didn't mean it. Therefore, she couldn't exactly get riled up when all she felt was love coming from him.

James looked over his shoulder at a sleeping Sophie. Although she had used little power on their excursion, she was still exceptionally drained. James wondered if it was because of the picture Karmen had drawn.

"Karmen," he whispered to the little girl who was rocking and watching cartoons on the television. Karmen didn't make eye contact with him, but tilted her head slightly to show she was listening. "Watch Sophie for me," he said, holding out his fist to her. "I have an errand to run, and I know she'll be safer with you."

Karmen grunted a laugh as a smile spread wide across her face. James kept his fist held out, and for a quick second, Karmen fist bumped him before focusing back onto the cartoon before her. James smiled and gave her an approving nod. Then he grabbed his jacket and slipped out of the room quietly.

James pulled out his burner phone.

We need to meet. Now. -J

He pulled his hood up over his head and went to meet with the enemy.

"So," John stated softly. "You're the intruder roaming my realm."

"You are the keeper," Shyera replied. "I'm not here to do harm."

John put his hands up in a truce. "I am learning that," he answered her. "But I need to know what's going on, so I can protect my own. Surely, you can understand that."

Shyera's nose wrinkled. "I do," she finally supplied with a quick and affirming nod.

"They failed at finding Rebecca, and I'm truly sorry for that. It must make your job that much harder," John offered cautiously.

Shyera put her hands on her hips as she took John in. "Not so impartial, are we?" she drew out slowly. The alarm in John's eyes gave her the answer she needed. "Who changed you?" she asked in a quiet whisper.

"Sophie," John supplied wearily.

Sophie. That name definitely kept coming up, but she had not crossed her yet. *Was she not here?* "Where is this girl?" Shyera asked, trying not to sound too invested.

It was John's turn to take Shyera in. "She doesn't reside in here," he said cautiously. "I think the reason you can't find your raven is because they're not here either."

"Impossible," Shyera said, shaking her head. "That is not how it works."

John laughed nervously. "I'm afraid several things haven't gone as they were supposed to." Shyera jerked her head up to stare at John, and he realized just how much of her attention he had. He sighed heavily. "I'll tell you what I know," he mumbled. "*IF* you return the favor," he added in more of a command than a request.

Shyera squinted her eyes at him. *It would save her time, but what did he really need out of knowing?* This was more than just keeping this realm in existence. Then she realized the price he paid. "This is your family," she said slowly.

John nodded. "Sophie is my granddaughter. Jack is my son. Jess is my daughter-in-law, and Rebecca was Sophie's grandmother on Jess's side," he whispered, barely audible.

Shyera processed the information he had given her. "The existing raven is..." was all she got out.

"My wife," John finished for her.

That was why he was chosen. Although the game board had been shaken up, and the pieces weren't where they were supposed to be, this man was here because he was a piece of the other half of the puzzle. Whether he knew it or not.

Shyera nodded, knowing the information she fed him would be filtered for his own protection. She smiled as John waved his hand and produced a couple of comfy love seats and took a seat. He held out his hand to Shyera to do the same.

Her smile widened, and she took a seat opposite of him. Shyera listened to him recount every memory he had gained since he was trapped with Sophie inside her own mind as she tried to process her own change. It was something she had never heard of a child doing before, and that made Sophie even more dangerous.

Shyera kept track of her reactions to not give that fear away. John didn't need to know that Sophie, herself, could still be the missing raven. Or something far more dangerous should she be forced to choose the other side. This would be something Shyera would have to process later. For now, she simply took it all in.

When it was her turn, Shyera explained just what Giselle had informed him of earlier. Shyera could see his mind, and knew what he already knew, so she simply confirmed it for him. The raven was a gifted spirit that could cross between the living and the dead without limitations.

If they chose good, they were to protect all realms and the creatures within them. If they chose evil, it could destroy every realm if the raven chose to do so, and nothing could stop her. Not even the brother of a psychopath that laid in hiding in the most godly of realms, preparing to take out the raven and the protector if it came to that.

"Melanie fears Sophie is not the raven, and something much worse," John countered with the information he had just been given.

Shyera raised her eyebrows at hearing the raven's human name. "Sometimes the raven's powers can skip a generation. Sometimes, a person can be chosen without the line, such as...Melanie," Shyera forced out.

John's eyes widened, but he didn't interrupt. So, he didn't know they had chosen Melanie against her will, Shyera realized. "Sometimes, when a raven is new, they are assigned a protector," she continued with caution. "It is too early to tell if Sophie would be the raven or the protector. Either way, the reason...Melanie," Shyera forced out again, "is concerned, is because Jessica should never have been enhanced. The powers above clearly could suppress them in Jess, but unable to keep them at bay in Sophie."

"So that makes her more dangerous?" John asked.

"The fact that she's tapping into them already, and unable to control them, makes her dangerous to herself and everyone around her," Shyera clarified. "Sophie clearly shouldn't be able to do half the things she's capable of doing," she added more sternly. "Adding the spirit of the raven to them makes her the strongest weapon in this realm, and all the others."

John sat back and digested that statement. He had watched Sophie consume Rein first hand. Even Rebecca had feared her after that, for the simple reason of not knowing how to control what she had already been given. There had been no reason to. They weren't awoke until then. Now, the one person who could help her was human and a blank sheet again.

"What can we do?" John asked in a shaky voice.

"There's nothing we can do," Shyera replied solemnly. "All you can do is deal with the disturbing increase of guests here," she said more firmly. "Something tells me that problem is going to destroy us all. I will take care of Sophie."

Blue flames ignited in John's eyes, but Shyera remained calm and held up her hand. "I'm not here to harm anyone," she replied flatly. "Rebecca will find her way to Sophie, even if she doesn't remember who she is," Shyera informed him. "I'm leaving your realm to watch over her," she assured. She would not promise she could keep her safe, because she knew that was a promise she might not keep. "If Sophie isn't the raven, then the new raven will also seek Sophie."

John ignited his flames and let his eyes return to crystal blue. "You think the psychopath knows about the raven? That they will try to corrupt them, and force them to choose the wrong side?" he asked in alarm. Shyera's eyes gave her away. John simply nodded. "That's what I thought," he added, deep in thought.

"Can you keep yourself hidden in here safely?" she asked him in a soft voice as she stood up.

"With all my power," John replied unconvincingly.

"Here," Shyera said, taking the necklace off from around her neck and handing it to him. It was of a silver moon. "Keep it under your robe."

"Is this how you hide from us?" he asked with a chuckle.

Shyera laughed in return. "Oh, Child, I don't need a necklace to do that," she smiled wickedly, before she turned and shot fire out of her hands that opened a portal that swirled with red flames. "Good luck, John," she said with a quick nod before she stepped through and the flames went out into nothingness.

She couldn't think about what would happen if the pieces kept going off their destined course. Or the fact that she would be the one sucking the life out of him if the raven ordered her to do so. She wouldn't be in control, but he wouldn't know that. So, Shyera left on good terms instead, and tried not to see the vision of her choking the life out of him with her bare hands float in front of her eyes.

Twenty-three

Clarice sat in a hole-in-the-wall bar chugging her whiskey. It burned her throat, but she didn't care. She hoped it was burning the ridiculous feelings she continued to have for people while it was at it, but she had no such luck. *How the hell could she have feelings for a dead guy, anyway?*

Who was she trying to kid? It wasn't just feelings like lust to fill a void when she got, well, frustrated. It was something much more foreign, and she did not care for it at all! She was missing the troll, giving a damn about some strange child, and even the thing she had hunted her whole life meant at least a little to her. "Fuck me," she mumbled as someone in a black coat sat down next to her.

"No thanks, I'm taken," James chuckled as he shook off his coat and flagged down the bartender. "Your best local beer, please," he said, giving the woman his boyish grin.

"What do you want?" Clarice growled as she held up her empty glass, signaling the girl to get her another. The bartender just frowned and walked away. "Lovely," Clarice grumbled, and set her empty glass on the bar. "Karmen okay?" she asked, trying not to sound like she cared. From the smile on James's face, she had failed miserably.

"Karmen's fine," James replied, nodding to the bartender. "Sophie's fine, too," he added. "Please get another for my friend," James told the bartender, nodding in Clarice's direction. The bartender lost the googly eyes and million-watt smile she had produced to James to glare at Clarice before rolling her eyes and heading off to get her another whiskey.

"So, I'm your friend now?" Clarice asked with a sneer on her face.

"Well, technically you're family, but we'll work our way up there," he laughed as he took a swig of his beer.

The bartender gave Clarice her whiskey with much less enthusiasm than she had served James with and stalked away. The boy was definitely a charmer. She could see why Sophie liked him so much. Even though the girls fell at his feet, he would see no one other than her niece. She was impressed and irritated at the same time.

"What's so urgent?" Clarice asked. "Being out in the open isn't good for either of us," she reminded him.

"I really need your help with something," he said, keeping his eyes forward and sipping on his beer.

"I love how you assume I do favors for you now," Clarice sneered, and took a sip of her whiskey. "Out with it," she ordered, watching his reflection in the mirror behind the bar while keeping an eye out for any redheads.

"Sophie seems to have some new tricks," James started slowly.

"So, I noticed," Clarice said flatly as she watched him struggle with his request. "She's not okay, is she?" she finally asked, breaking the silence.

James sighed and spun the beer bottle in his hand. "No. I don't think she is." He noticed Clarice sit up a little straighter. He had her full attention.

She pulled the glass to her lips. "Does Jess know?" she asked in a low tone before taking a small sip. She didn't look at him, but rather studied his reaction in the mirror.

"No," he said flatly as he took another sip of his beer.

Intriguing. Why not just tell her parents?

"We tried to see what the new...options were," he continued on carefully.

"And?" Clarice asked with interest. She stopped watching the room and put all of her attention on James's reflection in the mirror.

"They seem to be motivated by emotion," he said in a low voice. "But I only trigger one," he said with a frown.

Realization set in, and Clarice threw her head back and cackled. "You want me to piss her off, then?" she laughed as she sipped on her whiskey.

"Well, you do have the gift of riling her up," James replied with his best boyish grin.

"And who keeps me safe from the wrath?" Clarice laughed as she set her drink down and shook her head in disbelief.

"Well, that's the other part," he said cautiously with a shrug.

Clarice jerked her head up and narrowed her eyes to study his reflection. "No," she said in disbelief, as if she could read his mind.

"We need to figure out what we both can do," he said with a guilty grin as he took another sip.

"So, let me get this straight," Clarice said, as she tilted her head and popped her neck loudly. "I'm supposed to piss her off to see what she can do, and trust that you will be able to stop her?"

"Well," James said with a shrug, "yeah".

"I'm supposed to trust that you, of all people, would keep me safe. From her?" Clarice couldn't finish the sentence with a straight face. She held up the empty glass, and the bartender rolled her eyes, yet again, but made another.

"How many of those have you had?" he asked, suddenly realizing she may not be in the right state of mind to be discussing this.

"It's not your concern," she growled back, only looking slightly over her shoulder. "What else?" she barked out.

"That's it," James replied with a frown, trying not to look at her.

"You're a shitty liar," she said in a slur. "What. Else," she demanded.

James wanted to get up and walk away. She would not help them, and he was stupid to ask her to.

"Show her," he heard Corbin whisper in his ear.

"No," he mumbled back.

"Show her," he heard Corbin add more firmly. "She needs to know."

Clarice watched James ever so slightly roll his eyes to glare at the ceiling above them.

"Glad I'm not the only one they annoy," she cackled as she

grabbed the glass from the bartender before she could even set it down.

"That's the last one," the bartender warned, before stalking away.

James hung his head down and gave it a shake. Then he pulled out Karmen's last drawing of Sophie and slid the folded paper across the bar.

Clarice recognized Karmen's drawing paper immediately. "You said they were okay," she whispered in a cracked voice.

"Just open it," James said as he sipped his beer and kept his eyes front.

Clarice put her glass down and took the paper into her shaking hands. She pulled it under the bar before she dared to open it. It was Sophie, up in the air and in flames. That's not what scared her ironically. It was the fact that she was facing a much darker looking Sophie who grinned back at her from the ground. Clarice sobered up immediately.

"Two?" she asked. That wasn't physically possible. Clarice had spent her whole life not only hunting the original Sophie down, but she also made sure her father would never be able to clone her. *Had she failed and not known it?*

"Well, there's one physical version," James said slowly. "This is what Karmen saw while Sophie slept."

Clarice couldn't take her eyes off of the Sophie on the ground. She knew that smile. She knew that look in her eyes. That would be the version of Sophie had her father achieved what he wanted. Clarice quickly folded up the paper and shoved it back to James under the bar. "I can't help you," she said as she got up in a daze.

———

"We'll be in the mountains again tomorrow," he said in a raised voice as she was walking away. Clarice froze, but kept her back to him. "If it's any consolation," he said a little lower, "I'm pretty sure you're the only one who can. I'll send you the coordinates in case you change your mind." Clarice stalked off and James paid the tab and rushed back to Sophie.

He paused in the hallway before going to the room. "Any help you can give would be greatly appreciated," he said to no one as he stared at the ceiling.

"I'm working on it, Son," he heard Corbin reply softly in his ear. James knew he was telling the truth, but he wasn't sure anyone could get through to Clarice. No matter how much he found himself wanting her to.

James sighed heavily, and his shoulders slumped forward as he continued down the hallway. When he slid the door quietly open, he found Sophie cradling Karmen in her arms. He smiled and closed the door quietly behind him, before sliding off his coat and going to join them.

Despite her overwhelming guilt, Tina was out the second her head hit the pillow. However, when she opened her eyes, something wasn't right. She was surrounded by black fog. If this was the dream realm, it was a part she hadn't experienced yet. "Hello?" she called out cautiously. No one answered. "Jess?" she tried again.

"Stop your yelling, Child," came a deep female voice she didn't recognize.

Tina froze. Out of the fog strode a lusciously curved woman who looked like a queen, with skin autumn brown and as smooth as a moonstone, and hazel eyes that matched the sun. Tina took a few steps back as she approached and watched the woman calmly hold up a hand to stop her.

"You're not in any harm. Either of you," she said, nodding toward Tina's stomach. She threw a protective hand over it, regardless.

"Who are you, and what do you want?" Tina demanded.

"I've seen your fate, and I'm here to tell you not to be scared," the woman whispered.

"My fate?" Tina asked, half in alarm and the other half in anger. "What the hell is my fate?"

A black raven swooped in and landed on the woman's shoulder, clutching it hard. The woman winced before glaring back at the bird.

"I'm not allowed to say," she said through a clenched jaw, still glaring at the bird. "But it all has a purpose. Just like the little miss inside you, now," she replied, finally turning back to look at Tina.

"Little miss?" Tina whispered, looking down. They hadn't determined the sex of the child yet. She was just starting to show a tiny bump at twelve weeks. "How do you?..." Tina started.

The woman and the bird stepped closer. "Because there's a lot more to this world than people know," she replied in a motherly tone.

Tina stared at her blankly for a second before she doubled over and started laughing hysterically. The woman took a step back in surprise and concern as she watched Tina switch rapidly between laughing and crying hysterically. "Don't I know it!" Tina gasped out between laughs.

The woman looked at the bird, and it just raised its shoulders as if to shrug.

Tina straightened up, trying to collect herself again. "Sorry," she giggled. These hormones have me on overload. "And you are?" Tina asked, holding out her hand for a shake.

The woman looked her up and down before stepping forward again and shaking her hand. "Shyera," the woman said cautiously.

"Sorry," Tina said, wiping a tear from under her eye. "It's been a very long couple of months," she announced. "So, I take it it's not going to be pleasant," she added with a frown.

"Neither of you will be harmed," Shyera confirmed with a solid nod.

"And Sophie?" Tina asked as she rubbed her belly gently.

Sophie. There was that name again. "I haven't seen her," Shyera replied honestly. She really didn't care to lie any more than she already had. It didn't sit well with her inner spirit, even if it wouldn't have a choice soon.

Tina eyed the woman. "So, why tell me?" she asked more rigidly.

Shyera stared at the invisible floor, then brought her eyes back to Tina. "You're being taken out to hinder the raven. I need you to prepare in advance so that the line of destiny gets no more fractured than it already has been," she replied with a frown.

Was this what Donna had found? "Can you see where Donna is?" Tina asked urgently. The response of confusion gave her the answer.

"I only came to warn you. So, you could prepare," Shyera said truthfully.

"But how long will I be 'out'? What preparations do you need me to make? Are you sure this won't harm...her?" Tina asked, looking at her tiny bump.

Shyera smiled. "The puzzle solver," she nodded in her own recognition of why Tina was being removed. She turned to the bird. "They think she will know too much too soon, and that's why we have to save her?" she asked quietly, but not quietly enough.

Tina snapped her head up to stare at the pair. "Who are 'they'?" she demanded. The bird only squawked at Shyera, who nodded in return before turning her attention back to Tina.

"Prepare, Little One. She's coming for you, that's all you need to know," Shyera said confidently before holding out her hand as black fog circled around Tina and gave her a gentle hug before forcing her to wake up. She sat up, gasping for air.

"What's wrong?" Ben demanded.

Tina took a couple of deep breaths. "New player," was all she could get out before falling back onto her pillow into a deep sleep.

John met Jack in the realm of the slain lion. *Peter.*

"What are you doing here?" Jack asked, concerned. "Sophie?" he hissed outside of Jess's reach.

"No," John lied. "Why do you look for this 'Donna person' when there's more pressing matters in the realm?" he asked, concerned.

Jack sighed heavily. "That 'Donna person'," Jack mimicked his father's quoting fingers, "helped raised Mario. Who, in turn, raised your granddaughter and kept her safe," Jack replied softly. "We owe him that much."

John studied his son, trying not to let the pride show, but his eyes failed him. Jack caught it and put his hand on his father's shoulder.

"You remember?" he asked in shock.

John shrugged his hand off his shoulder and held his index finger to his nose. This was the sign he used to give Jack when he needed to stop asking questions out loud and do his own research. He watched Jack's mouth drop before he recovered quickly.

"Is the realm safe?" Jack asked worriedly.

"It's getting awfully crowded," John replied, with a line creasing his forehead.

"But Sophie," Jack started.

John held up his hand. "Everyone is a new face," he replied. "Apparently from some booktok community," John said with a shrug.

"A what?" Jack asked.

"It's a living thing," John waved his hand as if swatting away a bee. "Something called social media, where they don't actually meet in person, but through the web?" John remembered the internet. He remembered how much he despised Facebook, but this TikTok app was a whole different beast all together.

"You said booktok?" Jack asked, deep in thought.

"Yes," John replied in frustration. "A community of book lovers." His own comment made him think of Sophie sorting her memories into books that filled a glorious library within her head. "You don't think?..." he trailed off.

Jack scowled. "She stays off the grid, but if you were going to get her attention, going after people who loved books like she does..."

he said slowly. He looked in the direction John assumed Jess was searching and looked torn.

John put his own hand on Jack's shoulder. "She's being taken care of," he assured. "Find this," then he stopped himself. "Find Donna, but Jack," he warned. "What's your plan if she has to be replaced?"

Jack didn't take his eyes off from the direction of his wife. "I will take care of it," he said with determination.

John squeezed his shoulder. "Let's make sure it doesn't come to that," he whispered with a crack in his voice. Jack turned his head back to his father, smiled weakly, and gave him a nod.

"Go, before she sees you," Jack warned, and before he could say anything else, John was gone.

Jack knew there was more going on than his father was sharing, but knowing his father remembered like he had suspected gave him assurance that he would keep their daughter safe. Finding Donna meant leading them to Rebecca and her past. A past Jess deserved to learn, and he would give that to her. Even if it was the last thing he did.

Tina felt the blood pressure cuff squeeze her arm until it hurt and listened to the beeping of machines around her. "Benjamin," she whined as she rolled her head around, trying to make the room stop spinning.

Once her eyes focused again, she noticed she wasn't alone. Literally, everyone was watching her, and it was Daryl who gripped her hand, holding a rag on her forehead.

"I'm fine," she snapped as she tried to sit up, but Daryl's large hand kept her in place. "Unless you want to lose that hand, buddy, get it off me," she snapped. She felt the hesitation, but Daryl helped her sit up slowly.

"You're meaner, prego," he huffed out, before getting up to let Roger replace him.

Guilt consumed Tina. "I'm sorry, Daryl. It's really hard to have so many people manhandling me," she mumbled. "I'm just not used to it," Tina replied honestly, giving him her best puppy dog face.

"Knock it off," Daryl grunted. "You know you're still my favorite," he added with a smile.

"Likewise," she smiled sheepishly back.

"Could you two please stop flirting so my wife can tell us what's going on?" Ben asked sourly. Tina shook her head while smiling and grabbing her husband's hand in hers.

"I'm not sure, truthfully," Tina started. She described the woman she saw, and the raven. Tina left out the warning, and the gender reveal. She was pretty sure those messages were just for her. "She seemed friendly, but in this game, you just never know," she said with a frown.

Ben eyed his wife suspiciously. "So, what did she *really* want?" he asked, calling her out.

Tina rolled her eyes. "Fine. I asked her about Donna, and she didn't have a clue. I asked if she had seen Sophie, but she said 'no'," she replied in a huff.

"So, what did she want, then?" Roger asked, deep in thought.

"I think we met by accident," Tina said with her brows creased as she thought of the bird, who seemed to interrupt Shyera from telling her more.

"What do you mean?" Ben demanded.

"I mean, when I opened my eyes, there wasn't a door. Just fog. Only Sophie has done that a couple of times, and even Sophie doesn't know she does it," Tina offered while crossing her legs and resting her chin in her hands. "I'm pretty sure I was in the dream realm, but not brought in as we usually are. I think it was very unplanned and not supposed to happen that way," she continued in thought.

Sophie was scared of herself. That's why they weren't coming home. To keep Tina and her baby...girl safe. Tina uncrossed her legs and dangled them off the side of the bed. "We need to get to Sophie. I think something is coming, and people are changing without knowing what's going on," she added as she pushed off and got to her feet. Roger still held onto her.

"You're not going anywhere," Ben demanded.

The look Tina gave in return had even Roger dropping her hand and stepping back. "Sophie and James are family," she hissed. "We don't leave our family behind."

Ben gulped before he tried again. "I will go. Daryl will come, too. But I really need you to..." was all he got out before Tina was standing before him.

"Benjamin," she started in a warning motherly tone. "You will not smother me through this pregnancy. Besides," she added. "I'm pretty sure I'm supposed to go," Tina said truthfully. Even if the ending didn't sound like it was going to be ideal. "We don't need to fear Sophie. She does enough of that herself. We're her family. We are here to help ground her so she doesn't get lost in herself," Tina said softly, as she ran her hand down Ben's cheek. "I need us all to be together for

Christmas," she added pleadingly.

Ben's eyebrows came together. She knew he hated the idea, but she also knew she was right. And so did Ben. He forced a smile onto his face. "Let's go get the rest of our family," he replied, grinning.

Daryl slapped him on his back with a bag already on his back. "Wise choice, man," Daryl replied, winking at Tina. Sally held out Tina's bag for Daryl.

"We'll have the place decorated and ready for when you get back," Sally said with an authoritative nod.

"I seriously get no say anymore in this marriage?" Ben asked, sulking.

"Just wait until there's two of us," Tina said with a wicked smile and winking at Sally. She bit her bottom lip, knowing just what Tina was implying. The excitement spread across her face for just a second as she fought to contain it. Sally nodded at Tina and winked back. The three prepared to ride in search of their missing family that had been left behind.

Twenty-four

Claudia looked at herself in the mirror in front of her. She still looked the same, as far as she could remember, but she didn't *feel* the same. Not by a long shot. There was a loud knock at her door, but she ignored it. The door shook with the force of the knock on the other side, making Claudia just roll her eyes. "What?" she snapped.

The door opened, with Duke's oversized body barely fitting into the frame.

"What do you want?" she asked, intrigued, as she looked at the man's reflection instead of her own. The man never came near her. For being a *Men in Black* wannabe, he was very much a scaredy-cat when it came to Claudia.

"I have instructions to give this to you," he said with a tremor as he shoved a small black box in her direction.

"What is it?" she asked, eying it with suspicion.

"No clue." He shrugged and made another shove in her direction, not daring to enter the room.

"Tell Liz I don't want her sappy gifts," Claudia said as she went back to looking at her own reflection.

"It's not from Liz," Duke said, looking down at the box. "It's from your creator."

"Liz made me," she said in irritation as she looked back at Duke's reflection.

"No. She didn't," Duke replied, shaking his head at her.

Flashes of the old man holding her outside of the library as her body quickly became paralyzed, and the excitement that looked back at her was terrifying. "The man," she said slowly to herself.

"His name was Algos," Duke continued, "and he left this behind for you in case something ever happened to him."

Claudia turned to walk towards Duke, who took all of his strength not to step away from her and show fear, but she could smell it on him all the same. She looked at the box with a bit of excitement brewing from her core. She took the box gingerly from his hands and whispered, "Thank you," as she continued to stare at the box.

"You're welcome," he replied in a bit of surprise.

"I won't kill you, you know," she added as he turned to walk away. He froze immediately. "You're the only one who is honest with me. You are...my only friend."

Duke didn't move for a long time. He was paid to help be the muscle for the girls, but he was having a hard time wrapping his mind around her statement. "I'm designed to take care of you," he said quietly. "Not lie to you."

Out of the corner of his eye, he caught her slight nod before she closed the door. *Friend?* Duke only hoped that would still be the case once she opened the box. He didn't know what was in it, but coming from Algos, it wouldn't be anything good. Duke tried not to think about it as he hurried to put as much distance as possible between them.

Claudia never took her eyes off the box as she locked the door and carried it carefully to her bed. She sat down next to it and took off the lid with all the care she could.

There was a yellow envelope with the letter *C* scribbled on the front. It was thick, and she guessed there was another letter inside. She picked it up and saw a syringe with bright red liquid glowing from within it. "Interesting," she muttered to herself, before flipping the envelope over and opening it. The letter was several pages long and handwritten.

Dear Claudia,

If you have received this letter, it means I have lost my game of chess. However, I learned from an early age that no plan would be fully successful, and backups were always needed. You are my favorite backup of all.

I chose you for several reasons. Some being that you were well advanced beyond your peers, so you were smart enough to pull off the plan in place. You also look very similar to the daughter that held the most promise of replacing me in my death, but chose not to follow her destiny. Although my own daughters have done nothing but fall short of my expectations, I know you will be the daughter I was always meant to have.

The syringe contains a serum that will give you everything you need to finish what I started long ago. It would be a true honor to have you replace me in the game that I was always meant to win. One way or another. I'm sorry that I haven't been able to watch you turn into the best version of yourself, but fate had its own ideas. Of course, that doesn't mean that I'm done playing.

You are my legacy. My greatest creation yet! And the daughter I was always meant to have. Attached is the plan I expect you to fulfill in my absence in return for gaining all of your enhancements. Should you choose not to follow my plan exactly, know that you will not survive to see the end of anything.

I'm sure that Clarice has found your necklace I have left for you as planned. It will bide you time until you are ready to take it back for yourself. Don't let me down. I would hate to have you taken care of before we even begin.

Sincerely,

Algos

She held a few more pages in her hand that she casually flipped through. "Enhancements, huh?" Claudia announced with intrigue as she eyed the syringe. She was pretty sure that Liz knew as much about the mysterious red serum as she did, which made it even more enticing to have the upper hand for once.

Claudia frowned. Every gift had a consequence, and she had no idea what promises and curses the serum held. She flipped through the letter and realized that Algos had conveniently left any of that information out. Something told her that wasn't surprising.

Claudia held the serum to the light and only saw that it glowed bright red, with promise, evil, and intrigue. She laid down carefully on the bed in case it knocked her out, placed the needle on top of her good vein in her arm, closed her eyes and shoved the needle in while pushing the button down.

Her head flew back as she gasped from the pain. Her eyelids fluttered as her eyes rolled back before she collapsed onto the pillow behind her. It felt that her veins were on fire as the serum raced through them. When it reached her brain, she grabbed her head and fought not to scream from the pain. She drew her knees into the fetal position and sobbed as what goodness remained was killed instantly.

Claudia gasped for air as her heart rotted and all empathy, awareness of right and wrong, inhibition, and freewill were burned away by the serum. When she opened her eyes, they were black as coal, and her sinister smile had a life of its own. She sat up cautiously and looked at the reflection in the mirror.

She had longer hair. Her features were even more inviting. Claudia's soul was no longer in existence. "Well, hello," she said to the reflection in the mirror. It winked back and gave her a solid nod of acceptance. Her rebirth was complete, and the world was in a lot more danger....

"I have to pee before we go!" Tina called out, walking quickly to the bathroom.

"Again?" she heard Daryl whine and Ben apparently elbowing him in the stomach according to his grunt reply. Tina rolled her eyes and pulled out her burner phone.

"What's up, Boss?" she heard Stacey chirp gleefully on the other side of the line.

"Write this address down," Tina said in a quick, hushed voice. She rattled off the address of where they were going.

"What's this for?" Stacey asked in curiosity.

"If anything happens to me, and you don't hear from me in two days, I need you to show up here to finish the job," Tina hissed through the phone. She didn't want the boys to hear her.

"What?" she heard Stacey gulp on the other side of the line.

"Stacey, I need you to do this," Tina replied firmly. "I'm going to be okay. I just need you to come and finish what we started. Okay?"

"No, *NOT OKAY*," Stacey hissed back. "Most *DEFINITELY NOT* okay!"

"Freshman year," Tina said with a smile.

"Stop it! That's not the same!" Stacey snapped back.

"I'm pulling my card," Tina giggled at her. "But I have to go. Two days," she emphasized.

Stacey didn't respond.

"Two days," Tina repeated more firmly.

She heard Stacey sigh heavily into the phone. "Fine! Two days," she hissed back. "And you'd better be coming back!"

"Well, if I'm not, I'm hoping you'll help Sophie come get me," Tina said, staring at her tiny bump in the mirror. "You're the only one smart enough I trust to do so," she said with a frown.

"Two days," Stacey mumbled back.

"I love you!" Tina whispered into the phone before hanging it up, stuffing it in her backpack, and flushing an empty toilet for good measure. She washed her hands and left the bathroom with a smile on her face.

"You okay?" Ben asked her.

"I am now," Tina replied with a sigh. "Let's go get our girl!" She grabbed both men by the hand and dragged them out of the building behind her.

🔥

She ran until she found the road and threw her hand up to her eyes to shield them as headlights blinded her. She heard the wheels squeal to a halt before it nearly hit her.

"What the devil?" shouted an old man in his late seventies as he got out of his pickup truck. "Are you trying to get yourself killed?" he asked in frustration.

The woman looked around her wildly, trying to get her bearings. Her hazelnut hair with white streaks was pulled back in a ponytail and swishing around her face as she did. She had a "Be Kind" t-shirt on with jean shorts, and tennis shoes. Not proper attire for these parts during this time of the year.

The old man studied her, before asking her more gently, "You're not from around these parts, are you?"

The woman froze to stare at the man. His eyes were a gentle blue, and he had on a camo hat and matching shirt under a thick leather jacket. His jeans were worn, and his boots proved they had provided a lot of use for the old man. She gave a quick shake of her head "no". Her pure blue eyes were wide and full of terror.

"Well, you can't stay out here dressed like that," he said with a frown. "Come on, now," he ordered as he opened the passenger door. The woman shook her head "no" again, causing the man to put a hand on his hip. The woman saw the gun holstered at his side immediately and took a step back. The old man seemed to not notice.

"As a Christian man, I cannot leave you out here to freeze to death or be eaten by the wildlife," he commented as his white bushy eyebrows came closer together. He had a snow-white beard and mustache to match. "It would leave me up all night with worry, and I'm too old. My heart couldn't take it."

The woman looked down at his chest and listened to it tick slowly. She heard a delay in the pumping of the heart that was ever so slight, and she heard the minor blockage of an artery or two. Although his storm grey-blue eyes showed irritation that she was even thinking about this, they didn't hold any malice behind them.

Her hot skin was cooling off, and she could feel the chill in the air. The old man was right. She needed to get out of the cold. She hung her head down to veer off the gust of wind that suddenly whipped around them while a raven squawked from the tree above her. She nodded "yes" to signal to the bird she was going and climbed into the truck before the man slammed the door behind her.

Once inside, he turned up the heat and stretched his arm behind her. She flinched and response, but he said nothing as he pulled up a spare coat for her to put on. Once she had more layers on her, he tried again. "Do you have a name?"

The woman looked out the front window as her brows came together in concentration. She heard the name *Rebecca* be whispered into her ear. "Rebecca," she said slowly and in a hoarse voice.

"I always liked that name," the old man offered with a smile. "Where are you headed?"

She closed her eyes and searched the visions that floated quickly in front of her. A girl with a boy who held onto another little girl's hand got stuck in front of her eyes. The point of view shifted to be from the girl's as she looked down and saw the male hand that held her own. She felt the warmth and happiness that came from that single sight. However, it was quickly replaced with panic and then anger.

The old man watched as the woman tilted her head with her eyes closed, as if searching her memories. "Provo," she answered with determination once she reopened her eyes.

"Provo, Utah?" the man asked in surprise.

"Yes," Rebecca replied firmly.

He contemplated his options, but it didn't seem right to only take her part of the way and make her fend for herself. Something had clearly happened to her, and he felt a need to make sure she got to where she needed to go. "We're a day's drive away, but if that's where you need to go, I would feel a lot more comfortable being the one to make sure you get there," he finally answered.

Rebecca turned her head and flashed a big smile at the man. "Thank you, Bruce."

The man froze. "I don't remember telling you my name," he said with obvious terror in his voice. His eyes met Rebecca's, and they dilated to full on black.

"You did," Rebecca said sweetly. "And now you are taking me to Provo, Utah. I have very important business to attend to there, and you want to make sure I arrive safely," she added.

____

"I do," Bruce nodded, as if in a trance. Rebecca turned to look out the window next to her, and Bruce shook his head, trying to clear it. "Let's go to Provo!" Bruce announced eagerly, as he put his truck into drive and headed down the road again. Not sure why he was going there. Only that his life depended upon it.

Mario came up on a woman in a black t-shirt that said "Follow Your Dreams" on it, a pair of jean shorts, and some tennis shoes sitting on a couch. They really loved their couches around here. Her whitening bob framed her face ever so perfectly as her glasses barely showed over the book she held before her. *The Silent Patient* by Alex Michaelides.

There was something about her that was ever so familiar, although he was sure they had never met. Mario walked over and took a seat. "So, what are you in for?" he asked casually.

"Oh, the usual," she said, flipping the page. "Sacrificing myself to help people that typically proved not to deserve my saving," she ended with a shrug.

"You look familiar. Have we met?" he asked, turning to her.

The corner of her mouth curled up in a smirk. "You wouldn't remember if we had," she said slyly, not taking her eyes off the book.

"Ouch!" Mario claimed, placing his hand over his heart and faking pain.

"Your ego will be fine," she laughed and continued to read.

"Is it any good?" Mario asked, nodding his head at her book.

"For the most part," she replied flatly.

"Oh?" he asked in sudden interest. "What's wrong with it?"

She turned the page, clearly reaching the end before finishing the paragraph and putting it down. "How can I help you?" she countered.

Mario's brows furrowed. "Who said I need help?" he asked defensively.

"You're harassing me during my reading, clearly not taking the hint that I would rather read, because whatever you're struggling with is more important," she said flatly, but with her mouth in a smirk, accepting his challenge.

"I'm just not good at sitting around and doing nothing when I know the people I love are in danger," he huffed, sitting back and crossing his arms in front of him.

"Ah, yes," the woman replied, sitting back and mimicking his form. "It's incredibly frustrating when you've spent your whole life thinking that the rules don't apply to you, and you're suddenly forced to obey them," she replied condescending.

Mario laughed a big hearty laugh out loud. "So, we have met?" he said with an eyebrow raised.

The woman remained silent, but something told him they had. "Well, the best I can offer," she started breaking his train of thought, "is that when you stop fighting your destiny, it gets a lot easier, and life gets a lot more enjoyable."

"Life?" Mario cackled. "We're dead."

"Are we?" she asked, daring to stare him down. It sent a powerful chill down his spine. "There's a reason there are rules," she continued. "If everyone got to be an asshole that did whatever they wanted, thinking the rules never applied to them, the world would be the worst place to live in. Being ruled by bullies, with no balance, and no good left to fight for." She placed her hands on top of the book as she crossed her legs. "There would be no love, only bitterness and hate. What kind of world would that be for Sophie?"

Mario's eyes opened in shock. He hadn't mentioned Sophie. Ever. The woman simply held up her hand to stop him from speaking. *Why did all the women here think that was the best way to silence him?*

"I have ears, and I'm not Deaf, yet," she simply shrugged. "But from personal experience, a story will unfold in its own way, and on its own timeline. You can force it all you want, but you'll just be more frustrated the more you try." The woman looked down at the book, and then handed it out to Mario.

"I thought you said this wasn't any good?" he asked in confusion at her offer.

"Oh, it's very good," she corrected. "Well, until the end. The bad guy gets caught because he makes the most rookie mistake ever. All because he had no patience to wait and make sure his destiny had been fully fulfilled," she smirked and shoved the book at him. He took it and looked down at the title. "You should read it," she said firmly. "It's a real who done it, and you won't see the end coming, but it also shows just how important patience truly is," she beamed.

"I get it!" he said, exasperated. "I have to be patient!"

"No," she corrected as she stood up and put her hands on her hips. "You have to realize that some rules need to be followed in order to make those we love the most be able to do what they need to save the world. You're not above anyone. Especially not here. Do you not love Sophie enough to help her get to where she needs to be?"

Mario looked down at the book, but when he looked up, the

woman was gone, and the book seemed to burn a hole in his thigh. "What the?..." he mumbled, but the book flew open, and he felt something force his head down. "Alright!" Mario exclaimed, as he read the first page.

———

Twenty-five

Sophie slid out of James's arms and slinked off to the bathroom to put some clothes on. She should have felt guilty for sneaking away, but all she felt was hunger.

She finished lacing up her shoes and looked up at the bathroom mirror. Reine smiled and waved back at her. Sophie rolled her eyes at the image and opened the door. She had already gotten dressed in the dark as the cat in her helped her see, even in the blackest of nights.

She leaned her head against the frame and listened to James and Karmen breathe heavily as they slept deeply, their hearts beating slowly in unison. Her grin spread across her mouth as she crept to the front door and slid out without being noticed.

This sleepy town was already well tucked away for the night, minus the unholy side alley that held bars for the less religious types. The ones that weren't afraid to sin regularly, because they didn't believe in Heaven or Hell. They just believed in taking whatever they wanted when they wanted, and living life to the fullest until their time was up.

Sophie scanned the room quickly to make sure that Clarice wasn't around now that she knew she was in town. No sign of her auntie hanging out with her normal kind of crowd. Or at least Sophie assumed this was her normal kind of crowd. She didn't really know her aunt, other than how to hide from her. She saw an empty seat at the bar and slid gracefully onto it.

A redheaded woman sitting on the other side simply raised her hand and snapped her fingers. The male bartender came running. "A drink for my friend," she ordered without even making eye contact with Sophie. The bartender waited impatiently.

"Well?" he asked irritably.

The woman turned her head and gave him a look that had him retreating quickly.

"What would you like, Miss?" he tried again nervously.

Sophie was staring at the woman out of the corner of her eye, taking her in. "Vodka Cranberry," she said flatly.

"Top shelf," the woman added over the noise. The bartender nodded and raced off to make her drink.

"Have we met?" Sophie asked the woman, turning to look at her.

"You're welcome," the woman snorted.

"Thank you for the drink," Sophie replied in irritation. "Have we met?" she asked again, a little more forcefully.

"Nope," the woman replied as she took a swig of her drink. It looked like whiskey. She still didn't turn to look at Sophie.

Sophie tilted her head as she took the woman in. It didn't seem to bother her she was being eyed. She oddly looked like a livelier version of her mother. "You look really familiar," Sophie tried again.

The woman mused. "I get that a lot," was all she offered. "Out for a test run?" she asked casually.

Sophie froze. "Test run for what?" she asked in fake confusion. *How did she know?*

The woman took another swig of her drink. "I know that look," she replied with a shrug. "That feeling of knowing that if you don't feed that hunger, you're going to explode," she said, taking another sip.

Sophie stayed frozen, careful not to change her face.

"Relax," the woman half snickered as she turned to finally look at Sophie. "We all get an itch to be naughty from time to time, and this is the best place for it." The woman winked and gave her a sinister smile. She leaned in closer to Sophie and whispered, "We're close enough to Vegas. What happens in an alley, stays in an alley," she hissed.

Sophie relaxed, realizing the woman was talking about sex, and not what her inside was craving to do.

The woman shook her head at Sophie. "What?" Sophie demanded in response.

The woman gave her a pity frown. "How hard it must be being the 'good one' all the time," she whined while using air quotes. The bartender set down Sophie's drink and another whiskey and walked away quickly. The woman gulped the last of her current drink down and swapped glasses. "No one appreciates what we go through!" the woman wailed as she switched the glasses. Sophie nodded in understanding.

Although their situations were surely nothing of the same, Sophie had a lot of anger pinned up inside that suddenly demanded to be released. No one asked her if she wanted to have the responsibility of taking care of the world when she was little. It was just dumped on her. Her parents taken from her, and still nagging her all these years later. She didn't want to be the damn key! She couldn't control herself right now, anyway! Red flashed before her eyes, and she was losing her ability to see reason. Or anything at all, for that matter.

The woman leaned over and nudged Sophie toward the man sitting next to her. "Go ahead," she whispered approvingly. "Release the red and be free."

The man, who was around 6'3" with fading ash hair cascading down his muscular back and dressed all in black, turned on his stool to face her. Tattoos peaked out from the entirely too tight of a black t-shirt and went down to his fingertips.

"Well, hello there," said a husky male voice from the mouth only a few inches from Sophie's.

"Hello," she offered softly, giving him a shy grin.

"What are you doing out so late tonight?" he asked her as if he were an animal in heat.

As she leaned forward, her breasts pulled together, and she heard the sharp breath he took in as a response. "Just taking in the sights," Sophie replied with a sigh as she licked her lips seductively.

"And what sights would that be?" he asked breathlessly.

Sophie bit her bottom lip and looked him up and down. She saw him noticeably grow hard in his tight jeans. "You, for starters," she breathed out as she focused on his mouth. "Wanna show me something special?" Sophie added as she looked down at the bulge in his jeans.

"You think you can handle something so massive?" he asked her slyly.

"I'd like to find out," Sophie replied sweetly. "Alley. Now." And with that, she slid off the stool gracefully and sauntered through the bar and out the door toward the dark alley. She didn't have to look behind her. She knew he was hot on her tail.

Once in the alley, she felt him grab her by the wrist and push her up against the wall. He grabbed her by her jaw and began kissing her fiercely. He grabbed her free hand and shoved it up and down his hardness. She felt nothing. She only tasted the beer that he had just been drinking, but she moaned in fake pleasure all the same.

His quickening pulse dripped like honey in her ears as he lifted her and wrapped her legs around him. "Oh baby," he moaned in her ear, as he pounded his excitement up and down her sex in hard thrusts, grunting as he did. "I'm going to fuck you so hard," he growled in between thrusts.

"Oh, are you?" Sophie replied, surprised at how bored she was with his touch.

"You won't be able to walk out of this alley," he challenged.

That was it. That was what she needed. He didn't know what hit him. All he knew was that he was inches off the pavement as she crushed his back against the wall and his feet dangled beneath him.

Sophie held him by his throat with a single hand and was crushing it. The corner of her lips curled up. She heard the cracking of his windpipe and the sound excited her even more.

She had killed before. Granted, it was out of need, but

here...now...it was pure desire that fueled her.

"Put him down," she heard a female stranger order her. It wasn't a voice she knew, so she ignored it. "Child, this is not your path," she warned behind Sophie's back, but Sophie couldn't hear her over the rushing blood and laughter that filled her ears.

"ENOUGH!"

Sophie released him involuntarily and flew to the end of the dark alley away from the man, and landed with a thud against the dumpster, nearly collapsing it.

"Run," she heard the voice order the man, who scrambled to his feet and took off into the night. Sophie rolled her head back and forth as she attempted to recover her senses and open her eyes, the fire and hunger draining from her by whatever she had been struck with. She fought to open her eyes and saw the vague outline of a curvaceous shadow walking her way. "You have a choice," she hissed at Sophie. "I suggest you choose more wisely."

When Sophie finally got her eyes to open fully, she was alone in the alley. Not sure where she was, or how she had gotten there. Terrified, she forced herself to get up and race to the hotel, not stopping to look back. She wouldn't notice the redhead watching her with interest as she did.

Sophie snuck back into the hotel and sleeked to the bathroom, where she leaned onto the counter and looked up at her bruised face in the mirror. She only saw herself looking back. Suddenly healing quicker than she had ever done before.

"What's wrong with you?" she begged the reflection, but got no response. So, she slid down the wall next to her and curled up into the fetal position and cried herself to sleep.

Tina laid her head on Ben's shoulder in the backseat as Daryl drove them towards Provo, Utah. She had caught some chatter of a mysterious death of a man in the street by someone who matched Clarice's description, so they headed that direction. There was no mention of Sophie, but Tina wondered if there was a reason for it.

Many people interviewed had mentioned having a gap of memory, and could not remember what had led up to the killing or what happened after. Only that a man was dead, and someone who sounded like Clarice was next to him, then gone.

Tina didn't know what Clarice was up to, but it made her need to get to Sophie that much more. It was entirely too early for her to feel the baby move inside her, but she could definitely feel its...her...apprehension for some unknown reason. She rubbed a protective hand over her lower stomach to smooth the anxiety within.

"Everything okay?" Ben asked in a worried tone.

"Just gassy," Tina lied.

Ben just nodded and let it go for once. Probably because he was more concerned with what they were going to find once they arrived. Tina squeezed his bicep that she had her other hand wrapped around, and he gave her a weary smile.

"They're fine," Tina whispered to him. Ben just gave a silent nod in response and stayed deep in thought.

Mario paced in the makeshift white room. He had finished *The Silent Patient.* The woman was right. It was actually well written until the very end. A sit on the end of your seat kind of read, ruined because someone couldn't wait long enough to make sure their so-called destiny had been fulfilled. Forcing them to lose everything and pay the ultimate price.

He didn't want to admit it, but Mario could relate to the psychotherapist. Lord knew Mario seemed to be nothing more than a sacrificial lamb in this story, but everything that had happened had been to help Sophie get to the next step of her own destiny. So, if Mario had to be like a cat and give up nine lives to get his goddaughter to safety, then that was the price he would always be willing to pay.

Sophie's emotions were powerful and led to all of her actions, good or bad. She was a carbon copy of her mother in that way. Mario smiled, thinking back on some jobs he and Jess had done together, where Mario had to step in and calm Jess to help her regain focus. Well, until Jack came along. Then he repeated the process with Sophie. Talking a hormonal teenager off the ledge was no small task, that's for sure!

Mario thought of coaxing Sophie through her grief of losing him in the cabin. Death didn't give him that much advantage, and neither did Sophie's adulthood. She was still as stubborn as the rest of them, and it usually took a couple of tries to help get through to her. He shook his head as the memories flashed before his eyes.

And now, he had even less ability to help her than he had in the dream realm. *Why was that? If his destiny was to help keep her on track?* There had to be a way that fell within these so-called obnoxious rules that would help Sophie stay safe.

Being a raven sounded difficult and more dangerous than Sophie had ever faced. He needed to find out more, but he clearly would not get answers from Peter or Angie. It was time to make some new friends. Ugh, Mario hated making new friends, but he didn't have a choice. It was for Sophie.

Clarice did not know why she was driving to the coordinates that James had given her, but here she was. It was ridiculously colder in the mountains, but she understood why they were "playing" out here after seeing Sophie light up the other day. Which was another reason she couldn't believe she was volunteering to be the sacrificial lamb to someone who obviously had more "gifts" than she did. In fact, Clarice had nothing special about her.

Algos hadn't thought her worthy enough to enhance, so currently her only enhancements included a damn conscious that was becoming quite a problem for her. Not that she had developed an exact plan for what she was going to do in her father's absence, but helping the girl she had spent a lifetime hunting for him definitely was *not* on the top of the list.

But neither was caring about a ghost. Seeking out an autistic child to have to protect, and agreeing to "take care of" whatever her father had created to eliminate everyone, even the dead. *Damn it.*

Jess had mentioned there were several realms, but how many were several? She had been too distracted to ask, but it weighed heavily on her to find out the answer for some reason. Like it was going to be a choice to back out.

Jess knew she couldn't and wouldn't, knowing what little family she had left was endangered by the man who was dead and yet still kept trying to destroy her from beyond the grave. Clarice understood why he wouldn't be allowed to go play in the dream realm, but where did he go when she had taken his life? And why didn't it bother her if she never got an answer?

It was almost like jabbing the knife into his neck not only saved her niece, but it set her free at the same time. Free from his ongoing abuse and unrealistic expectations of her. And she was...happy...about it. Or at least this was what she assumed happiness might feel like.

She saw the empty Jeep on the side of the road and pulled up next to it as a fireball shot through the sky. "Well, at least I know I'm in the right place," she muttered to herself, as she forced herself to get out of the car. Clarice started dragging her feet in the light's direction when she felt two familiar arms wrap around her waist and squeeze hard.

"Karmen!" she heard Sophie yell from the distance.

"Hey, Little One," Clarice said, squeezing her arms back. She couldn't help but smile. She turned around and saw Karmen jumping around and clapping her hands in excitement.

"What are you doing here?" Sophie asked, with a hint of hostility in her voice.

"I was requested," Clarice said, as her smile quickly turned to a frown.

"By who?" Sophie demanded. "Come here, Karmen!" she called out, but Karmen ignored her.

Clarice laughed at the situation and saw Sophie's eyes ignite into red flames. "For that," she added, wiggling her finger at Sophie's eyes.

"What does that mean?" Sophie barked as anger filled her core, and her breathing increased.

Clarice suddenly wished she had brought a fire suit with her instead of her coat, but she felt a swoosh of air, and James was standing in front of her. "It means she's here to help you see what you can do," he added in a soothing tone. "I asked her to come," he added.

"Why would you do that?" Sophie snapped and moved closer to them.

"Probably because he knows I am better at pissing you off," Clarice said, watching Sophie with both curiosity and concern.

"Why would you piss me off?" Sophie demanded. The enjoyment of the heat consumed her faster the more she used it. "You only killed *EVERYONE* I loved," she snarled.

"Yep," Clarice nodded as she pushed Karmen behind her despite Karmen's protest and took a couple of steps back. "That's probably it," she said, shoving Karmen behind a boulder. "But I didn't kill *everyone* technically," Clarice added sarcastically, and dove to cover Karmen with her body as a fireball flew past them.

"Sophie!" James demanded in frustration.

"You wanted to see what I could do?" Sophie taunted. "Let's find out..." she said in a voice that didn't sound like hers at all.

"Sophie, no!" James yelled as he raced to block her, but she sidestepped him and used her cheetah speed to race around the rock.

Clarice shoved Karmen out of the way and stood up to face Sophie. Despite the terror she felt for the first time in...well, ever, she forced herself to cackle. "Oh my, has the apple fallen far from the tree," she said as she moved around the rock towards James's direction.

"Not really," said a deep voice that Clarice didn't recognize, but could guess what was fueling it. She knew from first-hand experience. The flames didn't live in Sophie's eyes, but they danced in her palms instead. Her eyes were completely black, and pure evil had taken over.

"Maybe you were my daughter instead," Clarice threw out as she raced around the rock and found Sophie had beaten her. She looked like a hungry animal that hadn't fed in years and was ready to eat. Sophie cracked her neck like an animal ready to pounce. "Or maybe you're just a freak of nature that gets *way* too much credit for doing absolutely nothing with her life," Clarice shrugged.

She heard an animalistic growl of irritation come from Sophie before James raced to carry her out of harm's way. Clarice tried to get the dust out of her mouth, and James glared at Sophie.

"Well, this is fun," Clarice offered sarcastically.

"I think we need to tone it down a bit," James said firmly.

"She's already past the point of return, you know that, right?" Clarice retorted.

"Not my girl," James countered and stood up to face Sophie. "You need to calm down," he demanded.

"Calm down?" the creature before him cackled. "You don't know who you're talking to," it hissed. Sophie wasn't available anymore. They both saw that.

"You have my girl, and I want her back," James said, lighting up into icy blue flames himself. Clarice shielded the light from her eyes.

"Karmen, Honey, I need you to hide!" Clarice called out in a slight panic since she was currently blinded and couldn't see the child. She got back to her feet and made her way back towards her niece. "So, who are we dealing with?" she called out curiously. "Cause you sure as hell aren't my niece," Clarice added.

The creature just cackled. "Oh, but I am. The better version, at least," she added with a shrug.

"Oh, I don't know about that," Clarice countered and took off her jacket as she continued to force herself to push through the heat that radiated off of them both. "You see," Clarice added as James watched Clarice out of the corner of his eyes but kept his attention on Sophie. "I know that look," Clarice said, waving her hand toward Sophie. Her body was oddly adapting to the heat. She must be dying, but kept going. "I know that thirst you're drinking on right now, and it's not that impressive," Clarice added.

Like an owl, the creature turned its attention to Clarice. It flicked a hand in James's direction, and he slid a few feet backwards.

Clarice forced a laugh. "The problem with the thirst is you're always thirsty," she continued, inching her way closer to Sophie. "It's never quite...satisfying. No matter how many lives you take," Clarice confessed. She watched the creature take great interest in what she was saying. This was what it needed to hear.

"Pretty soon, you just become bored, restless, and pissed off because even killing loses its excitement after the first few times," Clarice confessed. "You think people will see you. Notice you. But they don't. They still don't give a damn, and you're right back where you started," she said with bitterness oozing in her voice. "You have no purpose. No matter how good you get at it, or how 'creative' you try to be," Clarice said, adding air quotes in irritation. "The only thing you gain is irritation, boredom, and loneliness. And it's not all it's cracked up to be," she added.

James and Clarice watched as the blackness from Sophie's eyes retreated, and showing the smallest hint of blue returning. "But what if it's all you are?" she asked in a tone sounding more like herself breaking through.

"It's not all you are," Clarice said, staring at the girl she had hunted most of her life. "You're a brat that won't let yourself get caught, for starters," she threw out in irritation. "You're stupid-smart, and fast, and God knows you're stubborn," she said, rolling her eyes. James watched Sophie fight to find her way back and nodded at Clarice to keep going. *Damn it.*

"Fine!" she yelled back at him. "You're the best fighter I have ever come across," Clarice said exasperated. "And you're a carbon copy of your mother and father so much that it's disgusting," she said, sticking out her tongue. Sophie's breathing slowed down. Clarice sighed. "You found a family that loves you unconditionally," she said, jarring her chin in James's direction. "Who would do anything for you, no matter the cost? That's more than I ever had," she muttered.

Sophie heard her words. Felt her heart break on her last comments, and she knew that she just couldn't quite keep hating this woman. Despite taking Mario from her, she didn't understand the power of love, because she wasn't raised by anyone who could give it to her. She was only trained to find people's weaknesses and exploit them to get what she needed from them.

Sophie wasn't ready to give her a free pass for taking Mario's life, but she didn't believe the broken creature before her understood what she was doing. The price it cost her in the end.

"How do you not get lost in it?" Sophie whispered to Clarice, who was just inches away now.

Clarice looked down at her feet. "All I can tell you is once you cross that line, you can never find your way back. Take it from someone who knows," she said with a shrug.

"I'm not sure you can't," Sophie offered with a smile.

Clarice looked up to find Sophie's electric blue eyes and grin staring back at her. "Ugh! This is why I can't like you," she grumbled as she turned on her heals to put some distance between them and wipe away the tears that threatened to streak her cheeks.

Karmen ran up to her and hugged her once more. She clung tightly to Clarice as she turned around. "So, you clearly have some fun new tricks," she said to Sophie, studying her niece. "And you too," she frowned at James. "And I'm guessing that's why you won't get out of my hair," Clarice added in fake irritation.

Sophie tucked her hair behind her ear. "Not exactly able to be safe around others," she confessed in irritation.

"And when did this start?" Clarice pressed as an obnoxious teenager's mother would have.

"When we left the bunker," James confessed. Sophie gave him a shocked looked, and he shrugged. "It's a little hard to hide after all of this, Babe," he shrugged.

"Your hesitance will get you both killed," Clarice snapped at James. "It's why you couldn't stand your ground."

"I didn't hesitate," James protested.

"Bull shit," Clarice said with her face full of doubt. "What did Algos give you?" she demanded.

"Nothing," James answered her honestly.

"And I'm supposed to believe y'all are just lighting up the world from free will," she stated sarcastically. However, when neither answered, and they stared at the ground beneath them, she froze.

"Shit," she gasped. She looked down at Karmen. "And you let me leave a child with you?" she demanded in anger.

"He did." Sophie quickly pointed at James and giggled at his shocked face.

"This isn't funny!" Clarice barked.

"Well, aware," James cut in before Sophie could say anything.

"I think this is enough for today," Clarice stated firmly. "We're going to get the fuck out of the cold and you're going to tell me everything," she ordered as she spun on her heels and dragged Karmen behind her. "The kid is staying with me," she added over her shoulder.

Sophie and James looked at each other and James shrugged. "I think we need help," he thought to himself.

"I know, but Clarice?" she asked him.

"What?" James asked, startled.

"You said, 'I think we need help'. I agree, but I'm not sure Clarice is the best choice," Sophie said, shaking her head.

"Soph, I didn't say anything out loud. I was just thinking about it," James said slowly.

"Move it, you two!" they heard Clarice bark at them, making them look in her direction before they looked back at each other.

"Okay," Sophie offered slowly. "We do need help. And it's not safe enough to involve Tina, so I guess this *is* our best option," she said nervously.

"Come on, before she comes back to get us," James said, grabbing her hand as they raced past Clarice and laughed at the look of shock on her face as they got in the car.

___

Twenty-six

Mario walked for what seemed like forever before coming across a single person. No one seemed to be anywhere in this realm, but it didn't feel right at all. It had gotten much darker, and the air felt cooler than the warm white light that usually greeted him. The only time he had encountered anything different was when he was realm hopping with Peter. Mario froze immediately. He looked cautiously around him, trying to recall when the scenery had changed exactly.

There was a red glow ahead of him. It called to him like a siren calling to the sailors of the sea. Ahead, he found an African American woman standing with her back to him. She had a Seminole Indian mix as she stood at 5'7", with a short black afro, and skin autumn brown and as smooth as a moonstone. She looked like she was a queen of some sort. A raven sat on her shoulder and squawked, forcing the woman around. Her eyes were a blazing hazel as she looked him up and down, studying him.

"This is not your place, Child," she breathed. Her gold hoop earrings swayed in slow motion as she shook her head disapprovingly at him. She was curvaceous and warm.

"Who are you?" Mario asked against his own will.

"I am not your concern," she whispered as she backed away.

"That's a raven," Mario said, dumbfounded, and pointing at the bird. It flapped its wings angrily.

"It's not nice to point," she replied sternly. "And yes, what of it?"

Mario shook his head, trying to break himself from the trance. "I seek answers," he said more sternly.

"That is not your role," she answered in shock.

Anger ignited in his core, and she watched his eyes light up in red fire. She cackled in response and grabbed her stomach as she bent over. "What do you know about my role?" he demanded.

"Child, put your power away," she sighed as she waved her hand at him.

"Power?" Mario asked in confusion. Shyera straightened up immediately.

"You don't know," she said in sudden sympathy.

"Tell me what's going on," he snapped, trying to stay focused.

Shyera sighed heavily, and the bird flapped its wings and screamed at them both.

_____

"Oh, hush, you," she said, waving at it, forcing it off her shoulder. "You know it's difficult being blind. Stop being so damn fussy," she snapped.

The bird took a perch regretfully on a tree that appeared out of nowhere.

"What's your name?" Shyera asked him.

"What's yours?" Mario countered. She laughed at him before offering her hand.

"My name is Shyera," she said with the softest of smiles.

"Mario," he said, taking her hand cautiously.

"Oh!" she exclaimed. "I have heard grand stories about your bravery," Shyera offered. "And your stubbornness," she added in dismay.

"From who?" he demanded, taking his hand back.

"Easy, Child," Shyera said sweetly. "You're very popular in the dream realm."

Mario couldn't help but smile. "Oh, yeah?" he asked.

"Giselle told me all about your sacrifice to, what was his name, again?" she asked, falling into deep thought.

"Algos," Mario replied bitterly.

"Oh, yeah," Shyera replied, snapping her fingers. "That must be why you were chosen."

"Chosen?" Mario asked, caught off guard.

"A compass of the protector," she said with a nod.

Sophie. "I thought Sophie was the raven?" he asked in confusion.

"They can be one in the same," Shyera said with a shrug. "But it's still too soon to know if she is just one or both."

"And what do you know of this?" Mario demanded.

Shyera's shoulders sunk a bit. "Because I am also a part of the raven's army. It's my job to locate her and help her with her transition."

"Transition to what exactly?" Mario asked, more curiously than demanding. "I thought Rebecca was the master or whatever."

Shyera raised her left eyebrow at him. "So, you know more than you let on, soldier," Shyera offered with a sly smile. "The half raven must pass on her powers to the next. I assist in that transition. She chooses her protector to keep her balanced, and you, my friend, make sure she's always safe and stays on the path she has chosen."

Mario's shoulders pulled back in approval. "But how am I supposed to do that when I can't access her? Or am confined by rules that can destroy us all at the same time?"

Shyera's lips curled up on the ends into a wicked smile. "A rule breaker. How interesting," she grinned. "First," she said sternly, "you must come to terms that some rules simply can't be broken. Even if it seems like they will be more beneficial for you to do so," she warned, shaking her finger at Mario like a scolding mother. "You could destroy her and everyone else altogether."

Mario's stomach dropped. *Destroy Sophie? He could never.*

As if reading his thoughts, Shyera continued. "That is why you were chosen, Child," she assured him. "I understand that patience isn't your strong suit, but hasn't that always been the case with Sophie?" Her words couldn't ring more true if she actually was there while Mario raised Sophie all those years ago. Shyera nodded in confirmation.

"Unfortunately, this is where you have to wait," Shyera offered with a tilt of her head, and the most motherly warning ever. "It's not your time to react. Not yet."

"If you know so much, then why don't you just tell me what it is I'm supposed to do?" Mario asked in frustration.

"Because it's your connection with Sophie that always tells you when it's time to react," Shyera said simply as she shrugged. "No one knows her like you do, so only you can answer that question."

"You make it sound like it's a onetime deal," Mario stated suspiciously. Shyera knew she had to be careful with her answer.

"Our loved ones never truly leave us. Not even in death," she replied in a trancing calmness. "Have you not seen that?"

Mario frowned, knowing her answer wasn't an answer at all.

"I know. Not the answer you were looking for," Shyera giggled at him. She reached out and put her hand on his shoulder, and ease washed over him. "This is the part of the story where you take a break. Rest. You don't know what the future holds, and it's best to be as prepared as possible for when your time comes."

"What does that?..." but Mario didn't get to finish his question. He was forced into the deepest sleep ever, as he waited to be awakened again when the raven revealed herself.

Aimee Mae walked casually around the operating table. She was 42, with brown eyes, and shoulder length silver hair with blue tips. She was average in height, but fit to match her career path. Aimee stared dreamingly down at the twenty-nine-year-old woman, struggling against the cuffs she was currently in.

Tiana Cannon's dark brown eyes were wide and staring back at Aimee through her red glasses. They were a brilliant match for her long, dark brown hair and her lighter complexion. She may only have stood at 4'10", but people loved her for being her usual Latina sarcastic delight. However, right now, she was scared, but becoming madder by the second.

"If you think dealing with children, all day didn't prepare me for the likes of you," Tiana yelled at the top of her lungs in the abandoned warehouse.

"You literally know no one can hear you, right?" Aimee offered dryly. "I was too lazy to even blind fold you. Like, come on," she said with an eye roll.

Tiana glared at Aimee. "Let me guess, not enough love as a child?" Tiana replied, returning Aimee's eye roll with one of her own.

"Far too much," Aimee replied beaming.

"Clearly," Tiana stated sarcastically.

"Ooo! You are a delight!" Aimee countered with fake enthusiasm, as she filled a syringe with some dark brown liquid and set it on the stand she was using. She took some duct tape and put it over Tiana's mouth as she got the drip ready. As much as she enjoyed the banter, she didn't seem much in the mood tonight for some reason. She felt Claudia's presence before she saw her. "And what do you want?" Aimee inquired over her shoulder.

"Just admiring your work," came a woman's voice from the dark corner.

"Thank you," Aimee said, taking an exaggerated bow. "Now," she repeated, "what do you want?"

A redheaded woman of around Aimee's height came into the

light of the room she was using currently as a torture chamber. "What's the liquid?" she asked curiously.

"Chocolate," Aimee beamed. She laughed heartedly with Tiana's immediate protest. "Well, don't tell me you hate chocolate next time," Aimee shrugged at her.

"Can you inject chocolate into someone's veins?" the woman asked curiously.

"It's not just chocolate," Aimee whispered sarcastically. "But it is a nice cocktail to permanently block her veins, and give her an embolism," she added with a wicked smile.

"Can I watch?" the woman asked her eagerly.

Aimee looked at her cautiously, but just shrugged and continued to slowly inject the syringe into Tiana's arm. When she was finished, she stepped back next to Claudia. "So, who are you supposed to be?" she asked.

Tiana's body convulsed, and she hyperventilated against the duct tape. "Hmmm? Oh. My name's Claudia," she said.

"Well, Claudia," Aimee said, watching Tiana's body flop around like a fish out of water. "I rarely get spectators. What brings you to the show?"

Claudia couldn't take her eyes off of Tiana. "Well, your work, as beautiful as it is, is causing me some grief. So, I'm gonna need you to be on your way tomorrow."

Aimee crossed her arms in front of her and gawked at Claudia. "And why would I do that? Because you can't play nice in the sandbox? That's like asking me to stop breathing. Screw you. I don't even know you, or have even heard of you." Aimee went back to watching Tiana struggle to get air into her lungs.

Claudia should have just taken her out, right then and there, and be done with it. Yet, there was something about Aimee that Claudia couldn't quite put her finger on, but liked all the same. "Then why not a partnership?" she asked, still staring at Tiana in fascination.

"I work alone," Aimee replied flatly as she went to unbuckle Tiana and start working on disposing of the body.

"What if you could work your magic, but on the people I give you? I kinda have a thing going on, and there are certain marks that have to be taken out," Claudia replied, watching Aimee carefully.

Aimee paused unbuckling Tiana, and stood tall for a second as she pondered the proposal. "So, you give me a name, and I get to do whatever I want to them?" she asked curiously.

"The means aren't as important as the who, my friend," Claudia answered with a smirk.

Aimee stuck out her bottom lip and wiggled her head from side to side as she thought. "And what exactly do *you* get out of all of this?" she asked Claudia, narrowing her eyes and taking her future partner in.

"Winning several battles to a very important war," Claudia offered with a shrug.

Aimee threw her head back and cackled before asking, "Who pissed you off?"

Claudia took a deep sigh but didn't reply, because the truth was no one. She simply had an itch that didn't stop needing to be scratched. Claudia wasn't killing a particular type of person over and over again to relieve some past trauma. She had none, minus her mother dying. Yet, a sadistic plan had been put into place by another, which she tweaked to her pleasure, but the answer remained the same...no one.

———

"That bad, huh?" Aimee asked.

"A story for a different day, my friend," Claudia replied.

"Oh, so we're friends already?" Aimee asked, half amused and half annoyed.

Claudia realized a few other things at that very moment. One, she had past loose ends that needed to be tied up before she got much further with her plan. Two, she currently had no friends left that truly appreciated her newly gained skills and thirst. Claudia still didn't have any trust in her creator, even if she was literally the only person she didn't have a thirst to completely mutilate. There was something about Liz she didn't like, and that was number three. Get to the bottom of Liz's secrets.

"Why should I trust you, anyway?" Aimee asked, breaking Claudia's deep thinking session. "I've never heard of you, or seen your work?"

It was true. Someone kept coming up behind Claudia and cleaning up her messes. She and Liz hadn't had the opportunity to stick around and see who the person was or find out why they were doing it in the first place. If Aimee was helping her, though, it would give Claudia the chance to do just that.

"Well, that's because someone keeps rudely cleaning up my work," Claudia added with a frown. "If you help me, I could get to the bottom of it," she added, crossing her arms in front of her chest.

"Wow," Aimee breathed out, nodding, and crossing her arms to mimic Claudia. She tapped her finger against her bicep in thought. "I need to know who I'm working with," she scowled. "*IF* I decide to take your offer," she added hastily.

A smile crept across Claudia's face. "I'll just have to give you a show that can't be missed," she said sheepishly.

"And how are you gonna do that with what's their name cleaning up after you all the time?" Aimee asked curiously.

Claudia shrugged. "Give them a mess they can't clean up," she replied innocently. "Keep your eyes open," Claudia announced as she turned on her heals and wiggled her fingers in a wave to Aimee.

Aimee stood slightly impressed with her conviction, and watched her leave. Then she looked down at Tiana, stating, "Well, this should be interesting." She reached over and grabbed the electric saw. "But we have a date first," she whispered excitedly.

No one suspected a psychopathic serial killer running around taking out booktokers. There was no reason to be alarmed, because no one's bodies were being found according to the news, lacking any proof they were connected. However, one person, besides Clarice, was putting the pieces together.

Shelly Balderas was in her early 40s, with salt and pepper curly hair, and curves for days. She was a hairstylist, an author, and a lover of her Latin/Indian/Irish/Scottish mix. She was a translator, painter, photographer, horse trainer, mother and grandmother. However, it would be her BS in criminal justice that had her putting the pieces together faster than most.

First, it seemed like nothing. People were just dropping off for what seemed to be a "break", only Shelly noticed they weren't finding their way back. She started to make a list of where they were originally located, and if it connected them in any other way outside of being on booktok. Nothing stood out besides the fact they left and never came back.

With the community being so close, it was common courtesy for people to make a video announcing they were taking a break and would be back so their absence did not alarm their followers. None of these booktokers made such videos. They were simply present one day, and gone the next. Some blamed the algorithm for never seeing their friends, but Shelly knew better.

The number of missing booktokers was growing, with no other connection outside of being on booktok flagging them. Most weren't even following each other. Shelly had to be missing a piece to the puzzle, but she would never find it.

In an attempt to collect it, she would reach out to a couple of her friends in their DMs and ask what they knew about the individuals on her list. When her friends asked why she was asking, she lied and said she was looking into making some new connections to help grow her own account. Three days later, Shelly would join the others on her list, and authorities would never find her list.

It would take two weeks after the initial missing person's report for a student of the University of Tennessee in Knoxville, TN to find her body staked with her tongue cut out, hiding in the body farm. Although there would be an investigation why Shelly's body was tortured and dumped in the body farm, no answers would ever come, making it a cold case for several years.

Twenty-seven

They sat in a booth in the back of a mom and pop diner, and Clarice listened as Karmen hummed and colored happily sitting next to her. James and Sophie sat opposite of them and were confessing everything they had experienced since leaving the bunker.

"And he didn't give you anything?" Clarice asked James, still in surprised.

"He never touched me," James replied honestly.

"But the fire isn't from what he did to your mother. He's not that good," Clarice said, shaking her head. "Did someone else give you that?" she asked her pointedly.

Sophie shook her head. "It didn't show up until I killed Reine," she confessed.

"And who the hell is Reine again?" Clarice asked, trying to wrap her head around everything that she was being told.

"She said she was the version of me if Algos had his way," she confessed in a low, disappointing voice.

"So, like a split personality?" Clarice asked, gazing at her. "Cause Lord knows there's plenty of crazy genes in *this* family!"

Sophie's eyes widened in terror, but James put his hand on her knee. "I don't think it's anything quite that severe," James assured.

"Severe?" Clarice laughed. "Cause flame throwing is a *normal* thing?" she hissed at him.

"I know this sounds stupid," Sophie whispered, leaning forward, "but it *does* feel like she's the pure evil side of me."

James squeezed her knee and smiled wearily at her.

"It's not stupid," Clarice muttered. Now she was on a topic she understood. "We all have evil in us," she continued, looking down at Karmen. "It's more of how we're raised and if we decide to tap into it regularly or not, that makes us who we are," she added in a sad tone. "Your parents didn't raise you to tap into that side, so it's foreign, I assume. Eager to be tried out like a new pair of shoes," she added for clarification.

"But mom was raised the same as you, and she came out...different," Sophie added cautiously.

"Your mother and I were *not* raised the same," Clarice cackled in almost hysteria. "You're not the only pawn Daddy Dearest played with," she hissed, rolling her eyes. "And your father came into play, much like I assume James, here, has come into play for you."

"Then who balances you?" Sophie asked before she could stop

herself. James kicked her under the table.

Clarice glared at her, then caught herself. "No one," she said flatly and looked in the window's direction. "Tina will come no matter what you tell her," she added as an afterthought. "What are you going to do, then?" she asked, still looking out the window.

"We're still working on it," James threw out.

Clarice half-laughed. "Good luck with that." Karmen's humming brought her back to the present, and her promise to track down her father's creation. "Someone needs to keep Karmen while I take care of something," she said as she stared at the child happily coloring next to her.

"What do you have to do?" Sophie asked immediately.

"Something that doesn't concern you," Clarice added with a warning. "But I can't have Karmen around me." She went back to looking at the child with a range of emotions she couldn't quite decipher, nor did she want to.

"We will keep her safe," James assured, but the look on Clarice's face showed she didn't believe him. "I give you my word," he added.

"Yeah, you've proven that," Clarice said, rolling her eyes.

"I'm not the one on the fritz," he offered.

"Hey!" Sophie exclaimed and went to slap him, but he caught her hand before she could. She pulled it out of his grasp and crossed her arms in front of her chest in a huff.

"It's all fun and games until you hesitate and let her go too far," Clarice warned.

"It's only because I could still feel her when you couldn't," he shrugged innocently.

"Okay," Clarice retorted.

"Listen," James said, leaning forward and lowering his voice. "Like you said earlier, I was brought in," he started, choosing his words carefully. "I grow stronger as she does, to give her...balance," James said, smiling at Sophie, who was too engrossed with Karmen's coloring to notice him. He put his focus back on Clarice. "Something is coming," he warned. "She's going to be a part of it, and I will make sure she succeeds," he said slowly.

He looked deep into her eyes. "Jack told me as much," he thought to her.

Clarice frowned. *Get out of my head!*

He blinked rapidly at the sharpness of her tone in his head.

"I get it," she sighed, still glaring at him. He darted his eyes in Sophie's direction, and Clarice didn't lose her glare, but he felt her understanding his need not to speak out loud.

"That's quite a picture you're drawing," said Sophie slowly as she attempted to mask her horror. There were about twenty people dressed in various Halloween costumes, swimming, and being eaten by what looked like crocodiles, but something else caught Clarice's attention.

In the middle, amongst the waves of the water, was Corbin laying on top of Clarice under sheets with what she guessed was no clothes on. It was ever so small, but it was there. Clarice snatched the picture away immediately.

"Hey!" Sophie protested. She was too focused on the faces to notice the hidden picture in the middle.

"This," Clarice said, trying to find her voice again. "This is what I have to take care of," she finally hissed, looking at James. He nodded in understanding. "Little One, I have to go," she said to Karmen, who only gave her a sheepish smile. "Not funny!" she hissed in her ear as she leaned over to give her a half hug, but Karmen just clapped in glee.

Clarice pulled back with a frown on her face and shook her head before shoving herself out of the booth and throwing some money on the table. "Enhanced or not, if anything happens," she warned, looking down at Karmen, who was coloring a new picture already. "I will end you," Clarice added as she stormed out.

"What's wrong with her?" Sophie asked.

"Probably just saw something she wasn't expecting," James said, winking at Karmen, because he had seen what Clarice had and loved watching this all play out. Sophie frowned and went back to watching Karmen color in glee.

Aimee wasn't a part of Algos's original plan, but something made Claudia have to have her. Like a toy at Christmas that a spoiled child demanded she needed. Only Claudia wouldn't throw a fit to embarrass anyone. After taking the red serum, her fits were murder sprees like no one had ever witnessed before.

The letter didn't say she couldn't get recruits to do her bidding. It just said who to take, and the end result of this game. No Sophie. No Clarice. No Jess or Jack. No one left of the bloodline. Just Claudia. It sounded just fine to her, too. But for now, she had work to do. *Well, it's not work when you enjoy it. Is it?...*

Mariska Proulox loved throwing murder mystery parties, and with Christmas just around the corner, this was her favorite time of the year to do what she loved the most. At fifty-three years old, it made for the perfect side hustle since she lived with her retired ex-navy husband, David, and had the added skills of crochet, cooking, and baking. When she was asked to throw this last minute murder mystery party, with the money to cover any problems she might face and then some, Mariska eagerly accepted.

The redheaded woman, Claudia, had been impressed with her years of swimming experience, and insisted that the party be held at a particular old high school where the gym floor opened up to double as the swimming pool. Not that they would use it, but Claudia had mentioned that *It's a Wonderful Life* was her favorite Christmas movie, with that being one of her favorite scenes. It would mean so much to her knowing they were in a similar-looking setup, so Mariska got to work.

When Claudia gave her a guest list, it was exciting to see many of Mariska's favorite booktokers listed on it. Claudia was doing a top secret get together of some hand-selected booktokers, and Mariska was not to tell a soul. The secrecy only made Mariska more giddy, and was given permission to do whatever she needed to get them to come.

"Let the games begin!" Mariska would whisper to herself before she started a new task for the party. She started following everyone she wasn't already following immediately, and Claudia came up with the perfect storyline for the party. One booktoker would be murdered, while the others showed up as a famous serial killer.

Mariska stood outside at 5'3", with her auburn hair down and just the sides pulled back, and dressed as Aileen Wuornos. Her periwinkle eyes shined as each booktoker arrived to be checked in.

- *Rosalyn Butler*
- *Sheyla Rochelle*
- *Dani Breault*
- *Tawni Hargis*
- *Sandie Buckley*
- *Holly Morrison*
- *Amanda Guinand*
- *Monica Rollins*
- *Olivia Clark*
- *Linda Dial*
- *Rachel Welch*
- *Nathalie Gibson*
- *Rachel Raikar*
- *Noel Ness*
- *Jeanie Dawson*
- *Elaine Dymond*
- *Terri Hinton*
- *RaeAnna Carroll*
- *Crystal Thomas*

Everyone was checked in and mingling amongst themselves at their assigned table. Booktokers from around the world, all in one room, and it was incredibly exciting!

"This is so awesome!" Holly exclaimed. She was a huge movie buff and loved history. Her amber eyes sparkled behind her glasses as she took in everyone's chosen costume.

"I wonder how everyone was chosen," pondered Olivia, being only twenty-four years old, and one of the youngest of the group. She was 5'3", with green eyes, beautiful curves, and short dark brown roots with blondish light pink hair cascading to her shoulders.

"Does anyone know why we're here?" Linda asked everyone at her table. She was thirty-two years old, and 5'5" with extremely short strawberry blonde hair. Her wide hazel eyes took in the room. Outside of being on booktok, she wasn't sure how her love of penguins, taking care of her grandmother, and being awkward as fuck made her important enough to even be invited to such an event. The eerie fluttering in her stomach wouldn't go away, no matter how much bread she tried to shove into it to make it calm.

"Does this feel wrong to anyone else?" whispered Crystal. She was always known for being extra observant, even at thirty-one. Her green eyes were weary, even though stunning with her dirty blonde hair. She stretched her neck to look around since she was only 5'2". Crystal knew she was socially awkward and uncomfortable, but there was just something about this invite, and the willingness to fly out anyone who couldn't afford to come just to make sure they were in this room tonight.

Daryl pulled up in front of their hotel and carried their bags inside, despite Tina's protesting. In a huff, she went to the front desk and checked them all in. Once they were settled in their rooms, Ben insisted Tina eat something, whether she felt like eating or not. It was a Friday night, and the sidewalks were very congested as they shuffled their way down to a restaurant. Tina found her body on fire and let go of Ben's hand to pull down her hood and take off her scarf.

Ben stopped immediately to inspect his wife. "What's wrong?" he demanded.

She laughed as Daryl helped hold her scarf while she unzipped her coat slightly. "Benjamin, relax. With this many people around, I'm feeling a bit warm, like a sardine in a can. I just need to unlayer a bit," she added with an eye roll. "You have me wrapped up worse than a capybara being squeezed by an anaconda!" Tina protested. She nodded her thanks at Daryl as she took her scarf back.

"You're a little flushed," Daryl noted.

"Just overheated, Bear," she said, patting his arm gently and taking Ben's hand back in hers. "Let's go there so I can delayer, please," she nodded to the bar just a few doors down. Ben looked at her and nodded again as he fell behind Daryl. He pushed a path for them all to head in the direction of the bar.

After a couple of steps, Tina came to a stop and placed a hand on the back of her neck.

"Tina, what is it?" Ben asked, turning around to gaze at his wife.

"Nothing," Tina said, shaking her head.

Ben frowned at her, and his eyes focused on the hand she held to her neck.

"It's nothing," Tina lied, smiling wearily and shaking her head. "You're right, I just need some food and a nice big glass of water." But that wasn't it at all.

Tina didn't see the redhead slip past her, and quickly jabbed a syringe into her neck from behind her. She only felt the quick prick of it, and the icy feeling that was quickly coursing through her veins. This was it. This was what Shyera warned her about.

_____

Tina put her hand over her abdomen and whispered, "Hang on," as she forced her legs to keep following her husband. Knowing full well, she would not be making it to the bar.

"What happened to this one?" Mason asked an old buddy of his who was processing the body.

"Hmm?" his friend asked as he carefully inspected the body for additional clues.

"What happened?" Mason asked more harshly as his pulse quickened.

"Oh," the man said, straightening up. "At first glance, you would think it was the massive amounts of random bug bites. We're still waiting for the entomologists to identify them all," he added with authority. "But it was actually a heart attack. Can't blame the girl, quite honestly," he added.

"Really?" Mason asked curiously as he stared down at the twenty-eight-year-old who's dead hazel eyes stared back at him. Her sandy blonde hair hung a little longer than her shoulders. She had a semicolon tattoo on her right forearm. A symbol that had become a badge of pride for those who struggle with depression, suicide, addiction, anxiety, and self-injury. Mason knew it well, although it still didn't save his sister. "Do you know who she is?" he asked softly as he stared into the hazel eyes that would haunt him until he found her killer.

"Jessica Padgett," his friend offered, knowing this would haunt Mason until it was resolved. "She teaches...taught second graders, and loved photography," he whispered. After a moment of silence, he dared to ask, "Why did you need to see her?"

"Military is tracking down a similar offender," he lied.

"Military?" his friend asked, surprised.

"Don't stress out the boys in blue. It's not our guy," Mason affirmed, still staring at the girl. The blonde hair made him think of Ashley. It was a distraction he couldn't afford at the moment. "Thanks anyway, mate," he said, slapping his friend on the shoulder. "Just crossing all of my t's," he said before he turned around to call Clarice. It went straight to voicemail.

"It's me," he said in a hushed tone. "I believe this is the one that came from the glass box that was filled with what I assume to be various flying insects. She was attacked by her own personal fear. A bit of a different M.O.," he added with a hint of irritation. "Looks like she's growing her team. I'll be in touch soon. And answer your damn phone! I'm worried," he quickly added before he hung up.

Twenty-eight

Monica Rollins shifted in her seat. She was uncomfortable around people in general, and a room full of booktokers didn't make it any easier. Her green eyes took in the surrounding room. Amanda Guinand slid into the seat next to her. "You're @motherofthekaijus, right?" she whispered to Monica.

Monica smiled wearily. "How did you know?" she asked, laughing a bit nervously.

"I have always loved your hair," Amanda replied shyly. Monica put a nervous hand to her head. At thirty-three, she was shaving one side of her head, and leaving the other side to shine in light and dark blue. "Honestly," Amanda assured her with a smile. Monica took Amanda in.

Just a few years older, Amanda was dressed as a goth serial killer with her dark brown hair hiding most of her face, but nothing could take away from her unique and beautiful eyes, one blue, and one green. Some of her tattoos were showing. Monica loved her instantly. "Thank you," she smiled back.

Rachel Welch slumped down in a chair at their table with her eyes changing from blue to green to grey as her mood shifted before them. Her dark purple hair framed perfectly around her stunning face. Her make-up was breathtaking, and her nails painted black to match her costume of murder.

"Not that I'm mad about being in this room right now," Rachel rambled off quickly before being fully seated, with one ear bud still playing her favorite villain playlist she had made herself, "but does this not seem totally weird to anyone else?" She quickly noticed that it was quite a room of random booktokers.

"What do you mean?" Monica asked, already knowing the answer.

"Look over there," Rachel answered, jerking her head at the table across from them. "People with various sized accounts, some authors, most readers, but some of these people don't exactly follow each other or read the same genres," she ended with a frown. "It's not like a convention or book signing, so why offer to pay people who can't afford to come? All for a random last minute party?" Rachel added in a hushed tone.

"You, too?" Amanda asked her. She couldn't afford to be here, and the next thing she knew she had a plane ticket in her name and everything was paid for by a pleading woman on the other line insisting she had to be here tonight. Rachel's quick nod was confirmation, but it didn't slow Rachel down one bit. She continued to give tidbits about everyone in the room, barely stopping to take breaths as more people sat down at their table.

"Stalk much?" Dani Breault laughed as they took a seat at the table.

Rachel shrugged and waved a hand at them. "Hey," she said flatly. "The theme is serial killers. I wanted to be prepared."

Dani shook their head and laughed again. They had also taken in the room with their blue, storm gray eyes before coming to take a seat. They also recognized the odd mix of booktokers attending tonight. They knew some people had been talked into coming with all of their expenses paid, which seemed awfully odd for a simple murder mystery dinner party. Some of these people were very far away from their current location.

"Welcome, my favorite serial killers!" boomed a woman dressed in a black sequined evening gown. She had freckles on her cheeks, and her shoulder length red hair was curled to perfection. "I hope you're prepared for quite an exciting evening!" she announced enthusiastically. Everyone looked around at each other in curiosity and excitement. No one recognized the redheaded woman. "I know I am!" the woman added as she pulled out a chair in the corner of the gymnasium and took a seat.

"What the hell?" Tawni Hargis muttered to the people at her table. Just then, plastic walls dropped from the ceiling, putting all the booktokers strategically in a plastic box. Literally. Some of the booktokers screamed at the loud thud that echoed around the room when the make-shift walls hit the ground.

"This isn't funny!" yelled out Nathalie Gibson as she jumped from her chair and panic took over.

"Let us out!" demanded Sandie Buckley, knocking over her chair as she jolted out of it and ran towards the redheaded woman.

"What's happening?" Rachel Raikar gasped grabbing her chest in panic. Her background as a data scientist had her quickly trying to calculate their survival rate. With the top of the box opened, there wouldn't be gas involved.

Noel Ness grabbed her head quickly. Stress didn't help her with her chronic migraine, and as much as she loved playing board games like *Hunt a Killer*, this was not her idea of fun. She tripped over her chair and nearly fell on her face. Her green eyes scanned the box they had been forced into as she stepped up to the wall and pounded on it with her fist. Incredibly thick, with zero give. "Not good," she muttered to herself.

"Who the hell are you?" demanded Jeanie Dawson. As a registered nurse, she was used to dealing with chaos. Right now, however, she was pissed and anger brewed from her core.

"Who me?" the woman asked innocently, as she took a bag of popcorn being offered to her by some other brunette. "The name's Claudia. And I'm the one person none of you dressed up as," she shrugged and tossed a piece of popcorn into her mouth.

Sheyla Rochelle, Mariska Proulx, Elaine Dymond, and Terri Hinton were closest to Claudia and froze.

"Did she just?..." was all Terri got out.

"Yep," Elaine replied grimly.

"I'm so sorry," Mariska whispered, looking around the room at all the people she had just brought to their death. That's when they felt the vibration beneath them, as the floor began to split.

"What's happening?" shouted out RaeAnna Carroll as she grabbed frantically for the table next to her.

"The pool is underneath us," Mariska announced, only heard by a few while the rest screamed in terror.

"Drowning? Lovely," Sheyla sighed sarcastically, trying to avoid her rising panic.

"Stay calm!" Mariska tried to call out, but the growled response stopped her. As she turned slowly to see what had made the noise, she saw some green round heads popping out of the water.

"Alligators. Even better," Elaine laughed in hysteria.

"Crocodiles," Claudia corrected, as she tossed more popcorn in her mouth.

"You're mad!" screamed Holly as she attempted to climb on top of the table with the others closest to her.

"Would you say mad, or genius?" Claudia asked the brunette.

"A little of both," the woman replied flatly with a shrug, before she turned her head to watch the horror play out.

"Help us!" screamed Tawni at the brunette.

"Oh, you don't want my help," the brunette replied. "I supported the choice of the crocodiles. In the name of science, of course," the woman added as if that made all the difference in the world.

"Liz supports all of my decisions," Claudia said with a sheepish smile as she popped more popcorn into her mouth. Some booktokers had fallen into the water, and were trying desperately to escape the crocs, to no avail.

Claudia tilted her head back and forth as she took in the sounds of the brutal screaming coming from the top of the plastic box. The sound of bones snapping wasn't exactly her favorite, she determined, but this was definitely better than any movie she had watched.

"What am I supposed to do now?" Duke muttered as he walked in behind Claudia. He turned his face from the gruesome scene of body after body being consumed by the eight crocodiles he had wrestled into the pool.

"Get rid of the wall and leave the rest," Claudia replied, engrossed in the spectacle before her. Her eyes gleamed in such excitement, it made Duke nearly throw up.

"Leave the crocs?" he asked shocked.

"Yep. I need to show Aimee I mean business, and if our cleanup crew wants to battle the crocs to hide my work, well...good luck to them," Claudia replied with a smirk.

She watched with mild fascination as a small group of booktokers lost their battle with staying on top of the table. The floor had opened to just the edge of the back plastic wall, forcing them all into the water.

Linda found herself trying to hold the croc's mouth open and at bay with her feet as she fought to keep her head above water. Dani grabbed a chair and just missed the jaws of another croc and shoved the chair in its mouth. It snapped the chair into pieces with a single chomp, and Dani took a broken piece and began stabbing back at it. They didn't see another croc dive under them. They grunted and blood filled their mouth immediately as they were dragged under water.

"Fuck this!" Rosalyn yelled out. "I'm not going out this way!"

"Dive!" they heard Mariska shout from the other side of the pool as she surfaced.

Rosalyn didn't bother to look back as she listened to a woman scream bloody murder as Linda lost her battle with the croc she was holding away with her legs. Rosalyn dove and just barely missed the croc, snapping at where her head was just at. The water was full of so much blood that she couldn't see and started to feel the vomit rise in her throat. She swam for the surface and gagged on the vomit that she was trying to force back down.

"Rosalyn!" she heard Mariska scream, when she felt something clamp onto her leg and drag her back under before she could call back.

"What a fighter," Claudia said impressed.

Mariska was in the middle of the pool, which was full of just as much blood as water. She watched in horror as the seven crocodiles chomped aggressively at various body parts surrounding her. *Seven?* She thought there were eight. Mariska was a swimmer by nature, but she couldn't tread water forever, and definitely not with seven crocs in the water with her.

"You know you won't survive this, right?" Claudia called out over the loud snapping that was echoing around the gym.

"Fuck you," Mariska mumbled as she looked around eagerly for possible options. She counted again as she turned herself around in a circle. Seven. They were all preoccupied. If she could just get to the top of the wall, then she could....

However, there would be nothing that Mariska could do, because the eighth croc had been weaving in and out of the chaos unnoticed, dived under, and came up just in time to catch Mariska by the waist with its jaws of steel. Her body was severed in two.

"We'll have to make sure Reece gets those two," Claudia thought out loud as she jerked her head in the direction of where Mariska and Rosalyn had fought to their death. Liz simply nodded and typed the note into her phone. Claudia sighed in disappointment and got up from her chair. She dumped the bag of popcorn into her chair and put her hands on her hips and frowned.

"Not my most creative work, but it will do," she said chewing on her bottom lip and tilting her head in thought. Then she turned on her heels and started to walk away, with Liz right behind her. She only paused to pat her hand against Duke's shoulder, who pulled away at her touch. "Have fun!" Claudia offered cheerily and nearly skipped out of the room.

Animal control would get numerous calls about crocodiles running loose in the small town. Duke had closed the gym floor half way to give the crocs an opportunity to make their way to solid ground. He lifted the wall and released them into the world to be someone else's problem.

Once they exited, he locked the doors behind him, and disassembled the wall and got rid of it. He fished out the larger body parts and laid them strategically on the gym floor. He left the pool water bloody, and closed the floor the rest of the way. Duke didn't take off his breathing mask until he was outside and locked the building up.

While animal control wrestled with crocodiles that didn't belong in this small town so far away from their natural habitat, a forensic team tried to piece together what exactly had happened with news crews outside demanding answers.

The few booktokers that had tattoos still showing helped to identify that there had clearly been multiple people in the gymnasium without a reason or purpose. There was no booking that showed anything had taken place. It would be months before all the bodies would be identified.

Giselle looked around in concern as a large group of women entered the dream realm. "Hello, and welcome to the dream realm," she said with a weary smile.

John stepped up next to her, looking like his son, but she read his energy and knew better. "Something wrong?" he asked her.

"Just an awful lot of newbies coming in, Sir," Giselle replied, looking around with wide eyes.

John drew his eyebrows together. "What do you mean?" he asked, ignoring that she saw right through his cover.

Giselle nodded as an average height woman with gorgeous bright blue eyes, curvaceous, and shoulder length rose gold hair walked by looking around her in total disbelief. She had an immortality symbol tattooed on the middle of her right wrist, and was dressed up as a serial killer that Giselle had studied in school over ten years ago.

Next to her was another woman about the same height, with hazel eyes, and multicolored hair hitting her mid-back. She was also curved to perfection, and had a pentacle tattoo on her right wrist, and a music symbol tattooed on her right calf visible beneath her current serial killer costume. She held two gauged earrings on each ear, both her upper and lower. "Where are we?" the dazed girl asked Giselle.

"You have entered the dream realm," Giselle offered kindly. "It looks like you were at a party," she stated cautiously.

"A party from hell," snapped the other woman. "Are we dead?" she demanded.

"Yes," John replied as gently as he could.

"Fabulous!" she snapped. "I didn't even want to *GO* to the damn party!"

"I'm sorry," John interrupted, holding his hand up to stop the women from walking away. "What party was this?"

"She said it was going to be a fun booktok party, but some crazy redhead had..." the second woman stopped to shiver. "Crocodiles in the pool underneath us," she forced herself to finish.

John tilted his head, trying to keep his alarm in check.

"I'm Sheyla," the second woman said, offering her hand to Giselle. "This is Terri," she added with a jerk of her head to the woman next to her.

Giselle took her hand and shook it while she asked, "And how many people were at this party?"

Sheyla looked at Terri. Terri gave an aggressive shrug. "Twenty, I think?" Sheyla offered.

"Twenty," Giselle said with a slow nod. She looked sideways at John.

"I think there were still some alive before we lost," Sheyla offered with some hope.

"Would you mind telling us more about this party, and who threw it?" John asked politely, trying to hide his alarm.

The women looked at each other and shrugged, before they began sharing their story of Claudia and her crocs.

James gripped Karmen's hand as he and Sophie worked their way down the busy sidewalk. He held onto Sophie's hand with his other, when he felt her come to a sudden halt. He squeezed Karmen's hand, signaling her to stop, too, and he turned back to see Sophie staring down at her free palm.

"Sophie?" he asked suddenly panicked. He felt her anxiety immediately.

"You know how you kept saying Tina and Ben would come to find us?" she replied weakly.

"They're here?" James asked her shocked she could somehow sense them. "How?"

"Long story," Sophie said, looking up at him in panic.

"You're fine," he said, squeezing her hand gently, sending blue light coursing through her veins faintly. "We're fine," James reiterated with his boyish grin.

Karmen tugged impatiently on his hand, trying to pull them forward. Sophie nodded slowly and started walking towards a fate she wouldn't see coming, but Karmen would.

"Hold on, Kid," James laughed at Karmen's impatience, but Karmen ignored him, and kept tugging urgently to get them to move faster.

When James looked up, he found Ben's hazel eyes staring at him just a few feet away. They were first filled with relief, then with concern as he had clearly seen Sophie, and confusion when Ben noticed the little girl tugging at them both. James gave him a big smile and a shrug as they continued to make their way closer to them in the crowd.

Sophie saw red shoulder length curly hair pass Tina, Tina grab her neck and panic, and in her palm she felt sudden ice where a tiny heartbeat had been beating. Sophie looked down at her palm again, and back at Tina in fear. Tina's eyes met Sophie's and didn't break. She shook her head, and James and Sophie both heard her tell Ben she was fine, but Sophie knew she was anything but.

"No," Sophie whispered to herself, just loud enough for James to hear her. "Tina!" she yelled out, but the crowd was too loud as the bar door opened and live music came barreling out. "Tina!" she cried out as her panic began to overwhelm her. She let go of James, and pushed her way through the crowd more aggressively.

James watched for a split second before looking down at a very distressed Karmen. He dropped to his knee and looked her in the eyes. "I'm so sorry," he told her as tears threatened to escape and run down his cheeks. He felt Sophie's distress so intensely it nearly killed him. "We have to get to them," he nodded at Karmen, who nodded back. She held on tight as they made their way to get closer to an angered Daryl and Ben.

Tina's legs gave out, and Ben had just caught her in time. The crowd continued to push their way past them, until Daryl was next to them, barking at people to step back and give her room. Room wouldn't help Tina, though. Nothing could.

By the time Sophie reached her friends, her eyes were lit up with red flames dancing wildly in her irises. "Get back!" Ben snapped at her, but Sophie ignored him and pushed next to her to grab her hand. She closed her eyes and tried to flow heat into Tina, but she was blocked.

"No!" Sophie screamed when she opened her eyes, and tears ran down her cheeks.

"I'm okay," Tina told her. "I'm just exhausted," she yawned.

"Stay with her," Sophie demanded as she stood up, but Clarice's hand pushed her back down. Sophie turned her rage onto Clarice, but Clarice squeezed her shoulder hard.

"I've got her," Clarice snapped back.

"To hell you do!" Sophie yelled back at Clarice as she heated up, and her hair flew in the wind that didn't seem to exist.

Clarice narrowed her eyes at Sophie. "You can go where we can't," she snarled, trying to control her irritation. "I've. Got. Her," she emphasized and took off through the crowd.

"Karmen!" James yelled as the little girl was yanked from his hands by a huge bald male, as Karmen whaled, kicking and screaming in his arm.

"Mason!" Clarice snapped as she locked her eyes on Claudia weaving in and out of the crowd.

"On it!" he called back into her ear piece.

Crystal blue flames ignited in James's eyes as he locked on the guy pushing his way through the crowd with a fighting Karmen, when he felt a stranger's hand on his shoulder.

"Sophie needs you," the man demanded. "I've got Karmen," he said through a clenched jaw, with eyes fully dilated. "*Sophie* needs *you*," he snapped again before he took off, weaving through the crowd towards Karmen and her assailant.

"James!" he heard Ben call out to him, and he jerked his head to see Sophie closing her eyes, as shimmering waves of heat rippled around her. It forced Ben and Daryl to back away, unable to handle the heat.

"Sophie," James warned, pushing his way towards her. "This is exactly what they want," he yelled, knowing she could easily hear him.

"No!" he heard her protest. "They're in trouble," she growled.

"I know, Babe, but you told me you don't want to hurt them," he thought to himself. He knew she could hear him, but Ben wouldn't. "Please," he begged, as he continued to fight the people who seemed to collect to watch what was happening in fascination, and purposely blocking him from her. "Sophie," he begged out loud, feeling the one thing that scared him. Her enjoyment of being angry. "This isn't who you are," he thought.

"Isn't it?" she replied in a voice that even scared herself.

"Once you cross that line, you will never be able to find your way back. Take it from someone who knows...."

The vision of Clarice holding her head under water flashed before her eyes. Watching her kill Mario in front of her, and the enjoyment that had flashed wickedly across Clarice's face. Even watching her kill her own father, without a single care in the world. Slicing the man's neck outside of the bar, just because she could. Clarice had enjoyed all of it. Sophie had seen it in her eyes. But she had also witnessed Clarice come to Sophie's aide lately, more often than not.

Sophie could take out everyone. The woman who had endangered her friend. She could reach her before Clarice ever would and then focus on Tina, and helping to save her.

"Yes. Everyone," sang a voice that was tiny and unrecognizable. The faces of Tina, Ben, Daryl, James, and even Clarice flashed before her eyes. Sophie opened her eyes immediately, and the flames were ignited. The heat disappeared as quickly as it had shown presence, and Sophie stumbled back into James.

"I've got you," he whispered in her ear.

"I'm sorry," she gasped, shaking her head.

James spun Sophie around to look him in the eye. "You need to go in. See what's happening," he told her, nodding yes as he spoke.

"No, I..." she stammered.

"You can, and you will," James interrupted her. "We don't have Karmen," he reminded her. "And the baby might be in danger. I know you can do this. Tina is counting on you," James added, searching her eyes.

"What if?" Sophie whispered.

"You would never hurt your best friend," he assured her. Sophie nodded weakly and turned to find Daryl standing between her and Tina.

"I can't," he said, shaking his head.

"I know, Big Guy," Sophie said, frustrated. "I know, but we can't leave her in the street," she reasoned with him.

"Um, Babe?..." James started.

"Are you mad?!" Ben yelled, as he cradled his wife to his chest.

"I'm okay," Tina whispered, before closing her eyes to fall into the deepest sleep she had ever had.

"Make up your mind, Buddy," Sophie said, peaking around to look at Tina. "It's time. Now or never."

Daryl's eyebrows furrowed, but he gave her a solid nod.

"We need to get to the room," she called out over her shoulder to James. He fished out his key and started leading the way. Daryl knew the drill, spun on his heels, and peeled Tina out of Ben's arms to carry her through the crowd.

"No!" Ben screamed as he reached desperately for his wife and child. Sophie grabbed one of his hands and dragged him behind her. She waited until they were past most of the onlookers who made a pathway for the group as they made their way to James and Sophie's room. As much as Ben squirmed, Sophie's grip was just tight enough to give him no choice. She yanked him just enough to have him stumble up next to her.

"Brother, listen to me," she begged.

Ben refused to look at her, but he wiped the tears streaking his face instead.

"I need you to monitor Tina and the baby. If it becomes between the two of us, you *WILL* save our family. Do you understand?" she asked, keeping her voice so low that Ben almost missed what she said.

"I will do anything to save my family," he snapped back.

"Yes," Sophie said with a squeeze of his arm. "*Your* family. Don't worry about me."

Ben stopped moving his feet, but she yanked him gently to be back next to her. He knew exactly what she was giving him permission to do. "Sophie, I..." he said.

"You are a doctor," Sophie reminded him. "The only one I ever liked, quite honestly," she said with a smile as she kept her eyes forward and squeezed his hand. "And if I don't make it back, know I love you all."

"Soph," he breathed, as he jerked his head to catch the side of her profile. Sophie just gave him a shake of her head "no", and blinked back her tears.

"Let's go save our girl," she said with a determined smile, still not daring to look at him. Ben nodded and squeezed her hand as they climbed into the elevator with James and Daryl, and headed up to the room.

Ben felt the smallest pulse in Sophie's hand. Almost like it matched the rhythm of a baby's heart beating. He gasped, looking down at his hand and looking back up at Sophie, who simply smiled in response. She gave a gentle squeeze, and he looked at his wife's limp body. He didn't know how this was going to turn out, but if it started to go south, Sophie was going to find herself sleeping with Tina until he could figure out how to wake them both up safely.

Twenty-nine

Aimee walked around Claudia at the park, and whistled, "Impressive," before she leaned her arms on the bridge and stared at the water next to Claudia. The corner of Claudia's lips curled up.

"So, are you joining?" she asked Aimee, impatiently.

"I can do whatever I want?" Aimee confirmed.

Claudia gave her a brief nod to validate the agreement.

"I don't normally play nice with others when I work, but clearly you're worse at it," she said with a frown as she remembered their first meeting.

"Well, I do when it's someone I like," Claudia gave a flirtatious shrug. "You, I like," she added with a sassy grin.

"Well, that is a bit enticing," Aimee beamed back as she looked out at the water. "Partners it is," she said, sliding her pinky finger over Claudia's and giving it a squeeze.

A singe of electricity shot through Claudia's body and she licked her lips. "This is the start of a beautiful relationship," she said in a husky voice.

"Oh, you have no idea," breathed out Aimee.

Daryl laid Tina carefully on the bed, and Sophie laid down next to her, taking Tina's hand in hers. James laid next to Sophie and held her hand and gave it a brief squeeze.

"You've got this," he thought to her. Sophie squeezed his hand back and closed her eyes. She took a deep breath in and let it out slowly.

"I'm coming," she whispered in Tina's direction, and focused on finding Tina's stream of thoughts.

When Sophie opened her eyes, she found a beautiful blush wooden door. She smiled. *Of course, it was a shade of pink.* She looked over and felt James still holding her hand. He nodded encouragingly, and Sophie turned the doorknob slowly and pushed it open. It did not flood them with light like they were used to. In fact, it was quite dim. Like the ambiance of a candle lit restaurant. Sophie cautiously stepped through, but James was pushed back and the door was slammed immediately.

"So much for that," Sophie whispered to herself. She turned to find a champagne pink canopy bed. Black webbing was quickly consuming the room, the bed included.

"Sophie?" she heard Tina call out hysterically.

"I'm coming," Sophie yelled and rushed to the bed. She pulled back the drapes, careful not to touch the black webbing, and crawled in next to Tina. "I'm here," she tried to assure her friend, but when she looked down, Tina's stomach was huge and she looked like she was going to deliver any minute.

"Something's wrong!" Tina cried out in pain as she held her hands over her stomach and twisted around in agony. "Save her!" she demanded.

"I don't know how!" Sophie cried out, as she saw something bulge aggressively from Tina's stomach. It was mad, and it wanted out. Whatever *it* was....

"Save her!" Tina screamed.

Sophie's hands shook as she reached out and placed them on Tina's stomach. "I don't know what to do!" she called out in a panic.

"Save her!" screamed a voice not belonging to Tina. Tina's eyes were completely black, and bloody tear drops spilled down her cheeks.

Sophie closed her eyes and tried to focus. She saw the darkness consuming not only the room, but Tina's body as well. She saw it attacking Tina's neurons, blood vessels, and heart at an alarming rate. Sophie inhaled deeply, trying to calm herself. The second breath she took in, Sophie saw the darkness race towards her hands. *That's it. She just needed to absorb it.*

Sophie focused hard on the darkness and quietly called to it. "Take me," she whispered softly. "Take me instead." It eagerly complied. She slid one hand over to where the creature was trying to push out from. "Come," Sophie demanded. Not to the angry creature, but to the darkness that had quickly consumed it.

Tina's veins raced blue, and she seemed to start finding peace. However, Sophie's body was warming up in return. Too hot and too quickly. She was not only absorbing the darkness, but she was absorbing Tina's life and the life she carried inside of her. She threw her head back and gasped at the life that she was consuming. It felt euphoric, and Sophie couldn't stop herself.

"Sophie," Tina croaked, slapping her hand against Sophie's, trying to get it off of her, but she was already too weak to do anything.

Sophie couldn't hear her over the rushing in her ears. She licked her lips like a ravenous animal after eating its greatest kill.

"Sophie," Tina begged once more before passing out.

"ENOUGH!" shouted the voice that had stopped her in the alley the night before. Sophie felt her body be yanked away from Tina and thrown across the room and out the door with it slamming behind her. "You will not harm this child," she heard the woman hissed.

Sophie sat up, holding her swimming head when she was pushed back even further with another invisible blow. "Get out!" she heard the woman hiss. "You're not welcome here." Sophie was smacked again, and fell even further from the door, and when she opened her eyes, she found James staring back at her.

"What the hell happened?" demanded Ben as she tried to get her bearings.

"I...I don't know," Sophie answered honestly. He was buzzing around Tina and James held onto Sophie on the other bed. Separating her, but still protecting her.

"What happened?" he asked her quietly again. "Why didn't you let me stay with you?"

"It wasn't me!" Sophie hissed defensively.

James rubbed her arm and lit it blue. "What do you mean, Babe?" he asked her gently. "Was someone else in there?" he asked in a low tone that only she could hear.

Sophie just nodded, still holding her head. "But Tina and the baby are safe," she muttered. She wasn't sure what she was more annoyed about. A part of her was annoyed at being interrupted, but most of her was upset that she had put Tina in danger in the first place.

She held onto the fact that it was a good thing she was interrupted, and tried not to be terrified at how easily she lost her senses. How quickly she lost herself without anyone to anchor her.

Sophie didn't realize that James was reading and feeling everything. The information he was gathering from simply touching her was not only overwhelming, but alarming. He used his CIA habits and turned off his own emotions so she wouldn't realize what was happening by feeling his in return. However, James was panicking deep down. *No matter how much he changed to match her, would he really be able to save her from herself?*

It was just for a split second, but James felt just how much she had loved draining Tina of all the life she had to give. He couldn't blame her, because it felt euphoric to him, too. Yet, his will to save humanity remained stronger than hers in that moment. Maybe that was what he had to do. *Keep fighting for humanity when Sophie couldn't do it herself?*

Regardless, this was something he was going to have to digest at a later time, because if he could feel the anger brewing in Ben's core, then so could Sophie. He turned just in time to grab his best friend by the hands that were headed straight for Sophie.

_____

"You almost killed them!" he screamed in rage, as he struggled in James's impossible grip.

"Calm down, Buddy," James warned him.

"Don't tell me to calm down!" Ben snapped.

Sophie raised her hands in retreat. "Did Tina get injected with something?" she asked him eagerly, dismissing his rage.

"What? No! Of course not!" Ben hissed at her.

"Here," Daryl said. He was pointing at her neck at the small puncture wound. "Is that what's wrong?" he asked her.

"I think so," Sophie nodded.

"What?!" Ben yelled and looked at his wife. Daryl waved him back over and showed him the injection sight.

"There was a redheaded woman," Sophie started. "I've seen her a couple of times now." She turned to James. "At the bar," she said, thinking about the first time she had lost control in public. She stopped herself from thinking about the night in the alley before it was too late. "She walked by Tina," Sophie told James hastily, trying to keep herself from recollecting the night in the alley.

"What does she want with Tina?" Ben demanded, glaring back at James. He couldn't even look at Sophie right now.

"Maybe it has to do with what Donna was looking into that made her disappear?" Daryl offered in a sad tone.

"What?!" Sophie cried out in shock. "Donna's missing?" she asked weakly as James caught her and helped her sit back down on the bed behind her.

"Yeah," Daryl confirmed. "They were looking into Rebecca's background."

"Rebecca?" Sophie asked confused.

"We needed to know your background to make the serum," Ben snapped over his shoulder.

"What serum?" James asked, turning to look at his friend.

"Ask your girlfriend," Ben snapped.

"I'm asking you," James said in anger as he stood up and turned his full body to face his friend. "What serum?" he demanded.

"James," Sophie pleaded, standing up and grabbing his arm.

"To stop your out-of-control psychopath girl!" Ben shouted, squaring off against him.

"You what?" James hissed as his eyes lit up in crystal blue flames.

Sophie stepped in front of James, and Daryl took his place in front of Ben. They both held out their hands to stop the boys from attacking each other.

"Listen!" Sophie shouted. "There's too much going on right now to be fighting with each other!" she pleaded, as she found herself backed up to Daryl as they fought to keep the boys apart.

"How are her vitals?" Daryl asked, trying to distract Ben.

"What?" Ben asked, still glaring at James.

"Benjamin," Sophie ordered. "Keep your promise. What are her vitals?" she asked again.

He glared at the back of her head, but turned to look at his wife. "They're stable, from what I can tell."

"Good," Sophie said, as she pulled herself into survival mode. "Whoever is with her may not care for me too much right now, but she thinks she's protecting Tina and the baby, so she's on our side even if she doesn't know it."

"She?" James asked her, distracted.

"Remember the pictures of the woman with the hoop earrings surrounded by fog that Karmen kept coloring?" she asked James to refocus him.

"You met her?" he asked in shock and confusion, not forgetting about the serum despite her efforts.

"I think so," Sophie said, feeling him calm down enough to trust putting her hands down. "I don't think she's an intruder. I think she's here to help with whatever might be coming," Sophie whispered her conclusion.

"Who is Karmen and what is coming?" Daryl asked as he shoved Ben towards his wife. Ben gave him a sour look, but sat next to Tina and held onto her hand.

"Another ghostly war we have to fight?" Ben barked over his shoulder in bitterness.

"This attack was different," Sophie said, shaking her head. "I saw the redhead graze Tina's neck. Whatever she injected into her wasn't to kill her," she said, thinking back about the black spider web that was consuming her friend. "It was to change her. And maybe the baby, too," she thought out loud as she began to pace the room.

"Change her into what?" Ben demanded, forgetting to keep up his glaring contest as he stared at Sophie wildly.

Sophie froze. "Her mind."

"What?" Daryl and James asked in unison.

"Think about it," Sophie said, coming to Tina's other side and ignoring Ben's protest. "She fell asleep. Then when I went in, there was this dark black web spreading around her. Trying to consume her," she began retelling her experience in a rush. "Her eyes turned solid black, and she sounded demonic more than herself," she said, turning to

James and giving him a knowing look.

"What? Like Venom?" Ben asked, shaking his head in disbelief. Sophie looked confused, but having seen her experience replay.

"Yes," James confirmed. "Just like Venom, actually," he said, looking at his friend in fear.

Ben began to laugh and shake his head. Then he saw James's face. "Oh, you have got to be kidding me!" he shouted out his disbelief. Then he looked down at Tina. "What, but if..." was all he got out.

"I stopped it from consuming her," Sophie said in assurance. "But it started attacking me, and the woman Karmen's been drawing threw me out and locked the door."

"Locked the door?" Daryl cut in. "So, what? We can't access her?"

"Not necessarily," Sophie said, shaking her head no. "But we can't let her keep Tina sleeping for too long. It doesn't always end well," she said, giving Ben a look that had him hating her a lot less. He knew the same thing happened to Sophie. Only Sophie wasn't Tina, and Tina wasn't genetically altered to handle what was thrown at her. Neither was his unborn child.

"We need to get her back home," Ben said, jumping to his feet. "Roger will help me keep her safe while you fix this," he added, giving Sophie a glare.

Sophie simply nodded in confirmation.

"So, we're not going to talk about the serum that is meant to what I can only assume will kill you?" James asked as anger brewed within him.

"Sleep," Ben clarified. "Don't be such a baby," he said, pointing at his wife. "We know she can at least take it," he murmured.

James opened his mouth, but Sophie shut it for him. "Later," she said in finality.

"We're not done," he hissed at her.

"We never are," she said with a grin, and kissed him on his cheek.

Mason took off after the tall giant that was carrying a very distressed Karmen through the crowd until he dipped into the alley and disappeared. "Damn it!" cursed Mason as the giant threw Karmen in the back seat of a car and got in quickly to speed away. Mason looked around frantically as he spotted a motorcycle with the keys still in it. The owner was leaning against the post next to it and flirting with a pretty girl, completely distracted.

"Borrowing your bike," Mason growled as he hopped on, kick started it and took off after the car. He didn't pay any attention to the man yelling behind him. He leaned forward to pick up speed and raced through traffic heading into the outskirts of town.

Traffic was becoming less crowded as people got off the street to go to their final destination. Mason gained ground quickly until he saw the hand come out of the window and bullets started flying in his direction. He swerved to barely miss the first one.

"Nice try," Mason muttered as he swerved from side to side, avoiding the bullets coming his direction until the magazine ran empty. Mason chuckled as he closed the gap between him and the car in front of him. The car started swerving to prevent him from pulling up next to it.

"Child's play," Mason laughed to himself. He fell behind the car and kicked it into high gear as he hopped the bike onto the trunk, over the hood, and down the front of the car before racing forward and sliding sideways to a stop. He pulled out his 9mm and shot it through the windshield, hitting the driver right between the eyes.

The car lost control and skidded all across the road before coming to a complete stop. Mason smirked at his successful shot. He climbed off the bike and ran towards the car. He yanked open the back passenger door to rescue Karmen, but instead felt a sharp pain in his chest, forcing him backwards a few steps. Mason looked down as he felt the sticky liquid quickly soak up his shirt. It was dark and red. He'd been shot.

Aimee crawled out of the backseat, dragging a screaming and kicking Karmen behind her. She leaned down over Mason and looked at him with curiosity. "Nice riding," she professed. Mason's eyes were wild, like an animal, as he looked back up at her. "Oooo, you're not so happy, are you?" she asked smiling. "Relax. You won't die," she offered. "No organs were hit, but you are quite the bleeder," she added with fascination. "Maybe you will die."

Mason looked at Karmen, who looked at him and calmed instantly. She began shaking her head back and forth in a "no" motion.

"I will come save you," he growled as he dropped to his knees. It was getting harder to breathe.

"Oh, that's doubtful," Aimee beamed. "But I do applaud your enthusiasm."

Mason dragged his eyes back to Aimee. "How little you know," he laughed as he coughed out blood.

"Oh, okay," she said sarcastically. "Thanks for the bike."

Mason watched as she dragged Karmen away, kicking and screaming, shoving her on the bike in front of her, and taking off down another alley. He took a shaky hand and placed it over the wound. He fell over on his side and blinked rapidly as he fought to remain conscious. Mason heard a raven squawking at him as it hopped toward his face, tilting its head from side to side.

"I'm not dead yet," he muttered. The bird squawked loudly one more time and morphed into a tall, thin woman with black curls framing her face and cascading down her shoulders.

"No, you're not," the woman whispered. "We're not done with you yet."

Mason looked at her in shock and confusion. She placed her hand over the wound and closed her eyes. He was too tired and weak to fight her touch. He felt heat and warmth move quickly throughout his body. Something was being pulled through his chest. *The bullet?*

He closed his eyes and grunted in agony as it pulled back out of his chest. He felt the soft tissue and everything else damaged by the bullet be quickly stitched back together as if it hadn't sliced through him. The sound of metal hitting the pavement next to him forced his eyes to open and stare at it.

"Now," the woman declared. "Go save the girl." With her final words, she crouched down and morphed back into the raven. She squawked madly at him, ruffled her feathers wildly, and took off into the air.

"What the fuck?!" Mason coughed out in disbelief as he rolled over to his knees, took the bullet in his hand, and slowly stood up.

Even though the bullet wasn't still in him, his body still had some healing to do. He staggered to the car and pulled the tree of a body out and onto the street. He climbed inside and pushed through the pain as he kicked out the windshield so he could see to drive.

Mason leaned over the steering wheel and started the car, taking off in the direction he saw Aimee go down, realizing he just met one of the partners of Claudia face-to-face, finally. It wouldn't be the last.

He clutched onto the bullet furiously in his hand as he went to save Karmen.

<u>Thirty</u>

There was a knock on the hotel door, and everyone froze. James threw up his hand to stop Ben from getting up and jerked his head in Tina's direction. Daryl went to see who was at the door, but Sophie grabbed his arm and shook her head.

"Sophie, Ma'am," came a quiet female voice. "I have the chopper waiting to take Tina back to the lab," she called out. Sophie looked at James as everyone else stared at the door. The woman sighed impatiently. "Clarice sent me," she offered in irritation. "I'm Emma."

Everyone looked at Sophie, but she just stared at the door.

"If you open the door, I can explain," she said, clearly losing her patience.

Ben had the door opened before anyone realized he had gotten that close to it. He flung it open and yanked the woman into the room before shutting it. "Where's this helicopter?" he demanded.

The redheaded girl smoothed out her sweater and gave him a glare. "Not far from here, but you will need to stop manhandling me in order to gain access to it," she retorted.

"Who are you?" demanded Daryl.

"As I stated before, my name is Emma," she replied as she glared at Daryl. "I'm an assistant to Clarice. She sent me a message that we needed to get you a helicopter and get Tina to the lab to be treated by Dr. Jacobs."

"My wife doesn't need another doctor," growled Ben. "And no one is touching her but me!"

Emma turned her attention back to Ben. "Dr. Jacobs has very specialized skills, and will be able to help figure out what was done to her," she said, looking at Tina sleeping soundly on the bed.

"Where's Karmen?" James asked.

Emma looked over at James in confusion. "I have no orders for a Karmen," she stated very robotically.

James looked at Sophie, and Sophie nodded in confirmation. She looked at Emma. "Where is this lab, and is it fully equipped to allow Ben to monitor his wife?" Sophie asked.

"She's not going!" Ben shouted.

Emma ignored the outburst. "Top-notch," she confirmed with a solid nod.

Sophie looked over at Ben, but he was already shaking his head. "We have the equipment at the hotel," he protested. "And I'm not taking her to the lion's den!" he added in anger.

"We are not lions," Emma clarified as she stuck her chin up into the air, and Ben ignored her.

"Have you forgotten that this is the woman who has hunted you your *ENTIRE LIFE*?!" Ben shouted.

Sophie looked at him with sympathy. "No one is more aware than me," she said gently.

James put up his hands. "We're losing time," he announced. "Let's compromise," James offered as he looked at Daryl. "Can you get Cecil and everyone to meet you there, my dad included?" he added.

"I was not instructed to bring more than the five of you," Emma protested.

"This is non-negotiable," James cut her off. "Where is this lab?"

"Defeats it being a secret," Emma muttered with her eyes narrowing.

Sophie had her by the throat and up against the door before anyone could react. Red flames fired in her eyes. "Emma," she said in a low growl. "You can give us the information freely, or I can take it myself. I don't really care which you choose right now."

"Sophie!" James called out, but Sophie ignored him.

Sophie felt her disbelief, followed by terror. "Clarice will have my head!" she gasped as she tried to pry Sophie's hands away from her neck without any success. Sophie just laughed as the fire danced in her eyes.

"Clarice will be the least of your worries if you don't give us that address," Sophie growled before lowering the girl so her feet hit the ground fully again. Emma coughed as she rubbed her sore neck. "I will deal with Clarice if she gives you any issues," Sophie announced and Emma looked up at her shocked.

"No one deals with Clarice," Emma said in a hoarse and

confused tone.

"You haven't met us," Sophie said with her familiar grin.

Emma looked around the room as if she were calculating her options. "Fine," she said in defeat, and walked over to the table to scribble down the address on a piece of paper and handed it to Daryl. "We can inform them who is coming once we arrive," she said with a frown. Daryl nodded and gave her a weary smile. He turned and went to the bathroom to make the phone call.

"Great," Ben muttered.

"I know you're not happy, Bro," James offered. "But I think this will be the best thing for your family," he said, looking at Tina. Ben let out a heavy sigh.

"We must hurry," Emma ordered as Daryl came back from the bathroom and handed her back the piece of paper. She was surprised at the gesture, but couldn't process it right now.

"I've got her," Daryl said softly to Ben as he carefully collected the sleeping Tina into his arms. She laid her head against his chest and sighed in content.

"Let's go," Emma ordered. "The car is downstairs."

"Go ahead," Sophie said to Ben and Daryl.

"Wait, what?" Ben asked, whirling around.

"We have to get Karmen," James answered.

"You're sending us to God knows where alone?!" Ben protested in anger.

"He has a point," Sophie told James.

"I'm not leaving you," he said matter-of-factly.

Just then, there was another knock at the door.

"What is this? Grand Central Station?" Ben asked exasperated.

"Ben?" came the timid voice. He recognized it immediately.

"Stacey?" he asked in confusion. He pushed around everyone and answered the door. "What are you doing here?"

Stacey looked around the room until her eyes focused on the sleeping Tina. "Oh my God! What happened?" she demanded as she rushed to her friend.

"We don't know exactly," Ben replied. "Stacey," he said more firmly. "What are you doing here?"

Stacey brushed the hair from Tina's face before turning to Ben. Guilt consumed her. "She told me to come," she said, looking down at the floor. "Okay, so she told me to come later, but something just didn't feel right. So, I took off immediately and have been traveling nonstop to get here," she confessed.

"Who are you?" James asked, confused.

"Stacey," she said, holding out her hand, glad to not have to look at Ben. "I work with Tina at the FBI," she announced proudly.

"She knew," Ben said dryly as he turned to look at his wife, before turning his growing rage onto the new visitor.

"We really need to get going," Emma protested.

"How long have you been talking to her?" Ben asked bitterly, as his cheeks grew red.

Stacey slid behind Daryl despite his arms being full. "A while," she confessed nervously.

"How long is a while?" Sophie asked as she put herself in front of Ben to stop him from attacking the innocent girl.

Stacey gave a hard swallow. "Since she sent me the flash drive to keep it safe," she offered weakly as she crinkled her face up.

James, Daryl, and Sophie looked around at each other as Ben's eyes narrowed even more in Stacey's direction.

Emma stamped her foot down. "We will have to discuss this later. We need to go. NOW!" she yelled into the crowd.

"Oh, we will *definitely* be discussing this further," Ben hissed.

Stacey hid her face in Daryl's back, and he felt sorry for her, but his hands were full and they needed to get Tina help. Now. "Children, we need to go," he said as he looked down at Tina.

"Lead the way," Ben said, turning to face Emma, clearly deciding his wife and child were coming before his irritation with the secrets she had been keeping from him. Again.

"Nice to finally meet you," Stacey whispered to Sophie as she passed her, still sticking close to Daryl in case Ben decided to release his wrath on her again.

"Likewise," Sophie offered with a smile. "See you soon," she said with an encouraging nod.

Stacey smiled and nodded back at her. Sophie turned to James. "I'm a little worried about Ben," she confessed honestly.

"He'll be fine," he assured her. "We need to go get Karmen."

"We don't know where they took her," Sophie replied. "Where do we start?"

"Did I ever tell you I was a tracker?" James offered with a smile.

"Is there anything you weren't?" Sophie asked with a giggle.

James shrugged and tossed her bag to her as he threw his on his back. He took her hand, and they headed back to where Karmen had been yanked from his hands.

Clarice followed Claudia into an abandoned building on the outskirts of town. She slid into the lobby and waited for her eyes to adjust to the darkness. Claudia was leaning up against the reception desk, looking nonchalantly at her nails.

"Such a drama queen," she said, holding out her nails in front of her face.

Clarice forced her breathing to slow down. "I prefer grand entrances," she said flatly with a shrug. "What did you do to Tina?" she asked as casually as she could.

Claudia threw her head back and cackled wildly. A move Clarice usually made herself. "I don't like gnats in my way," she said calmly, studying Clarice as if seeing her for the first time.

"We have a lot in common," Clarice said, placing her hands on her hips, and taking in Claudia. *Could the girl even fight? That could be her advantage.*

"I told you we were sisters," she said, purring like a kitten. Her hair was pulled back into a ponytail, and although she had a similar build to Clarice, there was nothing genetically tying them together that Clarice could note. Although she did resemble Jess more than she cared for.

"Being daddy's science experiment and being blood are two very different things," Clarice said doubtfully. "And besides," she added. "I already have one sister, and she's annoying enough."

Claudia's lips curled up at the corners in a toothless smile. "And what if I could take care of that for you?" she asked, jerking her chin towards the sky.

Clarice swallowed the lump that suddenly appeared in her throat. "Can you?" she asked curiously.

"There's many things I can do," Claudia purred as she closed her fingers into a fist.

Okay. Maybe she could fight.

Clarice took a couple of steps forward. "What can a biologist do, exactly?" she laughed, crossing her arms over her chest.

Claudia put her hands on the desk behind her. "I love that you think that's all I am," she replied with a smirk.

"Oh, you're one crazy bitch. I'll give you that," Clarice sneered.

Claudia tilted her head as pride covered her face. "Thank you!" she exclaimed.

Of course, she thought that was a compliment. Clarice rolled her eyes. "You act like you're the only one he's ever done something to," she sighed, shaking her head.

Claudia's face fell flat. *Oh, she didn't like that.* Clarice noticed her jaw tighten and the sound of grinding teeth echoed the empty lobby.

"I know you have nothing," she snapped, and then, as if on cue, regained her composure. "But I will need my necklace back, now," she purred again.

The gold necklace suddenly seemed to burn Clarice's skin, and she placed a protective hand over it. *Why?* She didn't know. "It's not yours," she growled back.

"According to the letter, and the *gift* he left for me, it is," Claudia replied innocently, but emphasizing the word gift. Clarice didn't miss it. She just wasn't in the mood to process it.

"If you want it so badly, why not come and take it?" Clarice inquired just as innocently, and batting her eyes like she did before taking down her prey.

Claudia puckered her lips and made a tsk tsk sound. "It really would be a shame to kill you," she said slowly. "You have so much...potential," Claudia announced as she pushed herself off the desk and stepped closer to Clarice. "So, just hand it over, and I will share the *gift* father left for us," she replied, holding out her hand and walking towards her.

Clarice looked mesmerized at Claudia's hand as she drew closer. She reached behind her neck, pulled her hair over one shoulder, and unclasped the necklace before dropping it gracefully.

"That's a good girl," Claudia purred as she began to walk past Clarice.

"Or not," Clarice said, wrinkling her nose, grabbing Claudia by the ponytail and yanking so hard that Claudia found herself falling to the floor with a thud.

A grunt escaped her lips when she hit the floor. "Bad choice," she snarled as she flipped onto her stomach faster than Clarice had even seen Sophie move, reached out, grabbed Clarice by the ankle, and pulled her feet out from underneath her. Clarice managed to stumble backwards without falling to the ground. Claudia pushed herself back onto her feet.

"Correction," Claudia hissed out. "You *had* potential."

Clarice took stance like her and Jess used to in training, and she put her hands up, ready for the next attack. "Well," Clarice shrugged. "I've always been a disappointment," she sneered.

Claudia screamed out in frustration as she ran straight at Clarice. Unlike fighting with Jess, Clarice grabbed her shoulders and felt a force stronger than Claudia should be able to have, push them both backwards a few feet. Clarice jerked her head forward and head-butted her, forcing Claudia to stumble back in a daze. *Enhanced, but not a skilled fighter.* Clarice took a stance again.

"Bitch!" yelled Claudia. Clarice had hit her with enough force that blood was running down from her forehead.

"I get that a lot," Clarice sneered before racing towards Claudia. She took her right elbow and jammed it onto the top of Claudia's head and then up her chin. Her head bounced backward like a bobble head as she fell back into a support column. The building moaned with the force.

"Enough child's play," Claudia growled as she took off with an animalistic speed, and shoved her right shoulder into Clarice's stomach and wrapping her arms around her waist. Clarice grunted on impact. The women slid across the floor as Claudia crushed some of Clarice's ribs when her back hit the column behind her.

Clarice cried out on impact, and when she bent over to catch her breath, she wheezed out, "Déjà vu," in irritation, thinking of the first time she fought Sophie. Claudia kicked her in the chin with all of her might, sending Clarice across the room and into the wall behind her. The wall cracked in response, along with several of Clarice's bones. "So original," she groaned out once she was able to get to her feet.

"I know you're used to having the shit kicked out of you," Claudia cackled.

Clarice let out a laugh, but then winced in pain immediately. "I meant Algos mixing animal DNA with human," she clarified.

Claudia froze. *Was that what had happened?* But before she could process it, Clarice grunted as she smacked Claudia across the face with a two-by-four. "You think too much, Pretty," Clarice snarled as she wiped the blood from her nose that was running into her mouth.

Claudia cackled as she turned around to face Clarice, wiping the blood from her face. "Don't hate me because I'm beautiful and smart," Claudia taunted.

"Oh, I don't," Clarice sneered. "I hate you because you're a bitch."

Claudia laughed. "Good to know," she breathed out. "But you have a conscious and I do not," she smirked as she spun around and jabbed her foot into Clarice's stomach, sending her flying to the other side of the room.

Clarice was quickly calculating her options. Claudia was stronger. Faster. But she didn't know how to street fight. Clarice did. Claudia had the upper hand. Clarice knew how to get dirty. That made them pretty even. If she survived this, she was going to have to definitely rethink how she would kill Claudia, because today would not be the day.

"Nice move," Clarice coughed out the blood quickly filling her mouth. "So, you have been trained," she added, impressed.

Claudia gave that toothless grin as she stuck out her chin in pride again. "They made us take a lot of self-defense classes on the campus," she shrugged.

She never really thought she would use any of it, but here she was. Claudia walked up to Clarice as she waited for her to catch her breath. No fun just taking her out right away. She was still hungry. Claudia swung hard, meaning to knock Clarice right in the jaw, but Clarice ducked faster than she had expected.

Clarice popped up, and head-butted her once more, sending Claudia back a few steps before she grabbed her by the hand, and flipped her onto her back, snapping her wrist in the process. Claudia howled in pain as her bones cracked, and anger like she had never felt before, filled her body. Clarice put some space between them to catch her thinning breath, and Claudia scrambled to her feet.

Claudia charged, and Clarice side stepped, but Claudia grabbed her by the hand and crossed both of their arms over Clarice's neck as she dragged Clarice with her up against the wall, crushing her throat while she did. Clarice grasped for air as she used her free fist and slung it backwards right into Claudia's left eye. She howled like a wolf as she shoved Clarice off of her and pulled out the gun stuck in the back of her pants before Clarice could react.

Claudia emptied her magazine into Clarice's body. In the legs, arms, and chest. Clarice's body jerked with every impact, and she fell onto her knees and onto her face. She thought of watching her mother die before her as she heard Claudia's heels click across the floor. She was breathing heavily, but Clarice was in much worse shape. Claudia leaned down so Clarice could see her face. "Such a pity," she said with a frown.

The floor beneath Clarice's face was growing colder by the second. Claudia dangled the necklace in front of her eyes. "Thanks for the necklace, Sis," she purred. "Now, to take care of the rest of the family," she sneered as she stood up and brushed some of the dust off her sweater.

"At least she's not unscathed," Clarice whispered to herself, as she suddenly felt so tired that she needed to sleep. She closed her eyes and began drifting off.

Thirty-one

Jess stabbed a wooden stake through a very large wolf's heart, and smiled a wicked smile as she stood back up. They had been to several realms, but no Donna. Not yet. There was a sudden chill that consumed her heart. She jerked her head up in Jack's direction. "Clarice," she whispered, and was gone before Jack could catch her.

Corbin was in the middle of having a conversation with John, when his heart nearly stopped beating. "No," he gasped, and was gone before John could react.

Duke stood in the doorway of the empty office building. "Burn it," Claudia snarled as she walked past him.

"I thought you were leaving a trail?" he asked in confusion. The look he got from Claudia chilled him to his bones.

"I said...Burn. It," she hissed and tossed her loosened ponytail over her shoulder and stalked away.

Duke shrugged and walked to his black SUV as Claudia got into the passenger seat and waited patiently. He grabbed the gas can and went back inside. He didn't have the heart to actually set Clarice on fire, even though he was pretty sure that was what Claudia wanted.

However, he had watched Clarice be tortured enough by Algos and decided she didn't deserve that, too. So, instead, he doused the place around her, lit a match, and walked away. Never looking back.

Jess flickered into the space. "Clarice!" she cried out over the flames, trying to locate her sister. Jack appeared within seconds by her side.

"Where is she?" he asked, looking around the room anxiously.

"Clarice!" they heard Corbin shout as he appeared. "Where is she?" he demanded as he radiated ice blue flames around him.

"We don't know," Jack yelled over the creaking building that was threatening to collapse around them.

"Clarice!" Jess screamed as she raced to her sister.

Corbin followed her gaze, and found an unconscious Clarice laying face forward on the ground. Her life source quickly leaving her. He threw up his hand towards Jess and she found herself frozen. "Go," he snarled, still staring at Clarice. Beams on fire fell around her.

"Fuck you!" Jess screamed. "Clarice!"

Corbin looked at Jack, and he knew why Jess had to go. Jack closed his eyes and nodded before disappearing and reappearing behind Jess. "We have to go," he whispered gently in her ear.

"NO!" Jess screamed as her body ignited and matched the room around her.

"Please, Jessie," he begged, wrapping his arms around her. "Don't make me do something I don't want to do."

"GO NOW!" Corbin barked, locking his eyes back on Clarice.

"Jessie," Jack begged one more time, and Jess's knees gave out from underneath her as she fell back into her husband's arms, sobbing wildly before they both disappeared.

"Damn it, Clarice," Corbin hissed out, and disappeared, only to reappear right next to her. He could not carry her out of here. *Or could he?* He just had to get the portal close enough. *Then maybe?* He looked to the ceiling and gave a silent prayer, as he stuck his hand into the air and opened one right above them. Corbin thought of where he wanted to go, like Angie had taught him. Then he yanked the portal door down over them both, just in time to miss a large beam from falling and crushing her entirely.

Shyera entered the make-shift bedroom in irritation. "Just because I saved you once," she started, but froze at the scene before her. Corbin was nearly passed out completely, leaning his limp body over Clarice protectively. Both hanging on a string of life that was about to snap. "What have you done?" she gasped, unable to move.

"I will not let her die!" he hissed out his last breath and collapsed.

"He loves her," she whispered to herself, just as a raven flew in and perched itself on the table across the room from her. Shyera threw up her hand. "Don't start with me," she growled. "I know I can't save them both." It was time to take a stand and choose a side. The raven squawked at her and without any hesitation she whispered, "Him."

The bird ruffled its feathers and flapped its wings in fury, and Shyera's eyes lit up red. She turned her attention to the bird. "I save him, he saves her," she proclaimed as fire ignited within her palms. The bird was clearly displeased, but she didn't care as she raised her chin to the sky and closed her eyes.

Breathing in deeply, her whole body ignited, and she called out the words she needed. The temperature grew hotter as she gathered all the energy she could from the realm. With her eyes still closed, she brought her chin down and pointed it in Corbin and Clarice's direction. Still chanting under her breath, Corbin's body was lifted gently into the air to hover above Clarice's.

Shyera stretched her arms out in his direction and opened her eyes. She screamed, and all the energy she had gathered was poured directly into Corbin. Waves of power rippled through the air around them.

Blue light began to slowly race through his veins, chasing each other to the finish line until he was fully ignited and charged. When he opened his eyes, blue light flooded the room. The raven ducked its head under its wing to not be blinded. He raised his chin to the sky and gave out a yell as he absorbed every drop of energy now electrifying his body and soul.

When Shyera had nothing left to give, she dropped to her knees and her head dropped in exhaustion. Corbin dropped to the floor, landing on one knee and his head hanging low. Once he gathered his senses, all he could hoarsely whisper was, "Why?"

Shyera remained silent as she gasped air back into her lungs. Finally she replied, "Love." The raven squawked and flew away in irritation, and Shyera faded into a mist. *Clarice.*

Corbin quickly turned to the woman who was dying on the bed behind him. He inhaled deeply before leaning over to whisper into her ear. "I have to heal you now," he said softly. "It will be intense, but I need you to trust me," he informed her. "I won't let anything bad happen to you," he tried to assure her. "But you will have to let me in so I can save you."

He brushed his lips against her cheek, kissing her ever so tenderly before standing up straight and collecting himself. She would not die. Not on his watch. And if it meant giving her his last drop of life, then he would do it. Because he did love her. And he would pay any price to make sure she kept living.

"Here goes nothing," he breathed out before leaning down next to her again. He reached out and was thankful to be able to take her hand in his. He gently squeezed it before gently kissing the top of it. There was a blue glow on Clarice's body where he had left his mark.

Clarice heard the words he whispered in her ear, but she had no ability to respond. Even she knew she was dying, and she was pretty pissed off about it. Yet, even anger couldn't save her. Then she felt the softness of his lips against her cheek, and the memory of the day he seemed to suck the poison from her blood and heat came flooding back. How warm he made her feel, and the immense need of him she found herself consumed with while he touched her. *Well, if she was going to die, that would be one hell of a way to go.*

There was a moment when she felt nothing. *Great. He changed his mind, and now I have to die!* But she felt him take her hand in his and give it a squeeze, and somehow all of her worry evaporated. She only felt his lips leaving a gentle kiss on the top of her hand, and the warm burning sensation that was left on her skin when his lips weren't on her. Then she felt it again, a little further on her wrist.

Oh, just take me! Clarice's head was screaming at her after the fourth kiss, but Corbin couldn't seem to hear her, or was just blatantly ignoring her. Instead, he continued the slow, agonizing pace as he slowly moved his lips up her arm and to her shoulder. She thought she was going to explode once he got to the crevice of her neck.

Clarice's head turned ever so slightly to give him more access to her favorite spot. Corbin smiled against her neck as he kissed her.

"That's my girl," he whispered as he used his tongue to get an even better taste of her. She heard his whispered moan of approval, and he felt her shallow breathing skip in response. *Focus....*

He gently ran his nose up her neck, leaving a blue line of energy in its wake. He nuzzled her ear before gently nibbling on the lobe. She purred briefly like a kitten, and it made him want her even more, but he knew better.

Corbin traced kisses from one temple to the other, and he

caught her bottom lip, quivering as he did. The grin that was permanently plastered on his face grew wider, but he kept the pace as he nuzzled her other ear before gently nibbling on her lobe.

Are you fucking kidding me? Clarice was losing her mind! She was pretty sure he knew it too, because she didn't have to see his stupid boyish grin to know it was on the other side of her closed eyes waiting for her.

As much as she wanted to just take him and show him how to do this right, she also knew she still had no strength to even open her eyes, let alone lift her arms to pin him down and show him how it was done. She silently swore to herself that she would survive this simply to get even.

"Stop pouting," he ordered as he leaned down and kissed her furrowed brows.

Could he see how frustrated she was?

He nuzzled her neck and kissed and nibbled her, making her forget how irritated she was with him right now.

"That's better," he grinned before moving down her other arm. Only this time, when he got to her fingers, he gently put each of them into his mouth, sucking on them and moaning. He noticed she was trying to arch her back in response, and he gathered himself again. "Forgive me, but it doesn't work through your clothes," he said, obviously nervous.

Still unable to open her eyes, she did her best to nod and give him approval.

"I have to do this to save you," he said warily. "But I do it because I love you."

What?...

There was a deafening silence. Then she felt his hands gently rest on her hips.

Did he say he loved me?

She felt him nervously roll her top up, exposing her stomach. He paused briefly before he began leaving a trail of blue light from his kisses. Clarice tilted her head back and arched as much as her limp body would allow in pleasure as she absorbed the life he was giving her. The bullets pulled through her body and rolled off the bed onto the floor.

Corbin saw and heard her pleasure, but he also knew this kind of transference heightened desire. It wasn't how she actually felt, and he needed to remember that so that he didn't take advantage of her, even though he wanted nothing more. Just because he loved her didn't mean she loved him back, and he needed to not lose control right now.

He was surprised to feel her fingers running through his hair, encouraging him to keep going. Corbin jerked his head up to see her head tilted as she was watching him with a look he couldn't interpret exactly. *Was it acceptance?...* He cleared his throat.

"I need to keep going. This isn't enough, but..." he looked down, almost regretting he was having to do this to her. Corbin felt her tug on him, and heard her whisper hoarsely, "Up." A small smile spread across her lips.

Corbin had straddled her to pull her shirt up, so he let her guide him up to her until they were nose to nose. "Kiss me," she begged.

"Trust me," Corbin gulped. "There's nothing I want more, but what you're feeling is a side effect," he finished with a frown.

A tear ran down her cheek and he caught it before it got to her chin. "Please," she begged.

"I can't," Corbin said, shaking his head and dropping his eyes.

"But I want you, too," she croaked out her confession.

Want and love weren't the same thing.

"Seriously?" he heard her voice crack from dryness and irritation.

"It's not enough," he said, looking deep into her eyes. Clarice was pretty sure he was burning through her soul, if she actually had one. "I will not take advantage of you like that," he said sternly.

"So, let me get this straight," she said, squinting her eyes and dropping her hands from him. "You're going to let me die unless I tell you that I...well...you know," she growled.

"No," he said, giving her his stupid boyish grin that drove her nuts. "I'm going to save you, so that when you're back to being amongst the living, then I can make you fall madly in love with me," he replied with a sneer.

"I'm sorry, what?" she asked with a laugh before she winced in pain.

Corbin quickly placed his lips on her side and kissed the pain of her cracked ribs away.

"Can you even do things?" she asked. "Being dead and all?"

Corbin chuckled, trying to hide his nerves from her. He wasn't exactly sure how many lines could be crossed before he would have to pay the ultimate price. So, he simply offered her, "You're here, aren't you?"

"Huh," she said, a little surprised. *Had she just been fooling herself with the excuse that they could never be together?* "And what if I did? You know..." she asked, unable to look him in the eye. He could just be telling her what he thought she needed to hear because she was already dying.

Corbin tilted his head to study her. The corner of his lip curled up.

"I mean, if you save me and all," she pushed on. "I'm gonna die without you touching me regardless, and it will be your fault." The corner of her lips curled up.

He couldn't speak or move.

"So. Help. Me..." she growled, and before she could finish, his mouth was crushing against her and claiming it for his own. Their tongues swirled around each other as he held her face in his hands, and her hold around his neck became more fierce. He pushed his love out to her, and she absorbed it like a sponge. When they broke to get some air, she giggled like he had never heard her do before.

"So, can we speed this up so I can show you how it's really done?" she taunted.

"I will do my best," he chuckled and crawled away from her.

"Hey!" she whined, trying to sit up, but still too weak to do so.

"Do you want to show me up or not?" he asked with that stupid grin she loved so much.

She squinted her eyes at him before laying her head down and shouting, "Fine!"

"Try something new," she heard him taunt. "And actually enjoy the ride."

However, she was already plotting all the ways she was going to get him back to hear the words he was teasing her with. Clarice felt Corbin take off her shoes and tossing them to the side. Then he was back on top of her, unbuttoning her pants. He rubbed his nose at the hem of her underwear, leaving a trail of kisses and blue light. She squirmed under his touch.

He climbed off of her to study her. He knew it was hard for her to let her guard down. To let anyone in, let alone him. He would die again, trying to show her just how much she was worthy of love.

"What?" she finally asked self-consciously.

"Your pants are a little tight," he said in a frown. "I'm not complaining," he quickly added, "but we can't move you too much yet."

Before she could respond, she felt him jerk them off, similar to a magician yanking a tablecloth off a set table. It was so quick and shocking. Her jaw dropped. "Okay," she breathed out in lust. "One for the ghost man."

"Oh, we're keeping score, now?" he asked, tilting his head and eying her. Clarice's eyes widen. "Challenge accepted," he grinned before crawling up her like a tiger approaching its prey. Heat filled her core, and she squirmed eagerly in anticipation. He rolled up her top and sports bra, setting her breasts free. He sucked in his breath. "Damn, Clarice," he breathed. "You're gorgeous."

"No points for lying," she said with a frown.

He gently grabbed her chin in his hands, faster than even Sophie moved, forcing her to stare into his sapphire blue eyes. "I'm not lying," he said in a low growl. "I never want to hear you say that again." There was so much emotion flowing from his eyes that it caught her off guard.

"Okay," she breathed out the breath she didn't even know she had been holding.

He let go of her chin and stared into her soul. "You're beautiful," he insisted. "It's a disgrace that you don't know that, but I will never let you forget," he said in a low voice that made her wet in response.

"Okay," she repeated with a gulp. "Two for the ghost man," she whispered in a husky tone. No one had ever told her she was beautiful and meant it. It was fueling the heat in her core and between her legs. "Please continue," she offered in a shaky voice.

He gave a quick nod, as if recollecting himself, and leaned down to gently kiss her lips before pulling away. She groaned in protest at his break away, but he just smiled wickedly at her. "Patience," he taunted. "Can I touch you?" he finally asked hesitantly.

"That would be nice," she said sarcastically.

He reached out and cupped her breasts, running his thumbs in small circles over her firm nipples, forcing her to arch her back and mew in response. Corbin bent down and placed his mouth over one, sucking at the energy it eagerly gave back to him. Clarice's mouth filled quickly with saliva, and warm fluid soaked her panties in anticipation.

Hearing her approval made him even harder, and she felt the pressure against her leg, which made her smile in response. He nuzzled his nose against the hardened nipple and gave it a kiss before moving on to the other side.

"Touch me," she pleaded, and he didn't have to guess where. He slid a hand and found his way beneath her panties. A low grumble escaped as he felt her slick warmth eagerly awaiting him.

"Clarice," he moaned as he pulled away briefly from sucking the life she gave from her other nipple. "You're so wet," he offered, before opening wider to take her full breast in his mouth and suck harder to show his approval.

Clarice groaned in response as she pushed herself against his hand. He let his fingers wonder amongst her sex, making her wetter by the second. Her hands found his hair again as she tugged and let her eyes roll to the back of her head.

He kissed her lightly all along her collarbone before finding her neck again. "We're just getting started," he snarled in her ear, making her quiver and nearly coming in his hand right then.

No man had ever had such an effect on her before in her life! If this was love, she would gladly accept it with open arms. Then a finger slid into her throbbing opening, and she gasped at the sensation. She wasn't sure if the heat was from the energy he was giving her, but the words, "Fuck me!" escaped her mouth.

"Oh, I will," she heard his slow voice, thick with desire, answer back.

Gaining more movement in her arms, she pushed them down and eagerly pulled at his shirt. He only paused long enough to pull it off before he leaned down and kissed her deeper than any man had before. She responded just as eagerly with her tongue and moaned before biting and pulling on his bottom lip with her teeth.

He groaned and pushed his fingers deeper inside her, making her groan in response. She was gaining more strength and bucked eagerly against his palm as she arched her back and threw her head back. Digging her nails into his back and running them up and down.

"Clarice!" he called out, and began matching her rhythm so she could feel his erection growing larger by the second against her leg. "Are you trying to make me cum before I'm done pleasing you?" he breathed out.

"Maybe," she said with a sneer as her hands continued to explore his muscular arms, abs, and ass. "Damn," she breathed out,

"You're pretty in shape for a dead guy."

He let out a laugh that came from his gut. "I guess you can say I was working out a lot waiting for you," he said in a voice so low that it sent her quivering again. Before she could even think anymore, an irruption threatened to escape.

Corbin leaned down and whispered in her ear. "I can feel you. I'm going to raise your legs. Cum for me," he ordered her. He drew her legs up so he could reach deeper into her, and at his simple request, Clarice exploded as he crushed his mouth onto hers and kissed her deeply through her orgasm. When she stopped shaking beneath him, he kept his fingers in her but leaned up to give her air. "That's my girl," he growled his approval. "Now, let me finish saving you," he said.

When she opened her eyes, she found ice blue flames dancing aggressively in his eyes before he kissed her lips gently and withdrew his fingers from her. A smile was plastered on her lips, and he was proud to be the one who put it there. She was still panting from the aftermath as he kissed a trail of blue light straight down her middle and just about the hem of her panties. She was too full of bliss, heat, and life to even care what he did next.

Corbin paused to look at her afterglow, and it was the most beautiful he had ever seen her. And it was real, which made it even more beautiful. "We're not done," he told her, before gently pulling her panties off.

Clarice happily lifted her hips to help him get them off faster, as she pushed the wet hair away from her face and relished in all the things flowing through her body. It wasn't just the life he was giving her. She somehow could very vividly feel the love he so eagerly wanted to give her. Clarice wasn't sure why she wasn't scared or trying to escape. She would deal with it later.

Clarice felt kisses and warmth move from the top of her foot up to her sweet spot that still seemed to greet him with warm liquid, despite feeling like there was nothing left in her. *Had anyone been able to do that to her before?* She already knew the answer. *No.*

Thirty-two

Corbin brushed his nose over her sex and inhaled her sweet scent. He took a selfish sip of her wetness, and wrapped his mouth around her clitoris before giving it the deepest suction she had ever felt. Clarice gasped as her thousands of nerve endings were ignited at once.

Corbin knew it wasn't a requirement to save her life, but he would be damned if he left any inch of her untouched. He moaned in approval as she desperately grabbed at the sheets beneath her to hold her steady, and her head swung from side to side in pure pleasure.

Corbin felt his own warmth eagerly awaiting release, but he kept it at bay. He wasn't done with her. Not by a long shot. He laid her left leg down gently as he held the right leg up into the air, and kissed it eagerly around her thigh and down to her toes. She whimpered in protest as her knuckles turned white, fisting the sheets for stability. Her body began quaking underneath him. "Corbin!" she warned.

"I know, Baby," he whispered hotly against her sex. "You're mine," Corbin demanded, before taking her clitoris in his mouth and sucking hard. He cupped her ass in his hands. "Cum for me!" he demanded, and again, her body did as commanded. She arched her back and called out his name, as she shook in his hands and he eagerly sucked up the warm wetness that escaped her.

"Please!" she begged as she twisted in his hands. Corbin brushed the wet hair away from her face. "I need you," she whispered for the first-time in her life. "I..." but the words refused to form in her dizzy mind. He seemed to take pity on her, and she felt him crawl up her body and caress her face in his large, warm hand.

"I know," he whispered gently in her ear, before taking her mouth with his, and letting his tongue explore every inch of her. She moaned in pleasure and wrapped her legs eagerly around his waist.

"Please," she begged again, and this time, he didn't deny her. She felt something much larger than she expected slide into her, and she gasped. He gave her a second to adjust around him, and then gently began moving in and out of her. "Faster!" she pleaded as she reached up and drew his head down to her, crushing her mouth back onto his. She moaned her pleasure repeatedly with each thrust he made. She felt his hand roam down the side of her, before pushing her knees high into her chest.

"You're MINE!" he growled as he thrust deeper into her, hitting her G-spot dead on.

"Yes!" she panted back.

"Always!" he demanded, thrusting faster and harder.

"God, yes!" she screamed.

"There's no God here, Baby," he laughed huskily. "Just me."

"Corbin!" she warned, as her body quaked once again under him.

"Say it," he commanded as he continued to thrust faster and harder into her. "Say it!"

"I'm yours!" Clarice screamed out followed by his name. She heard him scream out her name in return, and felt him shake through his own orgasm with her, until he finally fell on top of her.

"Oh my God," he heard her whisper in his ear when her breathing finally slowed down. "That's like ten million for the ghost man," she giggled under him.

He chuckled a hearty laugh, pulled gently out of her. He laid on his back and pulled her on top of him. She swung her leg lazily across him and snuggled deep into him. Her hair sprawled over his chest. "Um, probably a little late to be asking," she said sleepily.

"Relax, Slick," he said, brushing the wet hair from her face, and enjoying their sweaty, naked skin touching. "Death makes me pretty sterile these days."

"Oh, that makes sense," she said as she drifted off to sleep.

He ran his fingers lightly down her sides and listened to her purr in approval. But when he got to her back, the terrain was less smooth. In fact, it was rigid from scar tissue. She felt his muscles tighten under her, which usually would have caused her to recoil, but she was too satisfied in sexual bliss to even think, let alone move.

"Clarice," he stated, with anger oozing in his voice. "Who did this to you?" He traced lashes, old bullet wounds, and what he was guessing to be cigarette burns along her back.

Clarice snorted. "Who hasn't?" she simply shrugged and went back to enjoying her bliss. Corbin wasn't satisfied with her answer, and pulled at her chin to force her to look into his eyes.

"Who did this to you?" he demanded. She saw the flames of anger ignite in his eyes.

"They're all dead, Buddy," she said, trying to keep her wits about her. "I already took care of them. One by one," she sneered in her sleepiness. *How was she this spent?* She felt his chest rise and fall rapidly underneath her, so she awkwardly patted it and rubbed small circles on his bare chest.

"Listen," she said as calmly as she could. "I had a life long before you joined Team Jack and Jess," Clarice stated, fighting to keep the bitterness out of her voice. "It wasn't pretty. Still isn't," she found herself confessing honestly. "I've done things that would have you kicking me out of this bed, but I'm too tired to tell you and really want to just enjoy this, please," she begged.

He could hear the strain in her voice. He could feel that she was surprised and overwhelmed by the emotions she was feeling. Corbin could also feel her exhaustion from sexual bliss that consumed her, which she desperately craved to hold on to. He also heard her thoughts and confusion from never experiencing something like this before. Corbin couldn't blame her. This was new territory for him, too.

He pulled her closer up his body, feeling her sex rub against his bare body, and making him wish he had better stamina. He put a hand on the back of her head and wrapped his free hand around her scarred back. Tugging her hair to make her look at him, made a moan of pleasure escape her mouth. *He would have to remember that next time, because there would be a next time.*

He waited for her eyes to flutter open, to stare into the icy blue flames that burned with passion and dominance. "You're mine," he growled, waking her body up all over again in her core. "No one touches you but me," he declared. She licked the wetness from her mouth away.

"Yes, Sir," she replied shakily. She was used to being in charge, but his dominance over her had her insides melting before she could force them to stop.

He moaned at her use of the word "Sir", but he kept going. "No one will hurt you again. Ever," he declared.

She tried to protest, but the tug of her hair to look him in his eyes again had her moaning in pleasure and forgetting what she was protesting.

"Clarice," he growled. She felt his lower half rumble beneath her, and it made her purr again.

Remembering his reaction to her the first time, she whispered, "Yes, Sir," more slowly. She felt him go mad as he released all his love into the best kiss she had ever tasted. Neither one was quite ready for a second round, so he pulled her head under his chin and moaned as she wiggled against him to find a sweet spot. She oddly fit perfectly in his arms.

"Sleep," he whispered softly, as he ran his fingers through her hair. Her body didn't hesitate to meet his command, and she gave her heart, soul, and everything else to the ghost holding her tightly as she drifted off into uninterrupted darkness.

Clarice awoke on top of Corbin and in more heat than she had ever experienced in her life. *How could she not get enough of this ghost of a man?* She shifted herself and rubbed her growing wet sex against his length, and felt it grow quickly in response. He was still somewhat asleep, but moaned his approval and began running his hands up and down her body.

Clarice reached down, and without any warning, she slid him inside her and squeezed her insides tight around him. His eyes widened in shock as he looked into her stormy blue eyes that raged like the sea.

"I need more," she growled, as she pinned him to the bed. "Let me show you what it's like when I'm on top," she sneered, and bent down to crush her mouth on his as she squeezed herself around him, making him insanely hard instantly. She smiled against his lips as he moaned his approval.

"We can discuss who is who's when you see what I can do," she said wickedly against his mouth and began riding him in an impatient pace that made him toss his head back and his eyes roll to the back of his head.

"Fuck me, Clarice," he moaned in ecstasy.

"Oh, I plan on it," he heard her breathe into his ear. "And then some."

He held onto her hips and began thrusting as deep as he could into her. It was a good thing he was already dead, because this girl would kill him for sure.

It was late, per usual, and Kevin Robertson was making sure his printing press was meeting its deadline. At fifty-one, he had already lived a lifetime as a teacher, and was currently living out his other dream, running a printing press. Although people usually found this 5'11" humble, dirty blonde, blue-eyed, stout man playing pool or guitar, when it was time for meeting a deadline, he was all hands on deck to make sure everything got done to perfection. This night was no different. Or so he thought.

He was walking the line as he always did, making sure everything was running smoothly, when out of nowhere a gorgeous redhead walked up towards him. "What are you doing in here?" he asked her, surprised.

She waited to speak until she was right up against him. She smiled ever so seductively before answering, "Looking for you."

"Do I know you?" Kevin asked.

The girl giggled innocently. "Not yet," she blushed, biting her bottom lip. His body reacted as all men did when she flirted.

He swallowed hard, trying to regain control of his senses, and cleared his throat before stammering, "How can I help you?"

Without hesitation, she took his hands and wrapped them around her lower back as she ran her fingers through his short hair and all over his body as she took his mouth and claimed it for her own. He froze immediately in shock, but it wasn't long before he took what she was offering. No man could ever resist.

She pulled him closer to her, felt him grow harder against her, as she rubbed up against him and moaned ever so softly into his ear. She bit his bottom lip, his ears, his neck.

"Why?" he whispered, trying to gasp for oxygen.

"Because I have had a crush on you for years, and you never see me," she growled as she took him into her hands and massaged him, forcing him to toss his head back and moan in pleasure. She moved his hands down to her ass and stepped closer and closer to the machine. He was too captivated to notice.

It would be too late for him to stop her from shoving his hand into the machine and watching it crush it as he screamed in brutal agony. He wouldn't notice that she had stepped away and watched with pleasure as he fought to save his own life. Or that her lips curled up into the most disturbing smile as he begged for her to stop the machine, and she did nothing. Forcing him to watch as the machine crushed his body to death.

No one would ever know what happened to Kevin Robertson. Only that the papers that came out printed in dried blood until the supply ran out had the headline of *Printer Gets Pressed For Story....*

Clarice woke up, once again, naked and on top of Corbin, entangled in his arms. *How long had she been here?* Panic set in, and she carefully slid herself out of his arms. However, Corbin caught her by her wrist, and without opening his eyes, just whispered, "Nope." He pulled her back into his arms and tightened his grip. She squirmed underneath his hold, but there was no escaping.

"I can't stay here all day," she protested.

"True," he responded flatly. "But you will stay until we talk through your panic."

She growled and tried to escape him again, but his hold made it impossible. *When did he become a straight-jacket?* He chuckled, and she got pissed. "Get out of my head," she warned. His face sobered, and he waited patiently for her to stop squirming.

"You can't run from me. From us," he corrected.

"Watch me," she grumbled, starting to wiggle beneath him.

He let out an exasperated sigh, and let her go free. As she scrambled away, taking the top sheet with her, and putting as much distance between them, Corbin pushed himself up onto his elbows and raised one eyebrow at her. "Okay, Slick," he said patiently. "I'm listening."

"For starters, stop calling me that," she grumbled, but he ignored her.

"I'm waiting," he replied more firmly, and something forced her to face front, but avoid his eye contact.

"We can't," she stated, as if that answered all the questions.

"Can't what?" Corbin pushed.

She glared at him, and for a split second, he thought he saw a quick red flame flicker in her eyes. But it was gone as quickly as it had appeared, making him second guess himself.

He frowned. "Your past means nothing to me," he assured as he sat up and crossed his legs, showing he was giving her his full attention. "I have my own," he said with a shrug.

She frowned in response. "Yours don't include taking lives," she grumbled.

"You don't know that," he said flatly. She paused only for a second before she began looking around the makeshift room to gather her clothes. He watched her, but didn't panic. He simply sat and waited for her.

"Stop it," she growled.

He tilted his head. "Stop what exactly?" he asked innocently.

"You know exactly what!" she countered, but he only flashed her that stupid boyish grin. "I don't even know what's going on, let alone where you fit in."

"How about right next to you?" he asked.

Clarice threw her head back and cackled. "And if I decide to go kill the woman who should have killed me twice," she snarled.

"Oh, that I would most definitely help you do," he replied honestly, with a hint of mischief.

She stopped collecting things and stared at him with her mouth hanging open, before she shook her head and yanked on her jeans. Corbin smiled as her breasts bounced joyfully with the action. Clarice huffed and turned around, making him stare at her scared back as she put her sports bra and shirt back on. Before she could pull her shirt all the way down, he was behind her, stopping her. Inspecting her with his eyes and fingers.

"I wasn't joking when I told you that you were mine, and I would do anything to keep you safe," he said, trying to swallow the bile from his throat. He helped her pull her shirt down. "I can try to take those away if you want," he offered more quietly.

Clarice snorted. "Scars are my armor," she sneered. She physically felt his heart break for her. "Why can I feel you more?" she asked, turning around to face him.

He lowered his eyes. "The cost of saving you means we share a piece of each other. I will always feel you and know when you're in danger. You're forever my responsibility," he said, looking into her eyes with a look that made her knees stupidly want to melt beneath her. *Was this what Jess always talked about having with Jack?*

"I belong to no one," Clarice found herself replying out of habit.

"Oh, you're mine, Sweetheart," Corbin grinned. "Whether you want to be or not. But I couldn't take you as many times as I made you cum if you didn't want me in return," he said in a cocky tone.

"What does that mean?" Clarice demanded, putting her hands on her hips. Corbin shrugged nonchalantly. "Corbin Dallas," she growled, and it made him glad she didn't know his middle name.

"We wouldn't be able to touch, if you didn't want me to," he answered as basically as he could. "There are rules, and we just broke a ton of them," he said, looking wearily at the bed. "Everything has a price," he whispered to himself. He felt panic rise in her.

"What's yours?" she asked cautiously.

He gave her his best boyish grin and replied, "To be determined."

"What the hell does *THAT* mean?" she asked, exasperated.

Before she knew what was happening, he pulled her into his arms and held her head to his neck. "It means we don't take life for granted, and enjoy every moment we have, because I would have done it no matter the cost," he whispered calmly in her ear. "In fact, let's do that," he said with his voice getting husky. Her core ignited, but the tears filling her eyes stopped her.

When she was quiet for far too long, he pulled her head back gently to see tears stained her cheeks. He brushed them away with his thumbs. "Shhh, now then," he said in a soothing voice. "You have rocked my world more than any living person did, and I'm dead," he said softly.

She blurted out a laugh and covered her mouth immediately at the shock of the sound that had just escaped her. He pulled her hand away. "I love that I make you laugh. Please don't deny me that," he said, licking his lips and staring at her mouth.

"Do you think of nothing else?" Clarice asked, exasperated.

"Not after tasting you, Baby," Corbin growled, and pulled her face to his, claiming her mouth as his. She moaned in appreciation until he pulled away. "But there's something else upsetting you. Spill," he ordered.

Clarice opened her eyes and scowled. "She's going after Rebecca and Karmen."

Corbin studied her. "Who's Karmen?" he asked, genuinely interested.

Clarice shifted her weight between her feet, while he still held her face in his hands. His patience was annoying, but if she was going to face Claudia again, she was going to need help. She placed her hands over his and winced a little. Clarice wasn't used to sharing with anyone, but she took a deep breath before she confessed.

"An innocent autistic child that can see into the dream realm and know what people do before they act on their decisions, and is currently in an unstable Claudia's care," she said closing her eyes at the end, realizing how selfish she had been in this war. Now, everyone was paying a price.

Corbin blinked a couple of times as he digested the information she spilled out. "So, what are we going to do about the girl who tried to kill you?"

He said we. And she didn't hate it. In fact, she fucking loved it.

Corbin saw the briefest flicker of a red flame, again, before she replied in a devious voice, "Kill her before she kills anyone else."

She had decided. Corbin wasn't sure just how much she realized she had in that moment, but she had decided. This was what he was sent to do. Help guide Clarice to this moment. Not that he would let her ever know that, but Clarice wasn't Team Sophie. She wasn't even Team Clarice anymore. She was simply, Team takes out the evil that threatened to destroy all realms, even if she understood the weight of her decision or not.

Clarice was no longer just the daughter of a psychopath, who had hunted Sophie most of her life, neglected to save her own sister, and took too many lives to count in between. None of that mattered now.

"Let me put some pants on," he replied. Pride filled his core, and he loved her suddenly even more than he thought he could. He turned to walk over towards the bed, but found her throwing him on it instead with strength that caught him off guard.

"Well, maybe just a quicky," she sneered before claiming his mouth and making him forget about the increase of abilities Clarice had unknowingly gained in the last couple of hours.

Viviana Gonzalez was thirty, stood at 5'5, had brown eyes that were framed by black square glasses and black, red, and violet hair. She tended to read lips when people talked to her, because it helped her stay focused.

She never knew it would be the thing that would lead her to her death, reading the conversation between an unknown redhead and an auburn-haired doctor as they planned a murder one day. Although

Viviana loved to Google random things from how to start a crime, to the different laws around the world, she was shocked to see it play out before her eyes while she was reading a book in her favorite cafe.

However, Viviana would never get to share this tale with anyone. Her body would be found days later, melted like a candle from the sulfuric acid, making her unrecognizable to anyone who saw her body in the morgue. A tattoo on her right inner arm of her mother's first and last name, written as a stem to missing tulips after her mother's passing, would be the only part of her body that would provide any sort of identity.

Thirty-three

Natasha Harrison-Bin loved her job at the library. She would live there if she could. Her auburn curly hair was tied up in a messy bun, as her hazel eyes scanned for last-minute stragglers. The library was closing, and it was her favorite part of the evening. When she had the whole place to herself. At thirty-four, some people said that wasn't much of a life to live, but to Natasha it was the best life, even living in the Land Down Under.

She was 5'5", voluptuous, and had a loving husband and two children that she loved to chase around on bikes from time to time and care for. Natasha loved playing sports and went horseback riding, but books were at the top of her list of loves. So, the job as a librarian was a perfect fit. She went around politely shooing everyone out and went to the desk when a redhead walked by and dropped a book on the floor.

"Hey, Miss! You dropped your book!" Natasha called out.

"So, pick it up," the redhead retorted as she continued to walk away.

"Seriously?" Natasha asked, dumbfounded. *Who would just toss a book and walk away?* She sighed heavily before walking around the desk and looking down at the floor. *Fahrenheit 451* stared back at her. Natasha's heart broke a little.

With all the civil unrest, and the current desire of some people to burn books, the title was a reminder of just how sad the world had become. It may not be 2049, but some people still refused to learn from this lesson.

"It's okay, I've got you," she whispered with care to the book and took it gently into her hands.

Natasha went to put it back where it belonged when her hands began to sting a bit. She looked down and noticed that the book had somehow combusted into flames. She gasped, dropping it immediately, took off her cardigan, and began to gently beat the flames out. Only they refused to stifle and just grew brighter and larger.

Natasha looked around desperately as the room began to quickly fill with smoke. She raced over to the fire extinguisher, broke the glass, and sprayed the book. However, nothing came out.

"Are you kidding me?!" she coughed in frustration.

The flames had spread quickly to other shelves, and the place was quickly filling up with fire and smoke. She was mad and defeated, but even she knew it was beyond time to call it quits. Natasha raced for the front door to find it locked. She jerked frantically at it as she coughed and her lungs filled with smoke.

In the split second that smoke cleared from in front of her eyes, she saw the same redheaded woman who dropped the book in the first place staring at her on the other side of the glass, waving at her with a wicked smile.

"Open the damn door!" Natasha screamed out, but the redhead just shrugged, turned on her heels, and walked away.

Not ready to have her life taken just yet, Natasha ran to the desk and grabbed the scissors. She cut off the bottom of her t-shirt and drenched it with what was left of the water in her water bottle as she held it over her mouth and dropped to the floor. She pulled her phone out of her pocket and dialed the fire department as she crawled to the nearest door. All were locked from the outside.

After letting the fire department know her location, she hung up and called her husband. She sat in the farthest corner of the room, and told him that she loved him as tears stained her ash covered cheeks. Then she quickly described the redheaded woman to him.

"I don't care if she's the raven or not. Tell Shyera to take that bitch out for killing me," were Natasha's last words.

Cassandra stared at the door nervously every time it opened, but Shyera never walked back through. Too much time was passing. When her second cell phone rang, she jumped, throwing her hand over her heart and gasping. She knew exactly who was calling her without looking. "Ali," she whispered into the phone.

"Natasha was killed last night," Ali confessed in sorrow.

Cassandra gulped. "Shyera still hasn't returned," she replied with a frown.

"Please don't make me the sensible one. You know my anxiety can't take it," Ali pleaded.

Cassandra shook her head in disbelief. "We're okay," she said in a low voice, more for herself than her friend.

"We are *SO* not okay!" Ali hissed on the other side. "Watchers are dropping right and left!"

"They call themselves booktokers," Cassandra corrected.

"I don't care what they call themselves," Ali replied flatly. "The raven is awake, and no one can find her. The realms are going to crash regardless, because watchers are being taken out faster than they are being born at this rate," she hissed in a panic. "War is here, and we don't know who we're fighting!"

Cassandra knew she was right, and her navy background kicked into gear. "It's time the Guild gets involved, then, isn't it?"

"The Guild?" Ali swallowed. "We haven't been involved in decades!" she hissed.

"I know," Cassandra assured. "But we don't have a choice."

"You know I'm going to be a ball of stress before I ever get there, right?" Ali whined.

Cassandra's phone pinged, and she looked down at the message. "Did you seriously just send me a picture of your mug saying to prepare for war?" she laughed in disbelief.

"It's a gift," Ali stated bluntly. "You know I need my coffee to make sure I murder the right people," she added.

"Boy, do I," Cassandra laughed. "And you are really scary when you're mad, so get mad and meet me in the courtyard," she told her friend.

"Did you not just hear what I said about the coffee!" Ali proclaimed, and Cassandra knew she was sticking her tongue out at her phone like Ali always did before hanging up.

Cassandra shook her head and let out a nervous laugh as she dialed her replacement. "Kimberly, it's time," was all she said before she hung up. She closed the library down early and shooed everyone out, claiming there was an emergency forcing them to close. She knew Kimberly would be prepared to open tomorrow and act like business as usual, so she headed home to collect her supplies.

The prophecy had been written in the books long ago. She had silently hoped it wouldn't play out while she was alive, but fate had other plans and it was time for war. She threw the backpack on her back, and grabbed the sacred book disguised as the latest bestseller as she went to the bus station and started her journey to Scotland.

Ali Kiki crinkled her face up as she paced her bedroom. Just having turned thirty, with dark brown hair flowing just past her shoulders with chocolate eyes to match, she pulled on boots and stared at her reflection in the mirror. *Ugh!* There was nothing warriorish about the 5'1" figure that looked back at her, other than the shit storm life kept wanting to throw at her in adulthood.

Ali never understood why she had been chosen to be a part of the Guild or anything else. She was an introvert that suffered from anxiety and always felt like an outsider apart from being with her mom. Now, she had to force herself to Scotland to save the world so her own family along with millions of others could keep breathing in this one.

"I could not go," she stated in hope to the reflection, who just scowled at her and replied, "You know that's not an option," back to her. Ali stuck her tongue out at the figure, who simply just rolled her eyes. "I hate you," she hissed as she grabbed her backpack in a huff and left the room. The figure smirked at her and wiggled her fingers in a sarcastic wave before disappearing.

Sophie was quiet in the Jeep as they drove in search of Karmen. They both saw the light blue hue that left a trail that started from the point she had been taken. Learning not to ask any questions, they started following it. James confirmed it did match where Karmen had been, so they traveled quickly, but cautiously.

James looked at Sophie briefly as he drove. He could feel her anguish, and it was damn near suffocating. "Wanna talk about it?" he asked gently, as he put his eyes back on the road.

"I don't even know where to begin," she breathed out. She couldn't keep this to herself. Not after what happened to Tina.

"The beginning is always good," he said, flashing her his boyish grin.

"It happened again," she whispered. Not the beginning, but where she could start, at least.

"What did?" James asked for clarification.

"Remember when we kissed outside of the bunker, and I just..." she started.

"Sucked the life right out of me," he chuckled.

She looked at him in shock, but he just smiled and gave her an encouraging nod. "Yes," she mumbled, looking out her window. Sophie sighed heavily. "I was absorbing whatever that woman jammed in her, and I guess I started to do *that* to Tina and her baby," she whispered as a tear streaked her cheek.

James knew better than to interrupt her.

"I heard her begging, and I couldn't stop," she confessed, her voice cracking. Then she shook her head no. "I didn't *want* to," she corrected herself.

James felt her pain, and the words didn't settle well. "Why didn't you want to?" he asked softly as he kept his eyes on the road.

"It's like," Sophie started, and then sat up straighter and brushed the tears away from her cheeks. "It's like ever since I killed Rein and collected her power, or whatever, once I'm mad enough, I just see red," she said, squinting her eyes in concentration. Then she turned her body to face him more. "Like I just lose all control, and I have no idea what the heck I'm doing," Sophie rushed on. "It's usually not until you or someone else stops me that I stop at all," she whispered, staring down at her hands.

"Why do you think I'm able to stop you?" he asked casually.

"Because you're lucky I like you," she giggled briefly, trying to ease the pain in her heart.

"You like Tina," he offered to her.

"I do," Sophie said. "But I don't want to get naked with her," she added, crinkling up her nose at the thought. James let out a laugh.

"Good to know," he added, and she gave him a weary smile. "You know what I think?" he asked her, flashing her a smile before turning to look back at the road.

"Please share," she begged, watching his face eagerly.

"I think there's nothing wrong with you," he stated bluntly, making her roll her eyes in response. "Honestly!" James protested.

"You're not being helpful," Sophie muttered, crossing her arms in front of her chest.

"Hear me out!" he pouted. She sighed heavily, but remained silent. "I think you are a very powerful woman," James started, ignoring her dramatics coming from the corner of his eye. "I think a lot of that power comes from your ability to feel so much. From within, and from others," he continued. "Even though emotions get away from you from time to time, they don't change the person you are at your core, which makes it easier for me to balance you out," James added with a shrug. He noticed her contemplating his words, so he continued.

"You act like you're the only person who has ever been controlled more by emotion than their rational thinking," he chuckled, and felt her glare, but they both knew he was right. "I think your ability to absorb people's emotions right now is to help give you the strength to fight and do whatever it is you are being called to do. Which *does* typically have to do with keeping the innocent safe," James emphasized. "And when you get lost in everything thrown at you, I will just remind you of how badass you are, and we can tackle whatever is thrown at us. Together," he added.

Sophie was silent as she took his words in. He wasn't wrong. Her emotions did get away from her, but it was because she felt so intensely. She loved as hard as she hated, and maybe that's why everything was happening.

Maybe that's why she was designed to live in the role of the protector, even though it wasn't her original choice. She just had to accept her weaknesses, and figure out how to make them strengths so they didn't make her as weak anymore. She wouldn't always win the war with herself, but she wasn't fighting alone, either.

"I knew I liked you," she giggled, as her smile grew wider. James just laughed and kept following the faint blue trail left behind by the girl he regrettably let go of when she needed him the most.

Clarice woke up startled. She had the weirdest dream. Karmen was taken by a woman, not the tree that Mason had chased in the opposite direction, and she sat rocking and humming herself towards peace. She was no longer in destress, which put Clarice's heart at ease. Then she realized why. Karmen knew Clarice was coming for her.

"Yeah, I am," she whispered. That was when she noticed she wasn't alone. She was twisted in Corbin's arms. He moaned with pleasure as he rubbed his nakedness against hers. "Get up," she giggled and tried to shove him off.

"You're mine," he growled. "I want to hear you say it."

Her cheeks flushed, and she tried to shove him off again. "We don't have time for this!" she protested. "There's a very special child that needs saving!"

"Then you'd better say it quick," he taunted, pulling her in tighter.

Sighing, she muttered, "I'm yours."

"Can't hear you," he sang in her ear, and tickled her.

"Fine! I'm yours!" she shouted as she tried to gasp for air from laughing so hard.

"Good. Now that you understand," he said, jumping out of bed and getting dressed faster than any human she had ever witnessed. "Let's go, slowpoke!" he ordered her, and spanked her butt when she got out of bed. The growl of approval almost had her pulling him back into bed, so she thought of Karmen instead.

It was as if she were looking through Karmen's eyes herself suddenly. She saw the room, the picture Karmen had been coloring. It was a Home2 Suites in Salt Lake City, Utah. "That's my girl," she whispered to herself before announcing, "They're not far. I need to get to Salt Lake City."

"We can do that," Corbin smiled his stupid boyish smile at her. There was that word again. *We.*

"Don't you need to," she said confused and holding her hands out, "stay here?" she finished.

"You're mine," he growled again. "I go where you go. Just in a different form," he added with a shrug. Clarice shook her head. She would have to process this later. He held out his hand, and when the portal opened, she noticed it was just across the street from where Karmen's picture stated she was.

"Another point for the ghost man," she breathed out, impressed.

"There's a lot you don't know about me," he said with a shrug, and held out his hand to her. She took it without even thinking and they stepped through.

Thirty-four

Cassandra looked out the window of the airplane as they flew over the water to the home of the Guild. She had watched the news as various booktokers fell to their deaths. No one had made a connection other than them using the same app, but Cassandra knew different.

She had been told the legend of the raven for as long as she could remember. She never believed the full raven would awaken in her time, though. There was no timeline stamped on the legends and the prophecies written to paper so many decades ago, but here they were.

Cassandra sighed heavily and tried not to think about the family she had left behind. She was well aware if she didn't fight this fight, no realm was safe. Including the one they lived in. The world had no clue what was going on, or what was at stake, but she did.

Although there were over billions of realms in existence, the one they lived and breathed in was one of them. Some had suspicions. They were viewed as being crazy, believing in aliens, Area 51, and all the other things that went bump in the night. But those things *did* exist. Just not necessarily in this one. That's why the stories were told, written down, and passed on from generation to generation. Only a few knew just how true they actually were.

It wasn't just random booktokers being sacrificed, and their unknown watchers wiped from existence without any clue. They were the gifted ones. The ones which gave the realms their much needed life support when they read them. Someone knew that, and was taking them out one-by-one, which could only mean they had compromised the Guild, and no one could be trusted.

Cassandra had watched Shyera leave to locate the new raven. She had many roles, and watching over Shyera was one of them, although Shyera never had a clue. Cassandra knew long before Shyera did that she was the chosen to protect the last known raven, although one had been born to replace her, but never quite made it. Melanie had been the rarely chosen raven. Rebecca was given the rights by birth, but it was a new line and she didn't have the power this current one did, whoever she was. Cassandra didn't know if that was more terrifying or not.

Although the raven typically chose the right side, and chose to protect the realms, the choice was not guaranteed to end the same every time. Should the raven choose to make her own path, no one was safe. She could destroy them all with a simple snap of her finger, which made her deadlier than any evil born thus far.

When she asked, Cassandra was always told it was to provide balance, no matter which side of the scale the raven sat on. That made little sense to Cassandra, and as a child, she was shushed into silence and not allowed to ask why ever again.

That was what Cassandra searched for during her entire adulthood. The why. She never found it, though. "Everything happens for a reason," was the only response ever given to her. Hence, why the prophecy was in play.

A chosen child would be created. Built to protect and destroy. The raven would awaken, choose her side, and the rest were left to fight based on her decision. It made no sense to Cassandra, but the Guild didn't ask questions. They dealt with the hands they were given and fought like hell to protect the innocent and try to survive the aftermath of the raven's decision.

She closed her eyes and tried to get some rest. She would need all that she could get.

They were on the rooftop of the building across the street. When Clarice looked down, she was surprised that her eyes locked on Mason's. He seemed to be as shocked as she was to see him. Mason was leaning against the building sipping on a coffee, and he nodded towards the building behind him. He was outside the tiny cafe attached to the hotel. She gave him a quick nod.

She heard the roof door open and Clarice didn't have to turn around to know who it was. Sophie and James joined her. Even though she couldn't see Corbin, she sensed he was still close by. "Took you long enough," Clarice replied flatly.

James grabbed Sophie's arm before she could respond. "We had to make sure Tina was safely on her way," he said, staring down Sophie while she glared at Clarice in irritation. "Thank you for the help," he added sincerely.

Clarice remained quiet, because it was the black SUV that had her attention, as the redheaded figure she despised climbed out of the passenger seat. Her wrist Clarice had broken was in a cast, and Clarice was pleased to see it. Sophie's head jerked to where Clarice was staring so intently, and her lips curled up in a snarl. "I'm going to take care of her," Sophie growled.

Remembering her last encounter with Claudia, she wasn't quite willing to put Sophie in that kind of danger. Not until they had more entail on Claudia's own enhancements. "We'll come back," Clarice snapped.

"Come back?" Sophie asked, already on the verge of hysteria. "I will *NOT* come back! She endangered Tina, and she has Karmen!" she hissed out as her eyes ignited.

Clarice turned around to face Sophie, her back sunburned from Sophie's heat. "We *WILL* come back, or you won't come *AT ALL*!" she challenged Sophie.

James wasn't sure what caused Clarice's sudden concern for Sophie's safety, or why she wasn't ready to face Claudia when they would already have the upper hand, but he felt the intensity of it and knew it was in Sophie's best interest not to face Claudia right now.

"She's right," he replied, pushing all of his love in her direction, but the red wasn't breaking in her veins. "Sophie," he begged quietly.

Clarice didn't want to share the one secret she knew would cause more damage than good, but she wasn't seeing any other options. "Eddie's alive," she muttered.

Sophie took a few steps back from Clarice, stunned. "What?" she gasped as the red dispersed immediately from her veins, but remained fierce in her eyes.

"Eddie's alive, and if you come with me right now, I will take you to him," Clarice blurted out in desperation.

"What do you mean he's alive?" Sophie growled at her. James stepped between them. Sophie went to shove him aside, but this time, James didn't hesitate. He remained in place.

Clarice closed her eyes in pain. "I found him in the explosion. He wasn't well. He's been in a coma. We've been trying to heal him. He's awake and alive. If you want to see him at all, you will come with me right now," she finished, opening her eyes and challenging Sophie.

"I can't believe you," Sophie whispered, covering her mouth.

James looked over his shoulder and saw the same man who chased after Karmen in Utah. "Karmen?" he asked, pulling his eyes up to meet Clarice's.

"Mason is very good at his job," Clarice replied, less harshly. "He will wait for an opening and get her when it's safe," she announced. Her pleading look surprised him, but she wanted them to leave for some unknown reason that outweighed going in for Karmen, and he found himself trusting her judgement despite their background.

"I trust them," he whispered in Sophie's ear, and her flames that remained in her eyes went out, leaving her baby blues in their wake.

"I want to see him," Sophie hissed as tears streaked her cheeks.

Clarice just nodded and walked around them both to lead the way to the extraction point. She pulled out her phone and sent a text to Emma, demanding they be picked up immediately. When she shoved it back in her pocket, she looked over her shoulder. Not at Sophie and James, but at the child she was leaving behind. Her heart ached, but there was nothing she could do. Right now, Claudia thought she was dead. And that was the only upper hand she had against the science project Algos had left for her to deal with.

Mason saw them snake around the building, and out onto the streets with everyone else bundled up, trying to shuffle to their final destination in the cold. His phone beeped, and he took off his thick glove to fish it out of his pocket.

Claudia is mine. Don't face her alone. -C

She could have Claudia. He wanted the woman who had shot a bullet into his chest and left him bleeding in the middle of the street. For now, he would shadow them, having finally caught up to them, and wait to see when he could collect Karmen safely and bring her home.

Rebecca jumped out of the truck, sticking her chin in the air and closing her eyes. She took a deep breath as the wind whipped around her. She still wore the jacket that Bruce had given her. After she had him give her all of his money, she released him and sent him back home.

So much had happened in this small town. The evil and death

burned the inside of her nose, and it oddly excited her. She let her head move from side to side as she searched for the one she needed. Fate had not been on her side, and she had just missed her. No...them. Visions flew before her eyes at lightning speed.

A tiny human with gifts that could destroy her. Another who had more power than even Rebecca did at this very moment, with a boy to match. One who was calling to her, and another who wanted to destroy her. And a fetus that scared her.

Too many things weren't right. It was time to make a choice. A raven on the top of the sign next to her squawked, forcing her eyes open. She studied it and nodded. Where she found one, she found the others.

Rebecca walked into the store and collected warmer clothing. She went to the fitting room and changed. When she stepped out of the dressing room, she bumped into a blonde muscular man walking past the fitting room. "Excuse me, Miss," he said and froze when his eyes met Rebecca.

Her eyes turned to black as she smiled innocently and asked in the softest of voices. "I need to go to Salt Lake City. You want to take me there. You want to go now." The blonde simply nodded in response, turned on his heels and led her to his Jeep. "You want to ask me no questions," Rebecca added before she leaned over to turn on the radio and leaned back to close her eyes.

The man shook his head and looked around to gather his bearings. He didn't remember needing to go to Salt Lake City, but suddenly it was the only thing he wanted to do. So, he leaned forward, turned the key, and got them going on their way while listening to Taylor Swift sing gracefully through his speakers. Rebecca kept her eyes closed and rested comfortably as she tapped her fingers on the armrest to the music.

Rebecca didn't know who she was giving her powers to, or that a trap laid waiting for her. She didn't remember her granddaughter, daughters, or even herself. She only knew that she had a limited time to give her powers to the next, or die trying, and she was late getting the process started.

Too bad someone who shouldn't have learned about the legend now knew her secret, and now held her life and everyone she loved in danger....

Legend of the Raven....

For as long as time has existed, there has been a war between good and evil, and a door between the dead and the living, with a spirit animal that could float easily between them. With more realms than any human could imagine, the raven was given power to control them or destroy them, depending on which side they were drawn to the most.

That's the danger of such power. It can consume you and cause you to get lost in it, which is what happened to the previous raven. Evil assisted in such a destiny, causing the raven to lose itself, and realm after realm was being destroyed in the process. Until fate stepped in, choosing another outside of the bloodline in order to create a new one.

As the bloodline grew strength, the chosen ruled in its place, waiting to be replaced by the next true raven. Only evil wasn't willing to just step aside and placed a child of Satan's in its path to be destroyed. However, before the act could take place, the baby raven gave birth to two daughters and a son. Only the daughters would survive. Evil strangled the life out of the raven, not realizing this new bloodline had a secret of its own. A new ability to be reborn as the fate of the world needed it to.

In the absence of the raven, the girls were raised by Satan's child. Unclear as to which daughter held the power to continue the raven's bloodline, one was enhanced with a manipulation trigger put into place, who would later give birth to her own daughter. The other was raised to hate everything in its path. However, the girls had a power of their own, even unknown to them. A power which would only be enhanced by love once they chose their lifetime mate. A power, evil would never see coming.

The manipulation trigger in the one daughter was easily broken by love, while the other daughter spent a lifetime of suffering, unsure if love was even possible. The enhancement in the second daughter was passed onto her own, and now she's more powerful than even fate was prepared for.

The raven's ability to unlock her power can only be accessed by the death of Satan's child, but that child had its own plan in place. A creation would be the raven's greatest downfall. The creation has awakened, as has the raven, but who has the power of the true bloodline, and who will fall to corruption? Power is a very dangerous thing. Especially when being evil feels so good.

Who is the true raven, with the power to rule the realms like never before? And will the creation take them down before they find their way? It's time for the raven to reign its new kingdoms.

Let the legend begin....

Did you enjoy this book?

Your feedback helps me provide the best quality books and helps other readers like you discover great books. Please be sure to leave a review.

If you want early access to future books be sure to subscribe to my newsletter at:
https://chasingstormillc.beehiiv.com/

<u>The Sophie Lee Saga</u>

The Key: Book One of the Sophie Lee Saga
The Protector: Book Two of the Sophie Lee Saga
Dead Draw: Book Three of the Sophie Lee Saga
Birth of the Legend: Book Four of the Sophie Lee Saga
Reign of the Raven: Book Five of the Sophie Lee Saga

<u>The Fate vs Foe Novella Series</u>

Fate vs Foe
Family of Blood
Family of Love
Family of Fate

<u>Other Books by Stormi Lewis</u>

Deck the Ex (2026)

About the Author

Stormi Lewis writes books—lucky for you, inconvenient for her characters. She's best known for her paranormal fantasy thrillers, **THE SOPHIE LEE SAGA** and the **FATE VS FOE** series, where folklore and bad decisions rarely survive unpunished.

She pleads the fifth on any BookTokers who don't make it out alive, but giving her milk chocolate could save your life. When she's not committing fictional crimes, Stormi advocates for mental-health awareness and lives with chronic migraines.

Stalk her for a change at https://linktr.ee/chasingstormi.

www.ingramcontent.com/pod-product-compliance
Lightning Source LLC
Chambersburg PA
CBHW060609300726
48975CB00005B/1497